CEONE FENN

Nicole,
Thank you for reading
my debut novel.
Enjoy! Ceone Fenn

the REAP *the* FINEST WHEAT

A Novel

outskirtspress
DENVER, COLORADO

To Reap the Finest Wheat
A Novel

v2.0

Outskirts Press, Inc.
http://www.outskirtspress.com

ISBN: 978-1-4787-6074-0

PRINTED IN THE UNITED STATES OF AMERICA

For my mother
It all began with her.

Chapter One

Clutching her satchel in one hand and a photograph of the stranger she'd agreed to marry in the other, Katerina stepped from the train. A loud hiss escaped from the cooling engine, startling her. The air, filled with roiling steam, smelled of burning coal. As her eyes adjusted to the midday sun, a clapboard station appeared, its white-washed siding pedestrian, its planked platform no more than forty feet long and sparsely occupied. Katerina thought of the art nouveau train station, with its magnificent archway and bustle of passengers, which she'd departed from in L'viv, Ukraine. She'd traded a vineyard for a raisin.

It had been a tearful farewell. She'd stood in the crowded station, grief-filled eyes searching for the two most important men in her life, her father and her priest.

"He isn't coming," Aneta had said.

Katerina hadn't been certain which "he" her sister meant. It didn't matter; neither had come. The memory stung like a slap.

Now she studied the small photograph, gripped so tightly she'd put a crease down its middle. The man appeared somber and young, although Danya had told her he was thirty-five. Maybe he looked different now, or maybe her brother-in-law had deceived her. Seeing no one who resembled the man in the photograph, she struggled not to panic.

Perhaps she'd misunderstood the arrival date. Katerina rummaged in her satchel. At its bottom, she felt her mother's sewing scissors, the possession she'd tenderly placed in a special velvet pouch made for its safekeeping. Touching it brought little comfort. Where had she tucked the confirmation telegram? Her hands shook.

The Psalter. She'd tucked it between the book's pages. She pulled out the telegram. September 10, 1925. No, she hadn't gotten the date wrong.

A worker on the platform lifted boxes from the train while another pushed a heavily laden cart toward the station's freight room. Cautiously, she approached the young man unloading freight. "*Vybachte*," she said.

The worker, more boy than man, stood and faced her. "Sorry." He shrugged and then turned away and continued lifting boxes.

Katerina froze. Her mediocre English, learned from a borrowed textbook in the months she'd been confined to Aneta and Danya's apartment, was suddenly as inaccessible as jewels in a vault.

This was not the reception she'd imagined. A hundred times, Katerina had rehearsed the moment she'd meet the man she had promised to marry. She'd pictured herself facing him, smiling demurely and offering her hand. At his greeting, she'd reply, "I am happy to meet you, Mr. Senyk." He'd warmly return her smile. "My journey was satisfactory, thank you." She'd meet his eyes but not too boldly, act cordial but not too familiar, be sociable but not loquacious. Would he find her worthy? She was certain Danya hadn't mentioned her crippled leg when he'd arranged this marriage. Her brother-in-law was too shrewd a negotiator.

Katerina straightened her back and lifted her chin, composing herself. She approached the man pushing the overloaded cart.

"Excuse me," she said, relieved to have found the words.

"Yes."

"This is Bilik?"

"Yes, miss," he said, pointing to the sign nailed over the station door. "Bilik, Saskatchewan."

"Thank you." She was in the right place.

"Viktor Senyk?" She showed him the photograph.

The man shrugged and turned back to his task.

Where was he? Katerina pressed her lips together to keep them from trembling. The weight of the situation settled on her shoulders and tugged at her limbs. Doubt wrapped its traitorous arms around her. She limped to the lone bench on the platform and sat down. The locomotive moaned and whistled a departure warning. Katerina eyed the conductor, who was preparing to close the door.

"Final call!"

There was still time to change her mind. She could get back on the train, take it to the end of the line, then turn around and retrace her path eastward to Halifax where she'd book steamer passage to Liverpool and, from there, make her way home. She'd suffer Papa's anger and beg his forgiveness. She'd tell her sister she'd made an awful mistake and reclaim her son.

The conductor stepped from the platform onto the train.

Katerina's heart beat double-time.

Stay or leave?

His fist folded around the door handle.

Decide.

Katerina knew she didn't have enough courage or money for the return passage. She wouldn't be going back, now or ever.

"Katerina Petrovna Danek?"

When she turned, Katerina saw that the voice came from a tall, ample woman with a broad, open face who strode toward her. She held a small child and a slightly bigger girl clung to the woman's skirt.

"*Tak*? Yes?"

"I'm sorry to be late. Vera," she said, nodding at the child in her arms, "had an accident. I thought you'd prefer meeting us without her soiled diaper." The woman's Ukrainian accent sounded both comfortingly familiar and strangely foreign.

Relief rippled through Katerina. Grabbing the back of the bench, she braced herself and rose, worried that her aching leg might betray her.

"Anyway, we're here." The woman set the toddler on the platform and hugged Katerina with her thick arms, kissing her three times on alternating cheeks. "Welcome."

"*Dyajytu.* Thank you."

"You're going to be staying at our house, Fedir's and mine, until the wedding."

Katerina's expression became a question mark.

"Oh, I'm Yana Panko. I'm so excited, I left my brain at home." The woman laughed with her entire body. "It's not every day Bilik gets a new face."

"Pleased to meet you, Mrs. Panko."

"We're going to be neighbors and friends, you and me. Please call me Yana."

The little girl peeked out from behind her mother's skirt like an actress from behind a stage curtain, her gaze traveling from Katerina's feet to her face. When Katerina smiled, the girl retreated behind the billowy skirt, burying her face in its folds.

"This is Marina, my shy one." Yana ruffled the girl's curly hair. "And this is Vera, my quick little rabbit." Yana scooped up the toddler before she could escape.

"You have beautiful children." Katerina's voice caught.

"There are four others, but they're in school," Yana said. "You'll meet them soon enough."

Vera sucked her thumb contentedly. Silvery drool escaped from the corners of her mouth, running down her chin and onto her mother's shoulder. Katerina studied the child's face: full-cheeked, soft, and innocent. Soon her son would be Vera's age. The realization ambushed her. She pulled a handkerchief from her satchel and dabbed at her eyes and nose.

"Are you all right?" Yana asked.

"I have a slight cold." It pained Katerina how easily she discarded the truth.

"With all your travel, it's no wonder. When we get home, I'll make some broth." Yana shifted Vera to her other substantial hip.

"Mr. Senyk is coming?"

"It's harvest," Yana said, as if that were sufficient explanation.

Katerina had steeled herself for this moment. Now, like a condemned prisoner who'd received a stay of execution, she would have to summon the courage to face him later.

"He's busy at the elevator, but you'll meet him tonight when he comes for supper."

"I don't want to impose."

"Nonsense, we're looking forward to having a guest. The children have been talking of little else. Besides, the room above the livery is no place for a woman to stay alone."

"I'm grateful for your kindness."

"You might be less grateful when the children talk your ear off." Wrinkles fanned out from the corners of Yana's smiling eyes. "You'll get married just to have some peace."

It felt unnatural to have this woman speaking of Katerina's upcoming marriage so casually. Until now, marriage had been only an idea, hatched by Aneta and Danya as a solution to a problem—not a flesh-and-blood event.

The worker pulled the last cartful into the freight room. The train whistle sounded, and the sun disappeared behind a bank of clouds, throwing the station into shadow.

"It will be warmer once we're moving. Come, I'll show you the town."

"Is there time?"

Yana chuckled. "You can walk from one end of Bilik to the other before the soup boils." She adjusted the toddler in her arms and started down the stairs with her other daughter still clinging to her skirt.

Katerina limped after her. "My luggage."

"Don't worry," Yana shouted over her shoulder. "The stationmaster will keep it, and Viktor can claim it after work."

Yana led Katerina across the rutted gravel road and headed due west down Main Street where none of the modest buildings stood taller than two stories. Bilik looked like a tree that had been optimistically planted but had never fully taken root, larger than a fork in the road yet far, far smaller than Katerina had imagined. There had to be fewer than two hundred people living in the town. The entire place could fit inside L'viv's Rynok Square with room to spare.

Barely a quarter mile from the train station, on the opposite side of the tracks, a red grain elevator with giant white letters painted on the structure, proclaiming the name of the town, towered over Bilik. As the train had sped through Canada, Katerina had seen many of these distinctively shaped buildings dotting the prairie, announcing towns no bigger than crossroads.

"That's where Viktor works," Yana said, pointing to the elevator. "He's pretty important around here. Farmers respect and trust him."

Katerina felt a flicker of unearned pride.

"There's the livery and the school next to it." Yana gestured north, up the street running perpendicular to Main.

For such a small town, the livery was surprisingly generous. A haymow faced the street, and, according to Yana, there must have been a room for visitors tucked behind it. She was right; it certainly didn't appear to be proper quarters for a woman. The single-story brick school just beyond it stood like an undecorated box as spare as the ground on which it sat. Katerina thought it a curious place to build a school, surrounded as it was by the unmistakable odor of horse manure.

"Viktor and Elena's house is past the school on the other side of the street," Yana said, nodding in that direction.

"Elena?"

Yana's hand flew to her mouth. "Oh my. I meant Viktor's house." She flushed. "Elena passed well over a year ago. Sometimes you get used to a thing, and it sticks in your head."

Danya had told Katerina that Viktor Senyk was a widower, but somehow hearing his name so effortlessly paired with his deceased wife's made her feel like an afterthought, something settled for when the genuine item is beyond reach. This was not how her life was supposed to unfold. She'd had grander plans, which didn't include being a second choice or living on a street that carried the stink of a livery. Katerina held her breath as they continued walking, until her insistent lungs forced her to inhale. Everything, it seemed, ran contrary to her intentions.

"You can see a bit of St. Kassia's from here. That's where you'll be married." Yana pointed over the rooftops at a dome, barely visible, crowned by a familiar patriarchal cross.

Katerina thought of the grandness of St. George's Cathedral—Meretin's architectural masterpiece graced by Pinsel's sculptures—the place she had always imagined she would be wed. By comparison, the silver painted onion dome of St. Kassia's looked like a dollhouse miniature.

The women passed a darkened firehouse and then continued on to the open yard in front of the blacksmith shop, where the smith rhythmically pounded the glowing tip of a long metal rod. Sweat beaded on his forehead and glistened on his arms, his taut muscles uncoiling and striking with such force that the boards beneath Katerina's feet vibrated. The man's eyes remained fixed on the anvil, and if he was aware of their presence, he gave no hint of it.

Gusting wind streamed through the open spaces between the buildings. Dust rose from the dry gravel road and swirled across the street and railroad tracks in a brown cloud. Katerina struggled to collect the hair dancing about her face. She tasted grit. Strands of Yana's hair, sprouting from beneath her scarf, flew frenetically, but she was too busy shielding the children with her broad body to notice.

Yana made neither comment nor inquiry about Katerina's limp, but when they reached Wozny's Dry Goods, she said, "Let's sit down and rest a bit. Vera's not the light bundle she used to be."

Katerina's leg throbbed. She was grateful for the rest.

Yana settled at one end of the bench whose gracefully arched wrought iron arms and legs seemed incongruous among the utilitarian surroundings. Katerina sat next to her, wondering if the smith was responsible for the artistry and questioning her future in a place that displayed so little of it.

Out of habit, Katerina eyed the fabrics displayed in the storefront window. If there was anything she was certain of, it was her ability to judge fine linens and silks and wools. Despite the ornate gold script spelling out the name of the store across the window, she was already certain the quality of the material would prove inferior and disappointing.

The women sat together quietly, Yana attending to the children, Katerina taking in the town. It was hard to imagine this insubstantial place as home. Katerina pictured L'viv's grand structures, which had stood for centuries. Longing, so powerful it felt alive, burrowed deep inside her.

Vera squirmed from her mother's arms and climbed onto Katerina's lap, tracing Katerina's mouth with her pudgy fingers, then curling her hand around the single strand of coral beads, the symbol of good luck and prosperity, circling Katerina's neck. Vera's silky skin and child's smell made Katerina ache.

"Be gentle," Yana warned.

Vera gave Katerina's cheek a wet kiss before climbing down to join Marina, who watched a woolly bear caterpillar hunch its way along the edge of the walk.

"Lots of black on that one," Yana said. "Means we're in for a harsh winter."

The few times a wagon or other vehicle bumped over the potholes on its way out of town, Yana waved and furnished an abbreviated history of the driver.

"That's Roman Klopoushak. Quite the lady's man," she said,

waving to a man driving the largest vehicle Katerina had ever seen. With its enclosed cab, huge tires, and wooden-framed bed, the truck looked as though it could do the work of a team of horses. "He's the most prosperous farmer around here. Couldn't settle for a Ford. No, he had to have a Gotfredson with a cast-aluminum radiator and a Buda engine, no less."

Katerina stared at Yana. "How do you—"

Yana's wide smile turned to a belly laugh. "I haven't the first idea what that means."

Katerina couldn't help smiling.

"Roman brags so much you wouldn't find a man, woman, or child in Bilik who couldn't recite every detail of his fancy truck."

The railroad tracks along Main's south edge stood empty now. Katerina watched as, in the distance, the locomotive shrank to the size of a worm as it inched its way toward Calgary. Plumes of black smoke rose skyward, riding the wind into nothingness. Her heart raced. She wanted to cry out. *Come back! I've changed my mind! Please, God, I want to go home!*

"I haven't asked you about your voyage," Yana said.

"I'm sorry. What—"

"Your voyage."

"Oh, it was long, but there wasn't any trouble."

"I can't imagine leaving everyone behind. I admire your courage."

"Sometimes you must do a thing because the other choice is far worse." Katerina's words floated on the wind toward the plains, escaping too quickly to pull them back. She looked down and stared at her folded hands.

"I was too young to remember, but I recall the stories my mother used to tell about the trouble she and my father had crossing the ocean," Yana said. "Mama told me she was sick the entire time. She didn't know she was pregnant with my brother and thought it must be the rocking boat that made her ill. When she found out, she feared that crossing the ocean while pregnant would bring the family bad luck. Mama was always superstitious. She worried her baby would die or that something terrible would happen to me or to Papa. She waited for tragedy. My brother was born healthy, I didn't die, and Papa is still alive, but when I was a little girl our house burned to the ground. I think Mama always felt guilty about that."

"Is your mother gone?"

"Five years now," Yana said. "And yours?"

"Since I was nine."

"Then you will understand Aleksandr."

"Aleksandr?"

"Viktor's boy."

"Boy?"

"Yes. Viktor has a son. You didn't know?"

Katerina shook her head. "How old?"

"Ten."

There had been no mention of a child in the bargain. A ten-year-old boy. Was this her brother-in-law's idea of a cruel joke, offering one son as replacement for another? Katerina's throat closed, stanched resentment threatening to overflow. Dumped in a thimble-size town on a godforsaken plain. A child. What other secrets had Danya kept from her?

Yana looked at her curiously, as though she couldn't fathom Katerina's circumstances. Just as quickly, the look vanished. Yana rose, gave Marina a kiss on the top of her head, and settled Vera in her arms. "It's time to go," she said. "There are hungry mouths to feed."

They walked past the small bank with a sign posted for the doctor's office located on the second floor.

"We're fortunate. Dr. Billings is often in town two days a week," Yana bragged.

A physician who was sometimes available two days out of seven. There was no reassurance in that.

They arrived at the general store, the last business on Main Street, a whitewashed, clapboard structure. Bracketing each side of a central doorway were large windows, which displayed wooden cigar boxes, potbellied stoves, and hefty wheels of cheese.

"We're here," Yana said, her voice full of cheer and welcome.

"This is your house?"

"This is our business. The house is out back."

In the unobstructed expanse alongside the building, the wind picked up, lifting Katerina's skirt and jostling her sideways. She struggled to keep her balance while limping behind Yana, who seemed unfazed. As they rounded the back corner of the structure, a startlingly blue house appeared. It shared a sidewall with the main structure, but its slanted roof, long front porch and jarring color gave the impression of a freestanding home. A garden worthy of a family of eight filled the yard. Katerina had never grown an edible morsel of anything. She'd never so much as pulled a weed from the ground. She despaired at how unprepared she was to live in this remote place.

But there would be no escape. This was it. This was the town where Viktor Senyk lived and the town in which she would live, perhaps for the rest of her life. She told herself she'd made the right choice, but she finally understood. Confession had cost her everything. Her punishment went beyond exile.

It was a death sentence.

Chapter Two

At 4:57 a.m., Viktor Senyk awoke in a mood as dark as the shadows lurking in his bedroom. He felt depleted but couldn't think why. He lay in bed, his head swimming through murky waters toward the distant, coherent shore.

Then he knew. Elena had appeared in his dreams again, dreams as unpredictable as prairie weather. She had stood in a fallow field, dressed in nothing but her flowing raven hair. He'd called her name again and again as loudly as he could until she turned to him. Her dark eyes glowered accusingly. When he'd tried to approach her to explain—what, he couldn't remember—she'd drifted farther from him, tauntingly, as if she'd wanted him to follow.

"What do you want?" he'd shouted, his dream voice sounding hollow in his ears.

She'd stood mute.

"Goddamn it, answer me!"

She'd smiled coyly and let him approach almost close enough to touch her. When she'd opened her mouth, instead of words spilling out, tongues of fire licked at the air. Viktor had shielded his face from the flames with his crossed arms, furious he'd been tricked into believing she could be trusted. By the time he'd dared look at her again, she'd vanished.

Viktor lingered in bed, sorting fact from fiction. This dream had been so real, he could have sworn he smelled Elena's flowery scent on his pillow.

He propped himself up on his elbows and looked around the room. The outline of the pitcher and basin sitting atop the washstand came into focus. From the mirrored wardrobe on the far wall, his tousled reflection—no longer young but still man enough for any woman—stared back at him. Elena be hanged. The metronomic ticking of the alarm clock on the table next to his bed counted off the seconds, making him edgy. It was harvest season. He needed to get to the grain elevator early. There was much work to be done. He had no time to lie around brooding and dwelling on foolish dreams.

As he waited impatiently for the buckwheat groats to boil, Viktor retrieved the envelope bearing the Ukrainian postmark that he'd tucked on the shelf between the flour tin and the sugar tin. He opened it but didn't bother rereading the letter detailing his marriage agreement with Katerina Danek. He knew its contents by heart. Although he had also memorized every detail of the photograph his uncle Demitri had sent, he studied it again.

Miss Danek sat with her ankles crossed, her back poker straight and her hands primly clasped in her lap. Her well-fitted clothes showed a slight frame. There was a look of privilege about her, unlike Bilik's leathery-faced farm wives, whose bodies showed the wear of childbirth and hard work on the land. Her upswept hair exposed a long, slender neck, and her dark eyes seemed to look beyond the camera. Viktor decided that only the width of her mouth kept her from being beautiful. When he met her tonight he'd judge her comeliness firsthand.

Viktor ran his thick fingers through his uncombed hair, then took a substantial swallow of tea. The whistle of the Canadian Pacific Railway train screaming through the middle of town interrupted his thoughts.

The porridge. *Shit!* He'd forgotten the porridge. As the mixture boiled over, Viktor grabbed the handle of the pan. "Damn it!" he cursed when the hot metal blistered his skin. He snatched a dish towel from the hook next to the sink and used it to push the pan to an empty burner. To ease the pain, Viktor ran his reddening palm over the slab of butter sitting in a dish on the table.

If he hadn't been so preoccupied with thoughts of Katerina Danek, he wouldn't have burned himself and his breakfast. If Elena hadn't left, he wouldn't have been thinking of meeting a new wife. If he didn't have a son, neither woman would matter. If.

His dream had already put him in a foul mood. Now this. He was looking at a long, hard day. He needed to have his wits about him. He also needed to leave the house with a full stomach.

Viktor scooped the porridge from the pan, taking care not to scrape the scorched groats at the bottom. He shook the sticky clump off the spoon into a bowl and poured milk over the top. The porridge was tasteless but filling. After cutting several slices of bread and cold sausage, he downed some, wrapped enough for his lunch, and set the rest out for Aleksandr, who was still asleep upstairs.

He'd been both mother and father to the boy for more than a year, and he resented it. Elena had wanted a child, but he'd never planned to be a father. His responsibilities at the elevator were plenty. True, at ten years old, his son got himself up, ate the meal laid out for him, and walked to the schoolhouse, barely one-eighth mile down the road. Still, there was more to caring for a child than he'd imagined or bargained for. Viktor was sick to death of women's work. He needed a wife. The boy needed a mother. That was all there was to it. That was why he would soon marry Katerina Danek.

When Viktor stepped into the cool morning air, he inhaled deeply, filling his lungs with the place. The aroma of ripened fields blew through town on the autumn wind. Whisper-thin clouds drifted high overhead. It promised to be a dry, sun-soaked day. Perfect harvest weather.

From his house, he drove his truck south along the gravel road for a block and then turned right on Main Street. He met no one but saw a light at the livery and in various living quarters above the businesses on Main. It was as if the town were waking up one window at a time. At the farthest end of the street, the eighty-foot grain elevator, with its characteristic shed roof, towered above everything like a secular cathedral.

As he approached the elevator, Viktor looked east and west along the empty railroad tracks before crossing to the office. He parked, unlocked the door, hung the keys on the hook just inside the entry, and rubbed his hands together against the chill in the room. He descended the stairs to the engine room. Today, the temperature promised to be seasonably mild. Come October, he'd be building a fire in the potbellied stove each morning. Viktor started the engine that moved the elevator's massive drive belts and powered the generator.

He climbed the stairs to the office and turned on the bare bulb hanging from a wire. The pressed-tin ceiling and silver-painted walls reflected the dim light, giving the small, utilitarian room a regal touch.

Gradually, as the sun cleared the horizon, natural light peeked through the windows. The planked floor creaked under Viktor's weight as he moved around the room. He opened the glass door of the small alcove housing the moisture tester and cleaned the cylinder. Next, he checked the dockage tester, the instrument that measured the percentage of wheat grain to waste and also determined the price a farmer would command for a load. Viktor prided himself on the accuracy of his measurements, believing his thoroughness was the key to the farmers' confidence in him.

Soon, a few farmers who owned the choice land closest to town would arrive. By midmorning, a crush of traffic would crowd the elevator entrance. Viktor stood perfectly still, savoring the quiet, letting the rising warmth from the engine room envelop him. Out of habit, he circled September 10 on the wall calendar hanging next to his scarred desk. He tucked the ledger under his arm and drew in a last full breath of dustless air before crossing the twenty paces to the elevator.

Although he'd already memorized them, Viktor checked the Canadian Wheat Board quotas and the distribution chart, which kept track of the bins where the grain was stored. He placed the open ledger on the shelf under the window overlooking the office and scanned the interior one last time. He was ready. At 7:00 a.m., when he opened the driveway doors, the first grain wagon approached from the west on Main Street.

As the farmers arrived, he directed them to the scale and weighed each load before dumping the grain into the pit. Then the motorized leg moved the grain in bucket loads up the length of the elevator to the distributing spouts, where it was channeled into the correct storage bins. Viktor took dockage samples and recorded the payment to each farmer before adjusting the numbers on the bin chart. How he loved the exacting nature of the work. No ambivalence. No guesswork. The world orderly and precise.

By midmorning, a press of wagons and trucks had funneled its way toward the driveway. Viktor stepped outside to take count. As he stood on the driveway looking down the line, he spotted a thin ribbon of smoke spiring above the third truck. His eyes narrowed.

"Zolyar, you damned fool!" he shouted.

All conversation stopped. Everyone turned to Viktor and then to Ivan Zolyar.

"Are you trying to blow us all sky high? Douse that pipe now or I'll put it out for you." Viktor pointed to the end of the driveway. "To the back of the line. You know the rules."

No one challenged Viktor. Grain dust was notoriously combustible. There'd been a major fire at Royceville less than six months earlier. Half the town had burned before they'd gotten the blaze under control.

Farmers intuitively understood the need for order. Harvest season was a ritual as familiar to the men as the Divine Liturgy. Gathering at the elevator was as much opportunity as it was necessity. Here, they discussed market prices, talked about the weather, argued about the newest farm machinery, and shared family news. The elevator was as sacred in small prairie towns as the church.

"Mornin', Viktor," Josef Sokur said, bringing his wagon to a halt on the scale. "Looks like you're puttin' in a pretty good day."

"Can't complain," Viktor said.

The men fell silent as they unloaded the wagon.

"Heard you're gettin' married," Josef said when they finished. He shifted the reins in his hands and the mules' ears flicked.

"You heard right."

"Heard she's comin' from Ukraine."

"She is."

"From whereabouts?"

"L'viv," Viktor said.

"City woman?" The farmer tightened his grip on the reins and steadied his team.

"Yup."

"Might be a little surprised when she finds out Bilik's got three streets."

"I expect she'll learn." Viktor kept his eyes on the ledger as he recorded the undersize load weight and quality in the correct columns. Sokur's grain proved inferior, as usual, but he kept the thought to himself.

"When's the wedding? I'll be ready to do some dancin' after I get the crop in."

"Depends on the weather."

Josef scratched his scruffy chin. "A man shouldn't be without a woman for too long."

"Nope."

"See you later this week, then, eh?" With that Josef gave the reins a snap and drove out of the elevator.

By midafternoon, grain dust hovered in the air like fog, clinging to Viktor's skin, rimming his eyelashes, and coating his mouth with paste. He stepped outside and squinted into the bright sunshine. Above him, he heard a familiar warble and spotted three barn swallows gliding near the driveway door, their iridescent bodies glinting in the light. Through the haze, Viktor watched a bank of gray-bottomed clouds gathering in the distance. A brisk prairie wind carried the dust eastward. He counted a half-dozen vehicles still waiting to unload.

At sunset, when all the deliveries had been recorded, the grain tested, and the ledger put in order, Viktor—tired, dirty, and hungry—headed to the train station to retrieve Katerina Danek's luggage. Afterward, he drove home to wash up and change his clothes. He was eager to lay eyes on her, but he was too damned tired to be sociable tonight. Yana, however, had insisted he come for dinner. Like it or not, tonight he would meet his wife-to-be.

Chapter Three

In the washstand mirror, Katerina nervously primped for her first meeting with Mr. Senyk, critically studying her weary eyes, creased forehead, and pursed lips. She gnawed bits of skin on the inside of her cheeks—a habit she'd acquired in childhood—and thought of Aneta, who'd always been more mother than sister and who'd scold her whenever she saw this same careworn expression. Half a world away, Katerina heard her disapproval: *It makes you look like an old crone. How do you expect to make a good impression with that sour face?*

Katerina's hair, pulled back and held by the silver clasp Stepan had given her last Christmas, escaped in wilted strands. She undid the clasp and examined its filigreed surface, remembering the pleasure on Stepan's face when she'd opened the gift, too overcome to speak. He'd embraced her, cupped her breasts, and brushed his lips along the nape of her neck. Prayers and distance had not dulled the memory. She sensed his presence, imagining his warm breath on her skin. She held the clasp next to her heart. It was wrong to keep it, she knew, and doubly wrong to bring it with her to Canada, but she couldn't bear to part with it. Without this tangible reminder of him, she feared her time with Stepan would be a dream.

There was a soft knock on the door.

Katerina dabbed her brimming eyes with the back of her hand and straightened her back. "Come in."

Lilia, Yana's twelve-year-old daughter, opened the door cautiously and peeked into the bedroom. "Mama sent me for your skirt and blouse so I can iron them. And she asked me to tell you that the broth for your cold is heating on the stove."

At first, Katerina was puzzled. Then she remembered her

improvised deception at the train station and resolved to be more truthful in the future. She glanced down the length of her body, taking a quick inventory of the clothes she'd worn on the train, clothes that looked as wrinkled and as tired as she felt.

"I don't want to put you to any trouble."

"You're not," Lilia said. "Mama's already set up the sadiron and board."

Katerina removed her blouse and stepped out of her skirt, handing them to Lilia, whose cheeks pinked at the sight of Katerina dressed only in her slip. Lilia averted her eyes and backed from the room as quietly as she'd entered.

Katerina raked her fingers through her oily hair. The skin beneath her eyes puffed, and a spray of blemishes covered her forehead. Nerves. Her belongings, including a change of clothes, were still at the train station. Bone weary from a sleepless night on the train, she wanted to weep. What she wouldn't give for a hot bath and a night's rest before meeting Viktor Senyk! What was Yana thinking, inviting him for dinner on the first night of her arrival? As soon as the thought formed, she heard her father quoting the Ukrainian proverb, "It is difficult to learn to thank God if we cannot thank people." Yana had shown her nothing but kindness. Remorse replaced ingratitude.

Scooping water from the bowl, Katerina lowered her face into the coolness, lingering a moment before letting it spill back into the basin, each time imagining her weariness washing away. She splashed water around her hairline, hoping to make it appear cleaner. As she patted her face dry with the freshly laundered towel, she closed her eyes and inhaled the scent of the outdoors, regaining her composure a bit more with every breath. She towel dried her damp hair. Finally, she looked in the mirror again, seeing, if not a relaxed face, at least a less anxious and unkempt version of herself. She practiced her smile and then pulled her hair neatly into a chignon. She sprinkled a touch of rosewater on her wrists and at the hollow of her neck.

There was a soft knock on the door. Lilia opened it a crack.

"Please come in."

At arm's length, Lilia extended the neatly ironed skirt and blouse. When she smiled, Katerina saw the promise of a pretty woman foreshadowed on the girl's face.

"Miss Danek?"

"Yes?"

"I'm—we're happy you're here."

Katerina followed the scent of cooked cabbage into the kitchen, where Yana stood at the stove, her back to the doorway, tending a skillet of frying meat. At a glance, she realized Yana planned a meal worthy of a religious holiday. Making an event of this first meeting did nothing to calm Katerina's nerves.

"You gave me a start!" Yana slapped a hand above her ample breasts. "I must have been daydreaming."

"I didn't mean to—"

"You just spared everyone a pauper's meal of bread and water." Yana laughed as vigorously as she stirred.

"What can I do to help?"

"You are a guest."

"I know a woman in another woman's kitchen can mean trouble, but I promise not to step on your toes. Please. I need to keep my mind and hands busy."

"There's an apron, then," Yana said, pointing to the hook on the door. "When it comes time to serve the meal, you become a guest again."

Yana's kitchen was a cheerful room. The whitewashed walls, each outlined in a thin red stripe, boasted a hand-painted border of gold vases filled with multicolored flowers. It was reminiscent of home except, instead of a traditional clay *pich*, a cast-iron stove anchored the room. A coal-burning compartment flanked each side of the oven, from which the aroma of freshly baked bread escaped. A sizzling pan or bubbling kettle occupied every burner on the stovetop.

"Your kitchen is very inviting." Katerina admired the comfort of the room with a twinge of envy. How different life must be in a house filled with love.

"We added the kitchen, dining room, and parlor. The family got too big to live upstairs. Now, only the bedrooms are above the store. It felt like a castle when we first added on. That was before Vera came along. I don't know how we'd manage without the extra space."

While Yana talked, Katerina listened, enjoying her distracting chatter. The women worked side by side companionably, chopping, stirring, baking, and frying. Katerina sipped her broth. Yana sampled everything, consuming an entire meal before the dishes reached the table.

A tall, solid boy entered the kitchen, followed by his opposite. There was no denying the taller child was Yana's. He shared her substantial frame and a face as round as a pie plate.

"Mama, when are we going to eat? I'm *starving*," he said.

"A watched pot never boils." Yana tweaked his ear.

"Aw, let's go outside." He motioned for the smaller boy to follow.

"I think you forgot your manners," Yana said, nodding toward Katerina.

"Sorry—I'm Lavro."

"Pleased to meet you."

"And this is Aleksandr."

"Viktor's son," Yana said.

It seemed impossible that the child, who would soon be hers, stood only a few feet away. Katerina wanted to stare at him and study him the way she might examine a curious object.

"Hello," she said. Unexpected resentment welled up in her like an underground spring. It was unfair, Katerina knew, to hold this child accountable for not being someone else, but how would she ever forgive him for not being Matviyko?

The boy stared at his feet.

His timidity made Katerina ashamed of her small-mindedness.

Lavro shifted impatiently from one foot to the other.

"Go already. And don't wander too far!" Yana called after the boys as they scooted out the back door.

Given Mr. Senyk's photograph, Aleksandr wasn't what Katerina had imagined. He was slight, and although he and Lavro were the same age, half a head shorter. His curly hair was dark, almost black, and his eyes were the color of earth.

"He seems very—delicate," Katerina said.

"Aleksandr is all boy." Yana flew around the kitchen, pulling bowls from shelves, opening the oven door to check the bread, and peering under the lids of steaming pots. "Losing his mother has been hard. He's a good boy and he'll come around in time. It will help to have a woman in the house again."

Before Katerina got the chance to ask more about him, Lilia walked in, humming. She grabbed a stack of plates off the shelf, pulled a mound of silverware out of the sideboard, and headed into the dining room. When she returned empty-handed, she was still humming. Katerina recognized the song and hummed along. Yana joined in, whistling.

Music soothed Katerina. She began to relax.

"Mama, are you ready for me to make tea?"

"I'll clear a place." Yana removed a pot from the front burner. "Lilia makes delicious tea, far better than mine."

An affectionate look passed between them. Regret clouded Katerina's memory of her own mother. During the year Irina Danek had been bedridden—when her skin had turned ghostly white and the room had filled with the stink of imminent death—Katerina had become invisible, not only to her dying mother but to Papa. *Be quiet.*

Don't be so thoughtless. Your mother needs her rest. It was as if Katerina had caused the cancer and her silence was the only cure.

"Viktor will be here any minute," Yana said, pulling Katerina back to the moment.

As promised, she hung her apron on the hook behind the door and limped into the dining room to await Mr. Senyk's arrival. The table was laden with braided bread, cabbage rolls, buckwheat sausage, cornmeal casserole, beets with horseradish, and crepes filled with mashed cheese. Katerina sat in the place reserved for her, next to Yana's husband, Fedir.

"So happy to have you with us," he said, rising. "Bilik can use a pretty new face."

"How kind of you, Mr. Panko."

"Fedir, please." The man's eyes twinkled when he smiled. His receding hairline, apple cheeks, and round eyes reminded her of a Raphael cherub. Although he stood at least four inches shorter than Yana, making the pair seem comically mismatched, Katerina decided their easygoing temperaments made them well suited to each other.

Despite Fedir's warm greeting, Katerina's composure evaporated. The import of the impending introduction set her nerves on edge. She gnawed her cheek and wiped her damp hands on her skirt. What if Mr. Senyk found her wanting? What if he decided her flaws outnumbered her assets? What if, once he saw her limp, he decided to return her like defective merchandise? She had nowhere else to go.

By the time Viktor arrived, everyone was seated except Yana, who was in the kitchen, adding dill and onion to the cream sauce to pour over the *pyrizhky*. Viktor entered the dining room, his cheeks scrubbed to a reddish sheen, his coffee-colored hair oiled and combed, and his clothes Sunday clean.

"I didn't recognize you. I thought Yana invited some dandy for supper," Fedir teased.

"Ach, don't mind him," Yana said, following behind him with the pitcher of piping hot sauce. "He's been married so long he doesn't remember the proper way to court a lady."

"Nonsense. I have plenty of romance in my soul," Fedir protested. He motioned for Viktor to take his place opposite Katerina. "Anyhow, Katerina Danek, I'd like you to meet Viktor Senyk. At least, that's who I think he is."

"Fedir, behave yourself," Yana scolded, but Katerina caught her grin.

"Miss Danek," Viktor said, bowing slightly.

"Pleased to meet you, Mr. Senyk." Katerina extended her hand, self-conscious of her clammy palms. She hoped he couldn't feel her trembling. His large, calloused hand surrounded hers, his touch firm and sure. Stepan had a cleric's hands, soft as summer grass, his touch light and tender. Silently, she apologized to Viktor for her disloyal comparison.

Viktor's freshly scrubbed skin had the masculine scent of unperfumed soap. He was ruggedly built—older and more seasoned than in his photograph—with deep, penetrating brown eyes. His thick mustache accentuated his full, sensuous mouth. Viktor Senyk was a handsome man.

Clinking silverware, lively conversation, and robust laughter filled the room. Like a symphony conductor, Fedir sat at the head of the table, wielding forkfuls of food. Yana sat at the opposite end, next to Vera, cutting the little girl's meat into kibble-sized pieces before spreading them on the highchair tray. Now, Katerina understood why Yana did most of her eating at the stove. Aleksandr fit quietly among the spirited Panko children, who squeezed in, elbow to elbow, along both sides of the table.

Despite the enticing fare and warm company, Katerina's anxiety dampened her appetite. She pushed the food on her plate from side to side, taking an occasional bite, hoping no one noticed. She felt Viktor's eyes on her, assessing her, taking her measure. When she turned to face him, however, he wasn't looking at her, and she wondered if his judgment was in her imagination. She tried to study him but dared look only in stolen glances. If he was aware of her scrutiny, it didn't show.

"By the looks of business at the store, the harvest is going well," Fedir said.

"So far." Viktor tore a large hunk of bread in two and slathered butter on each half. "The fields have been dry enough to get a good run at it."

"Let's hope the weather holds," Fedir said.

"We saw Roman Klopoushak driving his fancy truck in town. I figured he was coming from the elevator," Yana said.

"He's buying one of those new gasoline tractors," Viktor said. "Claims it's going to take the place of twenty men. Good news for Klopoushak, not for the threshing crews out of Thunder Bay."

"I was telling Katerina this is your busiest season," Yana said.

"On our walk from the station this afternoon, Yana pointed out the grain elevator," Katerina said.

"It's eighty feet tall and painted red. Pretty hard to miss." Viktor jabbed a large slice of sausage with his fork and scooped it into his mouth.

Katerina felt foolish. "I only meant that it's impressive."

"It was built new last year," Fedir said.

"I'm sure Katerina would like to see where you work." Yana wiped Vera's face with the corner of her bib. "She'll be even more impressed."

"No place for a woman, especially now." Viktor continued chewing.

Getting to know this man would not be easy. The fist in Katerina's stomach tightened. She moved the untouched cabbage roll to the other side of her plate and took a sip of tepid tea. Fatigue traveled through her body, settling at the ends of her limbs. She forced a smile.

"Then after the harvest," she said. "I will look forward to it."

Yana pushed herself away from the table. "Lilia and Sasha, I need your help in the kitchen."

The girls followed their mother. In a few minutes, they returned to the dining room, carrying a plate of honey cake.

"Who saved room?" Yana asked.

"I did!" Luka said.

"Looks as though you're full right up to your chin," Fedir teased. "I'm not sure there's room for anything sweet."

"Yes, there is, Papa," the seven-year-old said, his expression the picture of earnestness. "I saved this much room." Luka made a square with his thumbs and index fingers the same size as the pieces of cake.

Everyone laughed.

The plate passed first to Katerina and Viktor, then around the table. Katerina had no appetite for cake, but not wanting to appear impolite, she scooped a piece onto her plate.

"Papa, tell the story about the mule," Sasha begged.

"What mule?" There was mischief in his voice.

"You know, Papa. Jasper."

"Oh, that mule. Well, Jasper was the dumbest animal I ever saw, even dumber than a turkey in a rainstorm," Fedir said. "Back when I was wooing your mama, I tried to ride him to her parents' farm, but he wouldn't budge. I got so mad I painted Stupid on both sides of that cantankerous beast. The words didn't disappear for ten years."

"And, remember Papa, he bit you on your backside," Lavro added.

The children giggled.

"And you bit him back!"

Although Aleksandr grinned, Katerina noticed he was far more contained than the Panko children, who laughed as easily as they breathed.

"That's quite a tale," Viktor said.

"One he's told a hundred times before." Yana rolled her eyes. "Of course, the story stretches each time he tells it."

"I like to keep you guessing." Fedir winked at his wife.

Conversation around the table continued in a blend of English and Ukrainian. Yana explained that, although the entire community was made up of Ukrainians, by law, English was the only language allowed in Saskatchewan's schools.

"Like most people in Bilik, my family and Fedir's family settled here in the late 1890's," she said. "We try to help the children understand their roots and to keep our language alive, but they are more Canadian than Ukrainian. It won't be long, I fear, before they leave us behind."

"To tell the truth, my own memories of the old country seem more and more dream than fact," Fedir added.

Tonight, among these Canadians, Katerina's Ukrainian accent sounded heavy and old-world to her ear. During her months of confinement at Aneta's, she had diligently worked on her English. Still, reading was far different than listening and speaking. When the older children used English, they spoke so fluently that following them was like running after a galloping horse. It embarrassed her to think how feeble her attempts at mastering the language had been. She resolved to practice harder.

"Yana, you've outdone yourself tonight," Viktor said, patting his stomach and pushing away from the table.

Yana blushed. "Ach, it was nothing. Katerina did much of the work, and Lilia was a big help."

"Then compliments to all." Viktor raised his glass in a sweeping arc.

The parlor clock struck eight bells. The leftovers cooled on the table.

Viktor rose. "Fedir, Yana, Miss Danek, been a pleasure, but it's time to go home. There's school tomorrow and an early day at the elevator."

"It's been a fine evening," Fedir agreed. "Good food and good company."

"Aleksandr," Viktor said.

Aleksandr didn't look up. He and Lavro were hunched together conspiratorially, their heads almost touching.

"Aleksandr," Viktor repeated.

The boy straightened and rushed to stand next to his father.

"What do you say?"

"Thank you." Aleksandr stared at his shoes.

"And to Miss Danek?"

"Nice to meet you."

"It was a pleasure to meet you, too, Aleksandr," Katerina said, her heart softening.

As soon as they left, the chatter and activity at the table returned. Katerina, however, thought about the look on Aleksandr's face as he stood next to his father. What had she seen? A memory floated just beyond her reach. Then it came to her: a vision of the wounded bunting she'd found in the schoolyard when she was a child, its eyes wide, its wing broken, its song weak and pleading. She'd tenderly wrapped it in her handkerchief, taken it home, and hidden it in her bedroom in a box lined with twigs and fabric. For days, she had sneaked breadcrumbs and water into her room. Then one day, she'd found the bird's lifeless body in the box. It still bothered her that the bird might have lived had she known more and tried a little harder.

Chapter Four

Now that Katerina had found some time alone, she'd been hopeful the right words would come, but in the past half hour, she'd managed to scrawl only "Tuesday, September 29, 1925," at the top of the onionskin stationery. Since arriving in Bilik on the tenth of the month, she'd made several attempts to fulfill her solemn promise to Aneta to write every week, but she'd yet to complete a single sentence.

What could she write that wouldn't cause her sister worry or herself embarrassment? How could she explain that Viktor Senyk had come for dinner nearly three weeks ago, and that since then she'd waited on tenterhooks, hoping he would show some sign he still intended to marry her? How could she confess that each night at dusk, when he retrieved Aleksandr, Viktor greeted her with polite formality but without a hint of warmth, his handsome face always inscrutable? Should she admit that, despite the Pankos' benevolence, she grappled with constant loneliness and regret? Were there even words to describe such heartache?

Katerina knew she should be grateful for Aneta's willingness to raise her son and Danya's marriage arrangements on her behalf, but—God forgive her—she was bitter. How could she write that?

She stared out the Pankos' parlor window, watching the rain blend sky and land into a monotonous gray. Where only hours before there had been a faded carpet of dried grass, a soggy bog covered the backyard and garden. St. Kassia's dome, visible from the window, appeared lusterless. Despite the chilling rain, the parlor was warm. The black potbellied stove, on the wall opposite the window, heated the room and wrung the dampness from the air.

The house was unusually still. Fedir was stocking shelves at the store. The older children were at school, and the younger two were settled in for an afternoon nap. With everyone gone or sleeping, except Yana, the only sounds in the house came from the ticking pendulum clock and the occasional clang of pots and pans in the kitchen, where Yana was baking. Even the Berliner Gram-O-Phone, with its oversized daffodil bell, and the radio, which the family frequently gathered around in the evenings, stood mute in corners of the room.

The discomfort of silence surprised Katerina. When she'd first arrived, the noise in the household had sounded cacophonous, but quickly, she'd recognized the satisfying harmony of activity and voices and laughter. It was a startling contrast to her life in L'viv, where she had lived quietly with Papa, and then had lived silently with Aneta and Danya in a little apartment, made smaller by her large, pregnant stomach. Upon reflection, her entire life had been hushed and contained. Even her relationship with Stepan, which at first had made her want to shout for joy, had devolved into whispers behind closed doors. Her life had been a concerto played pianissimo. In contrast, the Panko family's collective lives were a symphony replete with fortissimos and crescendos.

Katerina lightly traced her finger over the date at the top of the page. Last September, Stepan had still been part of her life, albeit a secret part. Then, she had still believed her plans would turn out as she hoped. Stepan would leave the priesthood. He would choose her. From the first, he'd reminded her that although he had been married, according to church law, priests were allowed to take a wife only if they wed before being ordained. Stepan's wife had died, and he was never permitted to marry again. Still, she'd believed their love was so extraordinary that he'd choose her over his vocation. Surely, God could do with one less servant. Stepan would leave the priesthood and marry her. He was a brilliant man, who could teach or write or paint. How naive she'd been. So much pain freshly strewn behind her. So many things left unsaid.

Katerina wondered if Aneta knew Viktor had a son. Although she had no proof, she suspected Danya had known the truth and decided not to tell her lest she change her mind. His conscience wouldn't have suffered the slightest prick for his deception. She'd come to expect Danya's duplicity, but the idea that her sister might have purposely withheld this important fact was too hurtful to imagine.

The empty stationery served as a painful reminder of the gulf between sisters, a chasm wider than the ocean separating them. Once they'd been inseparable—Aneta the big sister and surrogate mother, Katerina the adoring shadow. There had been no actual falling out, no angry, irretrievable words spoken. Still, their once-solid bond had broken. The only way to restore it was through forgiveness. But who was to be forgiven? Her greatest sorrow had turned into Aneta's greatest joy. Who was to blame for that?

Katerina bowed her head and silently prayed to the Virgin Mary.

O Theotokos, teach me, who is a sinner in thoughts, words and deeds, to forgive that which to my hardened heart is unforgiveable. Have compassion on me. Guide me to a place of understanding. Soften my heart and set my mind at peace.

"Miss Danek."

Katerina startled. It was Viktor's authoritative voice coming from behind her. She turned to find him standing in the doorway. How long had he been observing her?

"I—I wasn't expecting you," Katerina said, flustered, searching for an adroit comment. Words and charm failed her.

Viktor strode in his stocking feet to the straight-backed chair beside her. His toes worked their way through expanding holes in each sock. His hair, finger-combed off his forehead, was as wet as if he'd just stepped from the bath.

"Closed the elevator early," he said.

"I see."

"Fields are too wet to harvest. Farmers won't be driving into town."

A single oil lamp glowed on the table between them, lending the room a shadowy intimacy. Katerina sat demurely with her ankles crossed. Viktor sprawled, his long limbs claiming the room. She watched him inventory her from head to toe in one scrutinizing pass.

She was a mare up on the block for purchase. Any moment now, he would inspect her teeth. Although Katerina resented his obvious evaluation of her, she also wondered how she fared in his judgment. She doubted he was equally concerned with her appraisal of him. Mr. Senyk appeared to be a very self-assured man.

"For you," he said. At the end of his outstretched arm he held a small brown paper bag.

Katerina took it and peeked inside. It contained licorice from the candy bins at Panko's General Store. Hope rose in her like a wildflower sprouting from newly thawed ground.

"It's not much," he said.

"Thank you. It's a very thoughtful gesture."

Viktor pulled a pipe and tobacco pouch from his shirt pocket, then reached into his pants pocket and retrieved a small jackknife and a match. With the edge of the knife blade, he scraped the residue from the bowl and tapped it into the ashtray on the side table before filling it with fresh tobacco, using his index finger to tamp it down. He cradled the bowl in one hand and, with the other, expertly struck the match head against his thumbnail, igniting a small flame in a single flick. Patiently, he held the flame to the tobacco until a smoke plume drifted upward. Viktor leaned back in his chair and savored the tobacco's sweetness. Little popping noises escaped from his lips as he drew smoke up the slender stem.

"I didn't realize you smoked a pipe," Katerina said.

"Why would you?" Viktor's brusque laugh wielded a sharp edge.

Heat rose to Katerina's cheeks. "Of course, you're right, Mr. Senyk. I was simply making an observation."

The acrid smoke seeped into her lungs. Katerina thought of Papa, who, for as long as she could remember, smoked a pipe at home but never downstairs in his tailor shop because it tainted the costly fabrics.

"How old are you, Miss Danek? Twenty-five? Twenty-six?"

"I've recently turned twenty-eight."

"Then why aren't you married?" Viktor leaned toward Katerina, his head tilted slightly like a hunting dog on alert.

She searched for some version of the truth, a half-truth that skirted Viktor's rudeness. Thoughts, impossible to share, whirled through her mind as she fumbled for an explanation. *Because I loved a man who was unattainable. Because the father of my child vanished. Because I was sent away to spare my family embarrassment.* "I haven't found anyone suitable," she said.

"No one has met your standards?"

"No."

"Or is your infirmity the reason?" he asked, gesturing toward her leg.

Although she'd endured the sideways glances and outright stares of strangers and dealt with inquisitiveness about her leg for most of her life, Viktor's bluntness wounded. She'd planned to broach this subject in her own way and in her own time. Katerina felt as exposed as if she stood before him naked.

"I can't answer that," she whispered.

She thought of Stepan, remembering how reluctant she'd been to let him touch her damaged leg, but, as always, he'd said exactly the right thing. *How could I expect you to love me with all my flaws if you were too perfect? Let's leave perfection to God.* He'd tenderly caressed her leg and, starting at her foot, kissed his way along its full length until he reached her inner thigh. The memory of it made her ache.

Viktor took a long draw on his pipe. Another smoke rivulet twisted toward the ceiling. "My uncle Demitri assured me you were agreeable to marriage," he said after a lengthy silence in which his eyes never left her face. "Is that your intention?"

"Yes."

"Bragged you were the best cook in L'viv."

"I daresay your uncle is given to exaggeration." Katerina offered no more, for fear he might be testing her.

"The size of my uncle's belly is proof he can judge a good cook." Viktor patted his flat stomach.

"You remember him well enough," Katerina said, allowing a slight smile. "I will do my best to satisfy your appetite."

"All my appetites, Miss Danek." Viktor raised his brow roguishly. "In exchange, you won't go hungry. You'll have a roof over your head." His eyes shone and his lip curled like a chess player who knows he's trapped his opponent's king.

Katerina's face burned. Before she could think of anything proper to say, Yana entered the room, carrying a small silver tray with two cups clattering against the metal as she walked. Obviously, she had unearthed her finest tea service for the occasion.

"Here you go," Yana said. "Nothing like a little hot tea with conversation." The lightness in her voice floated atop the palpable tension, which she didn't seem to notice. "Katerina, you're flushed. If the room is too warm for you, I can crack a window."

"The temperature is satisfactory, Yana. Thank you."

Yana set the tray on the table. "I was a blushing bride once myself," she said and touched Katerina affectionately on her shoulder. "I'll be in the kitchen if you need anything."

Although Katerina's throat was parched, she worried the nervous tremor in her hands would betray her, so she left her cup on the tray. Viktor, however, showed no reluctance. He shifted his pipe to his opposite hand and grasped the diminutive handle of the cup with the other. Katerina thought of a fairy-tale giant playing with a child's tea set.

In a few swallows, Viktor's tea vanished. "My boy needs a mother. He's weak. He needs a firm hand." Viktor emphasized his point with a fist on the table. The lamp flame flickered and Katerina's pen spilled droplets of ink as it rolled across the blank paper.

"He's still young." Katerina struggled to keep her voice even. "There are many ways to teach a child."

Viktor's jaw tightened. "The boy can't become a man if he's pampered and fussed over like a girl."

Katerina took a deep breath and willed herself to meet Viktor's glare. "I don't mean to quarrel with you, Mr. Senyk. I promise to be a devoted mother to Aleksandr. I will teach him and raise him as my own, but I am a woman, not a taskmaster. Perhaps he's—sensitive—because he misses his mother. I also lost my mother when I was Aleksandr's age. Such a loss is not easy for any child."

"If you're not up to it, Miss Danek, tell me now." Viktor puffed on his pipe and tapped his foot, rhythmically, against the floorboards, as if keeping time to a Wagner march.

Katerina hadn't noticed before, but now, as the sparse light angled perfectly across his forehead, she saw a crescent-shaped scar above Viktor's left eyebrow. So obvious. It was like an exclamation mark. How had she missed it? Until now, she'd been too nervous to look directly at Viktor's chiseled face; now she wanted to memorize it. She traced his ample mouth and the curve of his prominent cheekbones with her eyes. Her gaze involuntarily returned to Viktor's brow. So obvious, that scar. His imperfection made her buoyant.

"I am up to it," she said.

Aleksandr and his father walked home from the Pankos' house in darkness.

"Come on, boy," his father said. "I'd like to get home before dawn."

A thin line of clouds hung beneath the half-moon, and a north wind that had pushed the thick afternoon rain clouds southward swept across the prairie. They moved down Main Street along the wooden walkway, where water pooled in the depressions created by years of foot traffic. If his father hadn't been with him, Aleksandr would have stomped through the puddles, enjoying the thrill of seeing how high and far he could make the water burst. It would have been a satisfying cure for his sullen mood. Instead, he jumped over the puddles, considering every dry landing a small victory.

When they turned north off Main, leaving the shops that provided the only barrier against the wind, his father lifted his collar and thrust his hands deep into his pockets.

Aleksandr half ran to keep pace with his father. Hunger he hadn't noticed while playing with Lavro now poked at his stomach. His father had been at the Pankos' house when he and Lavro had returned from school. They'd been invited to stay, but his father had declined the offer. "Another time, thank you," he'd said. Why they had to hurry home to a cold, empty house for dinner, Aleksandr didn't know. Longingly, he thought of the tantalizing aromas escaping from Mrs. Panko's kitchen as he wrestled with the disappointment of another meal of bread and sausage he surely would be eating tonight. No wonder Lavro was twice his size.

It wasn't really the lack of a hot meal that bothered Aleksandr, however. Lilia had told him that Miss Danek was going to marry his father and become his new mother. The revelation made his head pound.

"No, she isn't!" Aleksandr had said, almost shouted. He'd lowered his voice only for fear his father would hear him. That would have led to an embarrassing reprimand but no further explanation, so he'd kept his voice down even though he'd wanted to scream *no* so loudly the roof would lift off the house.

"She is, too," Lilia had said. "Mama told us and Miss Danek said it's true."

He'd looked to Lavro for support, but instead, Lavro had shrugged his shoulders and said, "It's true. Mama told us."

Aleksandr had been stunned. How was this stranger going to be his mother?

"She's really nice. And Mama said Miss Danek comes from a big city, and she can sew beautiful clothes and sing," Lilia had said.

Why did Lilia know so much about this stranger who would be his mother—but he knew nothing? Resentment gripped his every muscle. It wasn't as if he didn't want a mother; he did—*his* mother.

It frightened him that his memory of her faded by the day. As his recollection of her features was reduced to her black hair and slender body, he held as fast as he could to his other sensory memories—the sound of her voice, the softness of her hands, and her sweet smell. Why was it that his mother had scrubbed herself with the same soap that his father did, but the difference between their scents was as stark as the contrast between a dirt road and a flower garden?

After her death, his father had removed all evidence of her—every piece of clothing, every photograph, and even the kitchen chair that had marked her place at the table. He had chopped it up and burned it, as though her disappearance from their lives had not been complete enough, as though death had not been adequate. And now, his father had chosen a woman to take his mother's place, as simply as he'd replaced the broken wheel of his truck with a new one.

It wasn't that easy with people. You couldn't magically replace them.

Still, Lilia's approval of her counted for something, didn't it? Everybody knew she was the smartest student in school, even if she was a girl. And every boy thought she was the prettiest girl, too, even though none of them would have dared admit it out loud; that would have led to more teasing than even the toughest boys could withstand. But saying a thing didn't make it true, no matter who said it. Being smart and pretty didn't make Lilia Panko an expert on mothers, especially his mother. If she thought this stranger was so special, Miss Danek could take her own mother's place.

When they arrived home, his father said, "Get some coal and see to the fire."

Aleksandr had been so lost in thought he'd forgotten about the cold wind. Now, it was piercing. He pulled his jacket tightly around his thin frame and slumped toward the rear of the house to the basement entry. It took all his strength to pull the right half of the clamshell door upward. When he finally managed to get it partially open, it caught like a ship's sail, standing upright in the wind. He pushed on it until it passed the vertical plane and fell open in defeat. His arms ached from the effort.

Aleksandr hated the dark, but it would have been no use protesting or confessing his fear. That was certain. He walked down four steps to the wall-mounted kerosene lamp and felt for the tin matchbox holder. He depressed the lever that raised the lamp globe, struck the match against the concrete wall, and touched the flame to the wick. When it caught, he adjusted the wick slightly. As soon as he released the lever and the enclosed flame lit the room, Aleksandr took a deep breath. He imagined the oily odor smelled like the center of the Earth.

An imposing mound of coal filled the bin. With the stubby-handled shovel, he scooped various-sized hunks of coal into the bucket, selecting the smallest pieces to tease the stove's remaining embers and the largest ones to pile on top to catch the fire. When he had filled the bucket, he hefted it with both arms and slowly made his way up the stairs to the lantern. Reluctantly, he extinguished the flame. As he placed both feet on each of the four remaining steps, he counted aloud until he broke into the open. The cold air was more welcome than a ten cent coin. He set the bucket on the ground and fought with the wind until the open half of the clamshell slammed shut. Then he closed the hasp.

It was only nine more steps to the back door, but it felt like fifty. When he opened the door, the wind pulled on it so forcefully that the door was nearly ripped from its hinges. Aleksandr scrambled to grab it before any damage was done. With his back against the door, he pressed with all his weight until the latch caught. Cautiously, he opened the door again, just wide enough for the bucket to pass through. He planted his feet, braced the door open with one knee, and pushed the bucket into the gap. Then he wedged himself through the slot and closed the door.

Staggering to the stove, Aleksandr dropped the bucket when his arms could no longer endure the strain. It thudded to the floor and tipped over.

"Aleksandr!" his father shouted from the kitchen. "What the devil are you doing?"

Aleksandr said nothing. He resisted kicking a chunk of coal across the room. Instead, he squatted, gathering each offending piece and naming a silent grievance as he dropped each one into the bucket. *My mother is dead. It isn't fair. I don't want a different mother. Lilia is stupid.*

"Hurry up! Stoke that stove and come eat," his father called.

Aleksandr knew he should hurry, but he also knew his father would be displeased if the fire wasn't properly tended. Besides, it wasn't as if a hot meal were sitting on his plate, getting cold.

Carefully, he used the poker to push the smallest pieces of coal on top of the glowing embers in the bottom of the stove. Then he spread several medium-sized chunks at short intervals on the grate above, as his father had taught him. He used the bellows to gently pump air until the embers pulsed with life, igniting the coal and sending the searing air upward. Aleksandr allowed himself a small satisfied smile.

By the time he entered the kitchen, his father already sat at the table, eating.

"Get the fire started?" he asked.

"Yes, sir."

His father's head bobbed slightly. An approving nod was the closest he ever came to acknowledging a job well done. Aleksandr received the gesture as if it were gold-plated.

"Then here's your supper."

His father shoved a serving of cold sausage and bread across the table. At least, it included a portion of Mrs. Panko's pickled beets. He didn't understand why they couldn't have stayed to eat a decent meal. It wasn't just that the food was better, although it was. Eating at a table with lively conversation and laughter was easier than being alone with his father. When he was at the Pankos' table, Aleksandr participated little, but just being there made him part of something, and, for a little while, he forgot that he didn't have a mother.

Aleksandr gobbled his food. The faster he ate, the sooner he escaped to his room.

"Slow down, boy. Your food isn't going anywhere."

Aleksandr forced himself to count to five between bites. Although they most often ate in silence, tonight his father seemed more distracted than usual. Out of the corner of his eye, Aleksandr studied his face. His mood was unreadable. That always made Aleksandr extra nervous.

In his mind, the boy shouted, *Is it true? Are you replacing my mother with some stranger? Is it true?* He had a right to know. The words stuck in the back of his throat, threatening to rush out. But if he asked, even in his most pleasant voice, his father would get angry. It was a rule that wasn't written anywhere, but he knew it by heart. *Do not mention your mother. Ever.*

Lilia could be wrong. Mrs. Panko could be mistaken. He didn't care if Miss Danek was nice or talented. He hoped she was just visiting and would go back to Ukraine, where she belonged.

It would be hard for Aleksandr to find the answer to a question he wasn't allowed to ask. He would have to stay constantly alert and pay very, very close attention.

Slumped in his chair next to the fire, smoking his pipe, Viktor downed his fourth shot of *horilka*, a distilled mix of grain, potatoes, honey and sugar beets. Biting and potent, it flowed down his throat with a satisfying burn.

He mulled over tonight's encounter with Katerina Danek. Overall, it had gone well. She wasn't what he'd expected, more complicated he supposed, but she was prepared to raise his son and fulfill her wifely duties. For now, that was enough.

Katerina was a well-favored woman, not beautiful, but attractive, even more attractive than her photograph. She had the manner and look of a pampered city woman. When she talked, her words came out precise and uppity. Unlike the farm wives, whose leathery skin was weathered by sun and fashioned by endless toil, hers was pale and as smooth as marble. He would bet that her slender, manicured hands had never touched soil. That would change when she began to tend their garden.

From what Viktor had observed, Katerina's breasts were merely adequate—disappointing, really. Viktor preferred a buxom woman with a bosom a man could get lost in. Elena had possessed tantalizing breasts, firm and full. When she'd been pregnant, they'd been as large as melons. He'd envied his infant son, suckling greedily on those engorged breasts, which had rightfully belonged to him. In the end, though, a large chest didn't compensate for disloyalty.

A man must play the cards he's dealt. Even though Katerina's breasts were not up to his standards, Viktor was eager to hold them, study them, and taste them. Perhaps she had large nipples that made up for their meager size. The prospect aroused him. He ran a hand between his legs. Closing his eyes, he savored the sensation. He'd been without a woman for too long. Fondling himself was a poor substitute for a woman's touch.

As quickly as the pleasure arrived, it vanished, the memory of Elena souring his reverie. Hadn't he provided a roof and food and security? What woman wouldn't have traded places with her? He'd made life too easy, and what had he gotten for it? Damned little. *If she were here, I'd take her now.* Did he mean Elena or Katerina? What did it matter? He needed a woman. Either would do.

Viktor took a deep pull on his pipe and swigged a fifth shot of *horilka*. It set his chest on fire. Maybe, as the myth said, *horilka* had been invented by the devil. And maybe the devil would someday claim his soul for drinking it, but tonight he didn't care. Viktor's head felt light, his eyelids heavy. Hell, he didn't need Elena; soon there would be a new Mrs. Senyk, and was she not a better woman? Besides, Katerina needed him. Twenty-eight-years old and still unmarried. Must be that damned leg.

Katerina might be citified, but he'd found her compliant enough, with the exception of her momentary indiscretion. Who was she to tell him how to raise his son? He'd let that pass but she would be well advised to mind her tongue in the future. Uppity Miss Danek should not make the mistake of thinking she was smarter or cleverer than he.

Until that moment, she'd been cautious, always watching, as if she were continually taking everyone's measure. Admittedly, her sudden flash of resolve had been erotic. There was something enticing about a high-spirited woman. Still, putting on airs would endear her to no one in Bilik, not to the merchants or the farmers. These were people from simple stock. Her refinement was out of place on the prairie. Stylish clothes counted for nothing. Book knowledge counted for nothing. Hard work and more hard work was the currency of the land. She must learn that lesson. He would school her. He would mold her like supple clay into the wife he wanted.

Katerina had her assets—a small waist and curvaceous hips. Viktor hoped that her hips didn't indicate that she was as fertile as Yana. He had no wish to sire a brood of children. Leave that to the likes of Fedir, who seemed not to notice the flurry of voices and demands that swirled around him. The number of children a man had was not his measure. He had only one child, and was he not more man than Fedir Panko? By God, he was. If Katerina became pregnant, so be it; but he had no intention of procreating like a rabbit. He had enough to deal with.

The real prize lay between her legs—one good, one defective. His uncle Demitri should have told him she was a cripple. It would have made him think twice about the agreement. But it was too late. Katerina was to be his wife. He would make the most of a less-than-desirable situation, but he would be less trusting of his uncle in the future.

Viktor's head lolled forward and then backward, his eyelids drawn like half-closed window shades and his pipe slipping from between his lips. He started and caught the pipe before it fell. A banging noise pounded in his head. It sounded too rhythmic to be his imagination. He listened intently. The rapping seemed to be coming from the back of the house.

Viktor hoisted himself out of the chair and staggered into the kitchen, drawing closer to the source of the thumping. It was coming from the shed, which was attached to the back of the house. Hanging onto the table, he steadied himself before crossing the extra twelve feet. From where he stood, he saw the back door was closed, but through the upper pane he watched the storm door swing freely on its hinges. *Damn it, boy, can't you do anything right?*

He lurched down the short staircase and opened the inside door. The wind caught the storm door and flung it against the house. He jumped, startled. As Viktor tried to reach for the handle, he missed and tripped over the threshold, tumbling outside and landing hard on all fours. Pain shot through his wrist. "Goddamn it!" The door swung back hard against his shoulder. "Shit!" After several tries, he managed to stand up. Mud clung to his hands and knees. He wiped his palms down the lengths of his thighs, leaving swaths of dirt on each trouser leg. One more damned thing to clean. Finally, Viktor grabbed the elusive handle and slammed the door so hard the glass rattled.

Holding onto his throbbing wrist, he stumbled back to the parlor. The clock chimes struck 11:00. Although it was still autumn, evenings could get cold, and getting up in the morning to an unheated house was always unpleasant. Viktor decided he'd best tend the stove before heading upstairs. One more job for a woman.

He shoveled a half bucket of coal onto the grate. When nothing happened, it occurred to him he'd overloaded the firebox. He should have paid more attention before creating twice as much work for himself. Thinking about women inevitably led to trouble. But it wasn't too late to salvage the fire. Thumb-sized, red-hot cinders still flickered below the grate.

This was a two-handed task, but Viktor's wrist protested when he tried to use his other hand. One would have to do. Piece by piece, he shoveled the largest chunks from the stove, frequently dropping them before they reached the bucket. *Damn!* He grabbed the wrong end of the poker and prodded the embers. The infusion of air made the coals dance. He stared into the firebox. The sparks floated upward and then rained down, reminding Viktor of shooting stars.

What was it about fire that proved so hypnotically satisfying? When he was certain the coals had caught fire, he haphazardly shoveled several pieces onto the grate and latched the iron door.

Sagging into his chair, Viktor grimaced when his shoulder pressed against the wooden backrest. If Aleksandr had done his job, there'd be no pain. If Elena hadn't left, he wouldn't be tending the pathetic fire.

Doing woman's work and raising a boy alone was no way for a man to live. The minute the last farmer brought his wheat to the elevator, there would be a wedding. He would marry Katerina Danek, faults and all.

The sooner he started teaching her to be a proper wife, the better.

Chapter Five

Katerina had expected to feel relieved when she finally completed her first letter to Aneta, but her words, so carefully crafted, fell flat and tepid on the page. They didn't come close to conveying the tumult inside her. Perhaps she'd hoped for too much. Explaining her new life was like trying to describe the Saskatchewan sky by sending a miniature photograph and expecting Aneta to grasp its enormity. Aneta preferred life to be neat and orderly, uncomplicated. She would welcome this condensed version, would want to believe Katerina was settled and content and that the untidy problem of her younger sister's indiscretion had been neatly put to rest.

Before news of her arrival in Canada reached Ukraine, Katerina would be a wife and mother. From this point forward, everything she shared with her family would be past rather than present. It wasn't as if she hadn't known this before, but the letter made the idea concrete; she could not ignore the pain of it. This was one more hurtful reminder of the price exacted for her choices.

The distance between Aneta and her could never be bridged. But like a runner who knows he may be the last to cross the finish line yet continues striding toward the goal, Katerina knew, futile or not, she must try to give her sister a sense of her world. It wouldn't be enough but it would be something.

She scowled at her neat script, its orderly lines belying the turmoil within. She blew gently across the onionskin stationery to dry the ink. The weightless paper seemed inadequate to its task.

Before sealing the letter, Katerina decided to reread it one last time.

September 30, 1925

My Dearest Aneta,

I arrived safely in Canada three Thursdays past.

Although the crossing from Liverpool to Montreal was long, it was without significant trouble. I was fortunate in that I escaped the seasickness that plagued many of the other passengers. So many different languages were spoken aboard ship that the entire world seemed to be my companion. I met several Ukrainians but, disappointingly, none of them were traveling to my destination.

Canada is more strange and beautiful than I can describe. Forests and plains stretch beyond the eye, and new cities seem to rise out of the earth. The train ride to Bilik, Saskatchewan, took the better part of six days, yet we had traveled only two-thirds of the way across this enormous land. It makes one realize how insignificant one is in the whole of God's creation.

Bilik is much smaller than I had imagined, more village than town, actually. There is one main street with a few businesses, a fire station, a bank, and a blacksmith shop. None of the buildings are more than two stories tall, and all of them, I daresay, would fit easily into a fifth of Market Square. There is also a school and St. Kassia's church, the footprint of which is not as generous as St. George's narthex. Most everyone lives on farms a good distance from town. Although the geography is far different than L'viv, there is comfort in being among others who speak Ukrainian. It lends this place a peculiar familiarity.

I am staying with a wonderful family. Fedir and Yana Panko have taken me in until the wedding. They have six lively children, four girls (Lilia, Sasha, Marina, and Vera) and two boys (Lavro and Luka). Fedir and Yana own the general store, where one can buy all manner of things. Their home is attached to the back of the building. It is small for so many people; still, they have been very welcoming to me. Fedir fondly calls the house an anthill because of the constant activity. It took some getting used to, I admit, but now I find warmth and comfort in it. I am sharing a bedroom with Lilia and Sasha, who laugh and chatter and ask so many questions there is scarcely any occasion to feel lonely.

I can hear you scolding me for keeping you in suspense about Viktor Senyk. It may sound immodest, but I must confess, he is far more handsome than his photograph. He is tall, with dark brown eyes and with a thick mustache above his full lips. He has a serious manner but is intelligent and quick-witted. His deep voice reminds me of Papa's.

Mr. Senyk is the grain elevator agent in town. I am told that recently the Saskatchewan Wheat Pool has been formed to secure better grain prices for the farmers, and, although I do not pretend to know the details of this, I understand he has been an important proponent of it. Yana tells me it is one reason he is well respected by everyone. The other reason, she says, is that the farmers trust him to be fair. I have not yet been to the elevator because it is harvest time, and he is very busy. For now, it is enough to know he is honorable and will be a good provider.

Mr. Senyk has a ten-year-old son. Imagine my surprise at this discovery!

Aleksandr is quiet and has the same intelligent eyes as his father. He is a thin, fine-boned boy, especially compared with the Pankos' children. He is well mannered, yet wary. He watches everyone and everything carefully, as if he is constantly studying all that is about him. I daresay it has been difficult for him to be without a mother. No one knows this loss better than you and I. With all my heart, I hope to be a worthy substitute.

Please forgive me, Aneta. Although I vowed not to, I am compelled to inquire after the baby. Is he healthy? Is he growing strong? Please tell me all that you are willing to share. You may judge it best to keep our pact of silence. You may think it will hurt me too deeply to hear about him, but I tell you honestly, it will hurt me far deeper if you refuse my request. I beg of you, dear sister, put my mind at ease.

Through her tears, the words bled one into another. Before she'd composed the letter, she'd sat for several minutes, pen frozen above paper, deciding whether to risk inquiring about her son. It was true that she'd promised silence on the matter. But it had been a hastily made bargain—the baby for a new, unencumbered life—struck with Aneta and Danya when she was at her most vulnerable.

In the months leading up to the birth, their excitement at the prospect of becoming parents had overshadowed her shame. At first, her pregnancy was a gift, repayment to them for taking her in and saving her child from the stigma of illegitimacy. Then, the baby had been mostly an idea, the physical manifestations of which were tender breasts and an occasional stomach flutter. But, when she'd held him, caressing the soft down on his head, inhaling the powdery scent of his skin, and fixing on his eyes—eyes that were unmistakably Stepan's—her heart had squeezed so tightly she thought it might burst. Never had she fathomed the immeasurable pain of her loss. Now, living without word of him felt impossible, like existing in a world without sufficient oxygen.

Katerina dabbed her tears with her handkerchief, fearing Yana would discover her wallowing and ask questions she was unprepared to answer. Silently, she chastised herself for her weakness. *Stop! You must stop this! What will you do, cry every time you think of him?* If yes was her answer, Katerina knew she would be crying every day of her life.

She took several deep breaths, trying to compose herself. Survivors didn't engage in self-pity. Survivors adapted. L'viv, Stepan, and Matviyko were her past; Bilik, Viktor, and Aleksandr were her future. The sooner she made peace with that, the better life would be. Katerina straightened her back, lifted her chin, and tucked her handkerchief inside her sleeve.

Despite her resolve, she was tempted to ask whether Aneta knew of Stepan's whereabouts, but she was 100 percent certain her sister would ignore any such inquiry. If she pushed, she would get nothing. Besides, even if Aneta was inclined to give in, she would consult Danya, and he would not allow it.

She imagined Danya's condemnation. *Behavior has consequences, Katerina.* She pictured his soldier's posture and set jaw, a look she'd come to loathe. *You should have thought of that before you sold yourself so cheaply.* She saw his eyes, fierce as Judgment Day. *You've made your bed.* He would have no patience for her unmended heart. By now, he would expect she'd erased Stepan from her daily thoughts, if not her memory. He would assume repentance and repudiation. But he would be wrong.

She couldn't deny she had regrets, but they were not the ones Danya assumed. She regretted the ecclesiastical laws that forbade Stepan from marrying her and raising their son together, but she did not regret loving him. If they knew, Danya would call her a fool. Aneta wouldn't understand. How could she? Katerina would never convince her that it was the very memory of being loved so intimately that allowed her to face every other trial. She refused to regret a single touch, a single transporting moment that had catapulted her to a place beyond herself. Her denial would make their love a dream, when she craved something real and tangible. To repudiate Stepan would be to deny the possibility of such intimacy. She couldn't bear that. It was a conviction buried so deep, no one could ever extract it. Her secret would be invisible to all but the Divine, and that was between her and her Maker.

Katerina heard footsteps in the next room and hurriedly finished reading.

Also, I must ask after Papa. How is his health? Does he speak of me? Please tell him I am well and striving to be worthy of his forgiveness.

I await your return letter with as much patience as I can gather.

Your devoted sister,

Katerina

Quickly, she folded the pages and tucked them into her pocket. It was as if allowing anyone to see a single written syllable would expose her secrets, and her world would unravel.

Chapter Six

On an unseasonably warm mid-October morning, Katerina sat at the dining room table among the chatter of the Panko family, fidgeting distractedly, awaiting Viktor's arrival. He'd shown so little interest in her, Katerina had begun to think he intended to marry her without overture or preamble, to simply show up at the church on the day of their wedding and claim his prize. But then he had invited her to accompany him to Weyburn—a town of several thousand inhabitants twenty-five miles west of Bilik—and she had begun to hope.

"I've some business to attend to," he'd said. "Might as well come along."

It was hardly the kind of invitation a woman expects from a suitor. True, theirs was more of a business arrangement than a love story. Still, Katerina hoped he'd exert some effort to woo her, to make her feel less like bought-and-paid-for merchandise. The man had much to learn in the ways of gaining a woman's affection, and, if all went as planned, she intended to teach him.

Yana, always the mother, insisted Katerina eat breakfast with the family. "It's a long drive to Weyburn," she said. "Get some hot food in you."

Katerina complied, but the butterflies in her stomach refused to settle. She gnawed her cheeks and picked at her food, absently pushing the eggs from one side of the plate to the other, wondering if impending marriage always made a woman this anxious.

She remembered Aneta's wedding day. Her sister, the portrait of happiness, had floated to the cathedral altar, smiling radiantly, her eyes locked on the groom as though no one else existed. At the time, she'd been glad for Aneta, although she'd thought Danya quite unexceptional. After months of living in their home, Katerina's opinion was no longer so benign. With the passage of weeks, love became more and more a mystery, a bafflement that one sister could love a man so completely, and the other, fruit of the same womb, could despise that same man so intensely.

For Katerina, there would be no floating down the aisle toward marriage. Hers was an arrangement of convenience contracted to repair broken lives. She wanted to believe it was possible to grow into love the way a girl grows into womanhood, the way a seed grows into a flower. It must be possible.

Stepan had been different. From the beginning, she'd known him intuitively. Their union had been born not out of necessity but out of an irresistible magnetic pull. There had been an inevitability about it. An inevitable coming together. An inevitable parting. Their lovemaking had been as combustible as lightning igniting a fire. God help her, embers of that passion still burned in her.

"Don't you agree, Miss Danek?" Fedir asked.

A ribbon of light shining through the east-facing window curled across Katerina's plate and onto the tablecloth. Vaguely aware she'd heard her name, Katerina turned in the direction of Fedir's voice.

"Pardon?"

"I was saying, I think Lavro has grown another inch since you've gotten here. Don't you agree?"

Katerina looked at Lavro, sitting across the table from her. A wide smile stretched across his broad face.

"Oh, certainly," she said.

"Son, you're putting the weeds to shame," Fedir said.

"Me too, Papa?" Luka asked. "Am I bigger?"

"How about me?" Sasha said.

Fedir scratched the top of his bald head, as if seriously considering their questions. "No, I think you're shrinking," he said, his eyes twinkling.

The children erupted in giggles.

Katerina laughed, too, grateful for the momentary respite from jangled nerves.

Soon, talk at the table turned to everyone's plans for the day. Lilia had a math test. Fedir expected a shipment of hardware. Yana would bake bread.

Scooping a forkful of egg into her mouth, Katerina swallowed without tasting. "Will you excuse me, please?" she said, pushing away from the table. "The meal is delicious; it's just that I'm on pins and needles this morning."

"I was wooed once myself," Yana said, winking at Fedir.

"Thank you for understanding." Katerina limped to the parlor window to watch for Viktor.

A gray rabbit hopped across the yard on its way to Yana's garden, where a line of seven-foot dried sunflowers stood guard like aging sentinels. A crow perched atop the clothesline pole, and the bedding, pinned to the line before dawn, swung slowly in the morning breeze. How impossibly ordinary everything seemed.

As promised, Viktor arrived promptly at 7:30.

Katerina smoothed her hair and skirt, pinched her cheeks, and hurried to answer the door.

She took several deep breaths. When she opened the door, Viktor held a bouquet of yellow flowers at arm's length, and Aleksandr stood stoically beside him.

Katerina accepted the flowers and cradled them in the crook of her arm. "It's so thoughtful of you to take the trouble," she said.

"No trouble," Viktor said.

"They're lovely."

"The boy picked them."

Aleksandr shifted from foot to foot and looked at his shoes.

"Then it's thoughtful of both of you," she said. "I've never had a bouquet of wildflowers."

"They're butter-and-eggs," Aleksandr mumbled, so quietly that Katerina wasn't sure she had heard him correctly.

"Butter-and-eggs?"

He nodded.

"What an interesting name. They remind me of snapdragons, only they're prettier."

The suggestion of a smile flickered at the corners of Aleksandr's mouth.

"Please, please come in."

The teasing aroma of fried potatoes and eggs enticed them to the dining room. Yana and Fedir looked up, but the children's patter continued. Aleksandr rushed to claim his usual place between Lilia and Lavro.

Yana eyed the bouquet in Katerina's arms. "If you get those flowers in water right away they'll last," she said, hoisting herself up from the table. As she brushed past Katerina to retrieve a vase, she arched an eyebrow and smiled.

"You're welcome to join us, too," Fedir chimed in between bites, pointing at Viktor and then at the bounty on the table.

"Another time," Viktor said, hat in hand, shifting from one foot to the other. "Big day ahead."

Katerina prayed that today everything would go well, that on her first journey with Viktor, they would discover a fondness for each other, that she would end the day ready to become his wife. For five weeks, she'd struggled to be patient with Viktor's preoccupation with the harvest. Now that he'd finally made time for her, the day assumed a disproportionate significance.

If Viktor was as nervous as she, he didn't show it.

"Let me carry that," he said. "You've packed enough for a week."

Katerina wasn't certain whether his comment was a compliment or criticism, so she said nothing. The picnic basket she'd prepared for their excursion overflowed with fare she hoped would please him: beet salad, cranberry *pyrizhky*, blood sausage, and apple bread.

Viktor set the basket on the seat of the truck and then circled his hands around Katerina's slender waist, lifting her onto the truck's running board. She could feel the heat of his hands through her blouse. Clumsily, she tried to pull herself up the remaining step, but it was too high. As he hoisted her into the truck, she was grateful her back faced Viktor so he couldn't see her embarrassment, and she couldn't see the disappointment she imagined was etched on his face.

He walked around to the driver's side. Effortlessly, he climbed into the truck. Despite his size, there was an alluring, self-assured fluidity to his movements Katerina found unsettling. His body, mere inches from hers, dominated the truck cab.

She watched as he skillfully turned the key, eased out the choke, and depressed the clutch. With his toes, he pushed down on the starter button and then pressed his heel on the gas pedal. When the engine caught, he pumped the gas pedal several times and gently revved the engine before disengaging the brake lever and putting the truck in low gear.

"Starting this vehicle takes an expert's touch," Katerina said.

"It's not difficult," Viktor said.

Despite his denial, she could tell he was pleased.

They pulled out of the yard and headed west. Behind them, the early morning sun glowed in the autumn sky. Within minutes, they were in the countryside. The truck clattered along the unpaved road toward Weyburn, kicking up clouds of dust, which floated on the gentle wind. Clusters of golden wild buckwheat lined each side of the roadbed. They passed between fields, some cleared and some still waiting to be harvested.

"That's the Klopoushak farm," Viktor said, nodding to the north. "Roman knows more about growing wheat than any ten farmers around here."

Katerina heard the respect in his deep voice.

"And that's the Zolyar farm to the south," he said, pointing to a house and barn about a hundred yards off the road.

"What's in that big white tent?" Katerina asked.

"Sleeping quarters for the threshing crew."

Katerina looked from one side of the road to the other and back again, taking in the vastness of the prairie. "There's so much land for every family," she said.

"Each homestead is a quarter section—160 acres. Takes a lot of acreage to make a living growing wheat."

"These farmers are very fortunate," she said.

"Some yes, some no."

"They certainly look prosperous."

"Takes three years of backbreaking effort, clearing and working the land, to make it pay," Viktor said.

"Then their reward is worth the effort."

"If they 'prove up' the land's theirs. If not, they're broke. Odds aren't great. Less than half make it."

The wind picked up speed along with the truck. As they approached twenty miles per hour, dust whirled through the open windows. Strands of Katerina's carefully coifed hair pulled loose from Stepan's clasp. The truck bumped along noisily on the ruler-straight road stretching to the horizon and beyond. A tower of dove-white clouds gathered in the distant sky. Katerina felt like a speck on this vast land.

"Red-tailed hawk," Viktor said.

"Where?"

He pointed skyward, where the bird glided in a tightening circle. "Looks like he's spotted a vole or ground squirrel." Viktor slowed the truck.

Katerina followed the length of his arm until her eyes fixed on the hawk, soaring above the undulating wheat. "He makes flying look effortless. I can't imagine such freedom," Katerina said.

"They're faithful birds. Mate for life."

For a long while, they rode in silence. Katerina wondered if Viktor was thinking about mating for life or if his thoughts had turned to more mundane matters. His clean-scrubbed, masculine scent saturated the air. She inhaled slowly. Sitting next to him in cloistered intimacy made her want to take him in, stare at him, study him, all with an urgency to know this man whom she'd pledged to marry.

Katerina's thoughts sailed across an ocean and traversed two continents. Although it had been more than nine months since she'd seen Stepan, she pictured him clearly, as if his portrait hung permanently in her mind's eye. She saw his slender frame, soft hands, and soulful eyes, remembering details known only to lovers: the taut smoothness of his chest; the zigzag scar on the collarbone, which he'd broken as a child; and the cleft in his chin, hidden beneath a beard smelling of spice and incense.

Viktor, with his substantial frame, work-hardened hands, and intense eyes, was his opposite. She and Viktor held no lovers' secrets. Everything she knew about the man sitting next to her was as visible to a stranger's eye as it was to hers. Knowing that would soon change made her flush.

Comparing Viktor with Stepan was as fruitless as it was painful. If she had it in her power, she'd banish thoughts of Stepan, build a wall—tall and impenetrable—that memories couldn't scale. Maybe in time, that would be possible. Maybe in time, she would stop longing for him. Maybe.

Katerina turned and stared at the unfolding landscape. Intense yellows and browns dominated the fields. Low-profile shrubs and trees faded to the color of unbleached linen. Like a prairie oasis, an occasional sward of deep green or pond of iridescent blue interrupted the russets and golds. Along the roadside culverts, cattails stood stubbornly erect against the wind.

"This land is so beautiful," Katerina said, more to herself than Viktor.

"Better than Ukraine?"

"It's a different beauty." In that instant, Katerina longed for the familiarity of L'viv—for the clanging streetcars crisscrossing the city; for the vibrant commerce in Ploshcha Rynok, the market square; for the narrow cobblestoned streets, where she had played as a child; for all the things she would never see again.

Along the roadside, hundreds of Canada geese rested on their southward journey, one multitude wading in the sprawling pond, another lounging on the matted grass.

"I've never seen so many birds in one flock," Katerina said, her voice breathless.

"Common sight here."

"But it's splendid. I can't imagine ever taking this for granted."

As the truck bounced along a washboard section of the road, gravel peppered the undercarriage, scaring up a flock of small, balletic birds, who swooped across the road and turned in perfect formation. The sun continued its ascent, making the truck cab as cozy as a woolen blanket.

In the distance, a dust spire rose from the road.

"Someone's coming," Viktor said. "Moving slowly. Must be a wagon."

Katerina squinted through the windshield, but all she could see was a cloud rising from the earth. She concentrated on the traveling cloud, and little by little, a mule-drawn cart appeared like an apparition.

"It's Josef Sokur," Viktor said. "I hear tell he thinks more of those mules than his wife."

Katerina looked skeptical.

"Know why?"

"No," she said.

"Because the mules are better looking."

To Viktor, the woman sitting next to him was a puzzle. On the one hand, Katerina's childlike appreciation of the most commonplace things amused him. On the other, the way she spoke and carried herself, almost regally, confounded him. He wondered how a woman whose body was so visibly flawed and whose circumstances were so obviously reduced could maintain such pride. She was unlike any woman he'd known.

One thing for certain, she was different than Elena.

Elena had been petite, quiet, and skittish, always darting into the shadows, especially in the end. It was only when it came to the boy that she had mustered uncharacteristic courage, offering herself up in his place. Perhaps that was why he hadn't seen the break coming. He'd always judged her to be more mouse than lion.

For several miles, Viktor and Katerina rode, each immersed in private thoughts.

Then a low-slung silhouette appeared along the horizon. "There's Weyburn," Viktor announced.

"When will we arrive?" Katerina asked.

"About an hour."

"That seems impossible."

"It's a fact."

As far as the eye could see, wheat swayed hypnotically, interrupted sporadically by a house, a barn, and a smattering of outbuildings. Occasionally, an automobile or a truck or a horse-drawn wagon passed by. Viktor tipped his hat and Katerina waved demurely, greeting these strangers who were neighbors by virtue of their habitation on the sparsely populated plains.

A stone's throw off the road, a farmer sat atop a tractor as it steadily chugged its way through the field. The tractor pulled three grain binders, with a laborer seated on each machine. Two more men, on foot, gathered the wheat bundles as they spilled from the binders. Each had a specific job to do. All of them wore wide-brimmed hats to shield their faces from the relentless sun, and all of them had arms the color of worn leather.

"Binders cut the wheat and then wrap the stalks into stooks," Viktor said, pointing toward the field, where the hourglass-shaped bundles stood drying. "Six men to do the work of what used to take twenty and in less than half the time."

"One can only wonder what inventors will think of next," Katerina said.

As they fell silent again, the truck settled into a rhythm as steady as a heartbeat. With each passing mile, the steel-gray outline of the city gained definition against the cobalt sky.

"The town looks much bigger than I expected," Katerina said.

"A hamlet by your standards, no doubt," he said.

"Standards, Mr. Senyk?"

Viktor looked sidelong at Katerina. Her head tipped slightly upward and her chin jutted in mild defiance, making her look like a willful child. Comic. Tempting as it was to take her on, to put her in her place, he thought better of it.

"Been a city only about twelve years," he said.

"That's impressive. Who would believe a city could grow as fast as a garden weed?"

"She'll be the largest grain-shipping station in Canada before long."

As if to emphasize his point, a Canadian Pacific Railway train suddenly appeared on the tracks next to the road. Pulling a line of grain cars a half mile long, the train pounded the tracks, racing toward Weyburn. Out of habit, Viktor silently counted the cars as they sped by, calculating the tonnage in his head, pleased by this evidence of the area's prosperity.

He shifted his attention to the road ahead just in time to steer the truck around a dead gopher lying in the middle of the road. Veering right, he narrowly missed a large pothole.

"Oh, that poor animal," Katerina said, bumping first into the door and then into Viktor.

"Biggest nuisance on the prairie." Viktor slowed the truck and pulled over.

"Why are we stopping?"

"To gas up."

Viktor climbed out of the truck and strode around to the passenger side. "Better stretch a bit," he said, opening the door and offering Katerina his hand.

Her skin felt cool and smooth to the touch. When she stepped onto the running board, he lifted her to the ground. For all her height—she stood several inches taller than Elena—she felt light and insubstantial.

Their eyes met briefly. Katerina looked away quickly, like a stranger caught staring a little too long. Perhaps she was embarrassed or perhaps she was simply being coy. Viktor didn't know which. He did know that the feel of her slender waist beneath his hands tempted him. He imagined running his hands under her blouse and over her pliable breasts.

Reluctantly, he forced his attention back to the matter of fueling the truck. Retrieving two cans from the bed, he poured the gasoline from the first spouted can into the tank, being careful not to waste a drop.

Katerina strolled along the edge of the roadside, singing softly: "There is a stream over there/ Go and drink/ And if you want to see my beauty/ Come to the garden."

Viktor recognized the traditional wedding melody, "Nese Galya Vodu." Katerina had a pure voice, as well placed on the prairie as the clear, whistled songs of the meadowlark. It pleased him to hear her sing. For a time, he forgot his task and stood listening for each perfect note. When the song ended, he looked at his pocket watch. It was 9:36, time to be on the move again. He emptied the second gas can into the tank.

"Careful of the snakes," he said, without looking up.

"Snakes?" Katerina said. "Are they poisonous?"

"Only if they bite."

Returning to Weyburn Mental Hospital was repugnant but necessary. Viktor hated going back to that freak show, but with his upcoming marriage, he needed an answer to his question: Would Jon ever be normal?

The most recent time he had visited, shortly after Elena had disappeared, her brother had lain curled in a fetal position in a corner of the dayroom, whimpering like a wounded puppy.

"Schizophrenic," the stout doctor in the white coat had said.

"Meaning?"

"It involves a significant disintegration of the thought processes. He suffers from auditory hallucinations, paranoia, and delusions. In simple terms, he cannot distinguish between reality and fantasy."

You didn't have to be a head doctor to figure that out, Viktor had thought. Annoyed, he had tried a different tack. "Will he recover?"

"That's impossible to say. So far, he's been resistant to traditional therapy. We've begun an intensive regime of hydrotherapy, the newest weapon in our arsenal." The doctor had looked up from the chart he held in his soft hands and peered at Viktor over his pince-nez glasses.

"Hydro—hydro—?"

"Therapy. It involves extensive exposure to varying water temperatures. I'm afraid the technique is a bit complicated to explain. Quite revolutionary, actually."

Viktor had recognized the doctor's type: superior and patronizing. The dandy wouldn't have lasted half an afternoon in the fields doing real work. If Viktor hadn't needed to make certain Jon was no threat, he wouldn't have spent a minute on the quack's hocus-pocus.

"So he's getting better?" he'd asked.

"To be candid," the doctor had said, peering over his pretentious glasses, "we haven't seen real progress yet, but that doesn't mean we've given up."

That trip had been a waste of a good day. He'd come for answers and all he'd gotten was double talk.

For days, he'd wrestled with what to tell Katerina about this visit to the hospital. He would explain that Jon was hopelessly mad, and this was simply a mission of mercy, fulfillment of a sacred promise he'd made to Elena. If Katerina became too inquisitive, he had resolved to pacify her with the skeletal story he'd rehearsed but omit the muscle and flesh of it. She could not accompany him because the man's condition was too fragile. That was true enough. And it was an act of charity to spare her the unpleasantness of life within the walls of the asylum. That was true enough, too.

Now, as they drove through the streets of Weyburn, Viktor turned the truck due north. They rode over bridges that spanned the Souris River and the yawning railroad corridor bisecting the city. They passed the New Royal Hotel, with its decorative peaks and white pillared porch.

"In L'viv, buildings have been around for centuries. Even the new opera house looks as though it's been there forever," Katerina said. "Everything here looks as though it was built yesterday."

"Because it was." Irritation edged his voice.

"Oh, I meant no offense by it. I'm just not accustomed to seeing everything looking so—new."

As they approached the northernmost section of town, a large copper dome with barely a hint of verdigris glinted in the late morning sun.

"I see the top of a cathedral!" Katerina exclaimed. "It looks as grand as St. George's."

"That's no church," Viktor said. "It's Weyburn Mental Hospital."

She looked at him, her head tilted and brow furrowed, reminding him of Queenie, the border collie he'd had as a boy.

"It's an asylum."

"Pardon?"

"For the insane," he said.

Her eyes widened. "But it's such a huge building."

"Biggest in Canada," Viktor bragged.

"Are we going there?"

"Elena's brother is a patient. I promised to look after him." Viktor kept his eyes on the road ahead.

At first, Katerina said nothing, and Viktor began to wonder if her silence meant she disapproved—not that her opinion would have changed anything.

"That's kind of you."

He'd been prepared for her objections, not her approval. Perhaps, because of her airs, he'd misjudged her. Perhaps Miss Danek would prove to be a more pliable pupil than he'd anticipated. Or perhaps she was simply being agreeable in an attempt to impress him. Either way, he would not be easily taken in by a little cooperation or praise. She had a lot to learn about becoming a proper wife, but he couldn't be bothered with that now. After the wedding, there would be plenty of time to teach her.

"May I ask what's wrong with him?"

"The doctor says he's insane, crazy, *bozhevil nyŷ*. That's all I know." His statement was as emphatic as a slammed door.

Katerina apparently took his meaning, because she asked no more questions.

They drove up a long road, past scores of flowerbeds, shrubs, and willow saplings. The approach resembled the driveway of an estate more than that of a mental hospital. Viktor recalled what the newspaper had said about the structure when it was built a few years earlier. The behemoth sat on 215 acres, with other, smaller buildings scattered about the property. It had taken two specially built spurs and a thousand railroad cars to haul the materials used to complete the hospital. Viktor thought it a pity to waste the building on nine hundred mental defectives.

He parked the truck in front of the sprawling, three-story brick building with its imposing facade and massive portico, crowned by a concrete coat of arms. As far as Viktor was concerned, the dignified exterior of the hospital gave an inaccurately favorable impression to the uninitiated. Somersaulting circus clowns would have been a more apt introduction to the freakish menagerie held captive inside.

Viktor pulled his watch from his fob pocket and studied it. "This could take a while."

"You needn't hurry on my account. It's a beautiful day and the grounds are lovely. If you'd be kind enough to help me out of the truck, I'll wait for you on that bench," Katerina said, gesturing toward a resting area surrounded by red osier dogwood, its fall foliage turned deep crimson.

When Viktor entered the lobby, he immediately recognized the chirpy woman behind the visitor's desk. Her protruding eyes and prominent beak were hard to forget. What such a homely bird had to smile about escaped him.

"Good day, sir. May I help you?" she asked.

"I'm here to visit Jon Blanek. He's a patient on 2F."

"May I inquire as to your relationship to the patient, sir?"

"Brother-in-law."

"Actually, your wife is listed as his next of kin and registered visitor. Is she with you?"

"No. I'm alone."

"Well..."

"She's ill."

"Oh, I'm sorry to hear that. I hope it's not serious."

The woman's interest began to annoy him, but he remained stoic. "While she's ill, I've agreed to look in on her brother."

"Very well, then. Please sign our log while I call up to the ward. You may have a seat over there while you wait," she said, gesturing toward a bank of wooden, straight-backed chairs.

After ten minutes, a woman wearing a crisp white uniform and a double-pointed nurse's cap arrived to escort him to ward 2F. She was pleasant but contained, her gestures small and her voice level—qualifications, Viktor assumed, for working with imbeciles.

As they rounded a corner and started down a long hallway, a guttural voice—more otherworldly than human—chanted, "Help me, help me, help me." Viktor looked around and saw no one, but the plea persisted. The nurse escorting him didn't break stride.

He fought the urge to turn and run, to escape to the outdoors, where fresh air awaited and the world made sense. It was eerie how merely stepping through the front doors of the hospital made him feel as though he were a patient, as though he might be mistaken for a crazy man and held against his will. The hospital was the stuff of nightmares. It was as if the institutional green walls, the polished terrazzo floors, and the ubiquitous smell of antiseptic, masking the odor of human decay, instantly made a person part of the place.

A stooped old man with skin like a dried riverbed shuffled along next to the wall. His lower lip quivered. He emitted a fetid odor. Viktor had been around farm animals his entire life, but he couldn't remember smelling anything as putrid. The man seemed to be rotting from the inside.

"Walter, you've had an accident," the nurse said gently. She took his hand and led him down the hall. "It's all right. Come with me. We'll find someone to change you."

Viktor continued to follow the nurse and the foul-smelling old man. He fought down the urge to vomit.

They passed a patient, who looked to be in his early twenties, sweeping the hallway. Except for his clothing, he could have easily passed for a staff member. He was trim, his hair was neatly combed, and he seemed aware of his surroundings. Viktor began to wonder if he'd mistaken him for a patient. The man didn't look crazy.

"You're doing a nice job, Michael. The floor looks very clean," the nurse said, patting him gently on the back.

He recoiled—whether from her touch or from the old man's repulsive odor—Viktor couldn't say. The patient kicked the dustpan, scattering debris in all directions.

The nurse spoke evenly. "It looks like there is more work for you to do now, Michael."

The young man began his task all over again.

From behind them, a loud cackle echoed down the corridor. Several patients milled about the hallway. Some strolled while others stood still, staring at nothing in particular. None made eye contact.

A uniformed woman emerged from the other end of the hall.

"Mildred, Walter has had an accident and needs changing," the escort nurse said.

Viktor decided that an invisible pecking order existed in the asylum because, without question or complaint, Mildred, who appeared to be a decade or two younger than the escort nurse, led Walter away. Viktor thought he'd rather starve than take employment changing old men's dirty drawers.

Relieved to be rid of the old man, Viktor wordlessly followed the nurse up a wide stairway. Finally, they reached the dayroom of ward 2F. At the entrance, a middle-aged man with large facial pockmarks stood guard, blocking the doorway with his stiffened arm.

"Bruno, we wish to pass," the nurse said.

Apparently, this ritual had been enacted many times.

"Y-y-you have to t-t-tell me the p-p-password," the patient stammered, looking around surreptitiously, as though someone might overhear the secret word.

"Venus," the nurse said in a loud whisper.

"N-n-no! T-t-that w-w-was y-y-yesterday's w-w-word,"

"Give me a hint, Bruno; I'm in a hurry."

The patient looked up as if the clue were written on the ceiling. "S-s-someone v-v-very st-st-strong," he said.

"Atlas," the nurse guessed.

"N-n-no."

"Hercules."

The patient's arm rose like a railroad crossing gate. "Y-y-you may p-p-pass."

"Jon is over there," the nurse said, pointing to a thin young man who stood in the corner facing the wall, his arms encircled in self-embrace. She walked with Viktor to the far side of the room.

"Jon," she said quietly. "Someone is here to see you."

He turned slowly, his eyes wide and unblinking, giving no indication that he recognized Viktor. Since Viktor's most recent visit, Jon's eye sockets had become more hollow, haunting. His cropped haircut revealed bare patches on his scalp where he'd pulled out his hair. Whatever hydrotherapy was, Viktor decided, it hadn't improved Jon's physical appearance.

"I'll let you talk alone. If you need me, I'll be on the other side of the room." The nurse inclined her head confidentially toward Viktor and whispered, "He's harmless, but it's best not to touch him or move too suddenly." Then she strode across the expansive room.

"Hello, Jon," Viktor said.

Jon stared past him and tightened his arms around his chest.

"It's Viktor, Elena's husband." At the mention of his sister's name, Viktor thought he saw a flicker of recognition in Jon's eyes.

"Do you know where she is?" Viktor tried to keep his voice steady.

Jon stared straight ahead.

"Has Elena visited you?"

Still nothing.

"Where is she, Jon? She wouldn't just leave you here to rot."

Jon began to rock from side to side.

"Where's Elena?"

"Gone, gone, gone," Jon said in a monotone chant.

"Where? Where has she gone?" Viktor's voice rose and his fists clenched.

"Gone, gone, gone."

"Where is she, Jon?"

"Gone, gone, gone."

"Come on, you sly son of a bitch," Viktor hissed into his brother-in-law's ear.

Jon stepped back and turned away.

Viktor followed him, stepping between Jon and the wall. He glanced across the room, checking for the nurse. She was preoccupied, coaxing a patient whose forearms covered his eyes like a blindfold.

"Don't play games. You know where she is, you crazy bastard," Viktor taunted him.

Jon bowed his head, rocked, and began to whimper.

"Then I'll tell *you* where she is," Viktor said. "Elena's dead. She's dead, Jon, and she's never coming back. Elena is *dead*!"

Jon unfolded his arms and covered his ears. "Dead, dead, dead," he chanted. Tears trickled down his cheeks.

Viktor glared at him.

"Dead, dead, dead."

Viktor's jaw muscles seized up, his neck veins throbbed, and his fists clenched tighter. It would be easy to eliminate this dangerous imbecile. His chest heaved and his breath escaped in emphatic bursts. "Goddamn you," he snarled. He turned and strode across the room toward the door.

"Wait! Excuse me, sir. You must wait!" the nurse called after him.

He didn't look back.

Viktor stomped down the portico steps and across the drive

toward the bench where Katerina sat waiting for him. His flushed face, sour expression, and emphatic footsteps told her his visit had not gone well.

"What happened?"

She wasn't certain whether Viktor didn't hear her or he chose to ignore her, but he didn't answer. His narrowed eyes seemed fixed on a point in the distance. She followed his line of sight, but nothing on the sprawling hospital grounds appeared changed since their arrival. The long silence grew uncomfortable. Katerina's intuition told her to hold back. She waited. She waited longer. Gradually, Viktor's breathing slowed and the redness drained from his neck and face, like gray disappearing from a spent storm cloud. Finally, he looked at her, his expression neutral, unrevealing.

When Viktor made no move to sit down next to her, she stood to face him. The uneasiness in her stomach reminded Katerina how little she knew this man. She seemed to be tiptoeing along a path littered with broken glass.

"Are you all right?" she asked.

"Yes."

"Did something happen?"

"Nothing that concerns you."

"I see."

"It's an unpleasant place; that's all."

"Perhaps I can help."

"Let it be."

"If that's what you want," she said.

"What I want is some food. Time to dig into that basket," Viktor said, his mood suddenly lighter, his features relaxed.

"The grounds are beautiful. We could set out our blanket under that tree."

"Not here."

"Wherever you please, then," she said.

They retraced their route through the streets of Weyburn until they found a small park on the south end of town, along the banks of the Souris River. There, in the tall grass, they laid out a blanket with flowers embroidered on each corner and sat under a spindly aspen, which, halfheartedly, shielded them from the late morning sun.

A girl in a pink pinafore, who appeared to be about ten, wore a blindfold and called to her playmates, who scurried to find hiding places behind the trees. The children romped and chased around and through a group of adults, who talked and laughed with easy familiarity. Although their voices carried, Katerina had difficulty understanding their rapid English. Happiness, however, needed no translation. Each joyful syllable served as a counterpoint to her loneliness. Would she one day have carefree children who frolicked in the park? Would she ever be so comfortably connected with friends and family? She tried to imagine it, but the faces that came to mind belonged to Stepan and Aneta and Danya.

An image of her infant son, Matviyko—she would never think of him as Petro, no matter what Aneta called him—appeared, as it always did at the sight of children. The only way she could envision Matviyko was as a young version of Stepan. She pictured him running and jumping and playing. She imagined the wind ruffling his mop of soft brown hair. She saw him looking up at her, his deep blue eyes large and pleading, his arms reaching out to her in the way a child does when he needs comforting. Then, predictably, the vision faded beyond reach.

The moment Aneta had taken Matviyko from her arms, Katerina had felt a fissure open inside her, a fissure as wide as the distance between sin and forgiveness. She'd thought of it as a barren place, deep and empty. Now, she realized that wasn't it at all. Her grief was a living, pulsating thing, roiling deep inside her, as much part of her as the blood coursing through her veins, as invisible as cancer and no less powerful. Automatically, Katerina silently prayed the same words she always prayed when grief overtook her: *Blessed Virgin, I gave my son to your care, as our Heavenly Father entrusted his only Son to you. Help me find peace in knowing that you are always watching over him.*

"Are we going to eat this food or just look at it?" Viktor said.

"I'm sorry. I was—daydreaming."

"A man can't live on daydreams. I'm hungry," he said, more teasing than cross.

She managed a faint smile.

"Hopefully today." Viktor's eyebrow, with the mysterious scar above it, arched rakishly.

Flustered, Katerina retrieved two plates and cups from the basket. Yana had given her the finest dishes in her cupboard, the ones with dainty hand-painted flowers curling around the perimeters. When Katerina had protested that they were too precious to pack in a picnic basket, Yana had shushed her. "Nonsense," she'd said. "I can't think of a better use for these fancy plates than a romantic picnic. They're not much use collecting dust on the shelf."

Now, Katerina filled Viktor's plate to overflowing with beet salad, cranberry *pyrizhky*, blood sausage, and apple bread. She took small portions for herself. From a canning jar, she poured tea into the delicate cups.

She sipped her tea but had little appetite. Viktor ate with relish. When he finished his plate of food, she dished out a second helping of everything. The fragile teacup disappeared into his palm. It took only a few swallows before the cup was drained. Katerina replenished his tea until the jar was empty.

"Fine lunch," Viktor said, after he'd devoured every morsel. "Mighty fine lunch."

How simple those words—"fine lunch"—but they were an offering as welcome as any compliment Katerina had ever received. It was as though she'd been holding her breath all morning and now could exhale.

In the distance, noon church bells chimed. The sweet fragrance of autumn drifted through the park on a mild westerly breeze. Yellowed aspen leaves rustled overhead. Light danced on the silvery water, and a bare tree branch bobbed in the river's current.

While Katerina carefully repacked Yana's good china, Viktor lay on his side, propped up on his elbow, head in hand, watching her. She pretended not to notice. When she finished putting the basket in order, she sat stiff-backed, her legs tucked demurely to the side as best she could, and soaked in the warmth of the sun.

"What unusual ducks," Katerina said, pointing to a pair of birds paddling along the river's edge.

"Scaups. See their dark heads and tails and the white bands in the middle?"

"You seem to know a lot about the natural world."

"Enough." Viktor pulled a single long blade of grass and put the end between his lips. A shock of hair fell across his forehead, making him look like a boy.

"May I ask you something?" Katerina said.

"About scaups?"

"No."

Viktor looked skeptical.

"It's a harmless question."

"I'll be the judge."

"How did you get that scar above your eye?" On impulse, Katerina reached forward, arm outstretched, stopping just short of brushing her fingertips above his left eyebrow, retreating when she realized the forwardness of her gesture.

Viktor caught her wrist midair and pulled it to him. He brushed the top of her hand with his lips, never taking his eyes from her. Turning her hand over, he kissed her palm, letting his lips linger until Katerina felt his full mouth sear her skin. She glanced around to see if the other picnickers were watching.

"We don't know them," Viktor said.

"But—"

Viktor guided her hand from his brow along the side of his face and neck, to his chest. She tried to pull it back, but he held her wrist fast. "Look at me," he commanded.

Katerina forced herself to meet his eyes. They were dark as prairie soil. His parted lips were moist and full, his breathing shallow. She recognized the look. Lust had stared at her before.

"I won't always settle for kissing your hand," Viktor said and released her.

Her cheeks burned. God forgive her desire. As if he had reached deep inside her, she felt Viktor take possession of her soul. She was certain he could see the stain of mortal sin upon it.

Chapter Seven

On the eve of her wedding Katerina spent a restive night. In the quiet hours, *forever* kept turning over and over in her mind. *Perpetual. Unending. Permanent.* The words gained power as the hours ticked by. *Everlasting. Ceaseless. Eternal.* She would marry Viktor in the Eastern Orthodox Church and be united to him through the holy mystery of marriage, not just in this life but in the next. Since Christ had defeated death by his crucifixion and resurrection, according to church doctrine, their bond could never be broken, even in death. For Katerina, age twenty-eight, it was hard to contemplate *forever*, but in a matter of hours she would irretrievably set her course toward that distant point.

It wasn't too late. She could admit she'd made a mistake, tell Viktor that she was sorry but she could not marry him. She could take the train to—where? She had a cousin, admittedly distant, living somewhere in America—Pennsylvania, she believed. She could find him and ask for help to—what? To return home, where a life of shame and recrimination awaited? At least she could reclaim her precious son, Matviyko—Matthew—her "gift of God." Her heart ached at the mere thought of him. But what kind of future could she offer her child? She loved him too much to consign him to a life as a priest's bastard. What chance would he have then? No, she'd done the right thing, leaving him with Aneta and Danya. Maybe she could go to Pennsylvania, find her cousin, and open a seamstress shop, but that would take resources Katerina knew she didn't have.

She glanced at the clock on the nightstand—almost quarter to four. Except for the soft sounds of the children's slumber, the room was quiet. Katerina, halfway between sleep and wakefulness, drifted into her past and the events that had brought her to this moment.

It was August. Hot. Muggy. Airless. She had been apprehensive about knocking on the rectory door, worried that the vestments she'd painstakingly crafted and carefully wrapped might not meet the priest's approval. To her surprise, when the door opened, instead of the housekeeper, Father Mihalik answered. She'd often observed him at St. George's Cathedral in his religious garb. Today, dressed in street clothing, he'd become, simply, a handsome man.

He invited her in and offered her tea. Although she was more anxious than thirsty, she politely assented. As he unwrapped the parcel and examined each of the vestments—chasuble, alb, stole, cincture, cuffs, and *palitsa*—all made of the highest-quality brocade and adorned with galloon made with golden thread, his face lit with pleasure. "Exquisite," he said. "Absolutely exquisite!"

At first, she thought his effusiveness was the generosity of a priest to his congregant. "Thank you for your kindness," she said.

"I say this with complete sincerity; I've never seen any…thing more beautiful!" The tender way he spoke and the way his eyes penetrated hers made Katerina believe he might not be talking about the vestments. Father Mihalik conversed with her as if they'd communicated effortlessly many times before, simply picking up where their previous encounters had left off. In her presence, he seemed completely at ease and talked of nothing ordinary. He quoted the poetry of Taras Shevchenko and Panteleimon Kulish.

"My favorite literary character is Mavka from *Forest Song*," Katerina confessed.

"Ah, the poetess and playwright Lesya Ukrainka. I have read her. Why do you favor her?" he asked.

"She understands love." The words escaped before she could pull them back. That he had read Ukrainka's works both pleased and unsettled her.

He foraged in the kitchen, brought cheese and bread into the sitting room, and poured her another cup of tea. With each passing minute, she grew more comfortable. As their conversation wove its way through the afternoon, time ceased. She lost herself in his voice, a voice that soothed like the sweetest concerto, sometimes its dynamic an intimate pianissimo, sometimes an assured mezzo forte.

"I want to show you something," he said, reaching for her hand and leading her into an adjoining room. On an easel in front of the south-facing window rested an unfinished oil landscape, alive with colors bleeding one into another, its romanticism evident in every brushstroke. "I've been working on this for weeks."

When Katerina looked out the rectory window, the only view evident was the brick face of the cathedral. "The painting is lovely. You're creating it from memory," she said.

"It's the meadow near my childhood home. It reminds me of a time when life was simpler."

Katerina heard the melancholy in his voice. His eyes were full of longing, and they glistened in the light. To her, in that shared moment, the priest had become the man, no longer Father Mihalik but Stepan.

Even though that first afternoon they did not embrace, she felt permanently connected to him. When she left—only because staying longer would have seemed improper—it felt as though part of her remained with him.

A few days later, Stepan appeared at the tailor shop, allegedly to order another set of vestments. "I wanted to see you again," he whispered when they were alone. "I finished the painting and thought you might like to see it."

For several weeks, their relationship inched from platonic to physical, the transition as natural as a bud blossoming to flower. Rather than furtive, their secret liaison felt preordained, a mere consequence of intimacy. Any qualms Katerina had about the rightness of their affair paled when compared with the depth of her need for Stepan. His smile warmed her like the summer sun. His voice soothed like a favorite lullaby. His caress enveloped her as gently as a love poem. In his soulful eyes, she saw her own reflection.

Then she missed her monthly bleeding. Though, at first, there were no other signs, she knew she carried Stepan's baby. She said nothing. Another month passed. And another. Still, Katerina kept her secret. She wondered if Stepan noticed the evidence of the child she carried in the slight swelling of her stomach, in her enlarged areolae, or her tender breasts. She tried to tell him, but the words wouldn't come. How could she reveal her secret—that concrete matter of a flesh-and-blood being growing inside her—when they never spoke of anything mundane? Theirs was a kingdom built on melody and verse, not on mortar and stone.

By the end of the fourth month, she worked up the courage to tell him, hoping he would give up everything for love, praying he could not fathom living without her as much as she couldn't imagine living without him. She went to the rectory to confess, not her sin but her secret. The housekeeper answered the door.

"I'd like to speak with Father Mihalik," Katerina said.

"I'm sorry. Father Mihalik is no longer here, but Father Burda, his replacement, is available if you would like to speak with him." The woman's voice was pleasant but formal, completely immune to the bottomless pain she caused.

"Where has Father Mihalik gone?" Katerina struggled not to choke on her panic.

"I couldn't say. All I know is he left three days ago."

The door closed. The Earth tilted erratically on its axis. Katerina couldn't breathe or think.

Life fluttered within while the world around her shriveled. She staggered home to her father's apartment above the tailor shop. He was downstairs, measuring a distinguished gentleman for a suit. Wordlessly, she walked by them, hoping Papa was too preoccupied to notice misery chiseled on her face. She struggled up the stairs to her bedroom, closed the door, and wedged a chair under the knob, barricading herself inside. The walls and ceiling pressed in upon her as she slumped to the floor.

Stepan loved her. She'd heard his whispers after they'd explored and satisfied each other. "I love you, Katerina. God knows I don't deserve you, but I swear I love you." She ran her hands over her breasts and stomach, reliving his words.

"What am I to do?" she sobbed aloud. Burying her face in her hands, she wept until she couldn't weep anymore.

"Katerina? Katerina, are you in there? Are you all right?" Papa said.

Those were the last tender words he had spoken to her.

Now, the memory of that time was almost too much to bear. Katerina, curled snail-like on the narrow bed, could not stop thinking about Stepan and all that might have been. Then, the realization struck her: she'd convinced herself that her mistake had been in loving too much. She'd believed it was her heart, over which she had no control that had brought her to this day. But in the darkness of the children's bedroom, surrounded by the gentle breathing of the innocent, she faced what she had refused to admit. Her failing wasn't a transgression of the heart but a sin of the body. It wasn't love that had brought her to this moment: it was desire. Shame weightier than Stepan's satiated body lying atop hers pressed down so heavily upon her that she struggled for air.

Love and lust. Never again, she vowed, would she confuse the two.

From the disquieting distance of Bilik to L'viv—4,900 miles—no matter how many ways she looked at it, her mortal sin cast a long shadow over all venial transgressions.

She was to blame. It was all her fault, every last bit of it.

Time moved by slowly until anemic light peeked through the bedroom curtain. With daybreak came clarity. Her eleventh hour angst served no purpose. No matter how many times she questioned her choices, the answer came out the same. Of course, she would marry Viktor Senyk. She would be a loyal, devoted wife and mother. She would accept this life as the consequence of her actions and she would accept it gratefully, embracing it with as much grace as she could muster.

By this time tomorrow, not only would she be a wife, she would be the mother of a ten-year-old boy. She would sleep in the intimacy of Viktor's bed. The prospect unnerved her. Would he be satisfied with her? Would he overlook her imperfections? She thought about the moment at the park, in Weyburn, when he'd looked at her with undisguised lust. The strength of his grasp and the warmth of his flesh had caught her off guard. The scintillating feel of her soft palm against his rough face had left her wanting more. But respectable women knew men preferred inexperience to wantonness in their wives, if not their lovers. Would he detect that she was not a virgin? She prayed not.

It was now 5:30. Katerina composed herself, moved quietly past the sleeping children, and limped downstairs to make a cup of tea. As she descended the steps, she heard activity in the kitchen.

Yana had already started the stove fire, and she sat at the table, sipping her tea. "You're up early," Yana said. "Did you have trouble sleeping?"

"A bit," Katerina confessed. She poured a cup of tea and joined Yana at the table. "Were you nervous before your wedding?"

"It was different," Yana said after a moment. "I knew Fedir since I was a child, and I always knew we would marry."

Katerina had lived in the Panko house almost two weeks before realizing Yana rose every morning before dawn. At first, she'd thought it was out of necessity, to get a head start cooking breakfast. Yana made motherhood look easy, as though it were the most natural thing possible, so it had surprised Katerina when, one morning, Yana confided how much she savored the peaceful moments without the children.

"They come downstairs, chirping like hungry birds waiting for their mother to come back to the nest with food," she'd said. "Sometimes the mother needs a rest from their open beaks."

On the mornings Katerina joined her, they often sat companionably, soaking in the quiet. Today was different, however. Yana seemed to intuitively sense Katerina's need for her counsel. In Aneta's home, despite their blood connection, she'd never felt comfortable. It wasn't just Danya's scowling disapproval. It was her swelling belly, an unimpeachable reminder of her fertility that stood between them.

Katerina looked at Yana, her round face, crow's feet, and substantial body showing the wear of bearing six children, and realized how much she would miss her new friend's company. Although they would live only a few blocks apart, she knew they wouldn't recapture the special closeness of these peaceful mornings when two women simply enjoyed each other's presence.

"You knew you were marrying a good man," Katerina said, her voice tentative. "Am I marrying a good man?"

Yana looked at her curiously. "Of course."

"I see what you and Fedir have together. You laugh and tease, and happiness fills your home. I want to love Viktor and be the wife and mother he desires, but Viktor is so different from your husband."

"Fedir was born with a smile on his face," Yana said.

"Viktor is very serious."

"He's been through difficult times." Yana placed her hand reassuringly over Katerina's. "The happier you make him, the less somber he'll be. You'll see."

"I'll do my best."

"Besides, seriousness is a fine quality in a man," Yana said, patting her hand. "Viktor has his faults, but he's responsible."

"Faults?"

Yana thought for a moment. "Oh, he can be a bit quick to anger, and sometimes he's too hard on Aleksandr, but things haven't been easy for him, losing a wife and raising a son alone."

"But is he a good man?" Katerina asked, wanting desperately for the answer to be yes.

"He's a man of his word, respected and held in high regard by everyone. He'll take care of you, Katerina. Of that, you can be certain."

The kettle rattled on the burner. Yana hoisted herself from the table, grabbed a potholder, and held the kettle away from the heat until the boiling water settled. From the icebox, she retrieved a bowl of eggs and a bottle of milk and set them on the table to bring them to room temperature. Katerina noticed Yana rub the small of her back and grimace.

"Are you all right?"

"Ach. Don't worry. I'm just getting old," Yana said, carefully lowering herself into the chair.

"What was Elena like?" The question came as much of a surprise to Katerina as it appeared to be to Yana. It had been in Katerina's head since the moment she first met Viktor, but she'd been afraid to ask.

Frowning slightly, Yana said, "This is not a day for remembering the dead. It's a day for celebration."

Katerina had seen neither photographs nor paintings of Elena. She was replacing a ghost. It was imperative to know what she was up against. "Please, Yana, I want to know. Was she pretty? Viktor is a handsome man. He must have had a pretty wife."

"This is a new day: a beginning not an ending."

"Please, Yana. I must know."

Yana hesitated, as though weighing the wisdom of honoring Katerina's request. When her words finally came, they leaked out in a trickle. "Elena was pretty in her way." Yana savored a sip of tea and inhaled deeply, fortifying herself before venturing into dangerous waters. "She was pale and had wide eyes, like she was surprised by everything."

Katerina leaned forward, as if she couldn't get close enough to the answer.

"She looked young, like a girl, really. Her body showed no signs of childbearing, at least none that I could see." Yana absently ran her hands from her ample stomach to her hips. "She was small and delicate."

"Like Aleksandr?" Katerina asked.

"More so."

"Was she a good wife?"

"Elena did her best. She kept a clean house and tended a fine garden and saw to it that Viktor and Aleksandr were fed and cared for."

"Did you know her well?"

"As well as anybody, but she kept to herself. Even in a room of laughing women, Elena seemed guarded."

"Did she love Viktor?"

"Of course."

Yana answered so emphatically Katerina was certain she found the question absurd or, at best, irrelevant. In the weeks that Katerina had lived with this stalwart woman, she'd learned that, to Yana, family—the tie of husband to wife, parent to child, and kin to kin—was unassailable. Family equaled love. The bond was unquestioned and breaking it unthinkable.

"Elena once told me she was unable to have more children." Yana lowered her voice. "Maybe that's why Elena suffered from melancholy."

"She was unhappy?"

"She had her struggles. It's understandable. I couldn't imagine my life with only one child."

Katerina's eyes moistened.

"Of course, you will give Viktor many fine, healthy children."

"I pray that's true."

"Enough about the dead," Yana said, getting up from the table. "This is a day for joy. Viktor and Aleksandr will be here in a few hours for the *blahoslovenya,* the blessing."

"Of course."

"It's a shame your parents won't be here, but Fedir and I are as happy for you as any parents could be."

Katerina brightened. Yana had a mother's gift for soothing.

"I have a surprise for you," Yana said. "Stay put."

She heaved her body up from the chair, lumbered out of the room, and returned, carefully holding two neatly folded cloths in her extended arms."For you," she said. "These are the *rushnyks* my mother gave me for my wedding. Today, you will use them. This one is to bind your hand to Viktor's in the 'Dance of Isaiah' procession." Yana unfolded the cloth so Katerina could appreciate the painstaking embroidery. "And this one is for you and Viktor to stand on," Yana said, offering Katerina the second *rushnyk,* decorated with boldly colored pairs of birds. "Remember to let him step on it first, so he knows he will be the head of your household."

"I'll remember."

"It will make your marriage strong and your body fertile," Yana said. "It's worked for me, heaven knows, and now it will work for you."

"They're absolutely lovely! I don't know how to thank you for your kindness. How will I ever repay you?"

"No need," Yana said. "You are family."

In St. Kassia's Orthodox Church, Aleksandr stood, grim-faced, watching his father marry Her. His new shoes squeezed his toes, and his tie pinched his neck. He'd never been more uncomfortable in his whole life.

Surrounding him was everyone he knew. The women and girls were dressed in traditional garb, blouses with abundant flowers rimming their necklines and sleeves, and triangular white scarves wrapped around their heads, with only a modest fringe of hair peeking out at their hairlines. The men and boys wore their Sunday-best trousers, pressed white shirts, and black ties, their hair parted and slicked for the occasion. Even Mr. Sokur and his sons, their usual dirt-darkened skin scrubbed pink, had on their best overalls and bowties.

Rings were exchanged in the church vestibule. Then the wedding procession, led by Father Warga, chanting a psalm—which one, Aleksandr couldn't remember—walked down the center aisle and stopped in the middle of the church. Mr. and Mrs. Panko carried icons of Christ and the Virgin Mary, and his father and the bride followed them.

Aleksandr heard his neighbors' murmured approval. "So beautiful!" "Viktor's good fortune." "A mother for Aleksandr." He'd never seen so many broad smiles. With all the fuss, you'd think the barnstormers had come to town. Was he the only one who felt as though he were attending a funeral? How had his father forgotten so quickly?

It had been less than a year and a half ago that they'd buried his mother from this same church with these same neighbors. That had been a day of tears and somber faces. Then, Father Warga had stood before them dressed in a black cape, reciting prayers Aleksandr hadn't heard and didn't want to remember.

At the cemetery, next to St. Kassia's, he'd watched as they'd lowered the wooden box, minus her body, into the ground. "Symbolic," Father Warga had said. After the drowning, her body hadn't been found. It drifted somewhere in the Red River's current.

It frightened Aleksandr when he thought about his mother, unable to catch her breath as the water washed over her face. In his nightmares, she appeared wide-eyed and unblinking. Her open arms reached toward him as if she wanted to hug him. When he tried to swim toward her, she floated farther from his reach, and when she tried to speak to him, tiny bubbles escaped from her mouth.

It wasn't that Aleksandr would have preferred to bury her. He didn't want to picture his mother in the ground either. He hated the dark and couldn't bear to think of her opening her eyes in a coffin blacker than coal. It was a foolish thought. Dead people couldn't open their eyes. It would have been better to think of her floating on clouds, where the sun shone and crisp air filled her lungs, but he couldn't erase the image of her tangled in the weeds at the bottom of the river.

Aleksandr had heard the story of his mother's passing so many times he could have told it by heart, the way he could recite the alphabet forward and backward. She had gone to Winnipeg to help his aunt Raisa, who had been very sick and expecting her third child. One afternoon, his mother had taken his cousins on an outing to the park. The littlest one, chasing the paddling of ducklings, had stumbled and fallen into the river. His mother had not been a strong swimmer, but she had jumped into the river to rescue him. A man had seen her struggling to reach the little boy and had dived in after them. He had saved the child but not his mother.

People had called her heroic. Father Warga had said her death was part of God's plan; she was in a better place. But how could that be true? Aleksandr wanted to believe in heaven, but how could he have faith that a better place was a place where she was without him?

Now, there was someone who breathed the air his mother was supposed to breathe and stood where his mother should be standing. No matter what everyone said, she wasn't his mother. He admitted that she was nice, as Lilia had said. When he had given her the flowers his father had made him pick, she'd thanked him sweetly and made him blush. He even thought she looked pretty in her white blouse and scarlet skirt. The veil and wreath, woven into her hair, made her look like a fairy-tale princess. Still, in his memory, his mother was prettier. He saw her reassuring eyes, dark as the night sky. He felt her lips, warm on his cheek as she kissed him good night. He imagined inhaling her flowery scent; but although he tried his hardest, he couldn't hear her voice. Every day he lost pieces of her. That bothered him most of all.

Father Warga's lips moved but Aleksandr wasn't listening. It occurred to him that this could be a bad dream. Maybe his mother was alive. Maybe he only imagined that his father was marrying the woman standing next to him. If he pinched his hand and it didn't hurt, this wasn't real. Aleksandr squeezed the fleshy part by his thumb as hard as he could. It hurt a lot.

He blinked away tears and stared at his father and Her. They had crowns on their heads and each held a lit candle in one hand. Their other hands were tied together by a white cloth. As if she read his thoughts, Lilia leaned toward him and whispered, "The *rushnyk* around their hands symbolizes the unity of marriage." Who cared? Lilia could be really annoying sometimes.

Aleksandr's neck itched. He considered taking off his tie, but he knew if his father saw it was gone, he'd be angry. Instead, he stuck his fingers under his collar and tugged, trying to make the opening bigger. A button popped and his heart sank. Now his father would be really angry. At least, the button landed next to his foot. He picked it up and put it in his pocket. Everything about this day was trouble.

He tried to pay attention to Father Warga, who read the Gospel story about the wedding at Cana where Jesus turned water into wine. That wasn't a very big miracle. What difference did it make if people at a wedding had to drink water? There were more important miracles, such as the time Jesus raised Lazarus from the dead. Why couldn't Jesus raise his mother from the dead? Aleksandr had prayed hard for his mother to be alive again, but nothing had happened. She was still gone and he no longer believed in miracles.

Father Warga blessed a cup of wine. "I shall partake in the Cup of Salvation, and I shall invoke the name of the Lord," he sang.

His father and the bride drank from the cup.

Still tied to one another, they followed the priest three times around the center table.

Mr. Panko walked behind them, holding crowns above their heads, and Mrs. Panko carried the candles. His father, a half step ahead, held the bride's arm and pulled her along. As they walked, Aleksandr studied her gait. Her shoulders and hips dipped to the left. Of course, he'd noticed it before; it was impossible not to. For a moment, he felt sorry for her until he remembered she wanted to take his mother's place. Today, the rhythm of her stride tapped in his head like a dripping faucet.

As they walked, people tossed rice and flower petals. The chorus sang in soft harmony. Their voices swirled around the church, reaching toward the blue-painted ceiling. Lilia hummed along in a voice half girl, half woman.

When the chorus stopped, for a moment, the church became perfectly silent. Then Lavro's breath escaped from his nose. Someone in the back of the church coughed, and behind Aleksandr, a baby fussed. The mother whispered, "Hush, hush, hush." Aleksandr wished his mother were here to soothe him. It was a silly thought. If his mother were alive, he wouldn't be at this horrible wedding. His feet ached from standing too long in his new shoes. Out of the corner of his eye, he watched Lilia pick up Vera—what he wouldn't give to be carried—and bounce her on her hip. Lilia's heels clicked against the floor like a ticking clock.

The priest led his father and the bride to the altar at the front of the church. On the floor was another white cloth, embroidered with brightly colored birds and flowers.

"That's Mama's *rushnyk*," Lilia whispered.

On the inside, Aleksandr yelled, *Shut up!* On the outside, he pretended to ignore her.

The bride hesitated. His father stepped on the cloth. She followed.

Murmurs of approval skittered around the church.

"Because your father stepped on it first, that means he'll be the head of the household," Lilia whispered.

Aleksandr couldn't imagine it any other way, no matter who stepped on the stupid cloth first.

The crowns were removed, their hands untied.

The priest held his arms wide.

A baby cried, getting louder and louder every second. Father Warga raised his voice, struggling to be heard over the bawling infant: "May their home...haven...spiritual values...holy principles... modeled...gladden them...grace and peace...with one heart...glorify You. Amen."

The priest called his father and the bride Mr. and Mrs. Senyk. Everyone excitedly pressed toward the altar to congratulate them.

It was done. Magically, she was no longer just Her. She was his mother. What was he supposed to call her? Her Christian name was Katerina, but his father probably wouldn't allow him to call her that. He certainly didn't want to call her Mother or Mama. Maybe, he decided, he wouldn't call her anything at all.

"Everyone!" Please!" the photographer shouted, clapping his hands above his head so furiously Katerina thought he might fly.

From her vantage point atop the steps of St. Kassia's, she watched everybody gathered in the churchyard ignore the gangly photographer. She scanned the crowd, looking for recognizable faces, half expecting to see Aneta and Danya and Papa. Yana and Fedir stood at the bottom of the stairs, conversing with a couple who looked vaguely familiar. She counted a handful of neighbors she remembered from the times, since her arrival in Bilik, she'd attended church with the Pankos. These neighbors had proven warm and welcoming, yet she felt herself a stranger among them, as though inhabiting a dream, where the figures in the vignette seem real but remain nondescript, unmemorable. Finally, she spotted Lavro among a group of boys, which meant Aleksandr must be nearby.

The photographer cajoled the crowd: "Everyone—before we lose the light."

Katerina thought of Aneta's wedding photograph taken on the steps of St. George's Cathedral, the setting grand and her place among family and friends taken for granted. Danya stood on Aneta's right, Papa on her left. Katerina posed next to her father, like an afterthought.

The photograph hung on Aneta's parlor wall in a gilded oval frame.

"Shortest to the front, tallest to the back!" the photographer hollered.

Gradually, boisterous chatter turned to subdued murmurs.

"Father Warga—next to the bride, please."

When Aneta married, Katerina was still a girl, who assumed life unfolded predictably—courting, falling in love, marrying, and having children. Her mother's death had shaken her belief for a time, but Aneta's coming of age had restored her faith. She'd witnessed the transformative power of marriage. With the priest's pronouncement, her sister had become someone else, someone who was no longer hers, whose loyalty and devotion belonged to Danya.

Before Aneta married, Katerina had believed the blood bond was unbreakable. But the marriage bond—an act of choice—had proved more powerful for its deliberateness. Would it be true for her as well? Father Warga had said as much when she and Viktor had met with him in preparation for their marriage. He had called marriage a sacred mystery, in which human love and divine love intersected. As she and Viktor had sat awkwardly next to each other, passively receiving the priest's instruction, she had silently questioned how such a tenuous union could possibly be a sign of God's living presence. Now, despite Father Warga's certitude, she stood next to a man whose tie to her felt as flimsy as an embroidery thread. Life was not predictable. Nothing was as she'd envisioned it. Nothing.

While everyone arranged themselves more or less according to height, Father Warga spoke to Viktor, saying something about a second chance and God working in mysterious ways. Their conversation fluttered over Katerina's head.

The photographer, perched atop a shipping crate, adjusted the tripod. Apparently dissatisfied, he moved the camera forward and a few inches to the side. He looked through the lens. "Mr. and Mrs. Senyk," the photographer said, gesturing for the bride and groom, standing next to each other, rigid as fence posts, to move together.

Each stepped sideways a whisker.

"Closer. Closer."

Viktor edged next to Katerina. The smell of antiseptic soap and hair tonic filled her lungs. Her husband wore his masculinity like a suit of armor, cutting a handsome figure in his polished shoes, charcoal pants, and white shirt.

A dull ache worked its way from Katerina's hip, down along the side of her leg, to the arch of her foot. She straightened her back and raised her chin.

"Look at the camera, everyone!" the photographer shouted. "Good!"

Light exploded from the flash-bulb.

The photographer slid the metal stylus from its mounting hoop. He opened the narrow hatch on the front of the camera to record the date on the film's paper backing. The stylus slipped from his fingers and rolled along the ground. Dropping to his knees, he scrambled to retrieve the stylus.

"Maybe you should let one of the children work that camera!" Viktor hollered. Laughter erupted. Katerina winced.

By the time the photographer had recovered the stylus, he'd lost the crowd's attention. "Everyone. Look this way. Please!" His voice was hoarse.

"Look at the poor man, so we can get this over with!" Viktor boomed.

Silence.

"One, two, three!" the photographer said. The light flashed.

"Let the fun begin!" Viktor shouted.

Katerina took a deep breath. What lay ahead she couldn't imagine, but it was enough to know that, like the wake of a ship, her past had disappeared behind her.

Rain, considered an omen of a rich life together, threatened: but so far, not a drop had fallen on Bilik. Under a ceiling of low-hanging clouds, Father Warga led the crowd to the community hall. Viktor and Katerina followed the priest—he with a confident stride, she with a reluctant limp. The pace proved too fast. Katerina stumbled. Viktor wrapped his work-hardened hand around hers and supported her while she regained her balance. It was strong and steady, the kind of hand a woman could rely on.

"Thank you, husband," she said. Her appreciation was for more than a simple kindness. Marriage to Viktor might not be what she'd hoped for, but he was providing her with a chance at a new life. She looked up at him and smiled.

Viktor squeezed her hand and let go.

The wedding couple entered the modestly sized meeting hall, greeted by evidence of their neighbors' generosity. Wheat stalks, multicolored tablecloths, and lit candles decorated the room. Tables swayed under mounds of roast beef, *kubasa*, cabbage rolls, and meat-stuffed *perogies*. Platters of tomatoes, cucumbers, onions, peppers, and pickled fruits proclaimed each gardener's skill like ribbons at a fair. The perfume of garlic sweetened the air. On a separate table, *korovai*, the traditional Ukrainian wedding bread, festooned with miniature birds and flowers made of dough, symbolically celebrated the birth of a new family and foretold future prosperity.

The entire town gathered among the abundance. Women shared the latest events and family news. Men talked about weather, crops, and current market conditions. Adolescents flirted. Children wove their way through the merrymakers, giggling and chasing and sneaking samples from the food tables.

Katerina spotted Aleksandr's dark curly head. He stood among a group of young boys. She'd caught him watching her with his old-soul eyes, so out of place on his young face; but whenever she would look at him directly, he would look away. She wanted to tell him she understood how hard it was to lose a mother and how difficult it would be for her to fill his mother's shoes. Impossible, truthfully. She wanted to assure Aleksandr that she would love him and care for him. In time, maybe she could say just that. But his expression warned her that it would take patience to get to know this boy.

The women of Bilik gathered around her, eagerly congratulating and welcoming her.

"You make a beautiful bride."

"Yana said you are a seamstress. Maybe you will teach me to sew better?"

"I'm sure you will make Viktor very happy."

Katerina smiled at them, thanked them, and tried to remember them—young, old, short, tall, thin, heavy, friendly, and shy. When she had the opportunity, she'd ask Yana about these women, certain there would be a story to tell about each one. She wondered who among them would become her friends. Were this L'viv, she probably wouldn't become acquainted with any of them, even gregarious Yana, who was at least ten years older than she. To Katerina, with her city sensibilities, Yana would have been invisible as they passed each other in the street or the marketplace. What a pity that would have been.

"I'm Svetlana Sokur. Josef and I have a farm about five miles from town."

Katerina turned to face the woman who'd introduced herself. An infant slept in her arms. She was thin, weathered, and plain. Her clothes were clean but worn and ill fitting. Although lines creased her forehead and fanned from the corners of her eyes, Katerina suspected she was younger than she appeared.

"Pleased to meet you," Katerina said. She tried to recall why the woman's name sounded familiar.

Svetlana glanced over her shoulder, as though checking for eavesdroppers. "Elena was my friend," she said.

"Oh?"

The silence between them grew awkward.

Then Katerina remembered. It was on the ride to Weyburn. Josef Sokur had passed by in his wagon, and Viktor had joked that the man's mules were better looking than his wife. Facing Svetlana now, Viktor's remark seemed cruel.

Her deep eyes met Katerina's. "If you need—I mean, if you ever want someone to talk to—" Her words disappeared as the band began playing.

"Thank you," Katerina said, stepping closer and talking louder. "I should find my husband."

Thankful for an excuse to walk away, Katerina looked around the room and spotted Viktor in the far corner, standing among a group of men. She threaded her way through the crowd, smiling at well-wishers as she went. The *troïstï muzyki,* an ensemble of three musicians on fiddle, drums, and hammered dulcimer, played Ukrainian folk music so sweetly that it brought tears of grief and gratitude to Katerina's eyes. The day she'd worked up the courage to knock on the rectory door and confess her secret to Stepan—a confession that had gone unheard—she'd learned that love and hate could vie for the same heart. It appeared that grief and gratitude could do the same.

Music swirled around the room in 2/4 meter. The middle of the floor cleared as people joined in dancing the *hutsulka* and then the polka. Prohibition, recently repealed and already forgotten, meant home-brewed *horilka*—distilled with one farmer's wheat and honey and another's sugar beets and potatoes—openly filled glasses again and again. Katerina didn't indulge but Viktor drained his glass quickly and took another. She had no idea how many he'd already drunk, but he, along with several others, became louder and more raucous by the minute.

"A toast," yelled Josef Sokur, his voice already fuzzy with drink "to Mr. and Mrs. Senyk! May your lives be long and your children be many."

Heat radiated up Katerina's neck to her cheeks. She swallowed hard. Even if God blessed her with a dozen more children, she'd never forget her firstborn. He would live secretly in her heart forever.

Glasses clinked and were drained in one swift gulp.

The drums announced the *kozak,* a fast-paced dance evocative of the Cossacks. The floor cleared. A circle formed. Men crossed their arms, squatted, and kicked their legs exuberantly. Onlookers clapped, keeping time to the rowdy tempo.

When the music stopped, young men bounded away to refill their plates and liquor glasses; old men bent to catch their breath.

Yana appeared, with Viktor in tow. "It's time for the veil ceremony," she announced.

Everyone gathered around, clapping in unison while Katerina, blushing, stood in the middle of the circle. Yana removed Katerina's veil, a tradition that claimed to protect the bride from evil spirits. She replaced it with a kerchief, marking Katerina as a married woman. A handful of husbandless girls vied for the privilege of wearing the veil.

Viktor put his arm around his wife and bent to her ear. "Now you're mine," he said, "only mine."

Katerina didn't know whether to be flattered or frightened. There was no denying he'd spoken the truth. She was Mrs. Viktor Senyk. She belonged to him in a way that she'd never belonged to any man. Stepan had owned her heart, but that union hadn't been sanctioned by God or the law. Before the entire community, she'd pledged herself to Viktor for eternity. But it wasn't the veracity of what he'd said that gnawed at her as much as the way he'd said it. No warmth. No romance. Only possession. She reminded herself that he'd had a lot to drink. Whatever he said under such circumstances had to be taken with a pinch of salt. What had Yana said only that morning? *He's a man of his word, respected and held in high regard by everyone. He'll take care of you.*

Wasn't that the reassurance she'd been seeking?

Katerina looked around the room at her neighbors' joyful faces. They were good people who toiled long hours, cared for one another, and loved life. She must try to be as appreciative and welcoming as they were. *It's a day for celebration.* Yana's words. It was a day for gratitude and optimism, not pessimism and doubt. Katerina resolved to put on a pleasant face and enjoy herself.

"Another toast!" Ivan Zolyar shouted. "To Viktor and Katerina."

Viktor raised his glass.

The band began to play again. Loud music filled the air. Viktor squeezed Katerina's shoulder and then swaggered toward the pride of men drinking in the corner. Feet tapped and bodies twirled. With each song, the *horlika* drinkers spun around the room a little more unsteadily. The men in the corner conversed so boisterously their voices carried above the music.

"Tonight's the night, you randy dog," Josef Sokur said, patting Viktor vigorously on the back.

Viktor wrapped his shoulders in a one-armed hug. "You're right, my friend."

The men laughed and raised their glasses. "Tonight!"

Katerina imagined every eye looking at her and picturing their marriage bed. Her good cheer dissolved. She was a cat among dogs, misplaced and out of step.

Yana elbowed a path to Katerina. "Ach, men," she said. "Not a brain among them. Let's go get some more bread and leave these fools to their drinking."

Soon Viktor staggered over to Katerina. "Come, we're expected to dance."

"I can't."

"Today you can," Viktor said as he grabbed her hand. He dragged her toward the circle of dancers and began to spin.

Katerina tried to keep pace with his flying legs, but she teetered clumsily, caught her shoe in her skirt, lost her balance, and landed hard, pulling Viktor to the floor with her.

First the fiddle and then the dulcimer and then the drums stopped playing.

She lay on the floor, stunned.

"Are you hurt?" It was Fedir's voice. He was on one knee, bending over her.

Her head pounded. She wasn't certain if she was hurt, but in her embarrassment, Katerina shook her head from side to side, trying to regain her pride.

Viktor rose clumsily. Offering Katerina his hand, he pulled her to her feet in one quick tug.

Her knees wobbled and the room tilted. For several moments, she waited. When she felt steady enough to move, she adjusted her skirt and retied her kerchief. The wedding ensemble she'd so carefully created wore a swath of dirt from shoulder to hem. Tears gathered ominously behind her eyes.

Yana pushed past everyone. "Is anything injured besides your pride?" she whispered in Katerina's ear.

"I don't think so." Katerina bit her lip, struggling not to cry.

Dusting off Katerina's clothes with one hand, Yana shooed Viktor away with the other. She brushed back a strand of hair that had sprung loose from Katerina's kerchief. "Then don't worry. The women will understand and the men won't remember."

Yana led Katerina across the room toward a small circle of friends.

Through tear-filled eyes, Katerina glanced out the windows at the silver sky. Still, not a drop of rain had fallen.

In the unfamiliar bedroom, dimly lit by a single oil lantern, Katerina strained to get her bearings.

"Come here," Viktor commanded, sitting on the edge of the bed, his arms spread wide. He still wore his wedding suit but had taken off his shoes and removed his tie. Muted light danced around him, casting his features in mystery.

"I haven't finished—preparing," she said, wondering if Viktor heard the quaver in her voice. Still in her undergarments, she had not yet donned the filmy white nightgown she'd saved for her wedding night.

"Never mind that. Come here."

Pressing her nightgown tightly against her body, Katerina cautiously stepped toward Viktor's waiting arms. She faced him, her eyes downcast. One by one, he peeled her fingers from the gown until it dropped, puddling around her feet. He slipped his hands under her camisole, the one she'd sewn specially for the wedding. His hands felt warm and calloused against her skin. When he cupped her breasts and circled her nipples with his thumbs, she gasped.

"You like that," he said.

Katerina flushed.

Viktor rose, tipping sideways, regaining his balance by clutching her shoulder. He tugged at her camisole, his seductive touch turning to frustrated groping.

"It has buttons," Katerina whispered.

"Damn the buttons." Viktor continued fumbling.

"Let me," she said, gently placing her hands over his.

When she'd unfastened half the buttons, Viktor impatiently pulled the camisole over her head and arms and let it drop to the floor.

Katerina heard a seam tear.

He ran his fingers through her hair and, clutching a handful, tilted her head upward. His mouth pressed hard against hers. She smelled liquor on his hot breath. When he pulled away, his eyes narrowed, like an animal fixed on its prey. She looked at the wall.

Viktor untied the drawstring of her pantaloons and, in a single motion, pulled them down around her knees. "Take them off," he commanded.

Katerina bit down hard on her lip and stepped out of her undergarment. He explored her with his eyes and hands. Part of her wanted to run from his touch, from the shame of standing naked before him. Another part of her wanted to move and sway and melt like warm butter. She willed herself to stand still.

Viktor ran his hands along her hips and between her thighs.

She closed her eyes. Her heartbeat thrummed in her ears. A moan echoed in her head. She heard Viktor mutter.

He struggled to unbutton his shirt and pants. "Don't just stand there, woman. Help me."

She reached for the front of his shirt.

He pushed her hands away. "I can do that. My trousers."

Katerina tried to drop to her knees so that the buttons would be at eye level. One leg cooperated, but the other gave way as she tried to kneel. Her feet caught in the garments gathered on the floor, and she fell into Viktor, pushing them both onto the bed.

"I'm sorry. It was clumsy of me. I'm sorry."

Viktor laughed. "Ah, you're so hungry you can't wait! So that's the kind of woman you are!"

"No, I'm—"

"Finish what you've started."

Lying on her side, facing Viktor, Katerina ran her hands from his stomach to his waist, finding the buttons on the front of his pants.

Viktor groaned.

Katerina's hands shook as she unfastened his trousers.

He roughly turned her onto her back. He tugged his pants and undergarment down around his thighs. Then he climbed on top of her, spread her legs with his knees, and entered her. Katerina arched her back and gasped. She stared at the ceiling, watching the light from the oil lamp flicker in an erratic circle as Viktor thrust and panted.

When he finished, he lingered over Katerina. Then he rolled down next to her, one arm slung across his forehead, while his breathing slowed.

Katerina lay still. Tears wetted her temples and cheeks. She thought of Stepan holding her after they'd been intimate, them lying naked together, her head nestled in the curve between his neck and shoulder, his hand stroking her hair. God forgive her for wanting him. She felt Viktor watching her.

"Always hurts most the first time," he said drowsily.

Katerina realized, with relief, that her husband had mistaken her reticence for inexperience.

Chapter Eight

Rap. Rap. Rap. Viktor heard muffled knocking and slowly opened his eyes. He rubbed his temples to clear his head, then rolled onto his back, brushing against Katerina, who lay curled on her side, lips slightly parted, breathing softly. Her hair fanned across the pillow, and her bare shoulder peeked seductively from beneath the blanket. She stirred but did not wake.

It had been a long time since he'd woken with a woman next to him and an equally long time since the fragrance of passion had lingered in his bedroom. Last night was more vague sensation than vivid memory, but as he looked at Katerina, he felt a reminiscent twinge in his groin.

Rap. Rap. Rap. Probably inebriated revelers from the wedding reception had begun the second day's celebration early, or they had come intending to play some damned fool prank. Either way, Viktor decided to put an end to the nonsense.

Rap! Rap! Rap!

"Hold on," he mumbled.

As he slid from beneath the covers, the bedsprings creaked; still, Katerina didn't move. His pants and shirt lay in a heap on the floor. He pulled them on and then padded barefoot along the hall, past Aleksandr's empty bedroom and down the stairs.

When he opened the front door, Lavro stood on the porch, his clothes and hair soaked from the pouring rain.

"There's been an accident," Lavro said, his voice strained and breathless.

"Where?"

"At the Sokur farm—but Yuri brought Mr. Sokur to our house. Papa says he's hurt real bad, and you should come right away."

"Tell him I'm right behind you."

Viktor took the steps back up to the bedroom two at a time, covering the hallway in four elongated strides and unbuttoning his shirt as he went. After hastily grabbing a pair of woolen socks from the dresser and a heavy work shirt from the wardrobe, he leaned over Katerina and touched her exposed shoulder.

She startled, blinking, as if she didn't recognize him.

"There's been an accident," he said.

She sat up, suddenly alert, protectively holding the blanket over her breasts. "Aleksandr. Is Aleksandr all right?"

Viktor frowned. "Nothing's happened to the boy. It's Josef Sokur. He's at the Pankos' house."

Katerina began to rise. Viktor placed a firm hand on her shoulder. "Stay here," he commanded.

"But maybe I can help."

"I have to go."

Before she could utter another word, he was out the door.

The rain fell in sheets. The gravel road percolated. Viktor trudged through boot-sucking mud toward Panko's General Store. When he reached Main Street, he ran along the planked sidewalk, which stood just a few inches above rivulets flowing on each side of the road. The town, bathed in gray, looked deserted.

As he neared the store, he saw Josef Sokur's wagon in the middle of the street. Yuri, Josef's oldest boy, drenched and looking dazed, held fast to the mules' reins. Fedir stood on the wagon's front wheel, his lower body exposed, his upper body hidden beneath the grease-stained tarpaulin covering the wagon bed.

Aleksandr and Lavro ran toward Viktor, both hollering at once.

"Mr. Sokur's in the wagon! He's not moving!"

"Mama's calling Dr. Billings!"

Viktor climbed onto the back of the wagon and crawled under the tarpaulin, where Josef lay unconscious. The vestige of his right arm twisted away from his body at an unnatural angle. His hand and forearm hung from the knob of raw muscle and crushed bone protruding below the blood-soaked tourniquet cinched above his elbow.

"We've got to get him in the house!" Fedir yelled above the sound of rain pounding against canvas.

Viktor placed his hand on Josef's chest, lowered an ear close to his mouth, and listened. "He's breathing!" Viktor shouted back. He stuck his head above the tarpaulin and barked orders.

"Lavro!"

"Yes, sir."

"We need your help to carry him. We'll lift him out of the wagon toward you. Hold tight to his legs. Boy, you can't let go."

"Yes, sir." Lavro obediently stepped to the back of the wagon and braced himself.

"Aleksandr! You hold the door and then help Yuri get the mules to the livery."

"Yes, sir."

Viktor untied a long piece of rope threaded through one of the tarpaulin's grommets, carefully strung it bellow Josef's torso, and tied it across his chest and right arm, securing his injured arm to his side. Then, kneeling behind Josef's head, Viktor carefully hoisted Josef's upper body while Fedir lifted his midsection and Lavro held his legs. Together, they lowered the body from the wagon and slogged around the building to the front door of the house.

As they eased through the doorway, Aleksandr lost his grip on the doorknob.

"Damn it, boy!" Viktor hollered. "Hold the door!"

Aleksandr grabbed the doorknob and stared at his feet.

"Dear Lord!" Yana gasped at the sight of Josef's bloodied half limb. "Lay him here." She pointed to the dining room table where she'd draped a thick blanket over its top. "I reached Dr. Billings' wife. He's in Hastings, delivering a breech baby. She's sending someone to get him but couldn't say when he'd get here."

Viktor and Fedir exchanged a look: Josef might not last that long.

Lilia entered the room, carrying scissors, towels, and blankets. At the sight of Josef lying on the table, she turned pale.

"We're doing everything we can, Lilia. The rest is in God's hands," Yana said, smoothing the hair from her daughter's forehead and gently taking the items from her arms. "You can help by keeping the little ones out of here."

"Yes, Mama," Lilia said, backing from the room.

Viktor untied the rope from around Josef's chest and arm. He cut off the tattered sleeve above and below his bicep, further exposing the mangled limb. The tourniquet held fast and appeared to have stanched the flow of blood from the wound. Once satisfied that the tourniquet was secure, he unfastened Josef's wet jacket and slowly cut it off his torso.

Yana removed Josef's boots and covered him with a woolen blanket. With the corner of a towel, she gently dabbed moisture from his face. "Be strong. Svetlana and the children need you. Be strong," she murmured, caressing his cheek.

Josef's eyes fluttered beneath his lids.

"Now we wait," Viktor said.

"And pray," Yana said.

The grandmother clock chimed the half hour. Viktor listened to the minutes tick by. He drew back the window's lace curtain. "The rain's slowed," he said to no one in particular.

Yana kept vigil, sitting next to Josef and holding the hand of his intact arm.

Aleksandr and Yuri appeared at the dining room doorway, each dripping a puddle onto the wooden floor.

"Did you get the mules put up?" Viktor asked.

"Yes sir," Aleksandr said.

Yuri stood motionless, staring at his father, who lay unconscious on the table.

"What happened?" Viktor asked.

"The water pump wasn't working. A big stick got jammed in the gears, so the windmill wouldn't turn, and Pa wanted to repair it before we came into town for the party," Yuri explained.

Fleetingly, Viktor thought of Katerina, at home in bed. This would not be another day of celebration.

"I went out with Pa to fix it." Yuri's voice sounded flat. His eyes blinked rapidly. "He put a pipe over the end of the wrench to make it longer, so he'd have more leverage. He told me to pull, but the pipe slipped."

Fedir put a hand on the boy's shoulder.

"When I let go, Pa lost his balance, his sleeve got caught in the gears, they started to move, and…and…" Yuri's lower lip trembled. "I had to cut his sleeve with the ax to get him out." Yuri's tears flowed. He wiped his eyes with the backs of his hands.

"It's all right, son," Fedir said. "It was an accident."

"But I cut off his arm!" Yuri buried his face in his hands. "I'm sorry. I'm sorry. I'm sorry."

"You did the right thing," Fedir said, putting his arm around the boy's shoulders. "You did the brave thing."

Yuri's shoulders shook as he cried silently.

Fedir pulled the boy into his chest and held him.

Viktor studied Aleksandr, standing in the doorway. He looked fragile, breakable. The boy had inherited more than his mother's small stature. Whenever confronted with difficulty, he stared at his shoes, as if by looking away he could become invisible. Such weakness disgusted Viktor. He envied Josef Sokur. Aleksandr would never have had the strength to do such a courageously terrible thing.

Heavy footsteps. Creaking floorboards. A slammed door. Katerina waited. When the only sound she heard was the ticking clock on the nightstand, she eased out of bed, walking softly at first, stopping between each step to listen like a disobedient child, wary but defiant.

She retrieved her nightgown from the floor and pulled it over her head. Then, limping to the window, she peered out from behind the curtain. Rain squiggled down the panes, distorting the outside world. In the distance, St. Kassia's dome shimmered like a mirage. Inside and out the air hung cold and damp, bathing everything in dreariness.

The soreness between her legs reminded her of last night's coupling. The image of Viktor hovering over her, arms locked, eyes closed, mouth open, and hips thrusting again and again until the moment of release, made her flush in a way that months of clandestine lovemaking with Stepan never had.

Stepan approached the carnal act as though it were a sacrament, replete with theater and ritual. He had worshipped at the altar of her womanhood, transforming her body from mere flesh into a consecrated vessel, from which he had drunk his fill. His pleasure had become a sacred offering; her pleasure had derived from fulfilling him. Theirs had been an eternal dance, in which he led and she followed.

How could something so natural have gone so wrong?

Katerina had always believed sin to be self-evident, so completely obvious that when it presented itself, she would know it. Sin and virtue would be as different as a starless night and a sunlit morning. Sin would appear gnarled, twisted, and ugly—virtue smooth, straight, and lovely. Instead, sin had come to her disguised as a gift, wrapped in beauty and gratitude.

When Viktor had finished with her, he'd lain on top of her, pinning her beneath him. Unable to move or breathe, Katerina had been afraid to tell him or nudge him, for fear he'd find her critical. She'd squeezed her eyes tight and counted the seconds, trying not to panic, until finally, he'd rolled onto his back. She'd prayed he hadn't found her wanting, that drunkenness had reduced their first intimate encounter to an egregiously vulgar act.

Now, Katerina unconsciously brushed her ring finger around her mouth, soothing the tender lips Viktor had kissed so urgently. She'd not been prepared for his overpowering need. Resisting would have been like trying to hold back a prurient animal, so she'd willed her body to be compliant, yielding to his touch. She must not assign the act more significance than it deserved. She must not turn a clumsy beginning into something bigger. After all, Viktor had said it always hurt the most the first time. Wasn't his assurance a version of tenderness and a kind of promise?

Katerina heard a creaking sound and stood still. She listened. The house groaned. She waited. Nothing but the clock spoke. Satisfied that the noise was nothing more than the wooden-framed house protesting the rain, she moved about the room, running her fingertips along every object and surface.

Last night, when she'd entered the bedroom for the first time, it had been dark and she'd been too nervous to notice anything but Viktor's expectant leer. She'd missed the peeling paint of the windowsill, the frayed edges of the quilt, and the faded cabbage roses of the wallpaper. Above the bed, next to the icon of Christ, there was a rectangular shape where the wallpaper still looked new, where another picture had hung beside the image, most likely, an icon of the Virgin Mary. Its absence threw the entire wall off balance. She wondered where it had gone.

Katerina shivered and wrapped her arms around herself. She turned in a slow circle, searching for Elena's presence, for evidence that a woman had lived and breathed and made love there. She looked for signs of warmth and contentment. But the room felt as cold as death. Even the lace curtains had a jaundiced cast. Elena must have touched everything in the place at one time or another, yet there was no indication of that. Was it really that easy to erase all traces of a life?

It had been very different when Katerina's mother had died. She and Aneta hadn't been allowed to handle any of their mother's possessions, as if somehow their touch would make the memory of her disintegrate. Papa had made the place a shrine, with reminders of their mother everywhere—her photographs, her clothing, and even her brush, with strands of dark hair still entwined among the bristles. When Papa had caught Katerina sitting at her mother's vanity, pulling the brush through her own hair, he'd struck her, sending the brush across the room. He'd scrambled to pick it up, as though the object needed comforting, not his child.

Now, at the washstand, Katerina searched for a clean cloth but found none and settled for the one floating in the basin. She bathed in the cool, cloudy water.

Her camisole lay on the floor. She stooped to retrieve it. Straightening, she ran her fingers along the torn seam. How hopeful she'd been when she'd sewn it, and how foolish to think that making something delicate to wear on her wedding day would make her feel innocent. The only clothing she'd brought besides yesterday's wedding attire was her nightgown and an ensemble for today's celebration. Now, the indigo dress she'd carefully selected seemed fussy.

Katerina pulled on her stockings cautiously, easing them over the deep scars on her shin. When she put on her shoes, she was reminded of how sore and weary they'd made her feet yesterday. She wove the laces around the eyehooks and up over her ankles, tying them loosely. Then, she brushed her hair and arranged it atop her head, fastening the upswept style with a half-dozen pins. From a satin pouch, she removed the three-stranded *korali* she'd intended to wear today for good fortune, placed the coral beads around her neck, and admired them in the mirror before returning them to the pouch. Today was not a day to tempt fate. Katerina adjusted her skirt, smoothed her hair, and straightened her back. She felt better. She sat on the edge of the bed and waited for Viktor to come home or to send word.

Two hours passed.

"Stay here," he'd said. Katerina weighed his words, turning them sideways and upside down. Certainly, her husband didn't expect her to remain alone in this strange house, ignorant of what was happening only a few blocks away. She couldn't stay. She must go to the Pankos'. She could be of assistance, if nothing else, by helping Yana with the children.

Viktor would understand.

Today was the third-worst day of Aleksandr's life. The worst had been the day they'd buried his mother's empty coffin; the second-worst had been yesterday, when his father married a woman to take her place. Those had been terrible days, but today was a special kind of horrible. The unthinkable had happened. Yuri Sokur had cut off his father's arm!

Aleksandr hovered in the shadowy niche between the sideboard and the corner of the Pankos' dining room, watching and listening. His rain-soaked pants and shirt clung to his skin, and his wet socks made his feet cold and clammy. His head hurt and stomach ached. He wanted to run. He wanted to stay.

His father stared out the window into the steel-gray light, quiet and distracted. Aleksandr remained wary, watching for warning signs—red eyes, balled fists, clenched jaw—attempting to anticipate his father's changeable mood, although he knew it was as impossible as predicting a thunderclap in a storm. Aleksandr held his breath, willing himself to be invisible, hoping his father had forgotten he was in the room.

Mr. Sokur lay on the table, breathing but not moving. Each time his chest rose, Aleksandr silently counted a beat until he reached ten and then started over. *One—two—three—four...*

He'd never seen anything so awful. Once, he'd seen a three-legged dog walking along the roadway. The dog hadn't seemed to miss his limb. And there was a brakeman working the rail through Bilik whose right hand was missing two fingers. When he'd asked the man how he'd lost them, his father had yelled at him and told him to mind his own business. This situation was much worse. He'd never known anyone missing a whole arm.

Ragged muscle and jagged bone stuck out below the tourniquet. Aleksandr swallowed the bile that crept into the back of his throat. Still he couldn't take his eyes from Mr. Sokur's arm. *Five—six—seven…*

Things had happened so fast, it made him dizzy. Before this morning, Yuri Sokur had been a shy, dirt poor boy, three years older than him, as big and strong as an ox, not mean, and not very smart. Mr. Marko often kept him in from recess to help him with his homework, which Yuri rarely did. But everything Aleksandr knew about Yuri had changed with a swing of an ax.

Aleksandr pictured Yuri's thick hands gripping a long-handled ax, swinging it high above his head, and in a blur, smashing it down with all his might. Had it made a sound like an ax thudding against wood, or did a blade cutting through flesh and bone make no sound at all? Maybe all Yuri had heard was this father's scream.

It had been strange to see someone as big and strong as Yuri cry. At first, he'd sobbed as though he'd never stop; but now, he stood silent and still as a statue, his face wet and streaked with blood and dirt. He kept his eyes on his father, as though nothing and nobody else existed. Mrs. Panko had wanted Yuri to go with Lavro to eat something and change out of his wet clothes, but he'd refused. Mr. Panko had just shaken his head at her, and she'd left Yuri alone.

When his mother had died, Aleksandr had cried at night, alone in his room, his head buried beneath his pillow so his father wouldn't hear. Just because he didn't cry anymore didn't mean he didn't think about her every day. He missed her so much his heart felt hollow. Maybe there was a limit to tears. Maybe it was possible to use them up. Maybe now he and Yuri would cry just on the inside.

Aleksandr wished there were such a thing as real magic—not the kind where a magician pulls a rabbit out of a hat—the kind that could actually make time disappear, eliminating entire hours from a day, days from a week, or weeks from a year, as though they had never existed. Voilá! Bad things that had happened would vanish. If Aleksandr had the power, he wouldn't subtract just the past two hours. He'd cancel the moment his mother had died and the year and a half after that. He'd especially erase yesterday, when his father had forgotten about his mother and married Her.

Mrs. Panko touched Mr. Sokur's forehead, bent over him, and whispered words Aleksandr couldn't hear. There was blood caked on the man's face and chest, not just on his sleeve where the ax had landed. When the blade had cut through his arm, blood must have splattered and gushed, exploding like a geyser and flowing like a river. Yuri's hands and clothes were covered in blood, too. *Eight—nine—ten...*

What would it be like to chop off his father's arm? It was hard to picture him weak and helpless, lying on a table, struggling to live. Then he thought of the grain elevator.

From the outside, it looked like a gigantic shed, but on the inside, it had a huge drive belt that ran the elevating leg, which moved the grain in big buckets to enormous storage pits. There were shafts where grain poured so hard, it could bury someone in seconds. Aleksandr pictured danger everywhere. There were fire hazard signs posted on doors and walls, and a sign nailed next to the lift platform that said, "Warning! This lift must not be used by anyone except the elevator operator!" He'd witnessed his father, protected by a single steel bar, ride the lift's open metal platform up the inside of the building until he disappeared eighty feet into darkness.

What if his father got his hand caught in the gears of the drive belt, and it kept turning and turning, pulling his wrist and elbow farther and farther between the gears? What if his father yelled for help, and the only one who heard him was Aleksandr? *One—two—three—four...*

Where was the ax? He couldn't remember seeing one anywhere at the elevator, not that his father had allowed him to go into every part of the building. There wouldn't be time to search. He'd have to run home to get an ax from the shed. He'd run back to the elevator as fast as he could. He'd get there just in time. He'd grip the ax handle with both hands and swing it above his head and smash it down with all his strength. There would be blood gushing from the place where he had cut off his father's arm. His father would cry out in pain, and Aleksandr would have to take a rope he'd remembered to bring from the shed and tie a tourniquet around the stump to stop the bleeding. He would save his father's life. He would do the right thing, the brave thing. His father would live. *Five—six—seven...*

What then?

He would blame Aleksandr for cutting off his arm. He would curse him and tell him he'd chopped off his arm for no reason. He imagined his father's voice: *You stupid fool! All you had to do was shut off the engine. You cut off my goddamned arm for no reason!*

Eight—nine—ten...

If Mr. Sokur lived, would he thank Yuri for saving his life? Or would he tell his son it was the worst thing he'd ever done?

Without warning, she appeared in the doorway, wearing a fancy blue dress.

His father strode toward her, eyes narrowed and jaw clenched. Aleksandr grimaced. He'd seen those eyes and that jaw many times. Consequences followed—a verbal battering at best, a beating at worst. No one else seemed to notice.

What had she done to make his father angry? Yesterday, he had been happy, celebrating and glad-handing everyone in Bilik. He couldn't remember seeing him smile so much, ever. She must have done something wrong. Why did she have to spoil things?

Aleksandr had vowed not to speak her name or call her his mother. He didn't want to feel sorry for her. In fact, he didn't want to feel anything for her. What he did feel was overwhelming gratitude that this time his father's narrowed eyes and clenched jaw weren't directed at him.

As if he were about to whisper a secret in her ear, his father leaned toward her. Aleksandr strained to hear.

"What are you doing here?"

"When you didn't come back—"

"I told you to stay home."

"I just thought…I could help."

"Help?" He stepped aside, gesturing toward Mr. Sokur, lying on the table. "How?"

When she saw the stump, the muscle and bone jutting from its end, her mouth gaped and face paled. She bent at the waist, holding one hand over her middle and the other over her mouth. Aleksandr thought she might vomit, but all that escaped was a punched-in-the-stomach gasp.

Mrs. Panko flew across the room, took hold of her waist, and placed a steadying hand on her back. "Easy now. Breathe. That's it."

"Are you all right, Katerina?" Mr. Panko asked, his arm still resting protectively on Yuri's shoulder.

She nodded but didn't look up.

From where he stood, Aleksandr could hear her breathing and see her hands shaking.

His father stared at her.

Gradually, she straightened, pulling her shoulders back and her chin up. Color returned to her cheeks. Her lips pinched. Her eyes glistened.

"I'm sorry," she said.

"There is nothing to be sorry about," Mrs. Panko said.

Before his father could say anything else to Her, Dr. Billings stepped into the room carrying a large, black leather case. "Sorry it took so long to get here," he said. "A difficult birth and this incessant rain slowed me down."

As far as Aleksandr knew, Dr. Billings was never in a hurry. Even the time he'd been punched in the eye and his mother had rushed him to his office above the bank, Dr. Billings had moved slowly and deliberately. Neither blood nor tears hurried him. Each painful stitch took forever.

The doctor bent over Mr. Sokur and touched the end of the stump. Aleksandr's eyes widened. How would it feel to touch someone's insides? Dr. Billings checked the tourniquet.

"The blood flow has stopped," he said, more to himself than to anyone else. He pulled a stethoscope from his bag, listened to Mr. Sokur's heart, and then cut the shirtsleeve around the arm. He took out a syringe, poked the long needle into a little brown bottle, and filled it with a clear liquid. Mr. Sokur didn't even move when it sank into his arm.

"The damage is extensive. We have to get him to the hospital." the doctor said.

Aleksandr noticed, although there were three other adults in the room, Dr. Billings spoke to his father.

"To Weyburn?"

"It's too far." The doctor wiped his forehead with the back of his hand. "The tourniquet stanched the bleeding, but if it's on much longer, he'll lose the whole arm or worse. Best take him to Kerryville."

"I'll drive Doc's ambulance, so he can ride in the back with Josef. Agreed, Doc?" his father said.

Dr. Billings nodded. He carefully wrapped a long white cloth around the bloody stump.

"Yana, you stay near the phone," his father continued.

"Fine, but someone should go to Svetlana," Mrs. Panko said. "The poor woman must be beside herself with worry."

"I'll drive out to the farm," Mr. Panko said. "Katerina, are you feeling well enough to come along? I think Svetlana's going to need a woman friend."

"If you think I can help."

Aleksandr watched the veins throbbing in his father's neck. *One—two—three—four...*

Josef Sokur's sod house sat wearily on the land. The front wall canted precariously, and the roof wore the same scramble of bleached prairie grass as the ground, reminding Katerina of a disheveled old man. Adversity, poverty, and backbreaking toil left their mark on every object and surface, natural or otherwise, and the skim of decay covered the entire homestead.

"It isn't what I expected," Katerina said.

"I suppose not," Fedir said. He pulled into the turnaround, maneuvering the Model T as close to the house as he dared without his tires getting stuck in the mud. "When they settled here, most farmers lived in sod houses due to lack of lumber and such, but now all but the poorest have built regular homes."

Although there was no judgment in his comment, Katerina understood his meaning.

The rain had stopped and timid sunlight peeked through the southeastward-drifting clouds. The air was still thick, and moisture clung stubbornly to everything.

When Katerina stepped from the car, the pungent smell of pigs and poultry assaulted her. A yellow, lop-eared dog with ribs like a paleontological specimen ambled toward her, barking. Katerina froze.

"Goldie's harmless," Fedir said. "That dog's so old, he's practically toothless."

Katerina kept an eye on Goldie despite Fedir's reassurances. As she stepped across the sodden ground, mud oozed over her best shoes and spattered her linen dress. It would take considerable effort to clean them, if they came clean at all. She felt guilty for her selfish thought and silently offered St. Augustine's prayer of forgiveness: *O Lord, the house of my soul is narrow; enlarge it, that you may enter in...*

At the wedding reception, Katerina had met so many neighbors that she'd struggled to memorize names and faces, but despite the briefness of their encounter, she hadn't forgotten Svetlana Sokur. Hers had been a sad island in a sea of joyful faces. What meager words of comfort could she offer a woman whose husband had lost his arm and might lose his life? Her stomach tied in a familiar knot.

She and Fedir approached the warped front door. The undersized windows flanking the entry promised darkness within. Katerina took several deep breaths, preparing for the worst. Fedir knocked softly. A boy close to Aleksandr's age opened the door a crack. He looked up at them with large green eyes.

"Kiel, we're here to talk to your mother," Fedir said gently.

The boy didn't speak but opened the door wide and stepped aside.

Svetlana sat at the table, her face red and her eyes swollen. An infant rested in her arms and a girl, perhaps five or six, crouched between stored sacks of flour and sugar under the oilcloth-covered table. It looked as though it was the only place where the ground remained dry.

Katerina surveyed the interior with a single glance. On the left, a wall separating a tiny bedroom from the rest of the space served as the lone partition in the house. The pich, a clay oven built against the back wall, still warm from the morning's baking, threw considerable heat into the damp house. White-painted newsprint covered the walls, which were sparsely decorated with religious icons and random sprays of hand-painted flowers. Lace curtains, yellowed with age, hung on the three small windows in the room. Overhead, sod poked through spaces between the ceiling's rough-sawn boards.

Svetlana looked up but said nothing.

Fedir knelt on the wet floor next to her and took her hand in his. "Svetlana, we've come to help."

"Is he dead?" she asked in a whisper.

Her directness unnerved Katerina.

"Josef is alive," Fedir said. "Dr. Billings is with him, and Viktor is driving them to the hospital in Kerryville. I came to take you there."

"But the children—"

"Yuri is safe and Katerina will stay with the others," Fedir said.

Svetlana's brow creased and her arms tightened around the baby. "The animals—"

"Don't worry." His voice remained calm and gentle. "Yana is finding someone to tend them."

Svetlana inhaled deeply, as if trying to steel her courage.

"Gather what you need. I'll go out and check the animals."

With that, Fedir left Katerina standing immobile, wondering what to say or do. Reassurances seemed false and anything else seemed inadequate.

"How will we live? How will we feed these children?" Svetlana looked from one small face to the other. "How will we survive?" Her voice quavered.

Svetlana's questions reached into Katerina's heart. *How will I live? How will I feed this child? How will I survive?* Those had been her words. She'd said them to herself a thousand times. In that moment, she realized she was more sister to this stranger than to her own flesh and blood. She hadn't acknowledged that when Svetlana had introduced herself or tried to tell her—what? She hadn't wanted to see her reflection in Svetlana's fearful eyes or in the defeat written on her anxious face.

"What use is a farmer with one arm?" Svetlana asked, her voice turning from desperation to quiet rage. "Tell me." Tears ran down her cheeks.

The infant whimpered and the little girl under the table inched back against the wall. Kiel stood at his mother's side and, in the softest voice, pleaded, "Don't cry, Mama. Please don't cry."

Something in the way the boy spoke made Katerina believe he'd soothed his mother with those same words before.

Katerina placed a hand lightly on Svetlana's shoulder. When she winced, Katerina withdrew her hand.

"Come now," she said tenderly. "Your husband needs you."

Svetlana looked into Katerina's eyes. "I don't care what he needs."

Bone weary, Viktor turned onto the Sokur farm well after midnight. Svetlana sat in the truck next to him, looking tired, defeated, and more haggard than usual. She hadn't said two words since they'd left the hospital, not that there was much to say. It appeared Josef might live, but if he pulled through, he'd be a one-armed farmer. He hadn't been a good farmer with two arms. In Viktor's estimation, he'd be better off dead.

A dim light shone in the house windows. The place appeared deceptively inviting, its decay erased by the moonless night.

When Viktor stepped from the truck, Sokur's mangy dog loped up and sniffed his boots and legs. Impatiently, he kicked the mutt, sending him rolling through the mud, whimpering. Svetlana paid no attention as she plodded to the house, head down, shoulders slumped.

A pre-winter chill rode in on a north wind and mixed with the pungent odor of pig manure, making Viktor grateful he lived in town. A rhythmic thudding disturbed the silence—perhaps a fence gate flapping on its hinges. Whatever it was, he wasn't about to go stumbling into the dark to search for it.

The front door creaked open. A single lantern lit the interior. Katerina sat at the table dozing, her chin resting on her chest, the baby cradled in her arms. Svetlana hung her coat on the hook inside the door and then stood in the middle of the small room, looking dazed, as if she'd wandered into a stranger's house.

"Katerina, wake up," Viktor called from the doorway, his voice crashing through the quiet. "Time to go home."

Her head lifted. She blinked sleep away. A look of recognition slowly lit her face. "How is Joseph?" she asked.

"Alive."

"Thank God."

Katerina rose quietly. The baby stirred. She hummed softly and rocked her. When she tried to hand the infant to her mother, Svetlana nodded toward the pich.

"She sleeps in the basket," Svetlana said.

Katerina placed the baby in the small basket perched on the stove's hearth. "Kiel and Inga are in your bed," she said. "Do you want me to move them?"

"No."

"Is there anything I can do for you?" Katerina asked.

Svetlana shook her head.

"Someone will be by in the morning to bring Yuri home," Viktor said.

Svetlana nodded. She managed a whispered "Thank you" to Viktor and Katerina before closing the door to her home.

The truck bounced along, splashing through invisible ruts. Although the rain had finally stopped, the cloud-filled sky blotted out the stars, making the night air as dark as ink. Viktor was tired of driving. It seemed as though he'd been on the road for days.

"At first, the children were very shy," Katerina said. "I imagine they were frightened after all they'd seen today. I told them stories to take their minds off their troubles. Gradually, they warmed up to me and ended up sitting on my lap."

Viktor was silent. Katerina continued talking, asking him about what had happened at the hospital. Her voiced grated on him. He was exhausted and hungry and in no mood to listen to a chattering woman. He stared straight ahead, ignoring her. Finally, she shut up.

When they walked into the house, Viktor cornered her in the entry. "I told you to stay here," he said in a voice as hard as flint. "Don't ever disobey me again."

She looked up at him, wide-eyed. "But Viktor, I just—I wanted—I—"

He grabbed her forearm and bent it behind her back.

"Viktor, please. That hurts," she whimpered.

He twisted harder.

"Don't contradict me. Don't think you're smarter than me. You're not." His face was inches from hers. "I've put a roof over your head. When I tell you to do something, you do it."

Chapter Nine

His gift was bewildering to Katerina, not only for its generosity but also for its timing. On November 24, her name day, Viktor had given her a bar of scented soap. For Christmas, he'd given her a bottle of toilet water. Both gifts had been purchased at Panko's General Store. Katerina recognized Yana's hand in their selection. Now, in late January, for some inexplicable reason, he had given her the perfect gift, a sewing machine.

There had been one other gift. After the first time he'd struck her, Viktor had left a small bag of licorice on the kitchen table, the same token he'd brought when they'd met alone at the Pankos' home, shortly after her arrival in Bilik. She hadn't told him then that she didn't like licorice and he hadn't asked. His assumption made her wonder if licorice was something Elena had favored. Although he'd never said, Katerina assumed the candy was an apology of sorts. She had no idea what her offense had been. He'd stumbled upstairs drunk and accused her of some unintelligible transgression. She'd begged him to tell her what she'd done. His answer had been a fist in her stomach. She'd promised never to do it again, whatever "it" was. Later, when she had mentioned the licorice, Viktor had looked at her blankly. "If only you'd learn not to provoke me," he'd said and then walked away, shaking his head. His voice had been devoid of sentiment or remorse.

The second time he'd crossed the line, he'd struck from the back, sending her reeling until she tripped, hit the corner of the dresser, and landed hard on the floor, causing black and blue marks on her shoulder and hip. Although her bruises were hidden beneath her dress, she'd been so ashamed, that in order to avoid encountering Yana or Fedir or the congregants at St. Kassia's, she'd feigned illness for a week. Aleksandr had said nothing but he knew. She'd seen it in his eyes, caught him staring at her in pity—or was it judgment?

Viktor had delivered lesser punishments, too—a forceful pinch, a grabbed shoulder, a twisted arm—no longer followed by gift or apology. Once, he'd squeezed her neck, circling it with his massive hands and pressing just long and hard enough to demonstrate he could choke the life out of her on a whim. He never struck her face. She was ashamed of her gratitude for that. Whether to hide evidence of his brutality or whether her disfigurement would have displeased him, she didn't know. Rather than lashing out at her unthinkingly, his retribution felt calculated, meted out more as a sentence than an impulse. Viktor's steely control terrified her most.

Katerina tried to please him, but no matter how determined her efforts, she hadn't learned how to avoid triggering his temper. How could she? The line between acceptable and unacceptable had no discernible boundary. Like a dark cloud, his disapproval blew in capriciously with the wind.

Since their wedding day, Viktor had accumulated a laundry list of her failings—her fancy ways, citified clothes, and superior attitude. When he wanted to hurt her deeply, he'd call her a cripple and remind her how fortunate she was to have any man look at her, let alone marry her. Resentment oozed from her pores. She feared he smelled it. Stepan had done far more than look at her. There were times when the temptation to shout, *I have been loved and bedded by a man ten times your better!* became almost too strong to contain. The words swirled in her stomach and head, met in her mouth, and threatened to escape. Behind clenched teeth, Katerina gated them, swallowed them, and commanded them back to an unreachable place; were they uttered aloud, she might not survive.

The seemingly random appearance of the sewing machine proved as baffling as the arbitrary punishments. Katerina studied Viktor warily, trying to gauge his mood.

"Well?"

"It's beautiful," she said and meant it.

The sewing machine was a work of art. Its wrought iron legs were ornate scrolls, and the wooden drawers, two on each side of the cabinet, curved in graceful arcs. Katerina mentally arranged the notions—threads, needles, buttons, pins, plus her mother's special gold-handled scissors—in the various compartments. She pulled up a dining room chair and sat. Pressing her foot lightly on the treadle, she tested its ease of motion. Her hands caressed the smooth finish of the brown oak cabinet, and her fingers lightly traced each cursive letter of the manufacturer's name—*E-A-T-O-N*.

"It's hinged," Viktor said. "See, you pull up here." As he lifted the sewing machine, the base tilted back on its hinges. He tucked the machine down into the cavity inside the cabinet. Then, he closed the wooden top of the cabinet over the machine.

"How clever! I've never seen one like it."

Viktor's eyes softened in a moment of unguarded good humor.

There were times when Katerina glimpsed the boy in Viktor. She wanted to keep those times close to her heart like a treasured locket. Her eyes glistened. This was the man she had envisioned marrying, not the miser who tallied her fictitious debts and tormented her. With this man, she could almost imagine being happy.

"May I try it?" Katerina asked.

"It's yours."

"I'll experiment on one of the old dish towels."

Without prompting, Viktor went to the kitchen and returned with several.

"Thank you."

"You'll need fabric," he said.

"I could use castoffs. I'm certain Yana has clothing the children have outgrown."

"Bilik has a dry goods store," he said. "Put it on account, but don't be foolish."

Katerina was already mentally walking the aisles of Wozny's Dry Goods, inhaling the scent of material. She'd gone by many times, never entering, fearing it would only make her homesick. Now, she could hardly wait. Tomorrow, she'd be their first customer. It wouldn't be the same as her father's shop, but it would be the next-best thing. What would she make first? A shirt for Viktor as a token of appreciation, she decided, and then something for Aleksandr. Maybe she'd even get around to sewing something for herself.

She dared not tell Viktor she had been used to working with the richest silks, brocades, and wools. As a child, she'd been schooled in her father's tailor shop, an enchanted space where Papa had transformed the bolts of cloth that lined every wall into the finest shirts, trousers, and jackets in L'viv. The most important men came to buy his suits—the best in the city, they claimed. How proud she had been to have a father with such magical hands. Papa had taught her to distinguish the choice wools from those that scratched the skin and quickly lost their shape in wearing. *Never skimp on quality, Katerina. Remember that and you will never want for customers.*

Katerina reached into her sewing basket for a spool of white thread. Her brow furrowed as she concentrated, examining various parts of the machine. "This is newer than the one I'm familiar with," she said. "It will take a while to figure it out."

"You're a clever woman. You'll manage."

Perhaps Viktor's comment was meant to be taken at face value. Perhaps. But she couldn't be certain. Ever. The tone of his voice made her believe she might have said or done something wrong.

Katerina rose and forced herself to look him in the eye. "Viktor, this is the most special gift I've ever gotten. I can't begin to thank you." She smiled at him and kissed him lightly on the cheek. In Katerina's estimation, her sweetness sounded cloying and false, but when a self-satisfied look crept across Viktor's face, she realized he detected only gratitude.

"The best Eaton's had," he bragged.

"I'm overwhelmed by your generosity."

Desperately, Katerina wanted to believe that Viktor's gift spelled a sea change in their marriage. How tired she was of living with regret.

"Have to get back to the elevator," Viktor said.

Katerina heard the front door close. Relieved to be alone and unobserved, she studied the needle mechanism, tension control devices, balance wheel, bobbin winder, and spool pin. The variety of stitch options pleased her, and the regulator seemed straightforward and easy to use. Before long, Katerina had the bobbin wound and a towel placed under the presser foot. She hummed to herself as she stepped down on the treadle, and the towel inched over the bed of the machine. The hypnotic punch of needle-through-towel, needle-through-towel produced a rhythm as soothing as a symphony.

Her thoughts wandered. She became a child again, with Papa standing over her shoulder. He smelled of sweet tobacco, her favorite aroma in the world. *Slowly. Guide the cloth gently with your fingers. If you press down too hard, the fabric won't keep up with the stitch, and the material will pucker.* She savored the sensation of the fabric under her fingertips. They knew the fabric as surely as a blind woman's fingers know Braille. The coarse towel became a fine piece of silk, its smooth, liquid texture gliding beneath her hands. *Close your eyes, kishka. Inhale.* Papa held a fabric up to her nose. *Which is it?* She inhaled as deeply as possible, filling her lungs with the hope she would know the answer that pleased her father. *Wool.* She opened her eyes and could tell by the smile on Papa's face that she'd guessed correctly.

Her imagination drifted further. It was the day she sold the first dress she'd ever created on her own. Mrs. Lubarsky twirled in front of the mirror in her new blue gabardine gown, admiring her reflection. Watching her, Katerina dreamed of becoming the finest dressmaker in the city. She had become a skilled seamstress under Papa's tutelage, learning to cut material with a surgeon's precision and matching her father's flawless handicraft, stitch for stitch. Her hands had become magical, too.

The parlor clock struck the half hour. Lost in memories, Katerina couldn't believe how quickly the afternoon had slipped away. Reluctantly, she put aside the towel, crisscrossed with stitches, and nested the machine beneath the oak top, as Viktor had instructed. She pushed her chair away from the machine. The winter sun, hanging low on the horizon, cast a pale beam through the paned window and across Katerina's foot, highlighting her worn shoes, scuffed by the unpaved streets and board walkways of Bilik. There had been a time when she'd daily polished her shoes to a glossy shine. But no longer. Viktor accused her of being high and mighty, no matter how hard she tried to adjust to life in Bilik. How was she to please a man who alternated between showing her off like a prize he'd won and berating her for her pridefulness?

The back door banged. Katerina startled. She listened intently. The sound of sole on wood wasn't heavy but child-soft. Her shoulders relaxed. Aleksandr was home from school. Within moments, he appeared in the parlor doorway.

"I don't imagine you're hungry for a piece of honey cake?" Katerina teased.

Aleksandr looked down and shook his head.

"Too bad," she said. "I think there are two pieces left, just enough for you and me."

Viktor paced across the undersized office, fuming and cursing. He raked his fingers through his hair with one hand and gripped a letter, with its familiar Winnipeg postmark, in the other. Like a viper, the letter had been lying in wait, hiding in a pile of official correspondence. The second he had seen it, he had known who it was from; Elena's childish scrawl on the envelope was unmistakable.

He'd read it three times, growing more agitated with each reading. *I beg you to send Aleksandr to me. You know he belongs with his mother.* Elena had lost claim to her son the minute she'd crossed the threshold of their home, determined not to return; in truth, she'd lost the boy the instant she'd decided to leave. If she thought he was sending his son back to her, now or ever, she was sorely mistaken. She'd been replaced. The boy had a new mother.

Viktor tossed the letter on his desk in disgust and stared out the south-facing window. Frost clung to the corners of the glass where the outside air seeped into the room. The outdoor temperature had dipped so low that the bottom of the door had frozen. He'd had to chisel his way into the elevator office that morning. He'd made a fire in the stove of the engine room, but the rising heat wasn't up to the task of warming the frigid air in the office. Viktor's anger provided all the heat he needed for the moment.

Elena had always underestimated him. Because she'd rarely stood up to him, she'd never seen what force he was capable of. Grudgingly, he admitted he had underestimated her, too—a mouse of a woman, skittering around the house, hiding in corners, squeaking in her timid voice. One act of defiance hadn't changed that. She was still a mouse. He'd be damned if he'd turn his son over to a weak rodent.

The wind howled, rattling the windows in their frames. He watched the north wind blow across the prairie, polishing the snow into drifts as high as waves in an ocean squall. Sheltered from the wind on the south side by the imposing elevator, the snow formed a V that protruded from the base of the office outward, reminding him of a ship's prow.

Life would be easier if he could sail away, the way Elena had, without thought or consideration for anyone but herself. How far had she gone? Was she in Winnipeg or somewhere else in Manitoba? Given her limited resources, it seemed unlikely that she had gone much farther, but he couldn't be sure. She'd simply vanished, leaving him with all the responsibility. Resentment filled Viktor's lungs.

It was more than a year and a half ago since he'd come home to an unnaturally silent house. It hadn't been unusual for Aleksandr to be at the Pankos' house, playing with Lavro, but he'd been confused when he'd walked in the back door and his wife hadn't been at the stove, preparing supper. He'd called out for her, but there had been no answer. Her silence had angered him. He'd looked on the table for a note. Nothing. He'd searched the parlor and dining room. He'd raced up the stairs and peered into Aleksandr's room, but still had been unable to find her. When he'd walked into their bedroom and discovered the newly vacant spot above their bed, where the icon of the Blessed Virgin Mary had hung, he'd known she was gone.

He'd had no idea how she'd managed to leave Bilik unnoticed. Elena hadn't given the slightest hint of her intentions. Bitterly, he'd wondered how many meals they'd shared and how many times she'd sat beside him in church, plotting. How many times had she lain beneath him, surrendering herself to him, all the while scheming to leave their marriage bed forever? Her duplicity had enraged him. *She'd damn well better hide.*

Viktor picked up the letter again. The return address was the same on each, but it didn't belong to any place he recognized. Every one of Elena's letters instructed him to reply to that address, but they warned him repeatedly not to search for her. *I have taken great care that you shall not find me, but I promise your message will be forwarded. I will send instructions where to send Aleksandr.* What presumption to think he'd bother to look for her, to imagine he'd actually want her back.

The day she'd left, Viktor had gone to Yana and Fedir's to fetch the boy. With each step, he'd swallowed his rage, squeezed his desire to hurt her into a morsel he could swallow. By the time he reached the Pankos' house, he'd appeared composed, his expression and manner revealing nothing. It could have been any of the hundred other days he'd collected his son. When he'd arrived at the back door, knocking with just the right force, so as not to alert them to any trouble, he hadn't given a hint his wife had left him. "I've come to retrieve Aleksandr," he'd said, his voice cordial, his smile practiced.

When he and Aleksandr had gotten home he'd said, "Your mother has left." He'd watched for the boy's reaction; he'd watched to see if his son was party to this deception.

"When will she be back?" Aleksandr had asked, his expression innocent.

Then, Viktor knew. The boy had no idea.

"Don't know." Viktor had said no more about the matter then. He'd needed time to figure out what to do, what to say, how to act. He'd needed time to weave a tale.

This was the sixteenth letter he'd received from Elena. It had taken two months before she'd apparently worked up the courage to write her first plea. Every month after that, another had appeared. He'd never written back. His silence had been answer enough. He'd predicted she'd give up, the way she usually gave up. But she'd persisted.

Today, Viktor had planned to repair the jammed pulley on the lift, but, in the unheated elevator, the circulation in his bare hands wouldn't last long against the frigid metal. He was too distracted to examine the ledgers; that would require his full attention. *Damn Elena!* She was as responsible for his inability to get work done as the severe weather. Finally, he settled on sealing the cracks in the engine room's exterior walls, where the heat from the stove would make work at least tolerable.

He pulled his hat over his ears, folded the letter, stuffed it into his jacket pocket, and put on his gloves. When he opened the door to the engine room, warm air floated up the stairs. He had to get his hands moving. He needed to forget about the letters. What were they to him? What was *she* to him? He had a new life, one that did not include the traitorous Elena. If she thought she could enter it again, even from afar, she was greatly mistaken. She'd be a fool to come back to Bilik, thinking she could take his son. He'd kill her first.

There was a soft knock on Aleksandr's bedroom door. Since marrying his father, she'd been appearing at bedtime, every night. Seventy-six nights she'd knocked, and seventy-six times he'd refused to answer. He was always careful to be as quiet as possible, holding his breath, as if allowing her to hear him breathing would be giving her too much. When he didn't answer, she'd say in the gentlest voice, "Maybe tomorrow night." He'd wait until her footsteps faded before he exhaled.

It had been getting harder to ignore her. Living in the same house and sitting at the same table day after day, acting as though she didn't exist, without setting off his father's fury, took great effort. And she was kind to him. That made him angry. It was as though she didn't know or care that he was punishing her.

Yet when she would give up and walk away from his door each night, he would feel as empty as a dry well. It was confusing to hate her while, at the same time, wishing she'd just open the door. He wanted her to see his misery and do something about it. He wanted to be comforted and told he wouldn't always be this lost. He hated her blindness.

Since his mother died, he'd been mad at the whole world. For the past five days, he'd been especially mad at Lilia Panko.

"She's nice and she's pretty. Mama says she's the best thing to happen around here in a long time," Lilia had said.

He'd wanted to choke know-it-all Lilia, to scream at her and tell her that she still had her mother.

"I heard them talking in our kitchen. Miss Danek—I mean your mother—told Mama you won't speak to her. Why are you so mean to her? What has she ever done to you?"

Lilia had no right to judge him. His mother had died and it had to be someone's fault. Who else could he blame? He'd wanted to defend himself, to say he hadn't been mean, to say he'd done nothing. That was what ignoring was: doing nothing. But he'd been too angry, too near tears to challenge Lilia, and he'd rather have died than cry in front of her. So he'd pretended to ignore Lilia, too, but her challenge had worked on him like a pebble in his shoe. Even though he made believe it wasn't there, it bothered him a lot.

That was why Aleksandr had decided the seventy-seventh night would be different. Tonight, when she knocked, he would invite her into his room. Besides, he had an important question to ask.

There was a second knock.

"May I come in?" she asked.

"Yes." He said it so quietly it was as though he hadn't said it at all.

"Aleksandr?"

"Yes. You may come in."

This time she heard him because the door opened a crack. She peeked in. At first, she looked uncertain, as if she couldn't believe that after all this time he had finally allowed her into his room. Like daybreak, her smile rose slowly.

Aleksandr sat in bed, propped against his pillow. She walked toward him, tilting with her familiar limp.

"Thank you," she said.

He wanted to say you're welcome, to tell her he was sorry for making her wait so long, but the words wouldn't come. After all this time, they were stuck in his throat, as if months of silence had stolen his voice. He nodded and smiled weakly.

"May I?" she asked, gesturing toward the edge of his bed.

He nodded again and edged toward the wall to make room for her. She sat down carefully.

"My mother used to tuck me in at night when I was a girl."

"You're not my mother!" he shouted.

She flinched, as if he'd struck her.

He'd spoken more forcefully than he'd meant to. He was embarrassed that his words had revealed so much, but he'd been holding them in so long that when they'd finally escaped, they'd spilled like hot lava from a volcano.

Her eyes glistened. "I know," she whispered.

Aleksandr felt terrible. For so long he'd imagined that wounding her would feel good, that it would make him feel powerful and blameless, but instead, he felt mean and small. Bitter words didn't make him feel better at all.

"I'm sorry," he said. "I didn't mean it."

"It's all right." She rested her hand on his.

He didn't pull away. Her skin felt warm and comforting. It had been a long while since he'd been touched so tenderly.

Aleksandr couldn't meet her eyes but he saw her. Her nightgown with tiny pink roses embroidered around the neckline made her look delicate and pretty. She smelled like a summer garden.

"I could never take your mother's place," she said.

He looked at her hand, still resting on his. The gold wedding ring circling her long, slender finger glinted in the lamplight.

"Do you know how I know?"

Aleksandr shook his head.

"Because my mother died when I was your age," she said. "I was nine, a year younger than you."

He looked at her skeptically. "She died?"

"Yes. And I missed her every day."

Aleksandr swallowed hard. "Did she drown?"

"No. She died of cancer. She was very sick for a long time."

Her sad eyes made Aleksandr realize he'd still miss his mother even when he was old. "Did you get a new mother?" he asked.

"No," she said. Her long brown hair, let down for the evening, swayed across her shoulders as she shook her head from side to side. "My father never remarried. My older sister, Aneta, took care of me."

They both grew quiet, thinking their private thoughts.

Aleksandr yawned.

She squeezed his hand lightly and eased from his bed. As she walked toward the door, she glanced over her shoulder. "I think I'll make *deruny* for breakfast," she said.

Aleksandr didn't know how she knew potato pancakes were his favorite breakfast in the whole world, but he hoped morning would come quickly.

"Sleep tight," she said and closed his door.

Aleksandr yawned again. As he nestled beneath his blankets and closed his eyes, he realized he'd forgotten to ask his important question.

Chapter Ten

Since the unforgettable day of Josef's accident, Katerina couldn't stop thinking about Svetlana Sokur. *Your husband needs you.* She'd intended her words as encouragement, as affirmation of a wife's value to her husband, as a reason not to despair. Fear had drained from Svetlana's eyes, if only for a moment, and flashed rage. The look had unnerved Katerina. Svetlana had turned pity back on Katerina like an unflattering image in a looking glass. She couldn't rid herself of the notion that she was meant to find a message in those eyes.

Dr. Billings had gone to the Sokur farm on several occasions to tend Josef's wounds. Fedir had made a delivery of winter staples. Katerina suspected it had been an act of charity, not a business proposition. Yana confided that, in Fedir's opinion, Josef was mending physically, but melancholia had set in so deep that he seemed barely able to get out of bed.

"Even on his best days, Josef wasn't much to look at," Yana said, "but now he's so thin and grizzled, Fedir barely recognized him."

Viktor had driven out to the farm to deliver Josef's meager crop payment. Katerina asked to accompany him, but Viktor had dismissed the request out of hand. "Nothing you can do," he had said. "You're needed here." Katerina had known better than to argue, but she'd at least convinced him to take the honey cookies and gingersnaps she'd baked.

When he'd returned home that night, tight-lipped as ever, Viktor had merely shaken his head and said, more to himself than to her, "What a sorry mess."

"How is Svetlana?" she'd asked.

Viktor had seemed confused by the question, as if he'd never considered the impact of Josef's accident on anyone other than Josef.

"As you'd expect, I suppose."

"And the children?" Katerina had pressed.

"Don't know."

"Aleksandr says Yuri hasn't returned to school."

"He's needed on the farm."

"He needs an education, or he'll be dirt poor the rest of his life," Katerina had argued.

"Josef can't handle himself, much less the chores."

"What about Yuri?"

"What do you expect them to do?"

"I don't know, but—"

"This isn't L'viv," Viktor had snapped. "You'd best learn that." He'd stomped away, ending the matter.

Throughout November and December meager news of the family had trickled unsatisfactorily into town. Other than a few drop-ins at the farm, no one had seen the Sokur family—neither at church nor at school nor at a store. It was as if they'd vanished.

The voices of Svetlana and the children kept Katerina awake at night. *How will we live? Don't cry, Mama. How will we feed these children? Don't cry, Mama. How will we survive? Please don't cry.*

Winter in southern Saskatchewan proved more bitter than anyone had expected. For weeks, temperatures had rarely risen above 0 degrees, even when the sun shone brightly in the ice-blue sky. Katerina pictured Svetlana and the children living in the crumbling sod house, stranded in the middle of nowhere, cold, hungry, and frightened. She worried about the little ones. She especially worried about Yuri. He was just a boy, carrying around guilt too heavy for a man. She understood the weight of guilt, how it made everything unbearable, how it lived in your mind and body, so even the smallest effort brought you to your knees. Yuri was shouldering his father's responsibilities, too. All this for a boy more than half a decade from adulthood.

One morning Katerina threw her coat over her housedress, pulled a scarf tightly around her unkempt hair, and headed to Yana's.

"Dear Lord, Katerina, what's the matter?" Yana said when she opened the door.

"It's the Sokurs." Katerina was breathless. "You should have seen them, Yana. When I was there with Fedir, you should have seen them…the children…and Svetlana…the place. We have to do something about them."

Yana didn't hesitate. "You're right."

That morning Katerina and Yana decided to organize a charity drive for the Sokur family.

When Katerina told Viktor about their plan, she presented it as Yana's idea. "She was so persuasive," Katerina lied. "I couldn't do less than agree to help."

Viktor's brow furrowed. "Fine," he said. "But you're fooling yourself if you think that's going to keep them afloat for long."

The next morning Yana telephoned Father Warga, who offered St. Kassia's basement for their collection efforts. At Sunday service, he made a special appeal.

"I know some of you have offered a hand," Father Warga said, "but I encourage each of you to examine your conscience, and ask if you have done everything in your power to help."

Heads bowed. Eyes lowered. The Sokurs, always on the bottom rung of Bilik's social ladder, were perpetually down on their luck and likely to stay that way. It was widely known that Josef had reaped what he'd sown through sloth and fondness for alcohol. The accident, although tragic, had hardly created a ripple in the community.

"Remember Matthew 25," Father Warga continued. "*For I was hungred, and ye gave me meat: I was thirsty, and ye gave me drink: I was a stranger, and ye took me in: Naked, and ye clothed me: I was sick, and ye visited me: I was in prison, and ye came unto me.*"

The church became unnaturally still. Neither cough nor whisper broke the silence.

"*Then shall the righteous answer him, saying, 'Lord, when saw we thee an hungred, and fed thee? or thirsty, and gave thee drink? When saw we thee a stranger, and took thee in? or naked, and clothed thee? Or when saw we thee sick, or in prison and came unto thee?'"* The priest paused and looked up, his gaze intent. He cleared his throat. Then he resumed speaking without glancing down at the text. "*And the King shall answer and say unto them, 'Verily I say unto you, Inasmuch as ye have done it unto one of the least of these my brethren, ye have done it unto me.'*"

Before they'd left church, Jakob the liveryman had volunteered the use of his wagon. Within a week, more food and clothing than Katerina and Yana could have imagined arrived at the church basement.

"I still say Roman Klopoushak could have opened the door to his larder," Yana said, frowning. "Heaven knows he has more means than anyone around here. The miser would rather food spoil than see it in someone else's mouth."

"Maybe he's never heard, 'Brotherhood is greater than riches,'" Katerina said.

"Oh, he's heard it all right; he just doesn't believe it." Yana pulled off her mittens and tucked them beneath her arm. She untied her scarf, readjusted it on her head, and retied the knot beneath her chin. "Won't His Lordship be surprised if Saint Peter turns him away at the gate."

"Looks like we're just about loaded," Jakob said, giving the chestnut horse a pat on its haunch.

"There's a little more room on this side of the wagon," Yana said, handing a crate to Lavro. "When you're done loading, you and Aleksandr can ride in back and keep an eye on the load."

"Aleksandr!" Lavro hollered, "Mama said we can go along!"

Yana handed a small box to Katerina. "Are you feeling all right? You look a little pale."

"Oh, I'm fine. I felt a little under the weather earlier this morning,"

Katerina said. “The herring we had last evening didn’t agree with me but I’m fine now.”

“You’re sure?” Her friend looked skeptical.

“Positive.”

Yana said no more and turned back to loading the wagon.

Katerina suspected her queasiness had little to do with the herring. She’d been through this before. The first time she’d been pregnant, from the moment she’d told the truth, her life had tumbled down a long, steep mountain, across an ocean, and landed on the Canadian prairie. Yana might be suspicious, but until Katerina was certain, she wouldn’t satisfy her curiosity. This time, she would handle things differently.

When the final box was loaded, Jakob helped Katerina climb onto the front of the wagon before helping Yana into the back, where she perched on an overturned crate behind the driver’s bench. With youthful enthusiasm, Lavro and Aleksandr jumped onto the wagon bed.

“We appreciate this, Jakob,” Yana said.

“It’s the least I can do. The Almighty knows we’re all just one tragedy away from the same situation.”

“How true,” Yana agreed.

“Everybody set?” With two clicks of his tongue and a flick of the reins, the liveryman set the horses to pulling.

The sun—its glow a faint yellow—shone through wispy clouds. The temperature hovered around 10 degrees. The wind, blowing unimpeded across the white plain, made the air sting. Along the horizon, sky bled into earth like a muted watercolor, blurring the difference between air and land and bathing the landscape in a winter palette so pale, it was as if the world were wrapped in gossamer. Vapor plumes escaped from the horses’ nostrils. Aleksandr and Lavro, bundled and lying atop the boxes on the wagon bed, giggled as they pretended to smoke invisible pipes.

Everyone was wrapped in layers of wool and fur, and Katerina and Yana each huddled under heavy blankets. Katerina gratefully rested her shoes on the charcoal-burning foot warmer, which kept the blood flowing in her feet. Her lungs filled with frosty air. It was the most alive she'd felt in a long while.

She turned to check on Aleksandr. As though he felt her watching, he looked up at her. She winked. He winked back. Katerina felt the door between them nudge open a sliver.

The wagon rode smoothly, its runners easily sliding over potholes filled by traffic-packed snow. Except for the farms, standing in stark relief against the winter-white ground, the landscape could have existed millennia ago, when the only tracks interrupting the unspoiled white would have been those of animals and birds. Even now, barely a foot had trod on the vast acres of pristine snow.

Katerina thought of L'viv, her memories defying time and distance.

January snow had fallen upon the city. The evening appeared enchanted, with haloed street lamps, candlelit windows, jingling sleighs, and laughing children catching snowflakes on their tongues.

Sometime in the hours between midnight and dawn—she could no longer recall—Katerina fled from Papa's to Aneta's in search of shelter. An icy wind lifted her coat collar and flattened her skirt against her thighs as she trudged more than a mile through unshoveled snow. Tears streamed down her ruddy cheeks like rivers flowing through winter fields. She headed south to Rynok Square, turning west at the Neptune fountain. The streets were quiet and nearly empty, with the exception of an occasional solitary figure, walking hunched against the cold.

Aneta answered the door, tousled and foggy-eyed, wearing the embroidered shawl Katerina recognized as their mother's.

"What are you doing here at this hour?" Aneta asked as she ushered her into the apartment she shared with Danya.

At first, Katerina stood, unable to speak. Her lips quivered and her shoulders shook.

"Katerina, what's wrong?"

"Papa banished me from the apartment," Katerina whimpered. "He said he's glad Mama is dead, so she doesn't have to bear the shame of having a worthless daughter. He told me never to come back!"

"But why?"

Every drop of moisture evaporated from Katerina's mouth.

"Why?" Aneta persisted.

Tears spilled onto Katerina's cheeks.

Aneta waited.

"I'm pregnant."

"But how? You haven't been keeping company with Taras for months!"

"It isn't Taras," Katerina said.

"Then who?"

"Stepan Mihalik." The name escaped in a whisper.

"The priest?"

Katerina nodded.

"Father Mihalik?"

"Yes."

"How could you!"

"I love him."

"Love?" Aneta snapped, her voice as hard as stone. "My God, love doesn't excuse you. It doesn't erase your sin."

Katerina's lungs shriveled. Panic radiated from every nerve ending. "What am I going to do? I have no one." She covered her face with her hands, like a child who pretends to be invisible.

"Have you told him?"

Katerina shook her head.

"At least, that's something."

Katerina felt herself sinking to the bottom of a deep, dark pit.

"How could you let this happen?"

"I didn't mean for it to happen. It just did."

"Nothing just *happens*," Aneta hissed. "Nothing."

Then it struck Katerina. To her barren sister, this pregnancy was more than a disgrace; it was a betrayal.

Jakob abruptly turned the wagon 90 degrees down a barely traveled side road, jarring Katerina from her painful memories. Unprepared for the change in direction, she clutched the bench to keep from sliding too close to the edge. Although months before she'd traveled this same route with Fedir, the dormant landscape now made the way feel unfamiliar. Regardless of season, to Katerina, the absence of city landmarks made every road on the flat prairie indistinguishable. How would she ever adjust to this place?

As Yana continued chatting amiably with Jakob, Katerina was content to ride in silence. The clomping of the horses' hooves created a rhythmic backdrop to Katerina's daydreams, which turned to Stepan and a morning like this.

Stepan stood, chin resting on his open palm, contemplating the unfinished painting on the easel, which canted toward the early light. Corners of the window glass were glazed with frost, yet Katerina basked in the warmth of his presence.

"Do you think so?" he asked, his lips upturned in pleasure.

"Yes, this landscape bears a distinct resemblance to Ivan Trush's work. The play of light reminds me of *Solitary Pine,"* Katerina said.

"Trush is brilliant. One of the exceptional impressionists. I fear I am merely a poseur."

She stood behind him, wrapped her arms around his waist, and leaned her cheek against the softness of his shirt, inhaling him, inviting his spicy scent deep into her lungs.

"Your work is wonderful, Stepan. You were born to create."

Together, they had created something more substantial than mere oil on canvas. She vowed to tell him soon. Not then, but soon.

Yana shifted her weight from one side of the crate to the other. As it rocked on its springs, Katerina experienced a wave of nausea and grabbed the side of the wagon.

"Are you all right, Mrs. Senyk?" Jakob asked. "I can stop if need be. The farm's another two miles yet."

"Thank you," Katerina said. "If it's not too much trouble."

Jakob pulled the right rein, coaxing the horses to the edge of the road, and then pulled both reins harder, bringing the wagon to a stop. He jumped down and helped Katerina over the side. Although self-conscious about her uncooperative leg, Jakob lifted her matter-of-factly, as if she were no trouble at all.

Katerina limped to the roadside and turned her back to the wagon. Her face was cold. Moisture gathered at the corners of her eyes. Air, escaping from her nostrils, made the inside of her nose sting. Unobtrusively, she pulled off her mittens and reached in her coat pocket for a soda cracker, taking the whole cracker into her mouth and putting her mittens back on quickly. With her first pregnancy, she'd found soda was the only sure antidote for nausea. In a couple of minutes, her stomach began to settle.

Once they were moving again, Aleksandr and Lavro bantered, and Yana and Jakob made small talk, leaving Katerina to her own thoughts.

Svetlana Sokur. There was something about the woman that evoked, simultaneously, sympathy and admiration. Katerina had taken one look at her haggard face and ill-fitting clothes and dismissed her. She'd been judgmental and prideful, feeling sorry for Svetlana and superior to her. But under the worst circumstances, Svetlana had been courageously defiant, and Katerina knew she'd misjudged her. The woman was a survivor.

Jakob turned the wagon south. In the near distance, a small unpainted barn and shed appeared. A gray windmill, its blades turning steadily, towered over the place. Katerina realized that this was the windmill that refused to turn when Josef's arm was severed. The memory of his bloody stump made her queasy. Who had cleaned up the blood and bone after the accident? Who had repaired the windmill?

Was it too much to hope that Viktor had been generous enough to fix it?

When she'd first seen the homestead, the sod house had been surrounded by uncultivated vegetation. Now, in the dead of winter, the low roof was hidden under a layer of snow. From a distance, it could be mistaken for a large snowdrift, save for the stream of smoke curling from its center.

"It's a shame they'll lose the farm," Jakob said, shaking his head.

"But when Josef recovers, things might improve." Katerina recognized the desperation in her voice, as though the stakes were personal.

"No, they'll lose it for certain. They've failed to prove up. Nothing will change that fact."

"Certainly, the bank will have some sympathy for their position. The loss of Josef's arm was an accident. You said yourself that we're all just one tragedy away from the same situation. Surely, there must be some consideration for that," Katerina argued.

"The accident has little to do with it," Jakob said. "They've not come close to making the land productive in three years. Even without the accident, they would have lost the farm."

Katerina fell silent.

The conversation with Viktor on their first drive to Weyburn, when she'd spoken effusively about the abundance of the surrounding farmland, came back to her. She'd marveled at the golden fields stretching as far as the eye could see and made assumptions about farmers' prosperity. Viktor had put an unpleasant face on it. Although 160 acres, in exchange for years of backbreaking toil, was theirs for the taking, he'd explained that fewer than half of those who attempted it actually proved successful. At the time, she'd thought him argumentative at best, cruel at worst. Now it appeared he had been simply right.

When Svetlana opened the door, her cheerless expression turned first to surprise and then to confusion. She looked nervously at her husband, sitting at the table on the far side of the room.

"Josef, we have visitors," Svetlana announced, as though the house were so large that guests at their door weren't obvious. "Please, please come in."

Svetlana's eyes scanned the room as though she weren't the home's occupant but a disapproving stranger seeing the lowliness of the place for the first time.

Pasha lay in her basket on top of the table, playing with her toes. Inga ran to her mother and stood shyly behind her.

Katerina bent to the little girl's level. "I'm happy to see you again," she said.

The child smiled cautiously, still clinging to Svetlana. Though much the same as Katerina remembered, her face looked thinner, or perhaps it was Katerina's imagination.

The interior of the house was also the same—newsprint-covered walls, yellowed lace curtains, and sod poking through spaces in the lumber-covered ceiling. Though anemic sunlight penetrated the mud-streaked windows, the interior of the house looked gloomier than on her previous visit, and the place felt smaller somehow, perhaps because Josef sat at the table, hunched and curled, more like an unsightly object plunked down in the room than a man.

"We've brought some supplies," Yana said, stepping forward. "Everyone at St. Kassia's contributed."

Katerina noticed the singular omission in her friend's white lie but was grateful Yana had chosen not to air her displeasure with Roman Klopoushak.

Svetlana looked bewildered. "Supplies?"

"Food and clothes, mainly," Katerina said.

"Jakob and Fedir will return tomorrow with feed for the animals," Yana said.

Josef stood, tipping. He braced his left hand on the table for support, while his empty right shirtsleeve dangled at his side. "So we're a charity case now," he said, his words slurred and his bloodshot eyes unfocused.

"Josef, please," Svetlana begged.

"This is my house," he said, staggering toward his wife.

Jakob put his arm around Josef's shoulders and steered him toward the bedroom. "You look tired," Jakob said.

"Everything...tired...of everything." Josef's head wobbled as he and Jakob shuffled toward the small partitioned bedroom.

"Let's have a rest, then," Jakob said.

Svetlana's eyes glistened. "I'm sorry."

"No need to be," Yana said gently. "Let's unload the wagon."

"Yuri and Kiel are working in the barn," Svetlana said.

"I'll get them," Jakob offered, closing the door to the bedroom.

As everyone pitched in, the mood brightened. Svetlana became more and more animated as she decided where each box belonged. Canned goods, along with several bushels of root vegetables, were stacked in a primitive root cellar hollowed out next to the house. Staples such as salt, flour, sugar, cornmeal, rolled oats, and rice, were dry-stored under the table. Canisters of split green peas, white beans, and peanuts were put on shelves near the pich. A jar filled with horehound candy, to be doled out sparingly, was placed high on a shelf, out of the reach of temptation. Yana fished in her pocket for the root beer candy Fedir had grabbed from a bin at the store, and she handed a piece to each of the children.

"What about me?" Jakob teased.

"Ach, you're too sweet already," Yana said, feigning reluctance before handing him a piece.

Yuri, who'd been in back tending the pigs and chickens, helped Jakob and the boys lift the heaviest crates and stack them in the shed. When Katerina had seen him last, Yuri had been a frightened boy, appearing as vulnerable as any child could. Since the day of the accident, he'd turned from child to man, looking as though he'd aged far faster than the passage of a quarter year warranted. He stood taller and thicker and had grown more stoic and careworn. At thirteen, he'd become the man of the house, responsible for tending the farm and keeping his family warm and fed.

Katerina thought of Viktor's words when she'd pressed him about Yuri's absence from school. *What do you expect them to do?* Now she understood.

The unloading completed, Jakob went to the barn to help Yuri repair the mule's stall. Aleksandr and Lavro ran in the yard, throwing snow and playing hide-and-seek with Kiel and Inga. Pasha, still in her basket, napped peacefully. Katerina, Yana, and Svetlana opened boxes of clothing, donated by the women of St. Kassia's, filled with shirts, pants, dresses, jackets, hats, and mittens of various sizes for the children, all used but laundered. One box included shoes for every member of the family. Two more boxes contained adult clothing. Svetlana held up one of Viktor's woolen shirts. Katerina pictured Josef wearing it, the left sleeve solidly filled, the right sleeve dangling by his side.

If Svetlana was embarrassed to be the recipient of her neighbors' used clothing, she didn't show it. Instead, she stacked the clothes in neat piles and ran her hands over the material, caressing each precious item.

Katerina saved the best box for last. She waited as Svetlana opened it and carefully lifted out a red woolen skirt and white blouse with matching embroidered trim. Moments passed while Svetlana stared at them.

"For me?"

"I sewed them for you."

Svetlana held the blouse next to her body and stretched a sleeve the length of her arm. "They're beautiful!"

"I'm pleased you approve." To Katerina, the expression on

Svetlana's face was worth every cut of the scissors and press of the treadle.

"I hate to end this," Yana said, hoisting herself from the chair and rubbing the small of her back. "It's getting late. Fedir and the children will be expecting supper."

"I...I'm...grateful to you," Svetlana said.

"We are neighbors." Yana kissed Svetlana on both cheeks before putting on her thick coat and heading outside to gather Jakob and the children.

After the door closed, Svetlana looked cautiously over her shoulder, lowered her voice to a whisper, and leaned toward Katerina. "I thought *I'd* be helping *you*."

"Helping me?" Katerina looked puzzled.

"I knew Elena." Svetlana hesitated, worrying her bottom lip. "And...I know Viktor."

Katerina's pulse raced. She swallowed hard. Her voice caught in her throat. She said nothing and thought everything.

"And I know a frightened woman when I see her."

Chapter Eleven

Sun glinted off the letter opener, creating a dancing pinpoint of light on the ceiling as Katerina carefully sliced through the top of the envelope. In the beginning, when Aneta's letters had arrived, Katerina had torn into the envelopes like a starving woman who'd found a breadcrumb. But today, she weighed the envelope in her palm and waited, not quite understanding her own hesitation.

She sat at the table, gazing out the window for a long time, the pages unopened. A trickle of water slid the length of a two-foot icicle hanging from the fascia of the roof. She watched as droplets shimmied at its tip before falling to the ground.

Strange how unpredictable life could be—how a woman could believe she was traveling one path, only to discover, beyond the point of no return, that she was headed on a completely different course. Strange how people you hadn't known six months ago could become family and the family you'd left behind could fade out of your life, becoming no more real than characters in a novel.

Finally, when she unfolded the letter, a photograph slipped from between its pages and landed on the table. Katerina's breath caught. Aneta, Danya, and the baby stared up at her from a photograph, looking for all the world as though they were the perfect family. Danya stood behind a seated Aneta, resting his hand on her shoulder, while she looked adoringly at the infant sitting on her lap. The Immaculate Conception. It could have been an icon of the Holy Family.

She turned the photograph over. "Danya, Aneta, and son Petro—age 5 months" was written in Aneta's careful hand. Katerina's eyes brimmed with tears. She turned the photograph over again and studied the child—*her* child. "Matviyko," she whispered and gently brushed her fingers over his image.

His round cheeks, large dark eyes—Stepan's eyes—and perfect mouth faced the camera. His swath of dark hair was smoothed flat against his head. Katerina pictured her sister fussing, wetting her fingers and gently raking them across his baby-soft scalp. Katerina's arms ached to hold him. She longed to kiss his velvety cheek and to inhale his baby sweetness. She closed her eyes, lost in the remembered sensation of his feel. Unconsciously, she ran her hand over her stomach.

Reluctantly, she opened her eyes, moved the photograph aside, and opened the letter.

December 21, 1925

Dearest Sister,

I hope this letter finds you and your family well and that you are surviving your first Canadian winter. Your descriptions of the country's vastness and climate have piqued my imagination. I picture you living under a mountain of snow.

Katerina scanned past news of friends and neighbors and Danya's recent promotion, searching for news of her son.

As you know, I have been reluctant to write about Petro, thinking it a bad idea, but because you have so earnestly implored me to share news of him, I have sent a photograph. Certainly, you can surmise from his contented face that he is happy and from our contented faces that he is a constant source of amusement and joy to his parents.

Yesterday, Petro turned over in his crib for the first time. Danya was so proud you would have thought his son had won first prize at the fair.

Danya's pride? Danya's son? Aneta's words on the page made her want to scream.

His hair is no longer all wisps and down. He is getting more atop his head every day. (I am referring to Petro, of course. Danya, I fear, is getting less!) He is a pleasant baby, who cries seldom and smiles often. I pray that means he will grow to be a tolerant and patient man.

Aneta would see Matviyko grow into manhood while Katerina would see begged-for photographs, sent from halfway around the world. Maybe someday her son would come to Canada to meet her, and they would be reunited as mother and son. But when she was brutally honest with herself, Katerina realized she would always be a stranger to him. Why would he come to see a stranger? Would Aneta ever tell him about his true mother, or would she keep precious Petro to herself and tell him stories of an "aunt" he'd never know? Katerina already knew the answer.

Papa suffered a cold at the beginning of winter but has recovered nicely. I think the pot of hot chicken broth I made, using Mama's recipe, was the reason. He is beginning to slow down, although he will not admit it. Despite his initial reluctance, I've convinced him to give me some of his smallest alteration work, to relieve his burden a bit. The time for Papa to live with us will not be long from now, I think.

Papa living with Aneta, Danya, and his grandson—minus his embarrassing younger daughter—made a cozy family portrait. It pained Katerina to think their lives were better, tidier, without her. They had little idea of what went on in her life, but she saw them clearly, Papa sitting and puffing his pipe, rocking in his chair by the hearth in his new home, telling "The Wolf and the Seven Young Kids" to Matviyko, Aneta and Danya contentedly basking in their son's delight. As a child, she'd begged Papa again and again to recite the tale until she'd memorized it. Now, the memory itself seemed an ancient fairytale.

The night she'd confessed her pregnancy, he'd called her a whore, banished her from the apartment, and shouted that she was dead to him. In truth, he'd been lost to her since she was nine years old. He'd been present in body, even taught her his trade, but when her mother had died, her father's spirit had been buried in the same grave.

Katerina continued reading.

Regrettably, he is not ready to give up his anger and disappointment. I pray the time will come when Papa can forgive you. I pray he will soften and open his heart to you again. Although he refuses to acknowledge it, he suffers from your absence, as I am sure you do his. You well know that Papa is a proud and stubborn man who has suffered much loss in his life. You must not judge him too harshly, Katerina. I beg you, be patient.

Katerina's jaw clenched. How could Aneta put such a premium on Papa's suffering but ignore hers? How could she plead for Katerina's forbearance but not expect better from him?

She'd withstood the harshest judgment from all of them. It hadn't been only Papa, Aneta and Danya, as well, had made a great display of her unworthiness. What harsher judgment could there be than sending your daughter or your sister to another country to marry a stranger? Why was she the only one forbidden to judge? *You must not judge him too harshly, Katerina.* As she reread the line again and again, her heart hardened. Aneta had been an apologist for Papa her entire life. Since Mama had died, Katerina had felt indebted to Aneta for being both sister and mother to her. She'd always assumed Aneta had sacrificed for love of her. But now it was clear, Aneta had cared for her out of fealty to their father. The revelation hit harder than a fist.

Katerina remembered the night before she had boarded the train in L'viv. In her dream, she'd dangled from the edge of a cliff, with Aneta grasping her hands to prevent her from falling into the mid-night blackness below. Her hands weakened, slid bit by excruciating bit. *Please don't let me fall, Aneta.* At first, the words were close and clear, but her hands had continued slipping, until she felt her fingertips against Aneta's fingertips. *Please don't let me fall.* Her voice had grown fainter and fainter as she slid away. She had woken shivering, her breathing shallow, hands aching. Even awake, she could hear her own voice pleading, feel her helplessness, her terror; but worst of all, she couldn't shake the feeling that Aneta had let go of her on purpose.

A loud burbling sound interrupted Katerina's thoughts and brought her back to the moment. Seconds passed before she realized she'd forgotten the pot of boiling potatoes. She shambled to the stove, but before she reached it, water spilled from beneath the lid, hissing as it tumbled and splattered against hot iron. With dish towel in hand, she turned her face away from the blasting steam, grabbed the handle of the kettle, and pulled it from the burner.

This was her life now. She was a wife and mother who boiled potatoes and wiped spilled water from the floor. Regret wouldn't put meals on the table or make her more accepting of her lot.

Blessed Mother, give me the strength to forgive as You forgave, Katerina prayed. Straightening her back and lifting her chin, she glanced at the clock. There was just enough time to finish reading Aneta's letter before she needed to start preparing tonight's supper.

She scanned the letter and found where she'd left off.

> *I eagerly await more news from you. Know that I miss you, dear sister. Not a day passes without thoughts of you. As I say my prayers each night, I pray to the Blessed Virgin to guide and protect you and keep you in Her loving embrace.*
>
> *With deepest affection,*
>
> *Aneta*

Katerina would write back to Aneta, telling her about the beautiful new sewing machine, a gift from her generous husband, who'd surprised her for no evident reason. She'd write that Aleksandr was a sweet boy who was beginning to feel more like a son each day. She'd include news of the Pankos' family and life in Bilik. When she wrote back, she'd put the best face on things and omit any hint of loneliness or discontentment. She'd tell about the coldness of winter weather but leave unmentioned how the biting wind and fierce temperatures left her heart colder than her body could ever be. There would be no mention of the heartbreak she felt, longing for Matviyko, hungering for Stepan, or pining for L'viv. There would be no confessing her husband's drunken temper, her stepson's reticence, or her own terror. She'd not mention Josef Sokur's horrific accident. The streets of Bilik would remain pastoral and welcoming, instead of pedestrian and lonely.

From now on, she was an actress hiding behind greasepaint, showing only the face she wanted her audience to see.

Her sweet voice drew Aleksandr to the dining room. He stopped short of the doorway and hid behind the wall, listening as she sang a song he didn't recognize but couldn't resist. Cautiously, he peeked around the doorway to see what she was doing. She stood bent over a large square of gray fabric lying on the table. Although her back was half turned from him, he could see her hands, palms flat, gently smoothing the fabric, stroking it like a much-loved dog. A loose strand of hair fell across her cheek. She brushed it away and tucked it behind her ear without thinking, as she'd done a million times before. With hands on hips, she straightened, arched her back, and sighed.

Aleksandr liked watching her when she was alone. She seemed different then, not trying to be what his father expected her to be; she wasn't pleasing anyone but herself. She was just her, the way she existed when only God saw her.

Maybe his mother was watching from heaven, too, from that "better place," as Father Warga had said. He wondered if she felt sad or jealous. Maybe his mother was happy that someone was looking after him. Maybe if she saw that his new mother was kind, she wouldn't mind and wouldn't worry about him. He hoped she would understand if he liked his new mother.

"Aleksandr?"

He heard his name and looked up. He'd been daydreaming. She was watching him, smiling, her eyes inviting him to come closer.

"How long have you been standing there?" Her voice wasn't mean or critical. It was just curious, the same way he was curious.

"Not very long. I—I came right home after school."

"Good. You can keep me company," she said.

Aleksandr pulled out the chair with the arms—his father's usual place—but thought better of it. He pushed it back and settled into an armless side chair. His new mother looked at him but said nothing.

On one corner of the table lay a pair of scissors with a gold handle, a pincushion filled with silver-headed stickpins, a thick pencil, and a measuring tape. On another corner, an Eaton's catalog lay open to a page of coats. His favorite brown flannel shirt, which was still a little too big, its arms spread as if flying, lay next to the catalog.

"Why do you have my shirt?" Aleksandr asked.

"It's supposed to be a secret." She tilted her head, putting her hands on her hips in a make-believe show of defeat. "I guess now that you've caught me, I might as well tell you. It's to find out what size to make your jacket." She turned the catalog toward him. "See the one with the large collar? I'm making that for you. Winter Fair is next Sunday, and I thought you should have a nice warm coat."

Aleksandr's eyes widened when he saw the $8.55 price listed next to the picture. "You're making this for me?"

"Yes. And now I have an assistant, that is, if you're willing to help me."

She sounded as though she really meant it.

"But I don't know how."

"I'll teach you."

Aleksandr was glad he'd decided not to play with Lavro after school. It was already snowing and the wind was picking up. Besides, he hoped his new mother would have honey cookies or something almost as delicious for him.

"I'm kind of hungry," he said, unable to think of a less obvious hint.

"There's a piece of cake on the counter and some cold milk in the icebox."

On the counter of the kitchen cupboard, a generous piece of cake with white icing was already cut and dished onto a plate. An empty glass sat next to it. Since his new mother had arrived, there'd been no more meals of cold potatoes and sausage. There'd been hot, filling food every night. The stove was stoked and the house was warm, no matter when he came home. And since the time he'd let her in his room to say good night, she'd come at every bedtime to tuck him in. He'd heard his father say, "The boy's too old for that." Aleksandr hadn't heard what she'd said back, but whatever it was had worked, because she hadn't stopped coming.

Sometimes his new mother was quiet and said nothing when his father ordered her around or said mean things to her. Unlike his real mother, who had acted afraid all the time, she sometimes stood up to him. One thing was exactly the same. The grown-ups thought he couldn't hear them if he was in his bedroom, but he heard plenty. He also saw plenty. Maybe his new mother's bruises were invisible to everyone else, but Aleksandr had seen the black and blue fingerprints on her neck. When she'd noticed him staring, she'd pulled her collar up to hide them, but he knew how she had gotten those marks. He pretended not to know because there was nothing he could do. He feared his father would turn on him and hit him, too. When he got older and bigger and stronger, he'd challenge his father. He'd hit back. Hard.

When Aleksandr returned to the dining room, his new mother was sitting at the table, drawing something on a small sheet of paper.

"I'm sketching the pieces needed to make this coat," she said.

The strand of hair fell across her cheek again, and she tucked it away as unconsciously as before. He noticed the bruises on her neck had faded so they were almost invisible.

"I was going to use your shirt for the pattern, but now that you're here, we can take your exact measurements."She asked Aleksandr to stand very still.

With the tape, she measured the circumference of his neck and the distance between his neck and shoulder. Each measurement was recorded on her sketch paper. Next, she wrapped the tape around his upper arm. Then, she had him stretch his arms out from his sides at shoulder height and ran the tape measure from wrist to wrist. "Forty-nine inches," she said and jotted down the number. When she put the tape under his arm to measure down his side, he flinched and let out an involuntary giggle.

"I see you're ticklish," she said, walking her fingers up his side to his armpit.Aleksandr squirmed and giggled harder. It felt good.

She laughed, too. "I guess that won't do. Here, you hold this end," she said, demonstrating by holding the tape under her arm with her opposite hand. "And I'll hold the other end of the tape by your leg. Ready?"

Aleksandr nodded.

"Fourteen inches," she said. "The next step is making the pattern."

She carefully folded the fabric and put it aside. Then she picked up the roll of newsprint leaning in the corner, let a few yards of it unfurl across the table, and cut off the needed amount.

"Why is your leg crippled?" Aleksandr hadn't meant to ask his very important question right then, but the words came out of his mouth before he knew they were there.

His new mother's smile disappeared, not into a frown exactly, but into a serious look. He wanted to take back his important question (even though he very badly wanted to know the answer) and go back to tickles and smiles. He didn't know what to do. Maybe he should pretend he hadn't asked, the way he would pretend not to hear his father's shouting. Maybe he should say he was sorry, but then how would he ever know the answer to his important question?

"I—I—" The words stuck on his tongue.

"It's all right, Aleksandr." Her voice was as soft as a hug. "I just wasn't expecting your question. I've waited months for someone to ask me but no one has."

Aleksandr wanted to look at her, but he stared at his shoes instead.

"Remember that I told you my mother died when I was nine?"

He wanted to say yes, but all he could manage was a nod.

"She was sick for a very long time. When she got really sick, the doctor came to our house. I heard him talking to my father." Her voice became even softer, as if her words were fragile.

Aleksandr looked up to watch the sounds form on her lips.

"I heard the doctor say that my mother was going to die. My father asked how long she had to live. The doctor said she wouldn't last until morning, and my father said that it was for the best, that it was too hard to watch her suffer."

She took her handkerchief from her pocket and wiped her nose.

"I heard my father say it was time for my mother to die. To my child's ears, his words were selfish and cruel. I ran from the house into the street. I just wanted to get away from him, from the doctor, and from my dying mother. I didn't see the carriage coming."

His new mother's voice became dreamlike. She wasn't looking at him anymore but at something only she could see.

"I fell."

Aleksandr held his breath.

"The carriage wheels ran over my leg. I heard it snap and snap again." She blew her nose. "The doctor said I was fortunate to keep my leg."

Aleksandr exhaled. He stood perfectly still. He didn't know where to look or what to do. It didn't seem right for the doctor to tell his new mother that she was lucky to have her leg. It would have been lucky only if she didn't have a crippled leg. He thought of Mr. Sokur's amputated arm. Would he be luckier if he had a crushed and crippled arm, hanging uselessly at his side? That didn't sound like luck.

"It was a long time ago," she said, straightening. "I can't do everything I want with my leg, but I can do enough." His new mother placed her hand gently on his shoulder. "Thank you for asking."

Aleksandr wasn't sure why she had thanked him, but it made him feel better. He was just sorry that his important question had such a very sad answer.

Chapter Twelve

Viktor looked with satisfaction at the smooth-as-glass ice. On winter mornings, when the Earth itself seemed asleep, he relished being in the cold, quiet outdoors. There was a ruggedness to it, something manly and invigorating. In the east, the suggestion of sun illuminated the horizon as if electric lights had been strung along the ground for a hundred miles. A beautiful sunrise beat a beautiful sunset a hundred times over, he thought.

Sitting on a bench alongside the rink, Viktor pulled off his mittens. He eased his feet, dressed in thick woolen socks, out of his boots, coaxed them into his skates, and tightened the laces to just the right snugness. He clapped his hands and rubbed them together to keep his blood flowing. In a single deep breath, he drew the crisp air into his lungs. *Until hell freezes over.* He smiled to himself. It would be worth the wait just for the satisfaction of a solitary skate on perfect ice.

The dugout behind the schoolhouse made a satisfactory ice rink. Viktor would have been happier if it were 200 feet by 85 feet, the dimensions of a professional hockey rink. At about three quarters that size, at least it was large enough for a competitive game. The main problem, considering its constant use, was keeping the pond ice smooth. It had taken Viktor, Fedir, and Jakob five nights, the borrowed firehouse pump, and 9,000 gallons of water to prepare the rink for Winter Fair. Luckily, the weather had been exactly right for flooding—little wind and daytime and nighttime temperatures well below freezing. After all their work, Viktor noted with satisfaction, not a single stone, crack, or blade mark marred the surface.

Once on the ice, Viktor skated around the rink's perimeter, gaining speed with each pass, soaking in the solitude before the rink filled with wobbling amateurs. Although the competition wouldn't be worth much, he looked forward to the afternoon hockey match. He imagined skating across the ice at breakneck speed and sending the puck sailing into the back of the net, past the goalie's extended leg and gloved hand, well before he saw it coming.

If circumstances had been different—if his father hadn't died unexpectedly, if he hadn't met Elena, or if she hadn't gotten pregnant at the wrong time—he could have played in the big league. He'd met Georges Vézina once—best damned goaltender to ever take the ice. Cool. Composed. Gutsy. What Viktor wouldn't have given to be his teammate, to play alongside him for the Montreal Canadiens. You had to be exceptional to be a professional. More important, you had to get the breaks. You had to be in the right place under the right circumstances. He'd never caught a break. That was why he had to be satisfied playing shinny on the frozen dugout, and that was how he had ended up operating an elevator in the middle of Nowhere, Saskatchewan.

Viktor spun and reversed direction, gliding backward down the middle of the rink. He didn't think about propelling himself across the ice; his body simply knew when to sway and tilt, when to apply force, and when to shift the pressure from leg to leg. He closed his eyes and savored the sensation of gliding effortlessly across the ice, feeling the wind rush past his body as though he were a bird in flight. He listened to the elemental sound of blades scoring ice. Skating restored him. He was a boy again—fast, free, and fearless.

With his eyes still closed, he aligned his skates and leaned his torso to the left while shifting his legs to the right. He savored the loud rasp of blades shaving ice as he came to a stop. When he opened his eyes, he saw that he had come within two feet of the rink's bank. Perfect.

Katerina would never know the pleasure of lacing a pair of skates and sailing, free as you please, across flawless ice. There were times when, for her, walking seemed an effort. Viktor had to admit, when he had first seen her limp across a room, leaning with each step as though she'd downed too much *horilka*, he'd considered calling off the whole marriage deal. But the bargain had been struck, and he was a man of his word. Now, he was glad he hadn't sent her packing. She was proving to be an adequate wife. There was a hot meal on the table every morning and evening and a decent noon meal packed in between. She kept the house clean and the fire burning. As far as he could tell, she was doing a sufficient job of looking after the boy, although he'd prefer she discipline more and pamper less. But if she wasn't capable of a stronger hand, he would provide that. Most important, his bed was warm again. She always complied when he had need of her, and if he discounted the damned leg, she had a body with which any man could find satisfaction.

The sun crept above the horizon now. The sky turned a muted blue-gray and the shadowy field surrounding the dugout softened to white. Reluctantly, Viktor glided to the bench and removed his skates. There was just enough time to eat a hot breakfast and get ready for Sunday service. He took a final look at the rink. The only blade marks scoring the surface were his. Perfect.

Viktor kept an eye out for Josef Sokur's wagon but didn't see it, and he couldn't recall seeing him or any of his family in church. Christ, what an awful mess. How was a farmer supposed to get along with one arm, not that Josef had been much of a farmer when he'd had full use of two arms.

It was unnerving, the difference a year could make in a man's life. He knew that better than anyone—one minute you had a wife in your bed, and the next minute she'd disappeared and left you alone to raise a child you'd never wanted to father. Twelve months ago, Josef had been flying across the ice, wielding his hockey stick as effectively as a weapon. Granted, he'd never possessed style; he'd always been more bull moose than elk. But he'd been a player you'd rather have with you than against you. Now, he'd never hold a hockey stick again.

It was too bad about Sokur, but he wasn't going to spend the day thinking about it or let it interfere with his enjoyment of Winter Fair. He and everyone he knew looked forward to this day for months. Excitement crackled around him. Winters were long and lonely on the prairie, and Winter Fair was a collective reprieve. The dead of winter. There was truth in the phrase, yet there was aliveness in the season, too. The cold invigorated. It awakened the senses. Drawing the frigid air into your lungs and then working every muscle in your body to the limit, until you felt steamy sweat trickling down your back, made a man feel alive. Viktor's heart pumped faster at the mere thought.

The temperature hovered near 25 degrees, but the warming sun made the air feel more temperate than the thermometer indicated. If Viktor had ordered it himself, he couldn't have asked for better weather.

After church, everyone moved to the school grounds. Bundled in wool or sheepskin coats, winter caps, scarves, boots, and hand-knit mittens, they milled about, exchanging greetings and news, their breath rising above their heads in vaporous clouds. Viktor spotted the Bandarek brothers' Chevrolet International truck, parked in front of the school. At least, they'd provide some decent competition.

A three-sided tent pitched in front of the school served as a makeshift warming house. In its center, a cast-iron stove provided heat and filled the air with the smell of burning coal. The enticing aroma of mulled cider and cooked meat wafted from the adjacent tent, where Yana and Katerina took the first shift, overseeing pots of borscht, sausage, and sauerkraut, simmering on a large coal-fired grill. Lilia sold candy favorites, such as Abba-Zaba bars, Dum Dums lollipops, and boxes of Jujyfruits candy from Panko's General Store.

Fiddlers played on a small stage between the tents, filling the air with lively folk music.

On the south side of the school, young children rolled boulder-sized snowballs for the snowman-making contest.

Junior boys, ages ten through fourteen, took the ice for the first hockey game of the day. Viktor noticed Yuri Sokur, suited up as goaltender, skating toward the far side of the rink. At age thirteen, he appeared to be a man among boys. At least, he was defending the goal for the team Aleksandr was on. Yuri had always been a strong skater—not the most agile, but there was no doubt about his courage. No one would ever question the kid's guts.

Viktor watched as the puck dropped. Aleksandr skated furiously toward it, controlled it, and sent it sailing to the left wing. Giving up six inches to Lavro and more to the older boys, he looked like a child come to play a man's game.

Katerina sat down on the bench alongside Viktor.

"Yuri's here," Viktor said. "Didn't see Sokur's wagon, though."

"Yana said Jakob drove out to get Svetlana and the children this morning," Katerina said. "She told me Josef wouldn't come along."

"Pity." Viktor shifted his weight on the bench. Katerina's thigh, draped in several layers of clothing, pressed against his leg.

"Aleksandr looks too small to be out there," she said.

Although Viktor thought the same thing, Katerina's mother hen tone irritated him. "He's got to learn to hold his own. Maybe a few bumps and chucks will toughen him up." He could feel Katerina's disapproving look. "I see he's wearing a new coat. At least, he'll look good when he gets pushed around," he added, his eyes never leaving the rink

It was true, Aleksandr was smaller than the other boys, and he was seriously outmatched in any maneuver or challenge that relied on weight and strength, but to Viktor's amazement, the boy had speed, out-of-the-ordinary speed. He was quick and agile and surprisingly fearless. As soon as he was knocked down, he'd scurry to his feet as though he'd never left his skates. And unlike the other ten-year-olds, he used his head, anticipating moves instead of frenetically following the puck like a lemming in search of a grub. Twice he led a breakout, and once he was credited with an assist. Not bad for a skinny little kid.

When the game was over, Aleksandr disappeared amid his teammates as they massed to center ice and raised their sticks in triumph, with Yuri Sokur standing tall in the middle of the pack. As the team dispersed, Aleksandr skated over to Katerina and Viktor, blood trickling from his nose.

Katerina gasped. "Oh my, you're bleeding!"

"You're not a hockey player until you've shed a little blood," Viktor said, bending down and scooping snow into his mitten. "Here, pack this around it."

Obediently, Aleksandr took the snow and held it to his nose.

"You looked pretty fast out there," Viktor said.

Aleksandr grinned.

"Of course, you need to get more aggressive."

Aleksandr nodded earnestly, a hint of a smile still curling the corners of his mouth.

"Let me see that," Viktor said.

When Aleksandr removed his snow-covered hand from his nose, Viktor touched the tip. "That hurt?" he asked.

Aleksandr shook his head.

"Looks fine." Viktor rose. "Have to go get my skates on; we're up next."

"Good luck!" Katerina called to him as he walked away.

"Takes more than luck," Viktor said over his shoulder.

He entered the warming tent and sat down on the long bench in the far corner, next to Jakob and Fedir, who were already lacing their skates. "Hear tell you drove out to get Svetlana and the kids," he said.

"I tried to talk Josef into coming," Jakob confided to Viktor and Fedir, "but he was having none of it. Worrisome situation, if you ask me."

"Yana says Josef has been hitting the sauce pretty hard," Fedir said. "Yuri's been taking care of the place."

"Svetlana's dumb on the matter." Jakob cinched his laces tighter. "Hasn't said where they'll go when they lose the farm, either. Has Katerina said anything?"

Viktor raised an eyebrow. "Why would she?"

"I don't know. It just seemed when we were out there Svetlana took a liking to her, is all," Jakob said.

Viktor frowned. Nothing good could come of that; however, he wasn't going to bother with it now. "Let's go show them how the game is played."

The men took the ice. Viktor stood in the center circle, adrenaline pumping, ready for the face-off against one of the Bandarek brothers—which one he couldn't tell, as the twins looked too much alike with their hats pulled down around their ears. When the referee dropped the puck, both men furiously fought for control. Viktor captured the puck, pulled it toward him, and shot it out to Father Warga on the right wing. After a couple of strides, he sent the puck to Fedir, who lost control, giving it up to the other team's defense. *Damn.* Fedir wasn't worth a nickel as a hockey player.

Viktor sped toward the opponent's center. Just as the puck arrived, he shouldered him, threw him off balance, and took command. He moved his stick from one side of the puck to the other, skillfully maintaining possession, skating toward the goal as the defensive players closed in on him. At the last possible moment, he pitched it to Jakob, who cocked his arm and, with a hard flick of his wrist, shot the puck. The goalie reflexively dropped his leg and extended his arm. Before he could block it, the puck careened into the back of the net.

Spectators cheered and clapped. Viktor had been so focused, it was the first moment he was consciously aware of anyone besides the men on the ice. He and Jakob took a jubilant spin around the rink.

In the next face-off, the Bandarek brother outmaneuvered Viktor and sent the puck up the middle. Viktor gave chase. Before he closed in, the puck was passed to a player behind him. Viktor slowed and intercepted it on the next pass. He spun around and shot the puck down the center to his teammate, who passed it back as Viktor outskated the first defender. When he broke toward the goal, the other Bandarek brother rushed forward, pulled his stick horizontally, clutched it with both hands, and blocked Viktor hard. Viktor's body jolted on impact. The puck flew out of his control. *Damn it!* The Bandarek brother was sent off the ice for two minutes on a cross-checking penalty.

With the other team undermanned, Viktor's team moved the puck, caroming it back and forth from one wing to the other and then to Viktor at center. He felt his skates score the ice as he sped toward the goal. Cheering loudly, the spectators urged him on. He set his jaw and took the shot. This time, as his knee hit the ice, the goalie deflected the puck.

The two-minute penalty passed and the Bandarek brother rejoined the game. With both teams at full strength, play became more aggressive. The opponent controlled the puck. Viktor watched the left wing's eyes glance at the center, signaling his intention to hand off. Viktor cut to his left to intercept the pass. As he leaned into the turn, the defenseman's stick hooked his skate. From that instant, time slowed. The body control Viktor had made look as natural and fluid as a bird in flight, was suddenly lost. The pointed tip of his blade grabbed the ice as he spun backward. His upper body twisted, the stick flew from his hand, and his arms spread like wings. Jolting pain gripped his ankle as he fell, face first, to the ice.

Katerina knocked on Yana's door and waited.

Despite the festivities of Winter Fair, the boredom and loneliness brought on by unrelenting winter threatened to smother her. She'd hinted to Viktor about buying a radio like the one the Pankos owned.

"Damned thing just buzzes most of the time," he'd said. "A waste of money, if you ask me." That had been the end of the matter.

After peeling potatoes, cleaning the kitchen, dusting every room in the house, stoking the stove twice, and mending a mound of socks, she'd found herself walking about the house, longing for noise, any noise. The house was so quiet that the slightest sound became magnified out of proportion, each drip of the faucet seeming to crash as loudly as thunder. When she was a child and her mother had lain in the upstairs bedroom dying, the house had felt the same—so quiet she'd imagined she heard blood flowing through her veins. She had to get away from Viktor's house or go mad.

Katerina knocked again. Still no answer. She opened the door a crack and peered inside. "Hello?" she said meekly. Then, more forcefully, "Hello? Is anyone home?"

"Come in!" Yana shouted. "I'm doing laundry."

When Katerina stepped inside, she heard thrumming close by. She set her parcels on the kitchen table, took off her coat, and hung it over the back of a chair before continuing to the small room off the kitchen, where Yana stood, laboring over the washing machine. The large copper tub, sitting atop a green iron stand, churned loudly. The floor was littered with piles of sorted clothes. Marina sat on the floor between the mounds, drawing. Vera nested in one of the piles, napping.

"Wash day's a bugbear," Yana said, loudly enough to be heard over the racket of the machine. Laundering was a tedious job for any woman, but with a family of eight, it was never ending.

"Today's Tuesday," Katerina said, suddenly feeling awkward. "I should have remembered."

"Ach, your company will make time fly," Yana said, feeding a shirt into the tub.

Marina edged toward Katerina and shyly held out her drawing.

"You're an artist!" Katerina exclaimed. "What a wonderful

snowman—and look, you can write your name!" She pointed to the large block letters stairstepping down to the bottom of the paper.

Marina beamed. Then, without a word, she returned to her spot on the floor and to her drawing.

"Besides, you saved me a trip to your house," Yana said, wiping strands of damp hair from her forehead with the back of her hand. "Alla Klopoushak wants to talk with you about doing some sewing for her."

"Oh?"

"When she sees what you can do with fabric and thread, she's bound to want more—and she'll brag to anyone who will listen."

Katerina felt a feather's brush of excitement.

"Alla couldn't keep her mouth shut in a dust storm," Yana said.

Vera uncoiled herself and rubbed her eyes with her tiny fists. When she saw Katerina, a wide smile erupted. She climbed off the pile of clothes and toddled toward Katerina with open arms.

"Hello, little rabbit," Katerina said, lifting her up. It felt as though Vera had gained five pounds since she'd last held her. Katerina thought of the photograph of Matviyko hidden in the bottom of her sewing basket and tried to imagine how he'd changed since the portrait had been taken. She quickly pushed the thought aside and smoothed Vera's hair, kissing her lightly on the forehead. In return, Vera planted a wet kiss on Katerina's cheek and then squirmed to get down. Katerina gently set her on the floor.

"Well, what do you think?" Yana asked.

Katerina hesitated.

"About meeting with Alla Klopoushak."

"It wouldn't do any harm to speak with her," Katerina said matter-of-factly. The prospect of earning her own money thrilled her, but she couldn't allow herself more than a thimbleful of hope.

The skeptical expression on Yana's face was the same one Katerina had seen when she'd lied about being ill the day they'd delivered food and clothing to the Sokur farm. It looked as if Yana was about to say something when Vera pulled at her mother's skirt.

"Potty, Mama."

"I'll be right back," Yana said, wiping her hands on her apron. "It's not wise to ignore Vera."

Katerina thought about the possibility of working for hire. She'd started as an apprentice in her father's tailor shop. It hadn't taken long before she'd begun getting requests from the wives of wealthy clients to sew custom-designed dresses. She'd grown used to having her own money and the independence it had brought. Now, she had neither.

Once she'd confessed to being with child, she'd been forced to stop working. Aneta had brought a few minor repair jobs home from Papa's shop on the pretext of doing the work herself, but Aneta's skills had never been a match for hers. Katerina knew that Papa would instantly recognize the quality of her work. He would know then that Aneta had been sheltering her. Upon reflection, Katerina wondered if that had been her sister's way of leaving a trail of breadcrumbs, of revealing what she hadn't had the courage to admit to Papa's face.

For the months spent living with her sister and brother-in-law, Katerina paid full room and board, watching her purse grow lighter each day with no means of replenishing it. The night she'd overheard Aneta and Danya discussing her circumstances, was a painful memory.

She'd sat uneasily on a straight-backed chair—a discomfort she considered emblematic of everything about her time spent in that apartment—huddled in the corner of her little box of a bedroom, pulling stitches from trousers she was clandestinely altering for a customer of Papa's. Her sister and brother-in-law had been in their adjacent bedroom, arguing. Despite their presumed discretion, Katerina had been able to make out most of their conversation through the paper-thin walls.

"Passage costs a small fortune. Katerina will need her money," Aneta had said. "She would never charge me if I was in trouble."

"You wouldn't be in *her* kind of trouble." Even through the plaster, Katerina detected the harshness in Danya's tone. His rebuttal had been laced with words and phrases such as "consequences," and "made her own bed." His aggravating sense of superiority, always on display, was something Katerina had come to detest. "Yes, Canada!" he'd snapped. "Senyk needs a wife. The money is *his* problem." That night had been the first time she'd realized that her brother-in-law had hit upon a tidy solution to the family's embarrassment. He'd found someone to marry her, and he'd intended to send her far, far away.

Silence.

Katerina had waited for her sister to defend her, to show loyalty, to stand her ground.

"Perhaps you're right," Aneta had said.

With those words, Katerina had been set adrift, cast off from the one person she had naively believed to be her unshakable ally. At that moment, she had understood she was utterly alone in this world, sucked into the wilderness with the Wila, joining the nymphs who floated between here and the afterlife, disconnected from living beings.

Yana returned with Vera in tow. "As I was saying, who knows where this project will lead?"

"Pardon?"

"Sewing for Alla Klopoushak. Who knows what might come of it?"

"Spoken like an optimistic merchant's wife," Katerina said.

What about Viktor? He was a prideful man, a controlling man. When he learned she carried his child, he might forbid her to work. Katerina wanted this opportunity. For now, it was best to keep her secrets; she'd figure out a way to deal with her husband, if it came to that.

"When can you meet her?" Yana asked.

"The sooner the better, I guess."

"When I get these wet clothes into the basket, we'll call her." Yana pulled several shirts from the tub and gave each one a healthy twist. "I'll hang these later," she said. "Let's go make that call."

With Vera toddling behind, Katerina followed her into the kitchen.

Yana cranked the phone, chatted amiably with the operator, and reached Alla on the first ring. "She must sit by the telephone, waiting for her subjects to call," Yana whispered, covering the receiver.

Katerina had to smile. Yana had a way of chipping away the hard edges, no matter what Katerina's mood might be.

"Hello? Alla? How have you been?"

As Yana spoke, Katerina thought about how she might arrange her days to design and sew while still managing all the chores and cooking, so that Viktor wouldn't object. She'd been tired lately; there were days when she was so fatigued she felt like sleeping in the middle of the afternoon. If this pregnancy followed the same pattern as the first one, however, she knew there would be months in which her strength and stamina returned. Taking on a single commission was a good idea. She could handle that much. It would be wise to have means of her own, just in case. In case what? A rainy day? What harm could it do?

"Katerina, would you be able to meet Alla at 1:00 tomorrow?" Yana asked, holding the receiver away from her mouth.

Katerina nodded. "Could we meet her here?"

Yana looked at her for a moment, her expression unreadable.

"Of course," she said.

It was better that way. No sense tipping her hand with Viktor if this idea came to nothing. Since injuring his ankle, he'd been in an even fouler temper than usual, and the less reason she gave him to quarrel, the better.

"Yah," Yana said. "I'll tell her…yah…good-bye." She hung the receiver on its cradle. "Her Majesty will be here tomorrow."

Katerina's heart fluttered as fast as a hummingbird's wings, yet all she heard coming from her mouth was a polite, "Thank you, Yana. I really appreciate this." When had she become so adept at covering her true feelings? Even Mary Pickford wasn't a better actress.

Before dawn, Katerina woke with a full bladder and a queasy stomach. She eased out of bed and wrapped her shawl around her shoulders, preparing to hurry downstairs and to the outhouse. After two steps, she knew she wouldn't make it. There was no choice but to use the chamber pot, tucked beneath Viktor's side of the bed.

She braced herself against his night table and clumsily lowered herself to the floor, one knee at a time. Viktor lay on his side, breathing heavily, his face mere inches from hers. Sour breath escaped in rattles and spurts from his open mouth. Katerina tried not to inhale and tried not to think about her stomach. She slid the pot from beneath the bed and removed the lid. The yeasty odor overpowered her, and, reflexively, she turned her head away from the stench. Lifting her nightgown, she positioned herself over the pot, all the while watching Viktor, praying he wouldn't open his eyes, praying he wouldn't witness her humiliation. Slowly, the pressure trickled away and relief took its place.

After Katerina put the pot back under the bed, she rose cautiously. Viktor didn't move. *Thank you, Blessed Mother.*

When Katerina reached the kitchen, she grabbed three soda crackers from the tin and downed them, one after another, closed her eyes and waited for the wave to pass. With her first pregnancy, bouts of nausea had been infrequent; this time, her upset stomach was as predictable as sunrise. Because her first pregnancy had been easier but had resulted in heartache, maybe the difficulty of carrying this child meant the opposite. Katerina wondered if she carried a son or a daughter. Wishing for one instead of the other might be courting disappointment; still, she couldn't help but think that a baby girl would seem to be less disloyal, less of a replacement and more of a new beginning.

How would Viktor react to her news? They had talked nothing of the future, living each day as if the succession of twenty-four hours after twenty-four hours—waking to sleeping and back to waking again—served merely as a demarcation point, rather than time connected by events that led somewhere. A child of their own could change that. Katerina longed for their lives together to be something more than the passage of time, so why was she so reluctant to tell him about her condition?

Katerina had learned that everything has its cost. Sometimes the price is immediate. Sometimes the toll comes when a person least expects it. The one certainty was that, with Viktor, the arithmetic was subtraction, never addition. He was a pragmatic man, lacking in sentimentality. How was a wife to share hopes and dreams with a husband who measured people and events the way he measured wheat grain to chaff in his dockage tester? She didn't pretend to understand him. He was water, she was air. He was night, she was day.

She'd loved a romantic man once, a sentimental man, one who'd whispered poetry in her ear, who'd expressed himself in art and idyll. Where that had led? Maybe Danya was right; maybe life wasn't about "what if" but "what is." She must tell Viktor that she was in a family way soon, very soon.

By the time he walked into the kitchen, fully dressed and supporting his weight on his cane, Katerina's stomach had settled.

"Good morning." She forced a lilt into her voice.

"Morning."

"How is your ankle feeling today?"

"The same."

Viktor had been limping around, favoring his right leg ever since the incident at Winter Fair. He usually wasn't one to complain about aches and pains—probably because he detested weakness in anyone—but he'd been cross for more than a week, as much out of frustration as pain, she guessed. The sprain hadn't improved; she wondered if he might have broken a bone.

"You're going to the elevator?"

"I can't sit around forever."

Katerina cautiously placed her hand on his shoulder. "I'm worried about you. Your ankle should be better by now. Perhaps a visit to Dr. Billings is in order," she said.

"He'll charge an arm and a leg and tell me there's nothing to be done about it."

"Still, it would be worth it just for peace of mind." Katerina ran her hand to the nape of his neck and rubbed gently. "You don't want to end up with permanent damage. You're too virile a man for that."

"Maybe."

"He'll be in town tomorrow. I'll stop at his office today and leave an appointment note on his door, if you'd like." Katerina hated the honey dripping from her voice.

"Fine."

"Viktor?"

"What?"

Katerina wanted to tell him. Her thoughts gathered and formed words. *I have something important to tell you. I hope the news makes you happy. We are having a baby.* She came within a hair's breadth of confessing, but the words buzzed around in her head futilely, like insects trapped in a jar.

"I—I'm glad that you're willing to see the doctor."

Katerina pulled her collar high around her neck as she walked toward Yana's. The wind had picked up, and the dense northerly sky had dulled to a whitish gray, a sure sign of an impending storm. At least, given the clouds' distance, the weather would hold until evening. In the city, the sky had appeared as slivers and patches between rooftops. On the prairie, where the sky could be seen without interruption, from horizon to horizon, weather announced itself well before its arrival. There was, in equal measure, majesty and intimidation in the vastness of the Saskatchewan sky.

Katerina was grateful that Viktor had gone to work and relieved that it hadn't been necessary to postpone her meeting with Alla Klopoushak. She hoped to get to work as soon as possible. There would be measurements to take, a design to settle on, and fabric to buy. This was territory Katerina had traveled many times before, and for the first time in a long while, she felt confident.

As soon as she rounded the corner on Main Street, she recognized Roman Klopoushak's showy truck, parked in front of Panko's General Store. She remembered Yana's words the day she'd arrived in Bilik, when they'd sat in front of Wozny's Dry Goods and he'd driven by. Yana had insinuated then he was a braggart and a lady's man. After being introduced to him, Katerina had to agree.

She'd encountered Mrs. Klopoushak on only a few occasions, not enough for her to render fair judgment. Yana, of course, had more than hinted that she and her husband were a matching pair, but Katerina would decide for herself. She'd dealt with many of the wealthiest women in L'viv and knew how to work with well-heeled clients. Admittedly, she felt a little nervous today, but she'd come prepared.

Yana answered the door after the first knock, almost as though she'd been standing on the other side with her hand on the knob. Katerina recognized Yana's Sunday skirt and blouse but not her coquettish hairdo. Instead of parting her hair in the middle, pulling it back tightly, and fastening it at the nape of her neck in a bun, as she usually did, Yana had parted her hair on the side and curled wisps of hair loosely around her face. The back was rolled under and pinned to make it appear shorter. Katerina guessed it was an attempt to emulate a bob, the latest fashion craze. It might have looked comic if it hadn't been so endearing. Katerina was deeply touched by her friend's effort.

Katerina put down her satchel. "Thank you," she said, taking Yana's hand in hers.

"Ach, no need for thanks," Yana said. "She's in the dining room. I was just getting some tea," she stage-whispered.

Katerina picked up her satchel and followed Yana inside.

The tray held Yana's finest service, including the cups she'd loaned Katerina for her first outing with Viktor. The house was unnaturally quiet. It occurred to Katerina that Marina and Vera were nowhere in sight.

"Where are the girls?"

"Fedir's minding the store and the children," Yana said. "It's good for him. He'll appreciate me more."

Together, they entered the dining room, where Alla Klopoushak sat, stiff-backed, in Fedir's customary place. Her hands lay on the table, primly crossed. A ray of sunshine streaked across her chest, highlighting her substantial bosom.

"Here we go," Yana said, placing the tray on the table. "I believe you've met."

"Yes," Katerina said, nodding politely.

"Indeed," Alla replied, extending her hand as though it were breakable.

Katerina took it gently in hers.

Yana poured tea all around and set the sugar bowl and creamer in front of her guest.

"We might as well get right to it, then," Alla said, ignoring her tea. "My husband and I will be traveling to Regina, and I haven't anything suitable to wear to my niece's wedding. A traditional dress simply wouldn't do given the caliber of guests who will be there. And ordering something from Eaton's catalog wouldn't do either; someone else might purchase the same ensemble. Besides, there's no guarantee it would fit properly. Their measurements chart is horribly off, I'm afraid." She looped her index finger through the delicately handled cup and rested it in the palm of her opposite hand but didn't drink.

"I noticed your son's coat at Winter Fair. I must say, it stood out from the crowd. And your wedding attire was splendid. Mrs. Panko said you designed and sewed it. She tells me you are a woman of considerable talents."

If Roman Klopoushak was His Lordship, Katerina decided, his wife was Her Ladyship. Her airs were as misplaced as a crystal chandelier hanging from a livery ceiling. Almost everyone Katerina had met during the months she'd been in Bilik was unpretentious—genuine, salt-of-the-earth country folk, who dealt with life and each other in a straightforward fashion. It was true that some were more prosperous than others, and some, such as the Sokur family, were plain unfortunate. Even at that, neighbors didn't flaunt their good fortune. In fact, they displayed extraordinary generosity.

Katerina pictured Alla Klopoushak among the patrons of L'viv's grand opera house. She'd be milkweed among roses. But the pretentious woman wouldn't recognize her socially inferior status if it stared her in the face. In Katerina's experience, those engaged in self-aggrandizing puffery rarely recognized their limitations. This, however, wasn't the time to concern herself with Mrs. Klopoushak's self-importance. It made no difference to her. If humbling herself before this woman led to employment, that was what she was prepared to do.

"Why, thank you for your kind words, Alla. May I call you Alla?" Katerina said with a deferential smile.

"Certainly."

"I hope you will find Mrs. Panko's faith in me well placed. I have many years of experience creating clothing for women of your sensibilities. Please tell me what you had in mind."

"I'm not sure what you mean," Alla said, her brow furrowing.

"There are several ways a woman decides what to wear to a special event." Katerina looked Alla in the eye, still smiling pleasantly. "She asks herself what image she desires, whether she wants to be subtle or bold, classic or modern."

"I see," Alla said.

"And then there's the matter of season and what style most flatters her figure."

Alla hesitated, seemingly at a loss. It didn't surprise Katerina. She could tell by Mrs. Klopoushak's attire she didn't know the first thing about fashion.

"Don't worry," Katerina said. "It's my job to help you make those decisions."

Alla sat up straighter in her chair, her haughty expression restored.

"I've taken the liberty of bringing some sketches to aid our discussion," Katerina said. "Any of them can be altered to suit your taste." She pulled three paper rolls from her satchel and placed them on the table. "I've drawn one traditional design, one contemporary style, and one that's a blend of both. You will see that they have several elements in common."

Alla stood and bent over the drawings.

"They all have a V neckline, a loosely defined waist, and a slight flare toward the hemline for balance. In my estimation, that is the best silhouette for your figure." She unrolled the first drawing. "Let's begin with the traditional design, shall we?"

Katerina reviewed each drawing, pausing to answer Alla's questions and patiently guiding her when she veered off course. After an hour, they'd decided on a design, settled on the appropriate fabric, and determined the fee for Katerina's services. With those decisions made, Katerina pulled a tape from her satchel and meticulously recorded each of Alla's vital measurements.

"It has been a most enlightening afternoon," Alla said as she prepared to leave. "I look forward to seeing your finished work." Alla extended her hand with the same effeteness she'd displayed at first. Now, when their eyes met, however, Katerina saw respect that had been absent before.

"It's been a pleasure," Katerina said. "I will do my best to create a special dress worthy of you."

Yana saw Alla to the door.

"Well, I'd say Her Highness has met her match," Yana said when she returned.

Katerina realized it had been more than an hour and a half since she'd heard Yana's voice.

"I'm sorry," she said, feeling embarrassed. "I'm afraid I quite ignored you. Yana, please forgive my rudeness."

"Ach, don't worry. It was more entertaining than a moving picture show."

Chapter Thirteen

In the middle of the night, snow began falling, first as solitary flakes and then dropping like a dense curtain over Bilik. When Aleksandr awoke, he padded to his bedroom window and stared at the falling snow, squinting, hoping that if he concentrated hard enough, he'd be able to see beyond the solid wall of white. But no matter how intently he stared, he saw nothing but white. Bilik wasn't supposed to look this way. In his whole life, he'd never seen this much snow. Overnight, the world had lost its color.

He realized there wouldn't be school that day or maybe for several days. It would take time for the farmers to dig their way to the main roads, and those roads would be covered, and it would be impossible to tell where they left off and the fields began. He was happy about missing schoolwork but disappointed because there would be no hockey played. The frozen dugout would be buried, and when it was unearthed—who knew when that would be?—the ice would be bumpy and pockmarked. Because his father had hurt his leg at Winter Fair and couldn't skate yet, he wouldn't be eager to repair the pond.

Snow usually meant fun—snowmen, snow forts, snowball fights. This was not that kind of snow. This was dangerous snow, with the wind howling, the snow drifting, and conditions whiteout-hazardous. It was the kind of storm where a boy could walk out his back door to use the outhouse and disappear into a world of white—the sky and the land the same color—and be unable to find his way back to the house. Everyone knew the story about the farmer who had lost his way coming back from the barn in a whiteout just like this one and had frozen to death before anyone found him lying twenty-five feet from his house.

Aleksandr remembered reading that this could happen in the ocean if you were tossed upside down by a wave. You could become confused and not know up from down. He wondered if that had happened to his mother. She hadn't drowned in the ocean, but maybe it was possible to become just as mixed up in a river. He imagined her underwater, grabbing and kicking frantically, thinking she was getting closer and closer to the surface. When there had been no more air left in her lungs and they had felt as though they were about to burst, she had probably paddled harder, thinking she was scrambling toward the surface. When she had realized her mistake, it was too late. She'd been clawing toward the river bottom, deeper and deeper, farther and farther from the air. There had been nothing to do but give up and let water fill her lungs.

Aleksandr's head hurt. It must have been terrible when she'd realized she had no chance. If only she'd swum the other way. If only. He wondered if she had thought about dying or about him or if she'd been too confused to think about anything. What had it been like to run out of air, to have nothing to breathe but water? Aleksandr felt pressure in his chest. His breathing grew shallower. Each time he breathed in, it seemed that only a small amount of oxygen seeped into his lungs. The less air he inhaled, the faster he breathed. The more he panted, the deeper panic planted itself in his imagination. He felt desperate, just as his mother must have felt desperate. He was drowning. He could feel it.

Finally, his lungs commanded him to breathe, demanded that he live. He gasped, inhaling air in hungry gulps and letting it out in swooshing huffs. His face burned. His hands shook. *Don't be stupid. You're in the house, upstairs in your bedroom. Don't be stupid.* He repeated this again and again in his head until, gradually, his breathing calmed. *Don't be stupid. You're not underwater. It's winter. It's snowing. Don't be stupid.* He closed his eyes and listened to his breathing grow slower and slower. *In. Out. In. Out. One—two—three—four...* He thought about snow. He knew that it was frozen water, but he didn't want to think of it that way because he loved snow. He didn't want his mother's drowning to wreck his love of snow. If he wasn't careful, his stupid thoughts could spoil everything.

There was a gentle knock on his door.

Aleksandr rubbed his hands over his face and tried to make his expression look as though nothing had happened, as though he hadn't almost drowned. He was a boy standing in his room, watching a blizzard, and thinking normal thoughts. "Come in," he said, pretending to rub sleep from his eyes.

His new mother opened the door and peeked in. She smiled. "There's no school today. You can go back to bed if you want. I'll make a late breakfast. Would you like that?"

She always spoke to him as if a loud voice could make him break. He could feel her words tiptoeing around him, falling off her tongue as bright sunshine and fluffy clouds. Sometimes, the way she spoke to him made him wonder if he *was* breakable. Could the wrong words make a person crack in two?

Aleksandr knew she didn't always speak that way because he'd been watching and listening to her very intently.

When she talked with his father, his new mother's voice became steady and formal with pleasantness sprinkled on top, like sugar over porridge, to make the ordinary sweeter. She paused before speaking, weighing her words, choosing them carefully, so his father wouldn't get angry.

Aleksandr understood because he chose his words cautiously, too. He pictured the gigantic shelf in his head, a library shelf that contained every word he knew. There were so many that sometimes deciding which ones to use got confusing. When he was forced to speak to his father, the secret was to select just the right words, avoiding anything that would make him mad and instead choosing only words that would please a father who was almost impossible to please. Sometimes, he guessed right. Too often, he guessed wrong.

When his new mother talked to Mrs. Panko, she spoke much faster. Her hands and arms moved as though they were free and happy to be allowed to do whatever they wanted. There were no long pauses before she spoke, no closed eyes trying to read the right words on the insides of her lids and no looks toward the ceiling, hoping to find the perfect words rolling through her brain. With Mrs. Panko, she laughed and her hand automatically covered her mouth, as if she didn't want all her laughter to escape at once, as if she had a limited supply and needed to save some for later.

When she spoke with Lilia or Lavro or any of their brothers or sisters, her voice played and danced. She didn't have to pretend to be happy. It was as if she could tell they'd liked her from the first. He wished he could tell her that he liked her now, too, that he was glad she was his new mother, but he didn't know how. If he admitted that his opinion had changed, wouldn't he also have to admit how much he'd hated her before? Wouldn't he have to explain that he still missed his real mother, from the tips of his fingers and toes to the middle of his heart? That would be impossible.

"Well?" she said in her soft voice. "Would you like to go back to bed?"

His father would disapprove. Aleksandr would get hollered at for being lazy. His father would have a list of chores for him to do, including loading buckets of coal from the cellar, which meant he would have to go outside and then down into the dark. He didn't want to face that, but facing his father's disapproval scared him even more.

"I don't know," Aleksandr said.

"You don't have to if you don't want to."

It wasn't that he didn't want to. The room was cold and his bed was warm and cozy and tempting. He stood as still as a block of ice, his mind ordering him to do one thing, his body wanting to do another.

"Your father has decided to stay in bed for a while," she said.

It was strange the way his new mother read his thoughts. Maybe it was because she was afraid of his father, too. He could tell by the way she looked at his father and by how different she was when he was gone. When he was at home, she was serious and busy, like hired help who had a job to do. She hummed softly but rarely smiled. He saw her eyes watching his father like a detective searching for clues. When he was gone, she moved and talked and sang differently. He liked her better then. He liked himself better then, too.

"I'll go back to bed," Aleksandr said. He climbed into bed, hunkered down beneath the covers, and tucked them under his chin. The warmth felt sweeter than a summer's day.

"I'll wake you in an hour." His new mother closed the door very carefully.

The last thing he remembered was her smile.

His father didn't just sleep late; he stayed in bed all morning. Aleksandr couldn't remember when that had happened before. Sometimes, when his father had drunk too much at night, he looked sick the next morning—his eyes red-rimmed and puffy, his hair uncombed, his features pinched tight against light and sound. But to sleep this late was unheard of. Aleksandr didn't know what to make of it. He'd have to stay especially alert.

It was almost as good as having him gone. Almost. His new mother acted somewhere in between cautious and happy. Sometimes she would start singing, and then it seemed that she suddenly realized his father was still in the house, and she'd just hum or stop altogether. Once in a while, she'd go upstairs to check on him. It was best to be careful where his father was concerned. There was always the chance he'd come downstairs when he wasn't expected, or maybe he could hear everything that went on in the house, no matter where he was.

Today was definitely a stay-in-the-house day. It was still snowing. Every business in Bilik would be shut down, and the streets would be deserted. The wind howled, whistled around the house, and rattled the windows. The fire in the stove burned hot, but a cold draft seeped through the slightest cracks, making every surface cold to the touch. Aleksandr wore his heaviest wool socks and put on an extra sweater.

At first, Aleksandr enjoyed the time to laze in bed, eat a late breakfast, and read a book. As the morning wore on, however, he became bored and restless. It wasn't much fun to play with his biplanes or tin soldiers without someone to fight against. He thought about going to the Pankos' to play with Lavro but then remembered he couldn't.

Curiously, there was a full bucket of coal next to the firebox in the parlor. He couldn't believe his good fortune. He wouldn't have to fight with the wind to open the cellar's clamshell doors or go down into the frigid darkness.

He wandered into the dining room, where his new mother was sewing. He watched as she concentrated on cutting a pattern precisely along the dark pencil lines, the way she'd done when she made his new coat.

When she finished, she put down her scissors and looked up. "Don't worry, this skirt isn't for you." She sucked in her cheeks, as if she was trying to keep from smiling.

Aleksandr chuckled. It was strange hearing the sound of his own laughter. At school or with friends, it wasn't so unusual, but in this house, his laughter was a foreign language.

"Can you keep a secret?" she asked, her voice a whisper.

Aleksandr nodded.

"It's a surprise for Lilia. I'm making a special skirt for her name day gift."

As she turned back to her task, she began to hum. Her fingers worked nimbly, fastening the paper to the bright blue material with long silver stickpins. Aleksandr remembered that blue was Lilia's favorite color and felt a twinge of jealousy.

"I didn't know you were such a good hockey player," she said, still concentrating on the pattern. "At Winter Fest, you were the fastest of all the skaters."

Her praise enfolded him like a warm blanket. He realized there were a lot of things she didn't know about him—that he loved airplanes even more than he loved playing hockey, that he wanted to be an aviator, that he could spell words backward as well as forward, and that he was the best reader in his class.

"I didn't know you could make clothes better than you can buy in the store," Aleksandr said as he inched near—but not too near—her.

His new mother paused, resting the material in her still hands. She tilted her head, like a puppy hearing a whistle. For what seemed to be a long time, she said nothing, as though she needed to wait until her words caught up with her thoughts.

"And I didn't know your favorite aviator was Ormer Locklear," she said, raising an eyebrow.

Aleksandr couldn't believe she knew that about him. How? He was certain he'd never, ever mentioned Ormer Locklear to her. Lavro must have told her, because he was the only one, other than him, who knew the name of his favorite aviator. It wasn't fair that his best friend had shared more with his new mother than he had. Lavro had his own real mother to talk to. Then a little voice reminded Aleksandr that he'd refused to talk to his new mother for a long, long time, and he decided not to be mad at Lavro.

"I didn't know you could sing pretty songs," Aleksandr blurted out as he crossed his arms over his chest and smiled. He enjoyed the challenge of this new game.

She set her pincushion down and turned away from her pattern. "I didn't know you could eat five potato pancakes at one sitting." She crossed her arms over her middle and nodded, signaling it was his turn in this game of one-upmanship.

Aleksandr looked at his feet, thinking. He realized that even though she'd been living in his house for months, he hardly knew her.

He knew the things she did, such as cooking and sewing and singing, but he didn't know what she thought or anything about her life before she had come to Bilik. One day, she'd just appeared, as though she'd fallen from the sky, bright and shiny but strange and alien as a meteorite.

"I didn't know you smelled like flowers," Aleksandr said.

"I didn't know you could touch your tongue to your nose," she said.

"I didn't know you were going to be my new mother."

Her expression changed. Her eyes weren't twinkling anymore, but she wasn't frowning either. He wondered if he'd said the wrong thing.

"I didn't know either."

He looked at her, puzzled.

"Until I arrived in Bilik, I mean. You were a surprise to me, too."

"I didn't even know my real mother was leaving," Aleksandr blurted out.

Instead of continuing the game, his new mother became very quiet. Aleksandr looked down at his hands, suddenly aware that things had taken a serious turn. Maybe she didn't want him to talk about his real mother, the same way his father didn't want him to talk about her. Maybe he'd ruined the game. Maybe she was angry with him now. He was sorry he'd said it.

Reaching over to him, she put her hand on his shoulder. "Aleksandr, you couldn't have known she was going to die. It was an accident. No one could have known," she said, soft as cotton.

"That's not what I meant. I didn't know she was going to Winnipeg to take care of my aunt. She didn't tell me. Mama never went anywhere without telling me. But she just left. When I came home from school, she was gone." His eyes grew moist and he swallowed hard. "She didn't even say good-bye." Aleksandr hadn't meant to tell her that. He hadn't told anyone before, not even Lavro. But his new mother had a way of getting him to say things that were buried deep in his stomach.

She was thinking. Aleksandr could tell because when she was thinking hard, she got a crease between her eyes and she turned her head to the side, as if she were straining to hear something in the distance.

"Are you sure she didn't tell you? Are you sure you didn't forget?"

The floorboards overhead creaked. Aleksandr looked at his new mother and then at the ceiling.

His father was up and walking around.

They both became very still.

Aleksandr held his breath, waiting for the sound to stop, for his father to go back to bed. Instead, the footsteps became heavier as they moved toward the upstairs hallway. He glanced out the window. The snow had stopped. Gray light had replaced the white curtain.

"I'm sure," he whispered.

Viktor woke to a headache that began at the base of his skull, pulsed through his temples, and settled behind his eye sockets. When he lifted his head from the pillow, he cursed, then vowed to lay off the *horilka*. The clock hands told him it was pushing noon. He rubbed his eyes and took a second look. He couldn't remember when he'd slept this late.

Katerina's side of the mattress was stone cold. No doubt, she'd been up for hours. It seemed she'd been getting up earlier and earlier. Sometimes, he was vaguely aware of the covers moving or the springs shifting beneath him as she eased out of bed, but most of the time he slept through it. Given her bad leg, it was uncanny how silently the woman moved about. This morning, she'd woken him by shaking his shoulder. He remembered because he'd been annoyed, and he recalled that she'd said it was still snowing hard. Anything else was long since lost in the haze of deep, dreamless sleep.

He stood gingerly, testing his sore ankle. It felt better—Dr. Billings had confirmed it was just a deep sprain that would take time to heal completely—but his body was stiff from being prone so long. He arched and rubbed the small of his back. It looked as though the damned storm had finally stopped. A little less than a foot of snow would barely warrant a mention in some provinces, but here, that much snow, scattered helter-skelter by the brutal prairie wind, wreaked havoc.

The floor was cold beneath his feet. As soon as he opened the bedroom door, the warmth of a well-tended fire, wafting up the stairway, greeted him. He massaged his temples. His tongue felt thick and his mouth drought-dry. What he wouldn't give for a strong cup of tea. He limped downstairs, still favoring his sore ankle a bit and then stumbled into the dining room, where Katerina worked on a sewing project. Aleksandr stood next to her like a shadow.

The dining room table was littered with fabric, not that it mattered. The table would be free of clutter and ready for the evening meal. He'd been clear about his expectations when he'd given her the sewing machine. Having it was not to interfere with her duties. At first, he'd been reluctant to buy such an extravagant piece of equipment, but Fedir had convinced him—although he had seen Yana's hand in it from start to finish—that it would keep his wife occupied and less homesick. Besides, the machine had practical value. It seemed Katerina could sew just about anything and sew it better than store-bought. In the long run, it would be a money saver if she didn't overspend on supplies. He'd have to check at the dry goods store to make sure she was living within their means.

"You're awake," Katerina said. "I trust you slept well." She looked bright-eyed and cheerful.

He was about to complain that he wasn't up to such cheer first thing in the morning when he remembered that it was already noon. He rubbed his stubbly beard and decided a shave could wait until later.

A clean-shaven face was the one thing Katerina requested of him before giving in to him in bed. One night, when he'd been on top of her, half crazy with need, she'd turned her face away from him whenever he'd brought his mouth to her lips. Irritated, he'd finally snapped, "What in the hell's wrong with you?"

"I'm sorry. It's your whiskers."

"Whiskers?"

"They hurt."

At the moment, her complaint had irked him. He'd pushed his frustration aside and finished anyway. Once sated, he'd thought it over. It was little enough to ask, he supposed, in exchange for having a compliant woman in his bed every night. Besides, he didn't want her turning her head every time his mouth got near hers.

"Your meal is on the kitchen table. I'll make some tea if you'd like."

Her morning cheer grated on him like a high-pitched whistle. *It's noon. Let it be.*

"Make it strong," he said, shambling toward the kitchen. "Aleksandr, the walkway needs shoveling. Get started. I'll be out soon." He didn't bother to look back. The boy's long-faced resignation would just rankle, although Viktor had to admit, despite his earlier reservations, lately, Aleksandr had been behaving more like the son he wanted.

At first, he'd thought maybe Katerina wasn't up to the task of raising the boy. She was obviously smart but young and citified, with an inclination to coddle. He'd watched for weeks as the boy acted cool as frost toward her, rejecting her motherly advances at every turn. She hadn't complained and hadn't asked for help getting Aleksandr in line. Viktor had been mostly silent on the matter, biding his time to see if she was capable of taking a firmer hand. Though she hadn't hardened, the boy finally seemed to be warming to her. It was about time, because Viktor had been losing patience. When Elena had left, he'd been tolerant, supposing any child would miss his mother some; but six months, a year, and more had gone by, and the boy had still clung to his grief like a baby to his mother's teat. Aleksandr would be eleven soon. Weaning was overdue.

A hot meal and strong tea went a long way toward clearing Viktor's head. Whatever cobwebs remained were swept away by the bracing cold that assaulted him when he stepped outside.

The low-riding wind had polished the snow's surface into a fine crust, but below that brittle layer, the snow lay feather-light. From the front porch, Viktor watched Aleksandr struggling to clear the walkway. With a hard down stroke, his shovel broke through the crust. He scooped a shovelful. The snow, as light as dust, blew off the shovel and back onto the path as fast as he cleared it. Still, he didn't give up. The determined little bugger kept shoveling, even when it was clear his efforts were futile.

"Shit," Viktor grumbled, leaning on his unused shovel.

Aleksandr looked up at him warily.

"It's no good. Have to wait until this wind dies down," Viktor said.

Aleksandr ran up the porch steps almost before Viktor had finished his sentence and leaned his shovel next to the doorway.

"You made short work of that," Katerina said when they stomped into the house.

"No use. Damned wind's too strong." Viktor kicked snow from his boots, pulled off his cap, and hung his coat on the hook. "No sense going to the elevator now either. Tracks won't be cleared, and there'll be a snowdrift the size of a mountain blocking the office door."

"Aleksandr, your cheeks are as red as apples," Katerina said, taking his face into her warm hands. She helped him take off his jacket and hung it on the hook next to Viktor's.

"Don't start fussing," Viktor warned. "He knows how to hang his own coat."

Katerina looked as if she would talk back, but she stepped away instead. "How about some tea with steamed milk and biscuits?"

Aleksandr nodded.

"We could take it by the parlor stove," Katerina suggested. "You both look like you need to thaw."

"Thought you had sewing to do," Viktor said.

"I can spare the time. We could play phonograph music and maybe even play a game of cards. Viktor, we do have a deck of cards in the house, don't we?"

He scratched the back of his head. Her enthusiasm began to soften him. "Some in the top desk drawer, I think."

"I don't know how," Aleksandr said, staring at his feet.

"I can teach you." Katerina was more animated than Viktor had ever seen her.

"I suppose it wouldn't hurt," Viktor said. "Understand, we'll have to quit when the wind dies down. A lot of snow needs shoveling."

Katerina clapped her hands together like a giddy girl. A phonograph and a card game. The most inconsequential things excited that woman. Damned if he understood her.

The wind calmed, and by late afternoon, Viktor and Aleksandr were outside again, shoveling. The sun dipped low in the sky, promising foreshortened daylight. Like sand dunes, which Viktor had seen only in photographs, the snow undulated across the land, in some places with drifts mounding as high as a yardstick and in others, barely covering the ground.

His belly was full and his headache long gone. An afternoon spent next to the fire, listening to music and playing games, had taken the spine right out of him. *Men of means, with nothing more pressing to do than lounge in fancy clubs, drink sherry, and play chess, always live the easy life.* Envy nipped at the edges of his thoughts. But such musings were a foolish waste of time. He was a practical man who had little use for daydreams and even less patience for frivolous talk. This was his life. He might not be a rich dandy, but he did well enough.

"Don't put so much on the shovel," Viktor said.

Aleksandr dug into the pile, scooped up half as much snow, and tossed it to the side. The boy looked at him expectantly, and Viktor offered a single nod of approval.

"You finish the walk, then start on the driveway," Viktor said. "I'll dig out the truck."

"Yes, sir."

The truck sat under a makeshift lean-to, which Viktor had rigged next to the shed attached to the back of the house. To get to the truck, he walked close to the house, along the south wall, where the snow was only a half-foot deep. He congratulated himself for having the foresight to build the lean-to on the side where the snow was generally shallower and protected from the wind. He shoveled around the truck tires to a steady rhythm. *Thrust—scoop—lift—toss—thrust—scoop—lift—toss.* In no time, a bead of sweat trickled down his back. On the west-facing side of the truck, the snow reached the front bumper. Viktor picked up the pace. *Thrust—scoop—lift—toss—thrust—scoop—lift—toss.* He stood upright, mopped his forehead with the sleeve of his jacket, and made one final effort.

Aleksandr had started shoveling by the road and was slowly moving up the driveway. The boy was only half as fast as an able-bodied man, but Viktor saw that he was making his best effort, and for now, that would do. Viktor started on his end and shoveled steadily until they met, about two thirds of the way down the drive.

"Good enough," Viktor said, digging a handkerchief from his pocket and wiping his runny nose. The clothed parts of his body were warm, bordering on hot, while his face and the tips of his fingers were cold, bordering on numb. "You can go inside."

Wordlessly, Aleksandr dragged his shovel behind him and headed toward the house.

Maybe there was hope for the boy after all.

"Don't forget to put that shovel away!" Viktor called after him.

By the time Viktor made it to the elevator, it was nearly dusk. As expected, from the street, he could see that the snow drifted high across the railroad tracks, crawled up the office steps, and settled on the landing, blocking the door. He lowered his shovel and pushed it ahead like a plow, carving a path across the tracks toward his office. It took fifteen minutes to clear the steps and the landing.

As soon as Viktor entered, he flicked on the overhead light, which swung from the rafter. The place was as cold as a whore's heart, but he decided not to bother with a fire. It was getting late. He perused the place in a single sweep, satisfied that everything looked intact.

In the distance, a train whistle blasted.

Viktor needed to vacate the office before the train reached the elevator. He didn't want to get caught anywhere near the tracks when the plow came through town, pelting snow like so much shrapnel. With his sore ankle, which now ached from overuse, he couldn't waste time dawdling. He quickly turned off the light and closed the office door, giving the knob a jiggle to make sure it was securely latched. Then he retraced his steps through the narrow path he'd shoveled and trudged across the street. Some of the walkway along Main Street had been cleared in front of businesses where the owners lived above their stores. The rest would wait until daylight.

As the train approached from the east end of town, he heard the huge blades of the rotary plow churning. There was still enough light to see the coal-black plume escaping from the push engine's stack and the dense, gray-white cloud roiling behind it. The gigantic rotor flung snow, cyclone-like, in every direction. It passed through, whistle blasting, leaving a cleared track in its wake.

Even though he'd slept until noon, Viktor was weary. The weight of winter pressed on his shoulders. His back ached and his stomach growled. He trudged home, anticipating a hot meal and, later, a willing woman in his warm bed.

Right now, he needed a drink.

Katerina sat on the edge of Aleksandr's bed, watching him sleep. His lips, slightly parted, made no sound. Without the anxiety that so often clouded his features, he looked peaceful, angelic. When she'd come to tuck him in, he'd already fallen asleep, exhausted from shoveling. It was no surprise—at the dinner table, he'd barely been able to keep his eyes open—but Katerina was disappointed that she hadn't been able to hug him and tell him what a fine job he'd done. Lightly, she kissed the top of his head and pulled the quilt up to his chin.

As Katerina stood to leave, she looked around his bedroom. The silhouette of Aleksandr's model biplane, sitting atop the dresser, made her smile. He'd been surprised that she knew about Ormer Locklear. She'd seen it on his face. There was much more hidden in those still waters that she hungered to know. It struck her, in a way that had eluded her before, that there was very little in Aleksandr's room that provided clues to his interests or dreams. She resolved to change that.

She carefully closed the door behind her and limped down the stairs to finish tidying up the kitchen and to stoke the stove before retiring for the night. Although she was tired, her step was light. She was in a very good mood. In the three and a half months since her wedding, this had been the best day of her marriage—not that anything extraordinary had happened. Quite the opposite. Although the intensity of the snowstorm had been unusual for Bilik—at least, that was what Viktor had claimed—the activity in the house could have happened in any family on any ordinary day. It was, in fact, the day's very ordinariness that thrilled her.

She'd prepared a late breakfast and had most of the morning to herself to work on Lilia's skirt. As snow had fallen, she'd watched the world turn brilliant white outside the dining room window, the purity of it cleansing her, making her feel unsullied and renewed. Her time alone with Aleksandr had been comfortable. Yes, that was it. Comfortable. They'd fallen into an ease together. If only briefly, he'd even allowed her to be playful.

Was this what being a mother was supposed to feel like? Was this what she had to look forward to with her own child? Katerina hadn't considered it before. Motherhood conjured up notions of protection, responsibility, duty, and love so fierce it could turn a woman to steel. But ease and whimsy? No, she'd never considered it, perhaps because she'd never had that with her own mother.

She and Viktor and Aleksandr had spent much of the afternoon together in the parlor playing a card game called three in the well. Viktor had taught them the rules. Aleksandr had caught on right away. Katerina had found the strategy a bit confusing. She had been delighted by the glee that Aleksandr and Viktor had shared when she had made a wrong move that had cost her the game. Their victorious conspiracy had seemed right somehow.

Best of all was the laughter that had erupted when they'd played the phonograph and taught her to sing "K-K-K-Katy."

"Please sing it again," Aleksandr had begged for the tenth time.

"If you insist," she'd said in mock resistance.

Viktor had moved the needle to exactly the place where the chorus began and lowered it onto the record. Gamely, Katerina had tried to keep pace with the words, twisting her Ukrainian tongue. Aleksandr had giggled harder each time as she stuttered through the lyrics.

At last, all three of them sang:

"*K-K-K-Katy, beautiful Katy,*
You're the only g-g-g-girl that I adore;
When the m-m-m-moon shines,

Over the cowshed,
I'll be waiting at the k-k-k-kitchen door."

When Viktor had returned home late, tired and hungry, she'd expected him—in fact, he'd looked so exhausted, she wouldn't have blamed him—to be demanding and crabby. Instead, he'd asked, "Are we eating in the d-d-d-dining room or k-k-k-kitchen?"

Her heart had lifted at her husband's teasing. She'd placed a steaming plate of pork and sauerkraut before him on the dining room table. "I hope you l-l-l-like it," she'd said.

He'd grinned at her, that boyish grin that appeared infrequently, that look she wished she could capture and save for the bad times.

She knew Viktor waited for her in their bedroom now. The look he'd given her when he'd snuffed his pipe and risen from his chair, without draining the last drop of *horilka*, was unmistakable. Tonight, she was determined to go to him, less through obligation and more through the desire of a wife to please her husband.

Before extinguishing the flame in the lamp, Katerina wiped her hands on the damp dishtowel and hung it over the lip of the kitchen sink. She headed into the living room, all the while thinking about the day, an ordinary day absent harsh words and constant dread, a day in which she had glimpsed what life with Viktor, Aleksandr, and a baby might become. It had given them something to build on, a foundation on which to create a solid family.

Katerina bent down and added a shovelful of coal to the stove. When she stoked the fire, sparks burst like fireworks from the flame and swirled inside the firebox. The stove door creaked on its hinges as she closed it and secured the latch. She exhaled, realizing she'd been holding her breath against the pungency of the coal. If this pregnancy followed the pattern of her first, she should be feeling better soon. Bracing herself on the arm of Viktor's chair, she straightened, arched, and kneaded the small of her back. She brushed the loose strands of hair from her forehead and then ran her hands tenderly over her stomach, remembering the first time she'd felt the flutter of life inside her and wondering how long it would be before she would feel this baby's movement.

Viktor would be getting impatient. Katerina took one final look around the room. Everything seemed to be in order. She extinguished the lamp. Pale moonlight shone through the windows. Softly, she hummed a lullaby her mother had sung a long, long time ago, a melody she hadn't thought of since childhood but which had somehow come back to her as clearly as though she'd sung it yesterday. Perhaps it was the thought of her unborn child or the boy sleeping in the room above her that had brought the song to mind. For their sake, she would bury her apprehension under a thin layer of hope. She would swallow her fear, which festered like an ulcer in the pit of her stomach.

Looking up the length of the stairway to the top of the landing, she stopped humming and took a deep breath. Gripping the banister, she pulled herself up to the first step. She hesitated, then took another step. Tonight she resolved to go to Viktor with forgiveness in her heart.

Chapter Fourteen

This morning, Katerina was especially distracted. She'd promised to meet Alla Klopoushak at Yana's in the early afternoon to deliver her new dress, but the hem was still unfinished. Ordinarily, an hour or so would be plenty of time to hem a dress—she'd done it a hundred times before—but the work took concentration, and right now all she seemed to be able to focus on was keeping the contents of her stomach down.

Katerina had been rising at 5:00 a.m., so that her stomach had time to settle before she began making breakfast. The slightest odor—foul or pleasant—would set it to tumbling and lurching. She would consume some soda crackers or baking soda mixed into a glass of tepid water and wait for the discomfort to pass. Today, she'd already eaten four crackers and drunk a concoction of soda and water, which was finally taking effect. If Viktor noticed her changed routine, he said nothing. As long as a hot meal was on the table, he seemed indifferent to what she did beforehand or afterward.

Familiar sounds overhead meant that Viktor and Aleksandr were getting dressed and would be at the kitchen table soon. She did her best to compose herself by counting and humming, and when that proved insufficient, she offered a silent prayer: *Grant me strength, O Lord, to face this day with grace and love and to be thankful for the life that grows within me.*

Katerina pinched color into her cheeks.

By the time Viktor appeared, dressed and ready for work, she was up to feigning cheer.

"Good morning," she said.

"Morning."

"You slept well?" She set a steaming plate in front of him.

"Can't complain."

Usually, his disinterest in being civil disturbed her. This morning, she was grateful. She turned her back to him and busied herself at the sink.

Within a few minutes, Aleksandr joined his father at the table.

"Good morning," she said, smiling at him and ruffling his hair. Showing affection for Aleksandr, at least, was one thing she didn't have to pretend.

"Good morning." He returned her smile.

Katerina savored it. To her, every one of Aleksandr's smiles, large or small, was a gift because she understood how dear the cost. A child losing his mother, she knew, counts on no one to protect him, not even God. If the most precious person in the world can be taken away, seemingly on a whim, life becomes an exercise in caution and vigilance.

She set a plate before Aleksandr.

"You're not eating?" Viktor asked.

"I couldn't wait." Katerina said. "I was hungry when I got up and fixed a plate for myself." She was embarrassed by how adept she'd become at telling lies and half-truths. She was sure God wasn't too pleased by it either.

Viktor looked at her a moment longer than was comfortable.

"Suit yourself."

Aleksandr concentrated on his eggs while keeping a discreet eye on his father.

"I won't be home for lunch today," Viktor announced. "Too much to do."

"I'll pack one for you, then," Katerina said, trying not to sound relieved. She'd been worried about feeding Viktor lunch without hurrying him out the door or letting on that she had somewhere else to be. Now, she wouldn't have to worry about making it to Yana's on time.

It was only after Viktor left the table that Aleksandr's body visibly relaxed and only after his father left the house that he began to speak.

"May I go to Lavro's after school?" Aleksandr asked. "We want to work on our fort. Well, it's actually an airplane hangar."

"Only if I get to peek inside when it's finished," Katerina said.

"I promise. Cross my heart." He put his dishes in the sink and hurried to get his coat.Katerina followed, as she did every morning, to see him off to school.

"Do you have your lunch?"

Aleksandr nodded.

"Your books?"

"Uh-huh."

"Your homework?"

"Uh-huh."

"Your brain?"

"Yes," Aleksandr said, grinning.

"Then off with you." Katerina pulled his coat collar up and gave his hat brim a gentle tug. She watched as he stopped halfway down the walk, giving a final wave before hurrying off to school.

Yana was right; Aleksandr was a good boy. Little by little, he'd allowed Katerina to edge closer. It was a delicate dance, bridging that distance between grief and healing, wariness and trust. Winning him was like enticing a sparrow to eat out of her hand, each day standing perfectly still, offering an open palm of seed and then waiting, waiting, waiting, until one day, the bird alighted to partake of the gift. It was a fragile acceptance, one that could be destroyed with a moment's distraction, an abrupt move, or a harsh voice. She recalled the day of her arrival, when she'd learned Viktor had a son. She'd told Yana about her mother's passing when she was a child, and Yana had remarked, "Then you will understand Aleksandr." She'd been right about that, too. For him, Katerina had all the patience in the world. She'd tasted his pain, felt it still.

There had been a turning point; exactly what had triggered it, she couldn't say. Aleksandr had decided to let her love him. He'd held out for a long time, watching her, testing her, taking her measure. Reluctantly, he'd become the sunflower in this thistle patch of a life she'd fallen into. Was it only a half year ago she'd known nothing of his existence? In that short passage of time, it had become harder and harder to picture life without him. It occurred to her that Aneta must feel the same way about Matviyko—her sister and she both destined to love someone else's child. Perhaps one day she could forgive Aneta for loving her son so deeply.

If only his father could see that Aleksandr was a good son, instead of enumerating the never-ending list of his imagined shortcomings. Viktor expected too much and gave too little.

Katerina couldn't stop thinking about Aleksandr's claim that he hadn't known his mother was leaving for Winnipeg. At first, she'd brushed it aside, only to have it gnaw at her.

Elena was so elusive, it was as though she'd never existed. All signs of her had evaporated, and any trail leading to her had been swept clean of footprints. Even Yana, who usually conducted a running commentary on friends' and neighbors' lives, had been reluctant to share anything about Viktor's fist wife. Svetlana Sokur had said she had been Elena's friend. Something about the way she had said it had made it seem more warning than fact. If Katerina ever found an opportunity to speak with Svetlana alone, she'd ask her about Elena.

For now, she had only a vague sense of Aleksandr's mother. Still, it was difficult not to pass judgment on her. What mother leaves, on what was certainly to be an extended trip, without telling her child she is going? It was possible that Aleksandr was mistaken. He had been only eight years old—with an eight-year-old's penchant for skewed memory—when she'd left, but he was not a child given to exaggeration or to tale-telling. He hid behind silence, not falsehoods. A quiet, persistent whisper inside her head wouldn't allow her to let it go.

Katerina's stomach fluttered. She reached for a cracker in her apron pocket and nibbled on it. It wouldn't be long before her condition began to show and she'd need maternity dresses. Right now, that was the least of her worries. She had to talk with Viktor. She vowed to tell him about her condition that evening.

The clock struck nine. The last cracker hadn't settled her stomach completely, but she had to get busy hemming Alla Klopoushak's dress, so she decided to start working on it and hope for the best.

Katerina pulled the garment from the wardrobe, carefully removing one of her own dresses that she'd hung over the top to hide it from Viktor. She examined Alla's dress with a critical eye. Light shimmered off the forest-green satin de chine. Given the time constraints and the inclement weather, she'd had to settle for an average-grade material purchased from Wozny's Dry Goods. Of course, she would not confess this to Alla Klopoushak because the woman probably couldn't spot the difference. If she commissioned more work, Katerina would make a point of securing a finer grade from the dry goods store in Weyburn. She'd purchased the best local stock available and pressed the daylights out of the seams to get them to lie perfectly flat. The delicate embroidery had turned out beyond expectation. Yes, it would do.

Katerina ate another cracker. The carnival in her stomach settled. She eased into a parlor chair to hand stitch the hem of the dress.

To keep the hem from puckering, the trick was to barely catch the fabric with the needle and to keep the stitches uniform, making certain the exposed outer material stayed in exact alignment with the folded inner material. *This is one of the most important lessons*, she could hear Papa saying. *A perfect hem separates superior from average quality.* She wondered if he was still sewing perfect hems or whether his arthritic hands and failing eyesight had forced him to turn the work over to younger hands and eyes. Had fate been kinder, Katerina would have been that someone.

As she proceeded along the hemline, the satin material slid easily beneath her fingers. It was less tricky to keep heavier material, such as wool, from slipping out of position. She compensated for the slickness of the material by checking the alignment of fabric—inside to outside—after stitching each inch of hem, working methodically, knowing that her creation relied on precision in the finishing details.

The hem completed, Katerina warmed the sadiron on the kitchen stove and set up the ironing board for one final pressing. She eased the dress onto the ironing board and placed a clean dishtowel over the hem to protect the fabric from scorching. Lowering the iron onto the towel, she was careful to apply enough pressure to set the hem but not enough to damage the material. When finished, she held the dress up to the light and examined it. Even Papa would not be able to find fault with its construction, she decided.

Although Panko's house was on the same end of town as the grain elevator, it was unlikely that Viktor would see her when she delivered the dress, since he would be preoccupied at work. However, she couldn't be certain. Her hands, usually sure and steady, trembled as she folded the dress neatly inside a blanket and placed some of Aleksandr's outgrown clothing on top of it. If she encountered Viktor and he inquired as to what she was doing, she would explain she was taking Aleksandr's used clothing to Yana's for Luca to wear. Hopefully, that would satisfy him. If not—she couldn't allow herself to consider that possibility.

She returned the ironing board to the closet and checked the dining room to make certain everything was put away.

It was time to head to Yana's house and Alla's verdict.

"I don't know what to say. I'm at a loss for words," Alla Klopoushak said as she paraded around Yana's dining room, wearing her new dress and an ear-to-ear smile.

"Well, there's a first time for everything," Yana whispered out of Alla's earshot.

Katerina hoped Alla would mistake her grin for approval.

"It fits like a glove," Yana said. "Of course, you do something for it." She turned her back on Alla and winked at Katerina. "I'll go get us some tea."

Although Yana was her cordial, mischievous self, this time she hadn't made a special effort to dress for the occasion or to shunt Marina and Vera off to Fedir at the store. Apparently, she'd decided entertaining a pretentious woman didn't merit the effort.

Alla extended her leg behind her and twisted her neck to look down at the hem. "It's a bit shorter than I'm used to."

"The hemlines have come up this year; they're now fourteen to sixteen inches from the floor. I chose fourteen inches so you would feel fashionable yet comfortable," Katerina said, feeling fraudulent, knowing that her limited knowledge of the latest trends had come from Eaton's catalog. "Besides, you have nice legs, and I believe a woman should show off her best assets."

Alla straightened to her full height and strutted with the air of a queen. Katerina made a circling motion with her index finger, signaling Alla to do a complete turn. As she twirled, the satin de chine reflected light in all the right places. The V-cut of the neckline elongated her upper torso, and that, combined with the drop waist, minimized her substantial bosom. Katerina had embroidered the wide waistband with a spray of pink and pale-green flowers, which drew the eye away from her chest. The slightly flared skirt provided the illusion of balance between her top and bottom halves. Katerina would have been willing to bet that this was the best Alla Klopoushak had ever looked.

Yana returned with teacups rattling on a silver tray. "Best change out of that fancy dress," she said.

"Let me help you," Katerina said to Alla. "I'll hang the dress so you can get it home without a wrinkle."

She and Alla retired to Yana's bedroom. Katerina noticed Alla's critical, roaming eyes.

"I don't know how she does it. Such a large family in these small quarters. To each his own, I guess," Alla said.

Katerina wondered if Alla's cutting remarks had been provoked by jealousy about her own childlessness or whether she simply enjoyed being nasty. In either case, her criticism rankled.

"Granted it's a lively household," Katerina said, struggling to keep the frost from her voice, "though I'm sure you'd agree there's never been a better mother or a more generous woman than Yana."

"Oh yes. Certainly, you're right. One has to admire her. I just cannot imagine it for myself."

Although a bit of wind had gone out of Alla's sails, when they finished, she cruised into the dining room and assumed a place at the head of the table.

"I was telling Katerina about the event Mr. Klopoushak and I will be attending," Alla said.

"Your niece's wedding." Yana poured tea and offered Alla and Katerina honey biscuits. She gave one each to Marina and Vera, who were playing tea party with their dolls in the corner of the dining room.

"Well, it's not just a run-of-the-mill wedding. The ceremony will be at the Church of the Descent of the Holy Ghost, a rather large and beautiful church, I'm told." She looked at Katerina. "Oh, of course, I meant no offense to you and your modest wedding at St. Kassia's."

"None taken," Katerina said pleasantly.

"The groom's father is a judge, and of course, he associates with all the best people. He's a member of the Assiniboia Club, and let me tell you, it's for the elite. I mean, premiers, lieutenant governors, and mayors have been members of that club. The reception and dance will be held at the City Hall ballroom, no less. So you see, it's essential to have a special dress, and I daresay I have one." Alla pursed her lips and took a small sip of tea.

"Well, you have Katerina to thank for the good impression I'm sure you'll make," Yana said.

"Certainly."

Katerina smiled at her friend.

Alla took a bite of her biscuit. The room grew silent.

Marina, seemingly oblivious to the adults in the room, chattered away in the corner. "You can't eat *all* the biksits," she admonished her dolls. "You have to save some for the *other* children."

"That sounded familiar," Yana said, raising an eyebrow.

The women laughed.

"By the way, have you heard about the Sokur farm?" Alla asked.

Katerina's body tensed.

"Only that times are hard," Yana said.

"They certainly are." Alla placed her half-full teacup in its saucer and moved it aside. She leaned forward conspiratorially. "My husband has made a bid to purchase it. We'll know by the end of the month if the transaction is approved, although I have no doubt it will be."

"Where will they go?" Katerina asked. She thought of Svetlana, sitting at the table in her dirt-floor sod house with four hungry children to feed and a drunkard husband with one arm.

"Well, I'm sure I don't know. I do know they can't manage that farm," Alla said.

Yana pushed away from the table and began to clear the teacups and plates, signaling the afternoon chat was over.

"Oh my, look at the time," Alla said. "I'm sorry I have to cut our visit short. I have other business that needs my attention." She pulled an envelope from her fur muff and handed it to Katerina. "The amount we agreed upon."

"Thank you," Katerina said. "I'm glad you find the dress satisfactory."

"'I'll be in touch with you after the wedding. I'm certain I'll need your services again." Alla wrapped her fur-collared coat around her and grabbed her matching muff.

As soon as Alla was out the door, Yana turned to Katerina. "That woman has got a head the size of a barn and a mouth just as big. She'd do us all a favor if she closed her mouth after hello!" A vein throbbed in the middle of her forehead and her cheeks burned red.

Katerina had never seen her so agitated.

"That business about buying the Sokur farm," Yana continued. "Maybe with a little help from the likes of the Klopoushaks and they wouldn't be losing it."

"I don't know, Yana. You've seen the place. From what Jakob told us, this has been a long time coming. I'm worried about where they'll go and how they'll live. Their situation is desperate."

"I know you're right. It's a pity." Yana shook her head. "I feel sorry for Svetlana. She's a hard worker who's being punished for a poor choice of husband."

Katerina felt the sting of her comment, certain Yana had no idea how close to home she'd struck. There was much more Katerina wanted to know about Svetlana and was about to ask when Vera, holding her miniature teacup, toddled toward Yana's skirt and latched on.

"Mama, tea?"

"In a minute, little rabbit."

"It's time for me to go home, too," Katerina said. "With all this sewing, I've neglected the house."

"Mama?"

Yana bent to pick up Vera.

"As far as I'm concerned, you can have Alla Klopoushak everyday of the week, including Sunday," Yana said, as though she hadn't heard Katerina. "I'm just sorry I pushed her in your direction."

"I'm not," Katerina said, dangling the envelope of money in front of her. "I'm not one bit sorry."

As he trudged home from work in the dark—collar turned up, hands in pockets, favoring his ankle, and thinking about his conversation with Roman Klopoushak—Viktor seethed. Since that arrogant sod had left the elevator at 3 p.m., his anger had been simmering. He'd be damned if he would make the same mistake twice. If Katerina thought he'd stand for replacing one deceitful woman with another, she was a bigger fool than he thought. If she believed he'd underestimate the power of a conniving woman again, she was dead wrong.

While lights glowed in the living quarters above some Main Street businesses, at street level, Bilik had already been put to bed. Overhead, Viktor heard the metal-on-metal screech of the sign hanging from Dr. Billings' office as it swung on its hinges. Preoccupied, he looked up as he passed under it, vaguely aware of the sound. Tonight, the town was backdrop to his thoughts. He had to nip Katerina's deceitfulness in the bud. The only question was how to go about it.

He felt something attach itself to the backs of his legs. The wind, blowing behind him from the west, had plastered a single newspaper page against his body. Irritably, he reached for it and flung it to the ground. As soon as he let go, the page caught the wind and somersaulted down the middle of the street like tumbleweed until it disappeared into the darkness.

He jammed his hands deeper into his into jacket pockets.

Should he confront Katerina right away, catch her off guard before she had a chance to concoct a story? Or should he bide his time? He had the upper hand, and he intended to keep it. There were advantages and disadvantages to both approaches. Either way, he'd outwit her. He decided to bide his time and let her hang herself.

Viktor opened the door and stepped into the house. Much about it felt the same as it had this morning when he'd left for work. The house was warm and the enticing smell of roasting meat greeted him in the entryway. As he'd expected, all evidence of her sewing project had been removed from the dining room table. It occurred to him that she cleared the table each day not out of respect for his wishes, but to keep secrets from him. The empty surface of the table mocked him.

Katerina was in the kitchen singing "K-K-K-Katy." Its high-spirited melody stoked his anger. She seemed to be celebrating her deception, taunting him with her good cheer.

Viktor stood in the kitchen doorway.

Aleksandr sat bent over a book, one elbow resting on the table, head in hand, concentrating. His son looked up at him with that whipped-puppy look he so despised and then looked down quickly, pretending to go back to his schoolwork. The boy could cower without moving a muscle.

Did everyone in the household—Elena included—take him for an imbecile who couldn't see what they did or how they conspired against him?

Katerina, still singing, stood at the sink with her back to him.

He took a critical inventory, moving from her legs to her back to the top of her head. He waited. Out of the corner of his eye, he saw the boy, head bowed and perfectly still, watching him.

"What did you do today?" Viktor asked.

As she jumped, her hand flew to her chest. She turned to face him. "You startled me!" she said. She dried her hands on her apron. "I was just thinking how much fun we had the other day playing three in the well together. It was a lovely afternoon. We should do that more often."

He wanted to slap the smile off her face. As if she could believe that an afternoon of playing games made up for her deceit!

"I asked you a question."

Her forehead creased.

"What did you do today?"

"Oh, I—I—"

Viktor watched her inventing a lie. So this was the hand she intended to play.

"I sewed for a while and then went to Yana's in the afternoon for tea."

"Is that all?"

Katerina looked nervous now. "Then I came home to start dinner."

"You're a goddamned liar," he said, his voice ice and his eyes steel.

"Viktor!" she gasped, nodding toward Aleksandr.

What did he care if the boy heard them?

"I didn't go anywhere else. I swear." Her eyes welled with tears.

"Roman Klopoushak was at the elevator today, killing time until *his* wife finished buying a dress from *my* wife."

Katerina blinked and bit her lower lip. She stood as still as death.

"Said she hired you a couple of weeks ago." Viktor's tone was as abrasive as sandpaper. "You've been lying to me for weeks."

"I didn't lie to you."

"Are you trying to make a fool of me?"

"Viktor, I—"

"The man tells me his wife has a business arrangement with you, and I know nothing about it." Viktor's jaw tensed and his fists clenched.

Aleksandr ran from the room. Katerina took a step, as if to follow him. Viktor moved toward her and she backed up against the sink.

"I buy an expensive sewing machine for you, and this is how you repay me?" Veins pulsed at his temples.

"I'm a seamstress," Katerina said, her voice quavering. "In L'viv, that was how I made my living, by sewing for hire."

He stepped closer and pinned her against the sink, creating a barricade with his long arms, his face inches from hers. "Do you think I give a damn about what you did in L'viv?"

"I'm just trying—"

"I pay for the food you eat and the roof over your head."

"I can help."

"Not if you don't have a damned machine!" he shouted. "Not if I make kindling out of that son of a bitch." Viktor turned abruptly and headed toward the dining room.

Katerina limped after him and grabbed his sleeve. He turned and pushed her. She fell to her knees.

"Viktor, please! Don't do this! Please!" Katerina begged. Tears streamed down her cheeks.

"You went behind my back."

"I didn't mean to."

"Ungrateful cripple. Expect me to trust you?"

"I'm sorry." She closed her eyes, still clinging to his sleeve. "Viktor, please. I'm sorry."

He looked down at her. She was a dog cowering before her master, a sinner pleading before her god. Viktor stopped, dropped his hands, and let his arms dangle at his sides. Katerina clung to him. A notion the size of a mustard seed grew into a thought and blossomed into an idea.

"Hand over the money," he said.

"I—"

"Give me the money."

"Viktor—"

"I know you've hidden it."

Katerina's tears flowed and her nose ran.

"Now."

Roughly, he pulled her to her feet. She teetered, trying to gain her balance, and limped to the sewing machine, which was pushed against the dining room wall. She looked smaller, diminished, defeated. Viktor followed her. She opened the top drawer and retrieved a white envelope with Katerina written on the front of it in Alla Klopoushak's looping hand. She handed it to him.

"If—*if* I let you keep the machine," he said, "things will be different." His voice was level now, fury replaced by calculation. "I will know who you are sewing for and why, and I will keep the money and pay the expenses." Viktor gripped her jaw and lifted her chin until she was forced to look at him. "And you will never lie to me again."

In Katerina's worst moments, night had never felt so dark nor home so far away. She lay in bed next to Viktor, he sleeping soundly and breathing heavily, she wide awake and staring at the wall, crying silently. Under the blankets, Viktor's body radiated heat. How could such a cold man give off such warmth?

Clearly, his aim was no longer mere intimidation; it was raw fear. Tonight, after bringing her to her knees, he'd sat at the table eating calmly, as though the trouble—once settled to his satisfaction—never existed. For him, the moon and stars were again aligned. Katerina had wanted to run and hide or, at the very least, retire to a place where she could cry alone and salve her wounds, but he had required her to sit at the table and take supper with him. They'd sat in silence. She'd pretended to eat, moving the food from one side of the plate to the other, never once looking at him. He seemed not to notice, or if he noticed, not to care. Apparently, it was enough to have the conquered submit to the conqueror.

He hadn't required Aleksandr to return to the table, a small mercy. At that moment, she felt that she couldn't have borne the immense fear and defeat for both of them. A muscle in her left eye twitched spasmodically. The time would surely come when she would have to bear the pain for herself, Aleksandr, and the child inside her. She couldn't fathom where she would get the strength.

Viktor had picked a battle over her failure to tell him she was sewing for hire. If he only knew, she thought bitterly, that he'd chosen to go to war over the smallest of her transgressions. The enmity he'd displayed over so minor an offense had knocked the wind out of her. What degree of malice would he be capable of if he discovered the worst of her sins? The thought chilled her.

Despondency threatened to devour her. She'd pledged herself to this man before God, forever. By her actions, she'd made this unholy marriage bed, and now she must lie in it. Despair threatened to build a permanent home in her heart. The room spun, giving Katerina the sensation of falling down a funnel toward a deep, black hole where there was no one to rescue her before she disappeared into the abyss. Sliding, sliding, sliding, she reached and flailed, her mind searching for someone or something to hold on to. Finally, she latched on to the only thing she could grasp—her memories.

She became eight years old again. Happy. It was after dinner. Papa sat in the rocking chair by the fire, smoking his pipe. *Come, kishka, it's time for a story.* She climbed onto his lap and leaned against his shoulder. *Papa, tell "The Wolf and the Seven Young Kids." Please, Papa.* His voice, more melodious than the sweetest music and more soothing than any balm, filled her head. Papa puffed his chest and narrowed his eyes, until his bushy brows almost touched his cheeks, and in his deepest voice, he transformed himself into the sinister wolf. Katerina pretended to cower in fear—this was a time when fear was still make-believe—suppressing laughter all the while. Then came the part she loved best: Papa imitated the mother goat, his voice reaching for soprano where none existed.

My kiddies own, my children dear,
Open the door, for your mother is here.
Open the door and you'll each have a treat,
For I bring you milk which is rich and sweet.

She could no longer suppress her giggles. *Again, Papa. Please, again! Tell the part where the fox fools the wolf.* He hesitated. Her anticipation tasted delicious. *Very well.* His eyes sparkled mischievously. She had known what was coming. The predictability delighted her. *And as for the kids, they remained alive and well. The end.* She laughed hard, barely able to get her words out. *Papa, you forgot the whole story!* He scratched his chin and feigned surprise. *Did I, kishka? Maybe you should tell it.* His smile swallowed her whole.

After Mama died, her father had never told that folktale again.

Katerina's childhood had been a peculiar mélange of security and neglect. She'd never been an indulged child, but she'd never wanted for any material thing either. Her family's quarters above the tailor shop, where her father still lived, had been cocoon like in its protection from the outside world; at least, that was the way Papa had made it seem. The bond between her father and her mother had been something a child could bask in. After Mama had died, her father, a passionate man, had been left with half a heart, and she and Aneta had been left with half a father and no mother. Never again had Katerina's father found it within himself to fully open his heart. Papa had worked and he had taught his daughters his trade, but the music and poetry had gone out of his life and his children's lives. Katerina had learned then that it was possible to love someone too much, to love that person to the exclusion of all others, even to the exclusion of children who longed for your love.

Now, Katerina carefully turned her head on the pillow and brushed a strand of hair away from her eyes. She watched a hint of moonlight kiss the windowsill, suggesting a break in the cloud-thick sky. She imagined drifting like the clouds, floating above it all, disappearing under the cover of night. Here today, gone tomorrow. There was nowhere to go, and even if there had been, she had Aleksandr and an unnamed baby to consider.

She thought about Aleksandr—shy, reticent, and defenseless. Yet he'd been the only one brave and honest enough to ask about her leg. She'd told him the truth, that she'd impulsively run into the street when she'd overheard her father telling the doctor it was best for her mother to die.

She closed her eyes and melted into a memory as fresh as yesterday.

She was nine years old. It was just before dusk or maybe midnight; Katerina couldn't tell because all the drapes in the apartment had been drawn, casting the rooms in timeless gloom. The house smelled of stale breath laced with a hint of decay. Aunt Sofia and Uncle Martyn and the Zelinskis, Mama and Papa's closest friends, were gathered in the parlor, whispering. Mama was dying. Katerina wandered among them, feeling as small as a forest creature among towering oaks. Her big sister, Aneta, sat in the corner dabbing her tears with one of Mama's embroidered handkerchiefs. That worried Katerina more than anything, because Aneta never cried. Father Sliva appeared—a strange sight, standing in her house instead of in church dressed in his vestments.

Aunt Sofia, her eyes red-rimmed, took her by the hand and led her into her parents' bedroom. Mama lay in bed, her face as white as an Easter lily, her eyes closed, and her head propped up on thick pillows. Papa knelt at Mama's bedside, holding her hand, his lips pressed to her palm. He didn't seem to notice anyone else in the room, especially his nine-year-old daughter, who had come to touch her mother one last time.

At Aunt Sofia's urging, Katerina stepped closer to the bed and stood next to Papa. Her mother's lips appeared dry, with white crust collected in the corners of her open mouth. Katerina listened to Mama's breathing. Each time she inhaled, something rattled at the back of her throat. *Don't go, Mama. Get better. Take care of me.* Katerina didn't know if she said those words or merely thought them. *Say good-bye,* Aunt Sofia said. *Good-bye, Mama.* The sorrow in her voice was solid, thick. Katerina was led from the room and back to the parlor.

Everyone ignored her. She was free to wander at the fringe, watching and listening. She sidled to the doorway. In the hall, her father spoke with the doctor. Most of what they said, she didn't understand. Then her father said, "I can't endure much more of this. It's time for her to die."

Katerina couldn't believe her ears. *Time for her to die!* How could he be so cruel? Didn't he know she needed a mother? How could he be so selfish? She refused to listen anymore. She refused to stay in a place where the air smelled foul and death clung to everything. She had to get out.

Katerina ran down the creaky stairway that led to Papa's tailor shop. The shop was dark. No matter. As she navigated the narrow aisles, her hands touched the bolts of woolens and silks like a blind woman feeling her way down a familiar alley. Out of habit, she fled to Mrs. Adamenko, the kind widow who lived across the street above the bakery. When Katerina opened the shop door and ran into the street, the rain poured down on her head. She blinked rapidly to see more clearly. Although the world blurred, she saw a light in Mrs. Adamenko's window. She ran. Slick cobblestones slipped beneath her feet. She stumbled. The last thing she remembered was jolting pain as the heavy wagon wheel cracked the bones in her leg.

Even now, Katerina winced at the remembered pain. But the harshest pain wasn't physical. She now understood that her father hadn't been protecting himself; he'd been protecting his wife. What he couldn't endure was not his suffering but hers. It had been time for Mama to die because she'd endured too much already. Letting his beloved go was the greatest act of love possible. The accident that had ruined Katerina's leg had been born of ignorance. The biggest wound of all was that Papa had never forgiven her for making him leave his wife's bedside to pay attention to a foolish child who'd impulsively run into the street. Her guilt was a private anguish that she hadn't admitted to Aleksandr or to anyone. Katerina had paid a heavy and permanent price for her naïveté.

Viktor rolled toward her. The mattress shifted and every muscle in Katerina's body tensed. His elbow poked the middle of her back. She considered getting out of bed and going downstairs but was afraid that if Viktor discovered she was missing, he'd be angry, and she didn't have the energy to endure another tirade. Instead, she slid to the edge of the bed, so far that her knees cantilevered over the side. Although she'd opened only a couple of inches between them, the chasm was as wide as a mountain gorge. Refusing to let him touch her as he slept was a tepid act of defiance.

When they'd first met, Katerina had thought Viktor was like her father—intelligent, strong-minded, difficult, and distant. Because she'd lived with that potent mix of admirable and disaffecting qualities, she'd made the mistake of believing that she knew her husband. In Viktor, those attributes appeared in a different guise.

From the first, he'd been difficult. Lately, however, there'd been signs that with the guidance of a patient and understanding woman, he could become the husband she'd hoped for. When he'd surprised her with the sewing machine for no discernible reason, she'd been touched by his generosity. She couldn't have imagined a more perfect gift. And he'd been softening toward Aleksandr, too. At Winter Fair, he'd been proud of his son for his skill on the ice. *You looked pretty fast out there.* Aleksandr's face had lit like a Christmas candle. On the afternoon of the big snowstorm, when they'd gathered in the parlor to play a game, they had been, for that moment, the family she'd imagined.

Tonight, she'd planned to tell Viktor she carried his child. She'd made his favorite dinner, spareribs and torte with custard filling and extra walnuts. She'd wanted her words to be exactly right. She'd rehearsed them again and again. *Viktor, I have joyous news. We've been blessed by God. I'm with child. Yes, I've suspected for awhile. I wanted to make certain. With this child, we are a family bound by blood.* Instead, she lay next to him, staring at the wall, her perfect words crumpled into a heap.

Katerina had been trying hard to make things right. It had been almost a week since she'd last thought of Stepan. Until tonight, she'd taken it as a sign. She'd thought that maybe it was possible to move forward into a life with Viktor, free from intrusion by her former lover. She could not forget him, yet maybe she could stop using Stepan as the yardstick against which she measured her husband. Maybe it was possible to let him go.

Instead, memories of Stepan flooded her thoughts. Tonight, she'd looked into Viktor's hard, dark eyes filled with judgment and fury and longed to look into Stepan's tender, intelligent eyes filled with mystery and passion. She'd been lost in those eyes once, uplifted and transported beyond herself. Even after he'd vanished, leaving her alone and pregnant, she couldn't picture betrayal in them.

When outsiders looked at Viktor, they saw an intelligent, capable, and respected man. She watched how they deferred to him, how they relied on his strength in times of crisis. Not even Yana or Fedir knew the private man. They loved Aleksandr, had all but adopted him since his mother had died. Any distance they witnessed between father and son they'd assigned to grief and the difficulty of a man raising a young boy alone. Katerina knew better.

Tonight, after he'd finished eating, Viktor had pushed back from the table, and without a word, retired to the parlor for his evening smoke and drink. He'd imbibed more than usual. She'd trodden lightly, avoiding him so that she wasn't in his drunken path. She'd cleared and washed the dishes and then taken a plate upstairs to Aleksandr.

She'd knocked on his bedroom door. Aleksandr hadn't answered but she'd entered anyway. He'd lain on his bed, face down, saying nothing when she'd spoken to him. He had been the living picture of despair: alone and heartbroken. She'd bent down and stroked his hair. "I've brought you some supper," she'd said. He hadn't moved. Although she'd known he needed it, deserved it, tonight she had no comfort to give. She'd turned and walked away.

As she lay on her side, Katerina slid her hand along her stomach. Where there had been hope, there was misery. Sadness coursed through her fingers and spread to her limbs. How could she bring a child into this loveless home? How would she ever bear watching her own child, the fruit of her womb, lying on a bed face down, heart broken to pieces by a father who created a world littered with land mines? How could she give birth to a child she could not protect? Her pregnancy, no longer the glue that would make them a family, had become a curse. God help her; she wished this child had never been conceived.

By the time Viktor had come to bed, Katerina had been already there, her back to him, pretending to sleep. Undeterred, he had grabbed her shoulder and turned her, reaching under her nightgown to her breasts and between her legs. She'd gasped when he'd fondled her tender breasts. It had excited him, as though he thought her sounds signaled pleasure and encouragement rather than pain and revulsion. She hadn't resisted when he'd climbed on top of her, hadn't protested when he'd moved and thrust against her pregnant belly, and hadn't gotten up to wash the evidence of his lust away. When he'd finally rolled off her and fallen asleep, she had been numb and grateful.

Katerina thought about Svetlana Sokur, a woman who wore her life on her careworn face, a woman whom she'd had the arrogance to pity. It occurred to her that the only difference between them was four children, a sod house, and an amputated arm. *Punished for a poor choice of husband.* Yana's words stung. She and Svetlana were both bound to unholy men.

On her most recent visit to the Sokur farm, she'd seen the look of desperation and defeat on Svetlana's face, the same desperation and defeat she now harbored. Was that what she'd been reduced to, a person for other women to pity? Svetlana's whispered confidences disturbed her. *I thought* I'd *be helping you.* At the time, those words had confused Katerina. Svetlana Sokur hadn't appeared to be in a position to help herself, let alone anyone else. She'd said the words despite her inferior education and lesser economic circumstances.

Viktor shifted his weight, pulling the covers toward him. He mumbled. Katerina held her breath and listened intently, hoping he wasn't speaking to her. Slowly, his garbled syllables trailed off into a loud snore. She exhaled.

Svetlana had met Katerina's eyes and then looked around furtively, making certain no one was within earshot. *I knew Elena.* During the months she'd been in Bilik, Svetlana had been the only person who'd dared to volunteer that. Everyone else, including Yana, had been content to pretend she'd never existed. Katerina's heart raced. When she'd said it, Katerina had assumed at first that Svetlana simply meant they'd been friends. *And...I know Viktor.* Gooseflesh crept along Katerina's arms. She tightened the blanket around her. *And I know a frightened woman when I see her.* Svetlana understood the kind of man Viktor Senyk was, saw beneath his public mask. She must find a way to talk with Svetlana Sokur alone.

The tinder-dry winter air evaporated Katerina's tears, leaving her head stuffed and making breathing difficult. Gently, she eased herself to her right elbow and doubled her pillow with the opposite hand. The sky beyond the window hinted at daybreak. Although she couldn't be sure, she thought the hands on the bedside clock pointed to quarter past four. She'd been in bed, awake, for almost six hours. Slowly, she sank back down onto the mattress, lying motionless, listening and waiting. Viktor didn't stir. Her body relaxed a little. Still, she couldn't sleep.

Aleksandr had told her his mother hadn't said good-bye before she'd left. When he'd confided that, Katerina hadn't been able to fathom why he'd said it. Not that she thought Aleksandr was lying, but it made no sense. Maybe other unshared memories of his mother would provide clues to this puzzle, but it might be unwise to probe for information. He'd barely trusted her before, and tonight she'd given him ample reason to believe he could never rely on her again.

Other details bothered Katerina. Viktor had erased Elena so completely that there was no evidence she'd ever existed. He'd barely spoken her name. At first, Katerina had believed Viktor was trying to start fresh, making it easier on his new bride by wiping the slate clean. Now, that idea seemed laughable. Katerina remembered she'd heard him say Elena's name just once, the day they'd taken their first ride to Weyburn together. She'd been surprised when, unannounced, they'd pulled up to the huge mental hospital. *Elena's brother is a patient. I promised to look after him.* Inexplicably, he had stormed out of the hospital, upset, but had refused to say why. To her knowledge, Viktor had never gone back to see Elena's brother. Besides, she doubted he'd ever voluntarily looked after anyone in his life. Now, Katerina questioned if Elena even had a brother.

Svetlana Sokur's words also pestered her like an itch in the middle of her back. *I knew Elena. And…I know Viktor. And I know a frightened woman when I see her.* Terrifying possibilities seeped into Katerina's mind. Had Viktor made up this brother? Had he actually had Elena committed to the mental hospital? Worse, had he killed her? Was Viktor capable of such vileness? The ideas were preposterous. She tried not to think them, but she couldn't help herself. *This is madness. You're frightened and not thinking clearly. Stop!*

Katerina had no idea what Viktor was actually capable of, although she knew he had a wide mean streak and the strength to be dangerous. In some part of her mind, she'd known it all along. Her pulse raced. She began to spin and slide toward the black hole again. She clawed, scratched, grabbed, and held on to the memory of the woman who had been strong enough to leave her family and travel alone across continents and oceans to claim a new life. She'd have to keep her wits about her and be careful. She must play her part, be the wife Viktor expected, no matter how frightened she might be now—not just for her sake but for Aleksandr's sake and the sake of the new life she carried.

First light shone through the window. As it approached Bilik, the 5:30 a.m. train bound for Edmonton blasted its whistle. Viktor would be getting up within the hour. She'd have to face him then, pretending all was well.

Viktor had accused her of deceit. Although she'd denied it for fear of what he might do, she *had* deceived him. Why? Viktor was right. He had fed her and put a roof over her head. He'd given her the means to clothe herself. She wanted for nothing material. So why did she feel the urgent need to do paid work?

Income promised salvation. Until this moment, she hadn't admitted that truth. She wanted her own money. She planned to accumulate it. She intended to hide it. That was the truth.

Chapter Fifteen

At the long table in the back of the classroom, Aleksandr, preoccupied, sat next to Lavro as they ate lunch.

"You want to trade an egg for half your dessert?" Lavro asked and wiggled his eyebrows.

Usually, Lavro's antics made him laugh, but he'd been glum all morning. He handed Lavro the slice of torte.

"I didn't mean all of it," Lavro said, although he didn't give it back. "What do you think I am, a pig?" He made a snorting noise, which made Sy and Max, sitting across from them, laugh.

Aleksandr accepted the hard-boiled egg and set it aside. Most days, he wouldn't have made such a lopsided trade, but today he didn't have any appetite. He tried not to think about the horrible scene at his house last night, but he couldn't help it. Gloomy thoughts seeped into his brain, no matter how hard Lavro tried to make him laugh or how hard Aleksandr tried to concentrate on other things.

He'd fled to his room like a frightened mouse, trying to escape his father's anger, but it hadn't worked. When his father got mean, dangerously angry, his temper was a volcano spewing scalding words in all directions, scorching everyone in its path. There was no escape. When his real mother had been alive, his father had been like that often; but with his new mother, he'd been nice, even bought her gifts sometimes. It had given Aleksandr hope that his father had changed, but just when everything had seemed good, he'd exploded like a stick of dynamite.

His father had a certain look and a calm way of speaking that sneaked up on you, trapped you when you didn't expect it. His new mother had gotten caught in that snare. When his father had come home from work yesterday evening, he'd stood in the kitchen doorway, looking at her and waiting. Aleksandr had been able to tell by the dark clouds gathering in his eyes that a storm was brewing. *What did you do today? Is that all? You're a goddamned liar!* That had been how quickly his new mother had gone from thinking his father was actually interested in how she spent her day to being struck by lightning. She hadn't seen it coming but Aleksandr had. He knew that tone and look. He'd recognized the trap the moment it had been set.

In math class that morning, when Mr. Marko had called on him, Aleksandr hadn't known the answer to the problem. He hadn't even heard the question. Instead, he'd been remembering how his father's anger had ruined everything, and how, after he'd run from the table, even with his head buried under his pillow, he'd heard yelling and crying downstairs. It had been a really easy multiplication problem, too—11 x 9. He had known that answer when he was in third grade. Now, he had to write the dumb equation ten times. Because Aleksandr was excellent at arithmetic, he was certain Mr. Marko knew it was simple for him; but the teacher always told the class he had to treat everyone equally, so Aleksandr would be copying it ten times.

That was the least of his problems.

Instead of standing up to his father or defending his new mother—who was very nice to him—he'd buried his head in his book when his father had called her "a goddamned liar." His father had shot him one of his hateful warning looks—his eyes became slits and his nostrils flared like a horse's. He'd wanted to yell at him, *I wish* you *were the one who drowned!* But he'd kept quiet. Worse, he'd run. If only he'd had the courage to do something, anything. Nothing was lower than being a coward. Everybody knew that. Although Aleksandr told himself nothing he could have done would have made any difference, shame flowed through him. Why couldn't he be brave like Yuri Sokur? Why did he have to be such a mouse?

"Well, are you in or not?" Max whispered.

"What?"

Lavro leaned in really close. He had crumbs at the corner of his mouth and on the front of his sweater. "Are you going to sneak into the horse barn with us or not?"

"We're not allowed," Aleksandr said. "Only the kids who ride to school and have to feed their horses are allowed in there."

"Everybody knows that," Sy said.

"C'mon, don't be such a chicken," Max said.

Aleksandr clenched his jaw and balled his hands into fists. "Don't call me that."

"Aw, he didn't mean anything by it, Aleksandr. We just want you to come along, is all," Lavro said.

Aleksandr wasn't going to let Max call him chicken.

After they finished eating, the four boys hurried to the cloakroom, which ran the length of the upper grades' classroom, to put on their coats, boots, caps, and mittens. It was Max's idea to take their hockey sticks along as decoys, so it would look as though they were headed to the dugout to skate.

"You're the lookout," Max declared, giving Aleksandr's shoulder a nudge. "You're the smallest and least likely to be noticed."

Max, the son of the town's blacksmith, had inherited his father's stocky build and strong hands. He'd gotten his bossiness from his mother—at least, that's what Aleksandr had heard grownups say. *We know who wears the pants in that family.* The combination made Max the toughest boy Aleksandr knew, other than Yuri Sokur, but Yuri wasn't at school anymore. Although Aleksandr hated being bossed around, nobody challenged Max. Besides, Aleksandr *was* the smallest, so it was hard to argue with his friend's logic.

"Okay," Aleksandr said, "but if you get caught before you get to the barn, you don't get to tell on me."

"Deal," Max said. He spit on his hand and offered it to Aleksandr, who spit on his hand, too.

Once outside, Aleksandr posted himself at the south corner of the building. The schoolyard was full of activity—girls playing tag, boys playing hockey. Some of the younger kids were having piggyback races. Miss Janko, the primary grades teacher, who was bundled up as though she were going to the North Pole, stood in the middle of the activity, supervising. She was bent over, her back turned to the building, temporarily distracted by two little girls, who were pointing in the direction of some boys. Older kids could be intimidating, but little kids were the worst because they were such tattletales. Aleksandr would have to keep a keen eye out for them. From the looks of things, nobody paid attention to the expanse between the school and the stable. He waved his arms, giving the coast-is-clear signal. Lavro, Sy, and Max skitter-hopped toward the barn, undetected.

Aleksandr made sure the teacher's back was still turned before he raced across the yard, looking over his shoulder every few strides, until he caught up with his friends. They opened the barn door a crack and slid inside. Feeding time was over, so except for the horses, the barn was unoccupied. To make certain they hadn't been followed, Aleksandr took one last peek outside and then closed the door.

He squinted into the dim light, which shone through dirt-streaked windows. Oat barrels flanked the doors, feedbags were draped over hooks next to each stall, and pitchforks and shovels hung along one of the walls. The aroma of hay and horseflesh lingered in the air. Although the barn provided shelter from the wind, the interior was still frosty cold.

Lavro pointed to Bogy Korol's chestnut gelding, Roper. The grin that broke out on Lavro's face was more contagious than measles, traveling first to Max and then Sy and then Aleksandr.

"My dad says that horse is slower than an old man on crutches," Max whispered.

For as long as he could remember, Aleksandr had seen the horse dawdling its way to school, and he couldn't recall a time when the animal had been speedier. Everybody joked that Roper should ride Bogy to school; they'd get there faster. Roper's big brown eyes blinked, and his ears twitched when the stall gate opened. As the boys sidled along the wall to the back of the stall, Roper sidestepped courteously.

Sy stepped into a fresh pile of horse manure. "Oh, gopher guts!" he yelled.

"Shut up!" Max said, his voice muted but commanding.

"I stepped in a pile," Sy complained.

Sweet stink filled the stall. Aleksandr, Lavro, and Max held their sides and their noses as they bent over, laughing.

"It won't be so funny if you step in it," Sy grumbled, giving Lavro a push.

Shoving Lavro was like trying to move a building. Sy keeled over backward, and his other foot landed in the steaming pile. The boys laughed harder.

"If my father sees these, he's going to have my hide!" Sy said.

Sy was the banker's son. Everyone knew he could afford a new pair of shoes, and everyone knew his father spoiled him.

"Aw, you can clean 'em in the snow," Max said. "He'll never know the difference." Max hiked his foot to the wooden crosspiece on the stall's half wall, grabbed Roper's mane, and hoisted himself onto the horse before pivoting, so he faced Roper's rear end.

The others crowded into the back of the stall.

Max reached down and grabbed Roper's stringy tail, lifting it over the horse's back. Intestinal gas leaked from Roper's hind end.

"*Peeww!*" Lavro said, holding his nose. "Equine gas."

"Let's see what happens when we light a little flame under him," Max said. He dug into his pocket and threw a small matchbox down to Sy.

"How come you have those?" Lavro asked, sounding skeptical.

"For smokin'." This time, Max's voice was louder, as though he'd forgotten they needed to be quiet.

Aleksandr didn't mention he carried matches in his pocket, too, as secret insurance against the dark in case the lantern blew out when he had to go into the coal cellar.

Lavro gave him a maybe-this-isn't-such-a-good-idea look but said nothing.

Sy struck a match and held it under Roper's lifted tail. The flame was small but burned brilliantly. As the heat inched toward Sy's fingers, he shook his wrist to extinguish the fire. After the flame went out on the tip of the match, blue, yellow, and pink fire fluttered in the air before disappearing. Sy lit another match and held it a little closer to the horse's bottom. The flame burned again, this time a little bigger, a little brighter, and a little longer. Roper nervously shifted his hind legs.

The game made Aleksandr nervous, too. He didn't want to be accused of being chicken, but he didn't want to hurt the horse or burn the barn down either. Should he say something or keep his mouth closed? Before he could decide, the bell in the schoolyard clanged loudly.

"Horseflies!" Lavro said. "We'd better hurry up or we're going to be late."

Sy dropped the match. Max slid off Roper's back, landing with a thud. The three boys dashed toward the barn door. Aleksandr bent down, scrabbling to pick up the burned matchsticks.

"Hurry up! We'll get caught!" Lavro said.

"I'm coming!" Aleksandr hastily pushed straw around with his foot, kicked dirt up to dust the straw with the toe of his boot, and stomped for good measure.

The three boys made a beeline toward the school. Aleksandr caught up and easily passed them. By the time they got inside, they were panting, but they'd made it. The classroom door closed behind them.

When he slid into his desk chair, Aleksandr realized they'd been in such a hurry they'd left their hockey sticks leaning against Roper's stall. His heart sank. Compared with the others, he stood to lose the most. If Lavro's father found out, Mr. Panko would probably make Lavro sweep the store for a week and then ask if he'd learned his lesson. Sy's father would probably buy him one less toy and warn him not to do it again. Max's father was so used to his son getting into mischief, he might just pat him on the back, relieved they hadn't burned down the barn. But if Aleksandr's father found out, *trouble* wouldn't begin to describe what would await him. No doubt whatever punishment he faced would be swift and brutal. Why had he gone along with that stupid idea? Nothing was going right.

Mr. Marko strolled down the middle aisle between the desks. "In 1608, Samuel de Champlain allied himself with the Algonquians and the Huron," he said.

Aleksandr tried to pay attention. It was embarrassing to get called on and not know the answer. Once today was enough. Still, it was hard to concentrate on the seventeenth century when he had so much on his mind. This morning, all he had been able to think about was his father's angry blowup at home; now, all he could think about was his father's rage if he found out about the barn. Aleksandr pictured his hockey stick, with his name carved in the handle, sitting against the stall like a gigantic sign advertising his guilt. This day might not be his worst ever, but it sure was near the top of the list.

As Mr. Marko made his way toward the back of the room, Aleksandr and the other students in the front half turned to face him.

"And in 1608," the teacher said, "Quebec City was established as a fur trading post by Champlain and the French colonists, creating the first permanent European settlement in Canada."

There was a disturbance in the far corner of the room, which distracted Mr. Marko. Students sitting near Sy held their noses or buried their faces in arms that lay crossed on the tops of their desks.

The teacher headed toward him. "What in the world—" When

he came within several feet of Sy, Mr. Marko crinkled his nose and turned his head away from the overpowering smell.

"Sy, I believe you have something foul on your shoes," Mr. Marko said.

Sy looked around sheepishly. "Yes, sir."

Though he wasn't sitting near the offending shoes, Aleksandr held his breath. He felt his heart beating faster. Adults were always saying it was best if you told the truth right away, although that wasn't accurate where his father was concerned. Maybe he should confess now. Maybe he should just tell Mr. Marko he had gone to the horse barn, where he had no business being, and take his punishment; but he couldn't move. If he confessed, his teacher would ask questions. *Were you by yourself? Who put you up to it?* Then, he'd be forced to choose between lying and telling on his friends. No. He would keep quiet. Certain his teacher could smell trouble, as well as Sy's shoes, Aleksandr waited to be found out.

"For now, Sy, put your shoes outside, next to the front door," the teacher said, backing away.

"Yes, sir."

As Sy slunk out of the classroom, giggles erupted.

"Enough nonsense. Let's get back to Samuel de Champlain," Mr. Marko said, walking quickly to his desk at the front of the class.

Aleksandr's heartbeat slowed. Now, he just had to figure out how to retrieve his hockey stick, and he'd never, ever sneak back into that barn again.

At the end of the school day, Aleksandr gathered his mathematics and history books and raced to catch up with his friends.

"We've got to get our sticks," said Aleksandr.

"We'd better do it now," said Lavro.

"No sense all of us going," said Sy.

"Aleksandr," said Max.

Aleksandr was tired of Max bossing him around. Besides, going into the barn hadn't been his stupid idea in the first place.

"I'll go," he said. He might be small but he wasn't a coward.

Aleksandr, Lavro, Sy, and Max ran to the back of the barn and hid until they were certain the farm kids had claimed their horses and mules. Then, Aleksandr skirted the side of the building and peeked around the corner to see if the coast was clear. When he saw no one, he willed himself to be invisible, bowed low, and scurried to the stable door. After unlatching it, he squeezed inside. Heart pounding, he squinted into the dimness. Even with the animals gone, the place smelled strongly of horseflesh. Remembering Sy's encounter with the fresh manure pile, Aleksandr scanned the dirt floor as he tiptoed. To his relief, the hockey sticks still leaned next to Roper's empty stall. Quickly, Aleksandr gathered the four sticks and slid out the door, latched it, and ran around the side of the barn to the back of the building, where the other boys waited.

"You did it!" Lavro patted Aleksandr on the back triumphantly.

"I've gotta go clean my shoes," said Sy.

"Watch out for horse apples," said Max.

"Shut up."

"You coming over?" Lavro asked Aleksandr.

"I'd better get home."

As Aleksandr rounded the corner of the barn, heading toward his house, he stopped in his tracks.

"Hello, Aleksandr."

"H—hello, Mr. M—Marko." Aleksandr felt heat rising to his cheeks.

"What are you still doing here?"

Aleksandr stared at his feet. He could tell the teacher he'd forgotten his hockey stick outside at recess. Aleksandr's gaze traveled the length of the teacher's body from his feet to just shy of his eyes.

"I left my hockey stick inside the barn," Aleksandr said.

"When?"

"At lunchtime."

"I see." Mr. Marko pulled on his beard. "You know the stable rules."

"Yes, sir." Aleksandr bit his quivering lower lip. "Please don't tell my father, sir. Please!" He didn't want to cry. Whatever he did, he didn't want to cry. A long silence ensued, during which Aleksandr imagined facing his father and enduring the whipping that was sure to follow.

"Did you go into the barn alone?" Mr. Marko asked.

It wasn't exactly a lie if Aleksandr said yes. After all, he'd recovered the hockey sticks on his own. But he was pretty sure that wasn't what the teacher meant.

"No, sir." It was Lavro's voice.

Aleksandr looked up to see his friend ambling toward them.

"I was with him."

Was that a faint smile on the teacher's face?

"Well, boys, what do you think would be a fair consequence for disobeying the rules?"

Aleksandr looked at Lavro. They were being asked to choose their punishment. All Aleksandr could imagine was a strapping. He shrugged his shoulders.

"Maybe we could write, 'I will not go into the barn ever again' one hundred times," Lavro said.

Mr. Marko stroked his beard, closed his eyes, and rocked on his heels. "I have a better idea," he said. "Tomorrow after school, you boys can muck out the stalls."

"All of them?" Lavro asked, his eyes wide.

Mr. Marko nodded.

"This time, we'll let it go at that. Next time, I'll have to tell your parents. Understood?"

"Yes, sir," the boys answered in unison.

Aleksandr wanted to cry from relief. He wouldn't have cared if they'd had to muck stalls for a month.

The boys stood, frozen, as Mr. Marko strode toward the school, and they waited until the teacher disappeared into the building before speaking.

"Thanks." The word escaped from Aleksandr's throat as he exhaled.

"Friends," Lavro said and spit on his palm.

Aleksandr spit on his palm and shook hands. As he ran home, half the weight of the world lifted from his shoulders.

Chapter Sixteen

It was a foul morning for hanging laundry, but Katerina was determined to get Aleksandr's shirt and pants on the line before the sleet arrived and before Viktor could become suspicious. Balancing the laundry basket on her hip, she made her way to the clothesline, fighting the piercing March wind. A thousand needles peppered her exposed skin. Only a few patches of snow remained on the ground, yet under her feet the brown earth felt as solid as concrete.

When she'd questioned him about the manure on his shoes and the smell of horses on his clothes, Aleksandr had confessed, tearfully, he and Lavro had mucked stalls as punishment for disobeying a school rule. He'd told her the story of their excursion into the stable and how Sy and Max had gotten off scot-free and how Lavro had owned up to his part in it.

The quaver in his voice when he'd pleaded with her not to tell his father had broken her heart. Keeping Aleksandr's trouble from Viktor required one more deception in a long trail of deceptions, but she had needed no convincing. Aleksandr had good reason to fear his father. Viktor was too harsh with his son for reasons far smaller than a forbidden foray into the school's stable. Katerina's inability to shield him from the worst of Viktor's temper plagued her. How was she to protect him or the unborn child she carried when she couldn't protect herself? Silence was her gift to them. It was the only weapon she possessed.

As Katerina bent to pick up Aleksandr's wet shirt, a sharp pain stabbed her lower back. This jab was much worse than the others. She winced, digging her fingers into her knotted muscles. Gradually, the pain eased to a dull ache. She'd been spotting for a few days, too. It had happened during her first pregnancy, so she'd figured everything was fine. Now, she wasn't so sure.

She bent over again, this time snagging the shirt and pinning the shoulders on the line. The wind caught it like a sail. Katerina's skirt billowed up past her knees. Reflexively, she pressed it against her thighs, although there was no one in sight.

Stubble poked through sparse patches of snow, and a crow landed on the garden fencepost. The garden had lain fallow since Elena's departure. Katerina was amazed at how quickly, in the absence of human interference, nature reclaimed its territory, as if to remind humankind of its tenuous hold on the land. Despite never having tended a garden, she knew she would plant one. Yana had promised to teach her, and Aleksandr seemed excited about the prospect of helping. She pictured herself in the warm sunshine, bent over a row of lush vegetables, her rounded belly as fertile as a Saskatchewan field.

Picking up the empty laundry basket, Katerina headed toward the back door. A cramp, this time in her pelvis, stopped her cold. She gasped, doubling over as though she'd been punched, and dropped the basket. She pressed her hands against her abdomen to ease the pain. It was ten more paces to the back door. She had to get into the house. She had to sit down. She had to make the pain stop. Inhaling deeply, she straightened slowly and limped to the house, as if both feet were made of glass.

In the kitchen, the smell of fried pork nauseated her. She'd continued making it for breakfast, fearing Viktor would become suspicious if she stopped serving his favorite meat. Holding her breath, she covered the grease can with a dish cloth and took it to the shed. She shut the door and leaned against the wall, fighting the urge to vomit. Closing her eyes, she counted to twenty before the wave passed.

For fourteen weeks, she'd struggled with this pregnancy. If Viktor had noticed her diminished appetite and frequent trips to the outhouse, he hadn't let on. At night, in their darkened bedroom, while he'd fondled her tender breasts she'd endured the discomfort, and he'd seemed to accept her gasps as evidence of pleasure rather than pain.

As she reached for the baking soda on the top shelf of the cupboard, her muscles contracted again. She bit down on her lip. The knifing stabs became knee-buckling cramps. *God, help me!* Her muscles squeezed in angry spasms. Her body folded to the floor. She brought her knees to her chest in a fetal curl.

Warm, bloody fluid leaked from between her legs and then a grayish mass. *Dear God, no*! Her body shook and shivered against the cold. Katerina lay on the floor in the red-tinged puddle, crying for what felt like days.

When she was able, she dragged herself to the kitchen table and into a chair, staring out the frost-edged window at the iron sky. Mind. Body. Soul. All were empty. She'd wished this child had never been conceived, and now, God had cruelly granted her prayer. He'd looked into her heart and decided she didn't deserve this child, whom she could not protect. This was her fault, all her fault.

Katerina wanted to sit, to feel nothing, but she knew she must act. The ground was unyielding for a full three feet under the surface. It was impossible, she realized, to bury the evidence. She must find another way.

She scooped the bloody mass into a rag and stared at the fetus, as big as the length of her palm. As she traced the minuscule arms and legs and toes with her eyes and saw its perfectly formed ears, the mass became more than blood and mucus and tissue, more than waste into which God had chosen not to breathe life. She hadn't intended to count its fingers, but she did. Emptiness, which began as a pinprick, grew and expanded until her entire body felt hollow. She did not think she had the strength to move, to do what must be done. Viktor must not find her like this. Whatever his reaction—blame or scorn or relief—she could not bear it. Carefully, she gathered the rag around the form, placed them both in an empty flour sack, and set a pot of water on the stove.

When the water boiled, Katerina wrapped a shawl around her shoulders and trudged the path to the outhouse, carrying the pot, the sack, and a broom. Sleet, pelting her with icy arrows, felt like justice.

She poured half the scalding water into the foul hole to melt the hardened excrement. A vile stench wafted upward from the dark pit. Katerina heaved. Bile rose in her throat. Despite the cold, beads of sweat bloomed on her forehead and dripped down her face, joining the salty tears spilling from her eyes. The outhouse door banged against the outer wall and flapped in the howling wind. She shook the contents of the sack into the hole and pushed it into the brown soup with the broom handle, pouring hot water into the hole until she was certain the waste was concealed. Then, she poured the remaining water onto the broom handle, wiped the handle on the sack, and limped back to the house.

In the distance, the first warning whistle blasts of the 9:37 a.m. train sounded.

Katerina's hair was wet. Mud clung to her skirt hem. She couldn't feel her feet. She began to shake—first her legs and then her arms and then her shoulders. A primordial sob, which began in a hidden place she could not name, burrowed into her stomach and lungs and throat and escaped from her mouth. Katerina cried until the sobs tapered to silence. She waited to be certain she could no longer hear the cries, as if the piercing sounds had originated someplace outside herself.

She stared at the bloody pool on the kitchen floor. *Erase it.*

Katerina took the pail from the back porch and filled the bucket with water and lye. On her hands and knees, she worked to scrub the bloodstain from the wooden planks, dipping the scouring brush into the bucket of lye again and again until her knuckles burned and her arms wouldn't move. Then, she emptied the tainted water into the sink and watched it swirl out of sight.

Katerina put another pot on the stove and washed herself with the scalding water. She scoured the tender folds between her legs until they burned. Her stomach's white skin turned pink, and then red, as she scrubbed away every trace of her pregnancy. She threw her skirt, her ruined undergarments, and the flour sack into the fire, encouraging the coals to obliterate all evidence of the life that had grown inside her.

One by one, she climbed the stairs, stopping frequently to hold the banister. When she entered the room she shared with Viktor, the bed mocked her. She pulled clean undergarments from the dresser drawer, a freshly laundered skirt and blouse from the wardrobe, and dressed herself. She brushed her teeth and then her tangled hair, barely recognizing the woman staring back at her from the washstand mirror. It was an older, more careworn visage than the one that had gazed back at her that night—was it only a half year ago?—when she'd first met Viktor Senyk. Was this the defeat Svetlana Sokur saw when she dared look in the mirror? The thought chilled her.

There was a knock at the front door; at least, that was what Katerina thought she heard. Perhaps it was her imagination. There was a second knock, firmer, louder. Who could be calling? Katerina had lost track of time. The bedside clock indicated it was well past noon. It must be Yana at the door.

Even for such a dear friend, Katerina was in no state for a caller. The miscarriage had left her mind and heart as empty as her womb. She needed to collect herself, to figure out what she felt, to grieve. It was tempting to ignore the knock. Later, she could explain she'd not been feeling well, that she'd lain down and not heard it. That, at least, would be a partial truth. Although weary from the physical trauma, Katerina was also tired of deception, falsehoods, and half-truths. Yes, she'd best answer the door. She would do what she could to cut this visit short and hope Yana didn't suspect anything or ask too many questions.

Katerina moistened her fingers and smoothed the damp hair from her forehead. She pinched her cheeks to bring color to them and forced, if not a smile, a neutral expression. As she limped down the stairs, both legs wobbled, each step reminding her of the rawness between her legs. She straightened her back and inhaled deeply.

When she reached the front door, a man's outline appeared on the other side of the wavy glass panel. Katerina opened the door. Roman Klopoushak stood there, hat in hand.

"Hello, Mr. Klopoushak," she said, startled.

"Good afternoon, Mrs. Senyk. I'd prefer you call me Roman."

"I'm afraid Viktor isn't home, Mr. Klo—Roman." She ran the tip of her tongue between dry lips.

"I know," he said. "His truck's at the elevator."

Katerina stared, confused. She peeked around him to see if Alla was in the truck. It sat empty.

"May I come in?" he asked, shifting his hat from one hand to the other.

"Of course." Katerina stepped aside but didn't offer to take his coat. She couldn't imagine he'd be staying.

He wandered into the vestibule and then into the parlor, looking around, obviously taking measure of the place.

"May I help you?" Katerina asked. Being cordial took almost more effort than she could muster.

"Alla wants to know if you have material left over from her dress."

"Oh?"

"She meant to ask you at church. You left before she had a chance to do so."

Material? Alla wants material? "I—I do have a remnant," Katerina said. "I'll get it." Before he could respond, Katerina limped to the dining room to retrieve the fabric stored in the bottom cupboard of the breakfront. She felt Roman's appraising eyes on her even as she turned her back. Heart pounding, she struggled to regain her composure.

When Katerina returned, she extended the green satin de chine remnant, offering it to Roman. Her raw-red knuckles glowed and her hands shook. His eyes met hers. She could see that the condition of her hands had not escaped his notice. She wondered which other of her distress signals he'd read.

"That won't be necessary," Roman said. "Alla wouldn't have the first idea what to do with it."

"I don't understand." Katerina's temples throbbed.

"I believe she has something else in mind for you to sew, a matching something or other. While I was thinking of it, I thought I'd find out if that was possible." Roman's eyes held Katerina's a little too long for comfort.

"I see," Katerina said, although she didn't. This seemed like a peculiar errand for a man as self-important as Roman Klopoushak. Her head filled with fog. She struggled to think. Perhaps she was making too much of his unexpected visit. Still. She longed to be alone. *Please, please leave.*

"Are you feeling all right, Katerina?" he asked. "You look—flushed. What's wrong?"

Katerina looked away, uncertain what to say. The concern in his voice made her uneasy. She didn't trust it. She didn't trust him. She didn't trust herself. And never mind that he wanted her to call him Roman. When had she given *him* permission to address *her* by her Christian name? When had she given him permission to ask such personal questions?

"I'm making you nervous."

"No, no," Katerina lied. "I—I have a slight headache." Her excuse sounded false even to her ears, and she wished she could take her lame explanation back. Silently, Katerina cursed the tears gathering, threatening to betray her.

"It's more than that. You're clearly upset."

Did he know? How could he? Control began slipping from her grasp.

He touched her shoulder.

She flinched. The gesture was so forward that Katerina could only manage to shake her head. Anything she said would only squeak out of her mouth, and Roman would read the profound loss strangling her voice. Anything she said would encourage him to probe further.

"You're a very special woman, Katerina." He stepped closer to her. "You should be treated like one." His hand still rested on her shoulder. His words slipped off his tongue like silk.

Her stomach turned end over end. At this moment, she felt the last thing from special. Part of her wanted to slap him for his impudence. Part of her wanted to fold herself into his arms and sob. He was standing too close to her now, his breathing audible, his breath steadily brushing her forehead. Her skin beneath his hand seared, yet she shivered. He was luring her toward the flame, inviting her to feel, enticing her into confession. *My life is sorrow. My future is hopeless. My husband is a monster.* She couldn't move. *Save me.*

"Tell me, Katerina, what a woman as exceptional as you is doing here, in this place, with—with an elevator operator." His tone teetered on a thin line between flattery and menace.

Unconsciously, Katerina ran her hand along the thigh of her damaged leg.

"Surely that's a small matter when it comes to a woman of your—talents, "Roman said, tracing the path of her hand with his eyes.

She stood mute.

"L'viv. That's where you're from? Not too difficult to find answers, you know." His look was penetrating.

All the while she'd feared Roman had been digging to uncover this morning's truth, he had been after more, far more. She'd hadn't the strength for Roman's game of—what? Seduction? Chess?

Danger stomped around her, threatening to crush her. She had to do something.

Roman stepped closer, both hands on her shoulders now.

Think.

His face leaned toward hers.

"Thank you for your concern," Katerina said finally, ignoring his last comment, forcing herself to meet his penetrating eyes. Her words were strained and false, something she prayed this conceited man would not recognize. Slowly, she stepped from his grasp. She had neither the energy nor the desire to play cat and mouse. She must be careful. A man of his ilk would punish her for rejection. Katerina pretended she didn't see his ulterior motive. She hoped that he would believe her feigned naïveté.

"You're right, Roman. I do not hide my emotions well." Her heart threatened to beat out of her chest. "I am beside myself with worry. My father is ill, and I fear I will never see him again." Another half-truth. Another deception. Another layer of deceit. "I appreciate your kindness," she said, touching his forearm lightly, her voice remaining soft and strained. Tears, the singularly genuine element of this encounter, flowed freely. Katerina did not stop them. She brushed them from her cheeks while demurely meeting Roman's eyes. "Please forgive me. As you've guessed, I'm very upset. I'm afraid I must lie down."

"Certainly."

She'd judged him well. Roman, disinterested in offering true comfort, was suddenly eager to escape. He was the kind of man lured by a woman's vulnerability and driven away by genuine need. From his expression, Katerina couldn't discern whether he fully believed her. What did his face telegraph? Disappointment? Frustration? Through her father's business, she'd had many dealings with wealthy clients. Her experience with men of means told her this one would not accept defeat easily.

"I will be sure to tell Viktor of your kindness," Katerina said. "I'm certain my husband will also be grateful for your concern."

After Roman left, Katerina closed the door and leaned against it for support. Exhaustion overtook her. Her legs folded. She gripped the doorknob with one hand and covered her mouth with the other as her body shook with dry heaves. Fluid leaked from between her legs and dampened her thighs. She rose, hobbled to the dining room, and slumped into a chair. Burying her face in her hands, she let go all control and sobbed.

She cried until she had no tears left.

Then she sat, paralyzed and drained.

Little by little, she began to recover.

Whatever his intentions, it was doubtful she'd seen the last of Roman Klopoushak. He was a man used to getting his way. His threats were thinly veiled. She must be very vigilant and extremely cautious where he was concerned. It would be a delicate dance to keep him close enough to watch yet not so close as to draw suspicion.

If Viktor found out about Roman, about her failed pregnancy, about everything… He mustn't, no matter the cost.

In her weariness, Katerina longed for succor.

She imagined Stepan's reassuring arms enfolding her. Although her yearning was so powerful she could scarcely breathe, she was grateful he could not see her at this low point. Stepan would not recognize her as the independent, confident woman he'd loved. She closed her eyes and felt her cheek resting in the hollow of his shoulder. His soft lips kissed her forehead, his warm breath teased her hair, and his sensual hands massaged her back. *You are safe. You are loved. I will protect you.* She waited for relief but found disturbingly little solace in this fantasy.

To love was to feel. Katerina realized she didn't want to feel. Oblivion tempted her. No sorrow. No regret. No fear. Smoke drifted into the sky and rain evaporated into the heavens, until they became invisible, so why not her? Why couldn't she simply stop feeling, stop existing? Why couldn't she just disappear?

Viktor stormed from the shed into the kitchen, where Katerina cooked supper. When would this woman learn? He'd made his expectations clear from the first. For someone so obviously book smart, she certainly was dense when it came to common sense. If she thought he would overlook her defiance of him, she was badly mistaken. He was master of his house. He'd had one wife who'd overindulged and overprotected his son; he sure as hell wouldn't have another.

Tonight, he didn't bother to change out of his work boots or clothes. Grain dust clung to his pants and shirt, and dirty boot tracks covered the floor. Without preamble, he faced Katerina. "You didn't think it was important to tell me the boy got in trouble at school?" His inflection spelled question. His glare spelled accusation.

"Trouble?" She stared at him as though she had no idea what he was talking about.

Her stupid expression galled him. Surely, Katerina didn't expect he'd believe this pretense. She could play the innocent but he knew better. She was always shielding the boy, going behind his back, keeping things from him, just as Elena had done. It hadn't worked for her, and it wasn't going to work for her replacement either. Didn't these women know they were no match for him? He always found out what they were up to, smelled their deceit a hundred miles away, saw their duplicity in the way they carried themselves and in the way they looked at him.

"Why do I always have to hear these things from someone else?" Viktor stepped toward her, backing her up against the stove.

Katerina's shoulders tensed. She chewed the inside of her cheek, the way she always did when she was nervous. If she thought she could stall for time to make up some lie, she was also mistaken.

"Fedir told me the boys got into trouble two weeks ago for sneaking into the school barn. Marko made them muck stalls. Two weeks ago.

Sound familiar?" Viktor crossed his arms over his chest, daring Katerina to challenge him. "I'll not be made to look foolish in front of our neighbors."

He could feel her fear.

"I'm sick to death of your coddling. The boy needs to be taught a lesson," Viktor said, turning to leave.

"He's already been punished," Katerina blurted out.

Viktor turned on her. "You knew."

He grabbed her biceps and squeezed until his fingertips threatened to touch bone. Katerina groaned and blinked back tears until he released her roughly. For all his bluster, Viktor hadn't been positive she was aware of the situation. Her hasty statement was her admission. She was no match for him. He'd trapped her with less effort than it took a spider to catch a fly.

Gravy bubbled over the side of the pan and sizzled on the stove burner. Reflexively, Katerina turned and pulled the pan to a cool spot on the stovetop. She kept her back to Viktor.

"And, you kept it from me."

She stood perfectly still.

"Damn it! Look at me when I'm speaking to you." His tone was harsh. He yanked her arm and spun her around.

"It was such a small thing," she said. "The boys didn't intend any harm. I didn't think it would matter to you."

Viktor exploded. "Think I give a damn about them sneaking into the barn?" The tendons in his neck protruded. He sneered at her. "About time the boy stopped acting like a girl."

The truth was he wished his son would quit being a little saint. It wasn't natural for a boy to be so careful. Viktor wanted him to mix it up, risk getting the tar beat out of him by some other kid, toughen up. He'd have been proud of him if he'd taken one of those nags for a ride and stormed back into the barn with his head held high, ready to take his punishment like a man. How much clearer could he be? She simply refused to hear him.

Katerina looked at him with that annoying confused expression that drove him mad.

"It's the lying I won't abide." The vein in the middle of his forehead pulsed. He fingered the scar above his eyebrow.

"I didn't lie to you."

Viktor leaned his face inches from hers. She was lucky he didn't knock her teeth out. In the palm of his hand, he cradled her chin and clamped his fingers, viselike, around her jaw. "Didn't exactly tell the truth, did you?" He glared at her, his eyes both fire and ice.

"You're hurting me."

Viktor gave Katerina's jaw an emphatic squeeze and a dismissive shove before letting go. "The boy needs to learn his lesson."

As he turned to leave, she grabbed his sleeve and met his eyes. "Viktor, please, he's served his punishment. He's learned his lesson. There's nothing to be gained by punishing him again."

Viktor jerked his arm from her grasp and looked at her with contempt. He hated her simper. "Baby him! Teach him to keep secrets from me! This is your fault!" he yelled. "He'll take *your* punishment, too!"

"I *promise* he won't go into the barn again!" She was near hysterics.

"Christ, how many times do I have to tell you?" Viktor was seconds from knocking her senseless. "I will not tolerate him lying to me, ever. Something you'd best learn, too."

"He was afraid. He's just a boy."

That was the wrong thing to say. Viktor was sick to death of the pampering and coddling. He strode through the dining room to the parlor, his footsteps emphatic.

Katerina limped after him.

"Aleksandr! Get down here!" Viktor bellowed from the bottom of the stairs. "Now!"

In seconds, Aleksandr appeared at the top of the stairway. Viktor pointed to the floor in front of him. Aleksandr's feet landed on each tread as if he were headed for the guillotine. When he arrived at the spot Viktor pointed to, he stood silently, staring at his shoes. His small, fine-boned delicacy disgusted Viktor. His shoulders slumped in defeat, beaten before the starter's gun had signaled the beginning of the contest.

From behind him, Katerina pulled on Viktor's sleeve. Easily, he twisted his arm from her grasp and grabbed a handful of her hair. "Stay out of this," he hissed before releasing her.

Aleksandr didn't move.

"Trouble at school?" Viktor asked.

"No sir."

"None?"

Aleksandr, staring at his shoes, shook his head.

"Nothing to tell me about the horse barn?"

Aleksandr's head jerked up, his eyes huge.

"Surprised?" Viktor's jaw clenched. His wet boot tapped out tense seconds on the floorboards. "One more chance," Viktor warned.

Katerina pleaded with him but he ignored her.

He could almost hear his son thinking, weighing whether to confess the truth or lie. The boy's gaze darted to Katerina and back again. His lips trembled. Viktor's fists flexed at his side. He was losing patience rapidly.

The boy just stood there. A tear dropped onto his shirt.

"Stop crying!" Viktor backhanded Aleksandr across the side of the head.

"Aahh…" Aleksandr landed on the floor.

With a single hand, Viktor hoisted him up by his collar.

From behind him, Katerina pleaded, "Viktor, no! It's not his fault. It's mine."

"Damn right it is," he snapped. Turning to her, Viktor gave her a hard shove, sending her toppling. "Stay out of this," he growled and then dragged Aleksandr upstairs and slammed the bedroom door.

When his father threw him, Aleksandr's body caromed off the wall and onto his bed. He was as light as a hollow-boned bird flying through the air. The impact of the wall hurt down his entire side, especially his shoulder. It felt like bone slamming against bone. It hurt a lot but he didn't scream. It was the only defense he had, to show no resistance, to make no sound at all. Even a peep would signal that it mattered, and although it didn't show on the outside, on the inside, Aleksandr's perfect silence was defiance. *One—two—three—four...*

Maybe this was it. Maybe this was the last time his father would hurt him, because maybe this time his father would kill him. There was a hard slap across the back of his head and another stabbing pain. *Five—six—seven...*

"You don't keep things from me, you sneaky little coward. Do you hear me?" It wasn't really a question. His father didn't want an answer. His father grabbed both his shoulders and shook him. "When you get in trouble, you'd better admit it or it's going to be a thousand times worse."

How could it be worse? Aleksandr couldn't fathom it.

He heard his new mother pleading outside his bedroom. Even though she was pounding on the door, there was nothing she could do. She was a woman with a crippled leg. His father's arms were bands of taut muscle wrapped in fury. When he was angry, he grew stronger. Resistance was futile. Aleksandr wished she would stop begging and crying. Didn't she know everything ended sooner by doing nothing? He wanted to shout *Stop!* to her, but he'd promised himself he wouldn't utter a single word, and he always kept his promises.

His real mother had known not to make a sound, to let his father's fists do their damage without interference, to let his anger wind down like a clock until he was worn out and tired of punishing. She'd wait until his father sat, drunk, by the fire or had fallen asleep before she'd come into his room and hold him and rock him. "Hush, hush; it's over. It will be better tomorrow, you'll see," she'd coo. And even though he would know it wasn't true, it would make him feel better when she said it.

Often, his real mother would step between his father and him and take whatever wrath his father's fists had to deliver. This had mostly worked when something wasn't really his fault. Plus, he had been littler then, and his father had rarely beaten him. The older he got, the worse it got. What was he supposed to do about getting older? If he lived through it, one day he would be old enough to fight back. He might never be stronger than his father, but he was quicker and more agile. Even if he couldn't fight back with equal force, at least, he'd be able to get away.

"Getting caught in the horse barn. How stupid can you be?"

Another question that wanted no answer.

Aleksandr wondered how his father knew about the trouble at school. His new mother had promised not to tell, and he believed her because it had been more than two weeks before his father had found out. Lavro must have confessed. It was hard to be too mad at his friend because he had no reason to be afraid of his own father. Besides, Lavro had no idea how mean Aleksandr's father could be. Even to his best friend, Aleksandr would have been ashamed to admit what happened at home.

A stinging slap across his back landed so forcefully, the imprint of his father's hand felt permanent, like an impression made in wet concrete, which would harden into a lasting reminder of his guilt. *Eight—nine—ten...*

"No supper and to bed."

The door opened.

"*Don't*," his father warned. His new mother must be in the hallway. "I expect supper in fifteen minutes."

The door slammed and then bounced ajar. Aleksandr curled on

his bed, his face turned to the wall, allowing tears now. His father would be angry if he saw them, though there was little chance he'd be coming back, since his father never set foot in his room unless it was to punish him.

Aleksandr heard his new mother limp into his bedroom.

"Aleksandr," she whispered.

He lay still, said nothing.

"Aleksandr."

He heard the regret in her voice. It made him even sadder. Though he wished he could, he couldn't help her. Inside and outside, he hurt too much.

"I'm sorry, so very, very sorry," she said.

Chapter Seventeen

After weeks of reclusiveness, on a sun-soaked fourth of May—one month to the day after Easter Monday—Katerina ventured out of the house, determined to resurrect her spirit.

Despondency had blown in with the March wind and stayed through April, claiming Katerina so completely, it had taken a gargantuan effort to get out of bed each morning. After her miscarriage, helplessness and hopelessness had become twin pillars of her grief. Guilt over her failure to shield Aleksandr from his father's temper constantly plagued her. It had taken every speck of energy she had to get through her days, cooking and cleaning and mothering.

When the townswomen got together, she hadn't participated in making *pysanky*, although Easter egg decorating had always been one of her favorite holiday traditions. Her sewing machine had sat in the corner of the dining room, untouched. The prospect of planting a garden had overwhelmed her. She'd even avoided Yana, whose good cheer fell on Katerina's ear like a flat note plucked on a violin string.

Today, when she'd woken, Katerina had sensed a shift. She couldn't explain it. Maybe it was the earlier arrival of spring's morning light. Maybe it was the sun's rays streaming through the bedroom window, shining optimistically on her face. Maybe, like influenza, the gloom infecting her had simply run its course. Whatever it was, today Katerina had decided to escape the house, to step into life.

The mail arrived on Mondays. She could fetch it from the post office, tucked in the corner of the general store, and get some air in the bargain. It had been several weeks since she'd received a letter from Aneta. If it simply contained routine news, it would provide a connection to things familiar, something she desperately yearned for.

The day would be even more promising if the letter contained news of Matviyko.

Limping along Main Street, Katerina recalled the day she'd arrived in Bilik, bewildered and frightened. She'd walked this same street, feeling conspicuously out of place, every crooked step she took punctuating her separateness. But from the first, Yana had ignored her impairment as if it were of no consequence whatever, and new friends and neighbors hadn't made much of it either. On the prairie, Katerina had discovered, a person's measure had little to do with vanity and more to do with being a skilled homemaker and a responsible parent, duties that were unaffected by her physical infirmity. She rarely worried how she appeared to others anymore. Of all the fears she'd harbored when contemplating a life in Canada, her imperfect leg had turned out to be the least important. Despite the bitter disappointment of her marriage, Katerina had found things to cherish in this place.

Still, nearly six months after her wedding, she felt like an interloper in Viktor's home. He'd tried to erase all evidence of his first wife, yet Katerina couldn't escape the notion that she was living another woman's life. Hadn't Elena listened to the same teakettle whistling and the same floorboards creaking? She'd hung her dresses in the same wardrobe and washed her face in the same basin. She'd looked out the same parlor window, waiting for Aleksandr to come home from school. When Katerina set the table, she would run her fingertips across the butter dish and wonder how Elena had chipped it. When she did laundry, she would picture Elena turning Aleksandr's socks right-side out. When she dusted the grandfather clock, she would see Elena's hand setting the pendulum in motion. Worst of all, when Katerina lay in bed, she would feel the indentation in the mattress where Elena's body had lain and where she'd had sexual intercourse with her husband countless times before her. As hard as Katerina tried, it was impossible to escape those thoughts. The ghost of that woman was nowhere and everywhere in Viktor's house.

As if it hadn't been difficult enough assuming another woman's place, Katerina's miscarriage had made it almost unbearable. Every time she walked into the kitchen, she imagined the red-tinged puddle spreading across the floor. Every time she stoked the fire, she saw her ruined dress burning to ashes. Every time she went to the outhouse, she pictured the bloody mass, evidence of a never-to-be life, disappearing into the stinking waste.

Today would be different.

The farther Katerina walked, the more the promise of warmer weather, floating on the spring breeze, cheered her. She inhaled deeply, inviting possibility into her lungs. Overhead, the sky, a robin's-egg blue, was covered with a film of clouds so sheer they could have been painted with a watercolor brush. Katerina remembered a day much like this, when she and Stepan had sat in the churchyard at opposite ends of the filigreed bench, pretending, for the sake of appearances, to be mere acquaintances.

"Those wispy-tailed clouds mean the winds are blowing high and strong," Stepan had said, pointing to the cirrus clouds swirling above them, as gauzy as a bride's veil. When she'd stubbornly declared she preferred to think of them as angel's breath, he'd thrown his head back, laughing, calling her a starry-eyed romantic, although he was as much a romantic as she. Her heart had surged with love for him, knowing it was their very romanticism that bound them to each other.

As she approached Panko's store, the sight of Roman Klopoushak's truck, parked in front, stopped Katerina cold. Since the day he'd appeared at her door, like a vulture circling carrion, she'd seen him only at church. There, he'd shown no evidence of his duplicitous intentions, and Katerina sometimes wondered if she'd only imagined them. She, too, had pretended the encounter had never happened, yet she remained aware of the danger of ignoring a man such as Roman.

She thought about backtracking to the dry goods store and browsing to avoid running into Roman, but then thought better of the idea.

Living in tiny Bilik, there was no way to dodge him forever. Besides, Fedir would be working at the store and would serve as a buffer. She straightened her back and continued down the street, determined that Roman wouldn't ruin her newfound resolve.

The overhead bell attached to the door tinkled when Katerina entered the store. She noticed Fedir's bald head barely sticking above the shelves in the hardware aisle. Standing next to him, Roman Klopoushak's full head of graying hair was clearly visible. Alla peered into the bins near the entryway, her hand gripping the handle of the Fig Newtons case.

"Hello, Alla," Katerina said.

"Oh—hello." Alla, caught in the act, adopted a stiff posture and a falsely prim expression. "I was just deciding how much pearl barley and popcorn to buy. Roman loves his popcorn in the evenings."

By the looks of him, Katerina thought it was more likely he enjoyed cakes and pies, but she kept the thought to herself.

"I haven't had the chance to tell you what a splash I made in Regina," Alla bragged. "I daresay my dress caused quite a stir."

Yana had pegged the woman exactly. Alla chirped on about how splendid she'd looked in the stylish dress she'd worn to her niece's wedding. Katerina decided she could probably gain a reputation as a quality seamstress through the sale of a single dress if Alla boasted like this to everyone in town. It was of little consequence, however, because Bilik was a place where fashion, like damaged limbs, didn't count for much. Since the hateful scene with Viktor, who'd stolen not only her earnings but the joy of making that dress, Katerina had convinced herself she would never again undertake such a project.

"How fortunate to run into you today. I've been meaning to speak with you. As I said earlier, I'll need your services again."

"Actually, Alla, I'm not—"

"Roman is taking me to Saskatoon for our anniversary. Of course, he has a little business to conduct, as well," Alla continued. "The green dress was perfect for the wedding, but for this occasion, I'll need something in keeping with the season, a lighter weight material, something that flows, perhaps."

"When do you need it?" Katerina asked.

"In a few weeks. Is that a problem?"

"No, not in terms of finishing the dress," Katerina said. "It's just that—"

"Just what?"

"It's just that..." It was Katerina's opportunity to decline, to steer clear of Alla and Roman, to retreat back into the shadows. "I would like a better grade of fabric than is available here, and it would take too much time to send for it."

"I see." Alla hesitated. "Would Weyburn have what you need?"

"Well—yes," Katerina said. "There's a dry goods store there with a far more extensive selection, but Viktor has no plans to go to Weyburn anytime in the near future."

"Let me speak with Roman."

Before Katerina had a chance to stop her, Alla sped down the aisle.

Katerina remembered Viktor's set jaw and clenched fists and knew she was wading into dangerous waters. But he hadn't forbidden her to take on sewing for hire; he'd only insisted that he be informed of every project and that he keep her earnings. Maybe he would soften in time, or maybe she'd just—

"Roman said he would be happy to escort us to Weyburn on Friday," Alla said, smirking.

"This coming Friday?"

"Certainly. That would give you sufficient time to complete my dress. You already have my measurements and know which styles flatter my figure." Alla had the look and tone of a woman used to getting her way. "It's settled, then."

Katerina couldn't believe she'd agreed to design another dress, much less ride to Weyburn with Roman. With Alla along, he would surely be on his best behavior, and she could continue to pretend that nothing had passed between them. Still, it would require her to be vigilant, to perform that delicate dance of keeping him close enough to watch, yet not close enough to draw suspicion. It would also require her to handle Viktor carefully. Tonight, when she told him about the plan, she would approach him with deference, making him believe she hadn't agreed to go without first seeking his permission. If he looked for evidence of duplicity, he'd find none. She would conduct her affairs openly. She'd be above suspicion. Her spine stiffened.

As he and Alla exited the store, Roman held eye contact with Katerina longer than was comfortable. She couldn't escape the notion that the look—direct, bold, and covetous—was meant as a warning. It reminded her she must never underestimate him.

Katerina pushed a wayward strand of hair from her brow and fought to regain her composure. She refocused on her errand, selecting the staples she'd come for: a quarter pound of almonds, two pounds of green split peas, two pounds of Louisiana rice, a round of cheddar cheese, a can of cinnamon, and a bar of Palmolive soap. Fedir threw in a licorice stick for Aleksandr.

"You spoil him," Katerina said, smiling.

"Only a little." Fedir handed her a small bundle tied together with string. "And here's your mail."

At a glance, Katerina recognized the *Grain Growers Guide* and Eaton's catalog. Several envelopes were sandwiched between them.

"I could get the boys to deliver the groceries after school," Fedir said.

"Thank you. I'll be fine," Katerina said. "It's manageable, and the walk will do me good." She slung the straps of her burlap shopping bag over her shoulder.

"Enjoy the beautiful day, then," Fedir said.

"I will."

It took every ounce of discipline Katerina had to unpack the groceries before looking through the mail, but she wanted to savor the wait, prolong it, the same way she anticipated the soothing warmth of a freshly drawn bath.

She put Viktor's magazine next to the small stack of bills on the table and set the Eaton's catalog aside for later. As she looked through the various envelopes, she was disappointed that none was from Aneta. Although her sister's letters were bittersweet, other than her memories, it was Katerina's only remaining connection to home. An official-looking envelope addressed to "Mrs. Viktor Senyk" caught her attention. Curiously, the return address was Weyburn Mental Hospital.

Why would she be getting correspondence from the mental hospital? It occurred to her then the envelope must be intended for Elena, the first Mrs. Viktor Senyk, and she suddenly felt like a foolish pretender. But Viktor had been to the mental hospital since Elena's death. Certainly, he would have notified them his wife was deceased. This didn't make sense.

Katerina hesitated. This was just one more example, among hundreds, of her stepping into another woman's life. Opening an envelope would seem to be such a simple thing, but even it was complicated. Katerina inserted the letter opener, made a tiny slit in the corner and then stopped. It was wrong to open another person's mail. It was against the law, wasn't it? Like trespassing on another's property. But she was the only Mrs. Senyk in this house, so she was entitled to open it, wasn't she?

With a long, deliberate slice, Katerina tore open the envelope, removed the single page, and read it.

April 23, 1926

Dear Mrs. Senyk,

I am responding to your recent inquiry regarding the condition and current course of treatment for your brother, Jon Blanek.

As you are well aware, there is no cure for schizophrenia. I was hopeful that hydrotherapy would benefit Jon, but, at first, it yielded limited results. Despite multiple treatments over a period of two months, Jon wavered between listlessness and bouts of uncooperativeness. His hallucinations continued.

Hydrotherapy was temporarily discontinued and then resumed again four weeks ago. As of late, I have some mildly encouraging news. Jon has begun to show some improvement. He has begun to answer basic questions and has been taking escorted walks on the lawn. Beginning next week, he will participate in occupational therapy on a trial basis.

If you are so inclined, I believe Jon is ready for a visit from you. Please advise me of your intentions.

Sincerely,

Herbert Fowler, MD

April 23, 1926. Katerina stared at the date. Surely, there must be some mistake. That was only ten days ago. It didn't make sense. The correspondence was intended for Elena, but how was that possible? Had a relative other than Elena made the inquiry, and the doctor simply assumed it had been from Jon's sister? Had he gotten confused and sent the letter to Mrs. Senyk, forgetting she was deceased, when he meant to send it to Mr. Senyk? Then why would he have referred to Jon as "your brother"?

Katerina's pulse raced. Suspicion niggled.

As she thought back to her ride to Weyburn Mental Hospital with Viktor, she tried to remember everything he'd said. She was certain he hadn't said anything about meeting with Dr. Fowler or any other doctor. When Viktor had come out of the hospital visibly upset, she'd asked him if anything had happened. *Nothing that concerns you.* Katerina remembered what he'd said because she'd been hurt by his dismissiveness. He'd given nothing away, instead deflecting attention to the picnic lunch she'd packed. At the time, she'd been glad for the diversion. Now that she looked back on it, she'd been far too timid for a woman committed to marrying a man she barely knew. It embarrassed her that she'd settled for so little.

Katerina had to find out what the dates on the letter meant. She had to find out why the doctor was inviting a deceased woman to visit her brother. Investigating would be risky. If he discovered her inquiring about Elena behind his back, Viktor would never forgive her prying. He'd punish her severely. The memory of him thrusting his fist into her stomach, knocking the wind out of her, made her shudder. She must plan carefully and watch every step. One thing was certain: On Friday, she had more important business awaiting her in Weyburn than buying fabric.

In the afternoon, Roman Klopoushak stopped by the elevator to talk with Viktor about releasing some of his wheat before the month was out. They agreed on an amount pretty quickly, which was unusual. Klopoushak was a man of growing means, who squeezed value from his money like water from a sponge, but once Viktor noticed Alla sitting in the truck, he understood why the man was so quick to agree. No doubt, Alla had plans for them that afternoon.

"We ran into your wife today," Klopoushak said, "at Panko's, buying supplies."

"Oh?"

"Looks as though Alla's hired her to sew another dress." Klopoushak stood at the office door, his hand on the knob. "I have to say, Alla never looked better than she did in that dress Katerina made." He patted Viktor on the back. "If Alla's happy, I'm happy, if you know what I mean."

Actually, Viktor didn't understand Klopoushak's attitude. He'd be damned if *he* ever let a woman run his life. In fact, in his book, any man who allowed it was a fool. What kind of spell Roman's gossip-of-a-wife had over him was hard to figure, but clearly he let Alla wear the pants.

On his walk home from work, Viktor thought about the first time

Katerina had sewn for hire. He'd had to get heavy-handed to make her understand. It would be interesting to see how she'd handle this latest agreement, to see whether she'd learned from her mistakes.

When Viktor opened the front door, the enticing aroma of cooked cabbage and freshly baked bread greeted him. This was the best part of coming home, when the smells of hearty food and Katerina's soprano voice, singing one folk tune or another, blended in welcome. She hadn't been singing much lately, but tonight she was obviously in a fine mood. Viktor savored the moment before he was forced to consider anyone but himself, before questions and answers and false cheer spoiled the perfection of it. He stood longer than necessary, escaping, if briefly, the demands of work, the responsibility of family life, and the nagging concerns over Katerina's trustworthiness. After hanging up his hat and jacket, he followed his senses into the kitchen.

Katerina turned to greet him. "Hello." She smiled and approached him with a buttered morsel of warm, fresh-from-the-oven bread. She placed it in his mouth, brushing her fingers over his lips, while the flavors teased his tongue. He closed his eyes. This was the wife he wanted, a woman whose purpose was to please him. He pulled her toward him and ran his hands down the length of her back and over her curves. She didn't resist.

"Supper will be ready in fifteen minutes," she said softly, "time enough for you to wash."

"How about I taste you instead," he said.

"Viktor!"

Katerina's embarrassment aroused him.

"Aleksandr is up in his room," she said. "I've already told him we'll have supper shortly."

"Send him to bed early," Viktor said and headed for the stairs.

Katerina was a changed woman. Ever since he'd confronted her and laid down the law, she'd been working harder to please him. Sometimes he saw fear in her eyes and knew she complied so he wouldn't discipline her, but that was fine by him. Fear could be healthy where a wife was concerned; it reminded her of her place. Now, Katerina had another chance to prove herself.

When Viktor arrived at the table, Aleksandr was already seated.

Tonight, Katerina had placed branches, tied together with a blue satin ribbon, in the middle of the table, another one of her citified ways. It wasn't just the ribbon; it was the way she took their everyday dishes and arranged them, placing saucers under the soup bowls and the cups and setting out more silverware than the meal called for, which made every night look as though they were expecting company. He'd gotten used to it and he saw no harm, as long as the food was hot and on the table when he was ready to eat.

While he ate, Katerina and Aleksandr talked about school. The boy liked book learning. In that area, he had more in common with Katerina than he'd ever had with Elena.

"And Phileas Fogg has to buy an elephant to get to Allahabad, because it turns out the train doesn't go all the way there," Aleksandr said. "Then he rescues Aouda because he feels sorry for her. Even though she's a girl, I still like that part."

Talking about the book, the boy became animated in a way that Viktor had never noticed before. Aleksandr, with his shy and nervous habits, had seemed almost simple. With Katerina, he appeared anything but. She had a way with him; that fact couldn't be denied.

"Jules Verne is a wonderful storyteller," Katerina said. "I like the part where Phileas thinks he's lost the bet but then discovers he's crossed the international date line, so he's actually won. I favor stories that have a surprise, where things are not what they seem."

Katerina turned to Viktor. "We've left you out, I'm afraid. Tell us about your day at work."

"Not much to tell." Viktor tore off a large piece of bread and slathered it with butter. "Definitely sounds as though we're going to throw in with the Pool."

"As I recall, you support the Pool."

"The Saskatchewan Wheat Pool is the future. Strength in numbers." Viktor scooped a forkful of cabbage roll into his mouth. "The government has set the Crow Rate at a point favorable to farmers. That means reduced rail rates for wheat shipped to the Great Lakes. Best time to be farming that I can recall."

"Things are looking up, then."

"So it seems."

After supper, Viktor retired to the parlor to have a drink and a smoke. Katerina entered, carrying a plate of hot biscuits and offered them to Viktor. He shook his head.

"Later," he said.

She sat down across from him, leaning forward in her chair. "I have something to tell you."

He took a long pull on his pipe and then let the smoke escape slowly from the corners of his mouth. "I'm listening."

Her eyes met his. "I went to Panko's today and ran into Alla Klopoushak. She asked me to sew another dress for her." Katerina looked at her hands. "I agreed—if you approve, of course."

Viktor sipped his *horilka*. He watched her gaze follow the glass from the table to his lips. If she disapproved, she knew better than to show it.

"Alla wants a special dress, which will require a high-quality fabric." Katerina bit her lower lip, as if working up the courage to continue.

"Hmm."

"She needs the dress quickly. It would take too long to order the fabric," Katerina explained. "Weyburn has a far better selection,"

"Can't take time to go to Weyburn this week."

"That's what I told her, so she asked Roman, and he volunteered to drive us there on Friday. I told her I could go only if you approve."

Viktor noticed Katerina breathing harder, her chest rising and falling in a faster rhythm, although he could see she was working to maintain control. He relished her discomfort, the way he relished the burn of *horilka*, drawing it out, making it last.

"Alla is going with you? Not just Roman?"

"Certainly. Alla is going to help select the fabric." She sounded like a salesman eager to close the deal.

"Wouldn't be proper to go that distance without her."

"Of course, you're right. I would never—"

"I wouldn't allow it."

She said no more, waited for a yes or no, her expression giving away little.

"And the price?"

"We haven't set it yet. It depends on the cost of the fabric we choose and the design," she said, meeting his eyes.

"You remember the conditions."

"Yes."

"Then you have my agreement."

Katerina leaned forward, closing the distance between them. "Thank you." She rose and left the room.

Viktor smiled to himself.

Weyburn Mental Hospital stood as imposing and impeccably kept as Katerina remembered it, as if external orderliness compensated for the inmates' internal chaos. The landscape, which in fall had been bathed in yellows and coppers, was awash in lime greens and pinks.

When Roman pulled his truck to the entrance portico, Katerina's every instinct told her to stay in the truck, but having enlisted the Klopoushaks to make this detour, she knew it was too late to turn back.

By spinning an altered version of her earlier trip with Viktor, she'd played on their vanity and sympathy. She'd explained her mission to check on Elena's brother, Jon, and said that she didn't want Viktor to know because it would disturb him. That had been true enough. It was the rest that made her ask the Lord's forgiveness. She'd flattered them, convinced them she believed they were most trustworthy of all the people she'd met in Bilik. Her husband was such a responsible man, she'd said, that he felt guilty for not strictly keeping his promise to his departed wife. It was little enough to spare him from self-recrimination. Work and weather and an untimely ankle sprain had all conspired to keep him from fulfilling his pledge, and there was nothing that meant more to Viktor than honor. She'd surprise him with news of her visit, she'd said, when he was in a better frame of mind, not now.

"He's an upstanding man, true enough," Roman had agreed. "Never has his thumb on the scale, and I've known plenty who have."

"He is indeed a man of integrity," Katerina had said. "It would please him to know how well thought of he is by such a successful man as yourself." She'd smiled a hypocrite's smile, certain he would believe her. Experience had taught her that the arrogant never recognize flattery for what it is; they take it as fact. She had felt guilty for misleading them, but she'd rationalized it to herself, convinced herself that this deception was the only means of getting to the truth.

The Klopoushaks had vowed to keep her secret. Because of Roman's game of seduction, his silence could be relied upon, but trusting Alla to keep quiet about anything was a gamble. Katerina thought of Yana's assessment: *If that woman had a choice between giving up gossip and giving up water, she'd surely die of thirst.* Katerina was tired of wallowing in sadness, sick to death of living in fear. It was a risk she had to take.

Roman opened the passenger door for her and extended his hand. She pretended not to notice when he held her hand slightly longer than was proper, but his boldness, so openly displayed, unnerved her.

"Thank you," Katerina said, stepping awkwardly from the running board. "I should be less than twenty minutes."

Ascending the stairs, Katerina grasped the brass railing to steady herself, smoothed her skirt, and took a deep breath. Once in the building, she glanced around attempting to get her bearings.

"May I help you?" the woman behind the reception desk inquired.

"I—I am Mrs. Viktor Senyk," Katerina said, struggling to keep her lips from quivering, self-conscious that her accented English sounded peculiar outside Bilik's Ukrainian enclave. "I am here about Jon Blanek, my brother."

"Certainly."

The woman's smile made deception difficult.

"I sent a letter to Dr. Fowler, but I have not heard from him." Katerina's heartbeat pounded in her ears. "Perhaps his reply was lost?"

"Oh, you want the Records Department. First door on the right," the receptionist said, pointing to a hallway behind her.

It wasn't too late to keep from opening Pandora's box. All Katerina had to do was turn and leave. She hesitated. If only the choice were that simple.

When Katerina found the Records Department sign posted above the first doorway on the right, she stepped inside and glanced around the room. On one dull-green wall hung the portrait of a somber, white-haired man with a look of authority about him; on another hung group photographs of women in nurses' caps. The dark oak woodwork, as lustrous as freshly shined shoes, lent the place substance.

A hefty woman, sitting at a desk behind a long wooden counter, glanced up, a scowl permanently fixed on her face. "Yes?"

Katerina repeated the words she'd carefully rehearsed. "I am Mrs. Viktor Senyk. I am here about Jon Blanek, my brother."

"Blanek?"

"Yes. I sent a letter to Dr. Fowler, but I have not heard from him. Perhaps his reply was lost?"

"Let me get his file."

The woman balanced her cigarette in the ashtray on her desk and rose from her chair, breathing heavily. As she waddled to a bank of filing cabinets on the wall behind her, she coughed every few steps. With effort, she bent to open the drawer—second from the bottom—in the first cabinet. "Blanek, Blanek," she said aloud, rifling through the tightly packed folders. "Ah, here it is—Blanek, Jon." She lumbered back to her chair. "Yes, Mrs. Senyk. Dr. Fowler sent a letter to you on April 23."

Katerina swallowed. "May I ask which address he sent it to?"

"Let's see." Squinting, the woman brought the copy of the letter to within six inches of her face. "The light in here seems to be getting dimmer every year," she complained. "The letter was sent to a Bilik address." The woman lifted another page from the file and held the two side by side. Her brow wrinkled. "I'm sorry. It seems there's been an error."

Katerina's heart pounded. She could walk away now, pretend she'd never received a letter sent to Mrs. Viktor Senyk of Bilik, and settle into her bargained-for life—or she could step off the cliff.

"I see you made a request that future correspondence be sent to a Winnipeg address," the woman said. "203 First Avenue, Winnipeg. Is that correct?"

Katerina's throat was as dry as winter grass. She prayed the woman couldn't smell deception.

"Yes."

Perspiration trickled down Katerina's back and between her breasts. She flushed, although she was certain it had nothing to do with the temperature of the room. *Two-zero-three First Avenue, Winnipeg.* She raised her chin, affecting a confidence she did not feel.

"Would it be possible to have correspondence sent to both addresses? My mother is not well, so I must travel often."

"Certainly, Mrs. Senyk, I'll make a note of it here." The woman penned the instructions on a blank piece of paper and placed it inside the folder. "At the reception desk, they'll call the ward to send an escort for you."

Lacing her fingers to keep them from shaking, Katerina stood rooted on legs as heavy as concrete posts. She forced herself to meet the woman's eyes, having heard somewhere that liars give themselves away by avoiding looking directly at a person. "I'm sorry; I haven't time to see Jon today. I'll inform Dr. Fowler of my next visit."

"As you wish." The woman's expression said she'd encountered other spineless relatives who hadn't the courage to face their defective kin.

"You've been very helpful," Katerina said. It was the first truthful statement she'd uttered since entering the hospital.

Two-zero-three First Avenue Winnipeg. Two-zero-three First Avenue Winnipeg. Two-zero-three First Avenue Winnipeg. Katerina repeated the address to herself again and again; still, it made no sense. She'd unearthed a clue, she was certain—but a clue to what, she couldn't figure. If she'd thought playing detective would bring peace of mind, she'd been wrong. It unsettled her completely.

What had she hoped to accomplish by going behind her husband's back, nosing around for information that made little sense? She'd set off on a trail without signposts or a discernible direction. Plus, she'd enlisted help from neighbors of dubious trustworthiness. What had she done? If Viktor discovered she'd gone to the mental hospital and inquired after Elena's brother, she didn't want to imagine it.

Unlike the first ride to and from Weyburn, in which she'd attempted to take in every sight and sound her senses could absorb, on this ride, she stared out the window, seeing little, feeling everything. The expensive Gotfredson rocked through ruts and potholes with Alla, wedged in the middle, bouncing toward one side and then the other, pinning Katerina against the door. The air became thinner and thinner in the claustrophobic cab, making it difficult for her to breathe.

"I was just saying to Roman," Alla prattled, "I couldn't be more pleased. I wouldn't have thought to choose lavender, but I think you're right. It enhances my brown eyes."

Alla's face was so close to hers that Katerina smelled the sausage she'd eaten at breakfast.

"I'm happy you're pleased."

Two-zero-three First Avenue Winnipeg.

"Have you decided on the design yet?"

"What? Oh. Well, I haven't put my idea to paper yet. I wanted you to choose the fabric first."

"Still, you must have some notion about the style," Alla said, her tone inching toward irritation.

Two-zero-three First Avenue, Winnipeg.

Because the letter from the hospital had arrived at the same time she'd agreed to create Alla's dress, Katerina had given the design little thought. She'd already decided that, in a pinch, she could use the same pattern she'd created for a patron in L'viv who had Alla's top-heavy figure.

"Can you give me a hint?" Alla persisted.

"Are you sure you wouldn't prefer a surprise?"

"Perhaps you're right."

Alla continued to chatter and Katerina's thoughts drifted.

Two different addresses for Mrs. Viktor Senyk. How was that possible? *Stop.* Katerina told herself to pretend she'd never gone to Weyburn Mental Hospital. She should forget the address, live the life she'd chosen, and quit borrowing trouble. *Still.*

Although to the entire town Viktor's first wife had become a heroine for saving a child, her story already woven into Bilik lore, Katerina knew very little about Elena. Aleksandr had once claimed he didn't know that his mother was going to Winnipeg to take care of his aunt. That was it! The address must belong to Elena's sister. It would stand to reason that the sister would look after Jon and communicate with the hospital. But hadn't the receptionist specifically said the request to send correspondence to Winnipeg had been made by Mrs. Viktor Senyk? Maybe her sister had simply forgotten to inform Dr. Fowler that Elena had died. That didn't seem plausible. If Aneta died, God forbid, Katerina would never send a letter in her sister's name or fail to mention her passing. The puzzle piece didn't fit, no matter how many different ways Katerina turned it.

"We grow the best wheat in the world right here in Saskatchewan," Roman said, his booming voice filling the cab. "Soon the land will be knee high in golden wheat as far as the eye can see."

Her focus turned to the fields, where shoots, barely visible, peeked from the fertile soil. This was Katerina's first prairie spring. How had so much happened in so little time? Only a year ago she'd still lived with Aneta and Danya. It had been after Stepan and before Matviyko. It had been before she'd heard of Bilik or Viktor Senyk.

"These days we grow mainly Marquis Wheat." Roman spoke with authority, a man proud of his business. "We used to grow mainly Red Fife, but the growing season here is only 110 days, and Marquis Wheat matures 10 days earlier than other varieties, making it perfect for this climate. It hasn't been around that long. Charles Saunders didn't develop the strain until 1904."

"Roman," Alla scolded, "Katerina doesn't want to hear chapter and verse about wheat varieties."

In truth, Katerina didn't want to hear about either lavender fabric or hybrid crops.

Alla gave Roman's knee an affectionate tap. "You'll have to excuse my husband," Alla said. "He's all business."

Katerina stared out the side window.

Chapter Eighteen

His father came home from the elevator in a rare talkative mood, which continued through dinner and into the evening. Aleksandr didn't know why, but it was best not to ask. Although his father had a drink sitting next to him on the side table, as far as Aleksandr could tell, he hadn't been drinking earlier. His father never, ever drank at work, because the elevator was too dangerous. Hadn't Aleksandr been warned a million times to be extremely careful there? *Don't touch that! Watch where you're going! Where's your head, boy!*

"Don't understand how you can tolerate working for that woman," his father said. He was talking about Mrs. Klopoushak.

"It's a business arrangement, Viktor. Besides, I've gotten other work because of her."

"Couldn't do it myself."

"What makes you bring up Alla?" she said. Her hands kept moving as she embroidered the collar of the blue dress she was making, but Aleksandr could tell she was paying extra-close attention because she looked at his father about every five seconds before looking back at what she was sewing. He could also tell from the cautious way she asked. Aleksandr understood caution.

The three of them sat in the parlor together, something they did, for no obvious reason, more frequently these days. His father had the *Grain Growers' Guide* open on his lap, although he only glanced at it as he smoked his pipe. Aleksandr pretended to read, too. It was important not to get too distracted; you never knew when there'd be clues that things were going to change for the worse.

"Roman came by the elevator today."

"Oh?"

Maybe it was his imagination, but Aleksandr thought his new mother looked worried. It was probably because the time that his father had threatened to destroy her sewing machine, it was Mr. Klopoushak's fault.

"The deal with the Sokur farm's gone through."

She looked up now and rested the dress on her lap. "So it's done?"

"Roman didn't waste any time discussing how much extra grain he plans to store come fall."

She sucked in her cheeks the way people do when they're trying not to laugh, although Aleksandr was pretty sure that wasn't the reason.

"Alla was with him. The woman never shuts up," his father said. "Don't know why he allows it."

Aleksandr wondered that, too. His father could make anyone be quiet, so why couldn't Mr. Klopoushak? Everyone knew he was rich, and a rich man should be able to make anyone do what he wanted.

His new mother tied off the yellow thread, searched in her sewing basket, and pulled out a hunk of red thread. "What else did they have to say?" Her hands were moving slower, and they shook as she tried to thread the embroidery needle.

"Only that he gave Sokur two weeks to clear out." His father set his pipe in the ashtray and took a large swallow from his glass.

Her hands stopped moving and she looked up. "That's heartless! How can he expect Svetlana, with her four children and her drun—her husband, to be ready to leave on such short notice?"

The crease between his father's eyes grew deeper. Aleksandr held his breath, waiting for him to get angry, but he didn't.

"Just business. This has been a long time coming. Svetlana knows that."

"Where will they go?" she asked. Her eyes glistened. She looked down and made three more stitches.

"Roman says Edmonton. Svetlana's got some distant family there."

His father took a long pull on his pipe and turned a page in his magazine. The smell of spicy tobacco drifted around the room. Aleksandr wondered if tobacco tasted the same as it smelled. When his father and his new mother grew quiet, he read several pages of *White Fang*, savoring the best part, in which the wolf-dog gets rescued from the cruel owner. Now and then, he peeked out of the corner of his eye for signs of trouble.

His new mother began to hum. She did that often, without thinking, the way some people bit their nails or pushed their glasses up their nose. Her beautiful voice was one of the things he liked best about her. The pretty melodies always made the house feel happier, at least for a little while.

She raised her head from her work. "Viktor, I'm thinking it would be neighborly to help the Sokurs," she said, her voice still cautious.

Aleksandr wished his new mother would keep humming and leave well enough alone.

His father drained his glass, tipping it until the last drop slid into his mouth. Then he looked at her, his expression unreadable, which made Aleksandr very nervous.

"And?"

"I'm not suggesting you go out there. I know you're far too busy at work."

A long, thin stream of smoke floated toward the ceiling as his father puffed in little spurts, saying nothing.

"Perhaps Jakob or Fedir could take me to the Sokur farm to help Svetlana," his new mother said.

"It's the Klopoushak farm now."

"Of course, you're right."

Without turning his head, Aleksandr looked from his father to his new mother, unable to predict what would happen next. The air suddenly felt thick.

"You won't neglect your work here?"

Aleksandr knew what that meant. His father's expectations were as plain as law.

She shook her head. "I won't." Then she smiled at him, not a big smile, just a pleasant smile. "Thank you, Viktor."

Aleksandr breathed again.

Despite all Katerina had endured in recent months, nothing was more disquieting than the atmosphere at the Sokurs' farm the June afternoon she and Yana arrived to help Svetlana pack.

At first, when Yana had insisted on accompanying her, Katerina had been disappointed, although she never would have said so to her friend. She'd hoped to spend time alone with Svetlana, lending a hand, but more important, getting answers to her questions before it was too late. Seeing the place again, she was grateful for Yana's presence. Weathering this without the comfort of her friend would have been unthinkable. Alone, she could not have endured witnessing Svetlana's heavyheartedness about leaving a home, humble as it was, with four children and a derelict husband. They would head, hat in hand, to live with relatives Svetlana hadn't seen since she was a child. Katerina's heart ached for all of them but especially for Svetlana.

Fedir let them off at the turnaround. "I'll be back after the store closes," he said.

Katerina and Yana walked toward the house on the narrow path worn through the tall grass. Kiel, who was at least a year younger than Aleksandr, hefted a water pail that seemed far too heavy for his stick-figure arms, lugging it to where Yuri tended the mules in the small corral attached to the barn. Katerina waved. Kiel smiled and Yuri tipped his cap, a gesture that no longer seemed out of place for this boy forced into manhood. Josef sat on a wooden chair just outside the front door, chin pressed to his chest, dozing. His daughter Inga played at his feet, entertaining her baby sister, Pasha, tickling her bare toes with a spray of grass. When Inga saw Katerina and Yana, she smiled shyly.

The place seemed unnaturally quiet, with only the cooing of the infant and the rasping of the grass in the breeze to interrupt the stillness. Katerina realized Goldie hadn't greeted them, and she wondered what had happened to the dog. Little was left of the dilapidated farm. The few chickens and pigs that had been there on her previous visit were no longer visible and had probably been slaughtered. Their absence hadn't improved the pungency of the place.

Katerina had entertained visions of helping Svetlana pack the household items they'd need to take to their new lives, but when she and Yana were greeted at the door, it became clear there wasn't much to do. What little there was, Svetlana planned to leave behind.

Tomorrow they would get on the train bound for Edmonton, carrying suitcases with a few family photographs, the *rushnyk* Svetlana's mother had made for her wedding, the clothes on their backs, and anything that would fit into a trunk and four small wooden crates. As if to underscore their misery, Yuri had been forced to make arrangements with Jakob to take possession of their wagon and mules as the final act before they departed.

Svetlana offered Katerina and Yana her dishes and pots and pans. "Might as well take these," she said, "instead of leaving them for the prairie dogs."

Neither Katerina nor Yana needed any of the items—they had far better—but to spare Svetlana further humiliation, they accepted them.

"Thank you, this will really come in handy," Yana said, holding a large, dented roasting pan and sounding as appreciative as if it were as good as new.

Katerina's heart swelled with affection for her kind friend.

Svetlana reached into the cupboard, where the cups still hung, and chose three without chips or broken handles. Everything seemed to be the same as last time they'd been there, as though the occupants planned to stay forever. She served them tea as if it were any other day and any other visit. This last bit of normalcy was the solitary grace note in a painful leave-taking.

Katerina had done this herself—packed for a life that lay ahead, as elusive as a mirage. Before she'd left Aneta's house, she'd packed her mother's scissors and surreptitiously taken the photograph of Mama from her sister's shelf. At the last moment, she'd stuck the silver clasp Stepan had given her, the one she'd planned to leave behind, into her satchel. She remembered feeling desperate to take something more permanent than her clothing, something that wouldn't wear out. Katerina wondered if Svetlana would do the same.

Over tea, they talked of ordinary things.

"We'll soon find out if Katerina's thumb is green or brown," Yana said, chuckling. "I remember the first time I planted my own garden. I'd grown up on the farm and helped my mother for years, but it's different being responsible for your own."

"Can you believe I've never tended a garden before?" Katerina said. "As a little girl, I remember my mother trying to raise tomatoes on the rooftop. We lived above my father's tailor shop. When the tomatoes ripened, she handled them as though they were made of gold. I almost felt guilty eating them."

As the three women conversed, a place deep inside Katerina opened. She searched for words to describe the feeling. *Comfortable. Companionable. Freeing.* That was it. Sharing memories with these women was so freeing, she regretted having guarded herself so completely. Even with Yana—guileless and warm Yana—she'd built a fortress around her memories, as if the mere utterance of them would have left her defenseless. Her life story was not all tragedy. It was more than Stepan leaving her and her leaving Matviyko. She'd been so afraid of revealing too much, she'd offered too little, and, at least where Svetlana was concerned, it was too late.

"Growing tomatoes on a roof," Yana said. "Now I've heard everything."

"It will be the first time I won't plant my own garden in as long as I can remember," Svetlana said.

It was surprising how matter-of-factly she said it, with as much emotion as if she'd said, *I won't be wearing that dress*, or *I won't be making that soup*. Katerina wondered if her detachment spoke of resilience or of defeat.

"If you'll excuse me, I need to use the outhouse," Yana said, pushing away from the table. "I'm getting old. These days, tea goes right through me."

As soon as the door closed, Svetlana turned to Katerina. "I suppose you've come to ask about Elena."

Svetlana's directness stunned her.

"I—I—"

"I figured as much."

Watching and listening for signs of resentment, Katerina saw and heard none.

"You've looked at me and wondered how a poor woman, who lives in such circumstances"—Svetlana's hand swept the room—"became friends with someone as well-off as Elena."

It embarrassed Katerina that she could not deny the accusation. "I know little about her."

Svetlana looked her in the eye. "You know enough."

Katerina wanted to argue that she'd asked questions no one would answer. She wanted to explain that Viktor had erased Elena from the house so completely, it was impossible to imagine her. But she knew what Svetlana meant. With certainty, she knew. Shame seized her.

Pushing up both blouse sleeves, Svetlana revealed arms full of bruises, some old, some fresh. Katerina remembered the time after Josef's accident, how Svetlana had winced when she'd lightly touched her shoulder, and a time at church when Svetlana's cheek and eye had looked bruised and swollen. Katerina had said nothing then.

"This is how Elena and I knew each other." Her eyes welled with tears, but they never left Katerina's. "Viktor has hurt you. I know it as surely as I know there is a God, who will someday punish men like our husbands." Her voice was quiet and steely.

I don't care what he needs. The day Josef lost his arm, Svetlana's vehemence had shocked Katerina. Now, she understood. Unconsciously, she touched her arm where Viktor had grabbed and twisted it only two days earlier. He had sat in the living room, drinking. "It's time for the boy to go to bed," he'd said, his brow furrowed, his words slurred. When Katerina explained Aleksandr was finishing an important school assignment and that it wasn't past his usual bedtime, Viktor rose, staggered into the kitchen, and pulled a startled Aleksandr from his chair. Katerina limped after him. "Viktor, please," she pleaded. "I'll make sure he goes to bed as soon as his assignment is finished." Viktor let go of Aleksandr's shirt, whirled around, and grabbed Katerina's arm, twisting it behind her back. "*You* don't tell *me* when my son goes to bed!" His breath smelled sour as he spat out the words. She cried out in pain when he twisted her arm farther behind her back. Out of the corner of her eye, she saw Aleksandr run from the room. Then Viktor let go and stumbled back to the living room to pour himself another drink, as though nothing had happened. His unpredictability had terrified her.

"I'm sure you want to know what really happened to Elena. Svetlana was speaking faster now and checking the door frequently. "I don't know what happened to her."

Deep disappointment gripped Katerina.

"I know everyone says she drowned. That's Viktor's story. The rest of the town may swallow it, but I don't believe a word."

Katerina checked the door. "What do you believe?"

"A couple of weeks before Elena vanished, she asked me if I'd ever thought of leaving, just picking up and disappearing," Svetlana said. "The notion seemed so fanciful, I paid it little mind. Since then, I've turned her words over in my head a thousand times. I think she was asking me to leave with her."

Two-zero-three First Avenue, Winnipeg. Katerina's throat closed. A cyclone whirled through her. *Two-zero-three First Avenue, Winnipeg. Dear God!* Was it possible Elena was alive? Her heart beat faster. She couldn't speak for fear of what might escape. *This is crazy. There's no proof. Svetlana is guessing. She doesn't really know anything.*

Svetlana took Katerina's hand in hers. "Are you all right?"

Katerina nodded, even though she was the furthest thing from all right. The world spun faster. The house grew smaller. She had to think. This was impossible. A man who already has a wife doesn't marry another woman. Svetlana must be mistaken. But even if Svetlana was right, maybe Viktor didn't know his first wife was alive. Maybe Elena had tricked him. Maybe he'd been told by someone—her sister, surely—that she'd drowned.

"Why didn't you go with her?" The words came as a whisper.

"She had one child. I have four."

"If you're right, she purposely left Aleksandr behind," Katerina said, more accusatorily than she'd intended.

"She loves that child. Maybe she couldn't think of any other way," Svetlana said. "Maybe she decided she could save him only by first saving herself."

The door opened and Yana walked in, her hair windblown and her shoes covered in dust. She bent down to remove them.

"Don't bother," Svetlana said. "Klopoushak will just let the place fall down anyway."

Yana looked from one red face to another. "You've been crying."

Katerina shook her head. "This is too hard," she said. "It's just too hard."

Chapter Nineteen

Saturday was Viktor's favorite day of the week. It was the day farmers came to Bilik to do errands, and as the preferred place to congregate, the grain elevator became the most important location in town. He was glad for the company of men, for time to talk politics, prices, and whatever topics came to mind. Mostly, he enjoyed Saturday because it was the day he took center stage as the authority on all things pertaining to the grain market.

The wives and children who accompanied the men to town strolled along Main Street, shopping and socializing. When their errands were completed, they gathered at Panko's General Store, sharing news and gossip. Fedir and Yana could tease even the most jealously guarded information from their customers. It was said if you wanted to know what was happening in Bilik, Fedir and Yana were the ones to ask. If they didn't know the answer, you'd asked the wrong question.

On this hot July morning, a warm wind blew from the southwest. Dove-white clouds stairstepped heavenward in a sea-blue sky, casting occasional shadows over the fields as they drifted beneath the sun. By midmorning, a bevy of cars, trucks, and wagons were parked at the base of the grain elevator, sunlight glinting off their metallic surfaces as if illuminated by klieg lights. A sizable group of men stood in the driveway conversing.

"Fifty more elevators have joined the Pool in the past couple of months, and that's only the beginning," Roman Klopoushak said.

"What guarantee do we have that the Pool's going to be any better than the privately owned elevators?" Tomko Usick had asked the question. Usick was the type to kick dirt onto any new idea.

"What guarantee do we have that there'll be enough rain this year or that it won't rain so much your crops will rot in the fields?" Viktor said. "A farmer is a gambler."

Heads nodded.

"You're going to get a fairer shake from the Wheat Pool than you'll get from those profiteers." Viktor shoved his hands in his pockets.

"He's right. The Saskatchewan Wheat Pool," Klopoushak said, gesturing up at the logo painted in huge white letters on the side of the elevator, "is the best thing to come along since the invention of the plow." Sweat trickled from his hairline and perspiration darkened his underarms. He wiped his face with the back of his forearm. "It's about time we used our collective power to command fair prices."

Roman Klopoushak held forth no matter the topic, and given his success, the others rarely challenged him. His rock-bottom bid on the Sokur place had jaws flapping around Bilik, but no one seemed ready to take him on face-to-face. Viktor had the standing to confront him, but on the Sokur deal—which, to Viktor, was simply good business—and the Saskatchewan Wheat Pool, they agreed, so he let him have his say.

"Anyone who doesn't join is a plain fool," Klopoushak added.

The men murmured agreement.

"It's the best chance we have to keep prices steady." The comment came from the Bandarek brother wearing the gray hat.

"It's the future," the Bandarek brother wearing the brown hat added.

The brothers were mirror images of each other. Vladimir's hair was thinning faster than Boris's, but with their hats on, Viktor was damned if he knew which was which. It didn't seem to bother the brothers that no one could tell them apart. In fact, they often used it to their advantage, playing pranks by impersonating each other. They'd been doing it since they were boys. It appeared nobody thought it peculiar for twin brothers, decades beyond youth, to be tied at the hip; or if they did, no one ever said anything about it. In Viktor's experience, every small town had its share of oddballs who were as much part of the place as Main Street and the church dome.

"Viktor, have you heard anything more about what's happening in the rest of the province?" Ivan Zolyar asked, working a straw reed between his lips.

Viktor paused for effect, scratching his chin and tipping his hat back on his head.

He thought of the autumn morning he'd called Zolyar out for smoking his pipe while waiting in line to unload his wheat. Every farmer knew grain dust is highly combustible—hell, all it would take would be a spark to send the place sky high—and, as far as Viktor was concerned, a man who tempted fate so carelessly wasn't worth his weight in air. Undoubtedly, Zolyar knew he'd been a fool, so he hadn't held the public rebuke against Viktor nor had any of the others. In fact, Viktor was certain the incident had gained him even more respect. The proof hung from Zolyar's mouth. Since that day, the man hadn't taken as much as a puff in Viktor's presence.

"There's been plenty of mail from the Pool coming across my desk," Viktor said. He pulled his hat brim down, leaned against the elevator wall, and crossed his ankles, a man totally at ease in his surroundings. "Looks as though they have their sights set on dominating the market. Been real aggressive in signing up farmers all over Saskatchewan. Hear tell the Pool's looking at the number of elevators reaching somewhere around six hundred by year's end."

For a moment, Viktor lost the group's attention as the men reacted to his generous estimate.

He waited.

"That's awfully optimistic," Usick said once the murmuring had settled. His eyes became slits as he squinted into the bright sun. "You think they can actually reach that?"

"Might be optimistic but it's also possible the number could go higher." Viktor had the group's attention now. "Private companies aren't taking too kindly to the plan. Been losing ground, left and right. But they're not getting any sympathy here. If they'd played fair all these years, there'd be no need for the Pool."

In the distance, a train whistle blasted like an exclamation point.

"I guess that settles that," Zolyar said.

The men laughed.

"I heard a rumor there's an implement dealer coming to town," the brown-hatted Bandarek brother said.

Viktor's eyes met Klopoushak's. They'd discussed this more than two months earlier, when Klopoushak stopped by after dropping Alla off to conduct business with Katerina. Klopoushak had sworn him to secrecy, and Viktor had been as good as his word. He guessed Alla had been wagging her tongue again, and he was pretty sure her husband knew that, too. Klopoushak nodded at him almost imperceptibly. Viktor took his meaning.

"Guess you'll have to ask Roman about that," he said.

Klopoushak strolled to the highest point of the driveway so he was visible to everyone. "You heard right. I'm fronting the business and my wife's brother will manage it."

"When's it coming?"

"Two weeks. In fact, I've already bought the first combine. It's going to make the threshing machine obsolete," Klopoushak bragged, "and it's going to eliminate the need to bring in seasonal crews from Ontario."

"Sounds like magic." It was crotchety Usick putting in his two cents again.

Laughter erupted.

"There'll be a demonstration at my place, so you can see for yourselves," Klopoushak said. "Then we'll see who's laughing."

Several conversations broke out at once. The men talked of machinery prices and debated Klopoushak's claims. Viktor knew Klopoushak was right. He'd seen what a combine could do, and he knew Roman Klopoushak wasn't a man to throw money after a fanciful contraption.

Soon, the exchanges turned to more personal matters, and the men splintered into twos and threes. By noon, they began to disperse, some bound for home and some headed to the general store to pick up their supplies and families.

Klopoushak was the last to leave. He turned to Viktor. "How are you doing with that pretty new wife of yours?"

Viktor felt a twinge of jealousy at Klopoushak's reference to his wife's looks. Had it been anyone else, Viktor would have set him straight. "Can't complain," he said.

"Alla seems to think she's part angel."

Viktor had to admit that in spite of Katerina's citified ways, people liked her. Hell, maybe it was her sophistication that drew them to her. The women, even Alla Klopoushak, looked up to her, admired her, as if she were some kind of exotic orchid among common prairie onions.

"Wouldn't go that far," Viktor said.

"A woman of her caliber doesn't come along every day," Klopoushak said.

"Suppose not." The man's interest began to rankle.

Privately, Viktor allowed that Katerina was smarter than most women. He'd never tell her that, of course; she was prideful enough. On the occasions he talked about work, she asked intelligent questions, not that she understood the specifics of market prices or the agricultural economy. But Katerina wasn't the ideal prairie wife by a long shot. In fact, she was downright inept at certain basics. When he'd told her he expected her to revive their garden in spring, she'd admitted she didn't know the first thing about planting or tending one.

"Suggest you learn, then," he'd said.

"I'll ask Yana to teach me."

Simple as that, the matter had been settled.

When they'd first married, Katerina would have challenged him. She was a willful woman; that had been evident from the first. He'd decided to put a stop to her arrogance before it got out of hand. Her defiantly raised chin—she had been spoiling for a fight—had initially caught him off guard. The next time she'd adopted that haughty attitude, he'd punched her. She'd gasped and fallen to the floor, her crippled leg instantly giving way. He'd meant to teach her, not knock her down. He'd purchased a bag of licorice and left it for her. That had been a mistake. She'd taken it as a sign of weakness, and his intended message had been lost. He hadn't made the same mistake twice.

Before leaving, Klopoushak extended his hand. Viktor gripped it firmly. There was a lot to a man's handshake. Klopoushak's was strong and sure. In response, Viktor tightened his grip.

"We'll be seeing you at church tomorrow," Klopoushak said, stepping up into his truck. "You take good care of that sweet wife of yours."

The man had nerve.

Viktor stomped to the elevator office, chewing on Klopoushak's comments. He didn't like any man showing interest in his wife. It wasn't *his* fault that Klopoushak had chosen to marry a well-heeled, prattling cow.

He tried not to stew about it, but found Katerina slipping into his thoughts despite his intention to focus on work. Somehow, she must have encouraged Klopoushak. After all, Viktor hadn't been present every time they'd encountered each other. There'd been the ride to Weyburn, and there'd been numerous times that Klopoushak had picked up Alla after she'd conducted business with his wife. If Katerina knew what was good for her, she'd keep her eyes to herself.

Viktor turned back to the open ledger on his desk, running his index finger down the payout column. He double-checked the amount of grain stored the previous year by Josef Sokur. Klopoushak was looking to quadruple that volume.

As of late, Katerina had been agreeable and trying hard to please him. She'd been turning into the kind of wife he wanted. He'd even gotten used to her damaged leg. It hadn't really interfered with her work or his pleasure in bed.

After all their coupling, he'd begun to wonder if she was barren. For a time, he'd suspected she might be pregnant, but obviously, he'd been mistaken. It wasn't that he actually wanted more children. It was more a matter of manly pride than the desire to father a brood. He'd already fathered a son, so any suspicion about infertility would fall on Katerina. Besides, Klopoushak had no children, and Viktor had never heard a word casting doubt on *his* manhood, although he'd heard plenty of doubt about Alla's fitness as a wife.

Klopoushak had a rich man's cheek. Money or not, he'd better not come sniffing around Viktor's wife like a male dog pursuing a female dog in heat. Vowing to keep a closer eye on Katerina, Viktor closed the ledger in disgust. No way would he accomplish any more book work today. Katerina and Roman Klopoushak had seen to that.

Approaching Viktor about the new opportunity Alla had thrown in her lap would require planning. If Katerina had learned anything in her marriage, it was that she would have to convince her husband this prospect would be more to his benefit than hers. She'd been waiting for the right moment to speak with him—when he wasn't preoccupied with work or inebriated—to explain Alla's offer of a business proposition that was too good to pass up. For two weeks, she'd watched for the right time, but none had presented itself.

Last Saturday, Viktor had come home from work sulky and aloof. Since then, she'd tiptoed around him, searching for the source of his pique; she was now no closer to discovering it than she'd been that night.

While she lay awake, unable to sleep, it occurred to her that she'd been trying to figure out how to approach Viktor on her own when the best chance for gaining his approval was to have the business proposal presented by someone else, someone whom Viktor respected—Roman Klopoushak.

She'd have to think this through carefully. There was danger in involving him. If she dealt with Roman directly, he would surely interpret it as a sign of her interest in him. Any hint of need on her part would expose her vulnerability, and he'd pounce upon his prey. She must convince Roman to intercede for her without him exacting some intimate payment. The only way was to enlist his help through Alla. Depending upon her was like relying on the weather, but Katerina was desperate for this opportunity. It held the promise of independence. She weighed the risk of seeking Roman's help and decided it was worth the gamble.

The next morning, she went to Yana's to use the telephone. It embarrassed her to impose on her friend again. Viktor had agreed to have one installed at their house—he had one at the elevator office—but so far he'd not made good on his promise, and Katerina was afraid to remind him. The one time she'd asked, he'd barked, "I'll get to it when I'm damned good and ready."

At Yana's door, the sweet, yeasty aroma of baking bread greeted Katerina. "I'm sorry to trouble you again. I'd like to use your telephone," Katerina said.

"Ach, what are friends for? You're just in time to help me sample the cinnamon buns."

While Yana slathered butter on the warm buns, Katerina called Alla. It was too risky to discuss her idea over the telephone; one never knew who might be listening on the party line. She simply told Alla she had something she wanted to discuss with her and asked when they might meet.

"We'll be in town on Saturday. How about then?"

"Perfect."

On the following Saturday, they met on the bench in front of the general store and devised a strategy to convince Viktor of Alla's proposition.

"Your idea is wonderful, Alla, but Viktor might not recognize that if I bring it up to him. Like many men, he has little faith in a woman's business sense. But he's sure to agree if the plan is presented by your husband, a respected businessman," Katerina said, her confident air masking her uncertainty. "We'll make an evening of it. They can talk over dinner."

"I'll speak with him tonight," Alla said. "Roman will think it's a splendid idea."

Katerina remembered Yana's assessment of Alla and smiled. *That woman's so persistent she could talk a cat into going for a swim.*

"I'll check with Viktor and let you know tomorrow which evening to come to dinner," Katerina said.

That night, after she'd finished washing the dishes, she took her embroidery into the parlor and sat in the chair across from Viktor.

"You seem to enjoy Fedir's company," she said.

"Better than most." Viktor continued reading his magazine.

"Alla tells me Roman has been taking you into his confidence," she said after a while. "He must trust your business sense."

Viktor lowered the magazine to his lap and met her eyes. He said nothing but Katerina thought she detected a slight frown.

Distracted, she poked her finger with the embroidery needle and winced. A pinprick's worth of blood mounded on her fingertip. Before the droplet could stain the fabric, she took a handkerchief from her pocket and pressed it against her finger.

Viktor turned back to his article.

Be careful. Don't press too hard. "We always have such a fine time with Fedir and Yana."

"Uh-huh."

Her mouth was desert dry and her hands trembled. "They've

invited us to their home often." Katerina put the handkerchief back in her pocket. "I was thinking..." She took another stitch. His liquor glass was still half full. She wasn't certain whether it was his second or third. "Yana and Fedir are our dear friends. They've been so generous with us; maybe we should return their invitation. Perhaps we could also include Alla and Roman as a show of gratitude for the sewing jobs she's brought my way."

Viktor set his magazine aside and rested his glass in his palm.

Katerina couldn't read his mood.

"The Klopoushaks as well as the Pankos?"

"Well," she said and licked her lips, "given how widely respected you are and how influential they are in the community, it might be advantageous to include them. Only if you agree, of course." She went back to her stitchery.

Viktor remained silent. His stoicism heightened her nervousness.

When she glanced up, he was studying her.

She forced a sweet smile.

"When?"

"Oh, no particular time," she said, taking another stitch. "Whenever you think best."

Viktor took a hefty swallow from his glass and turned back to his magazine.

Katerina thought he intended to ignore her. Perhaps he was punishing her, but for what, she couldn't guess. With Viktor, retribution was often delayed. He might say nothing now and then hurt her later. She bit the inside of her cheek.

"Next Saturday," he said.

Katerina exhaled. She hadn't realized she'd been holding her breath.

Early August, almost a year since Katerina's arrival in Bilik, was the first time she and Viktor invited guests to their home. Katerina wanted everything to be perfect. This was more than an ordinary gathering; it was hope masquerading as a dinner party. If Roman convinced Viktor to let her take this new opportunity, it meant she could secretly hide a small portion of the profits. She had no clear plan for the money, no idea how to change her circumstances or notion of how to face a future with a man of Viktor's temperament. This wasn't something she knew; it was something she felt. Katerina's intuition told her this opportunity promised salvation.

Days in advance, she scrubbed floors, dusted furniture, and beat carpets. She planned the menu as though she were serving a holiday feast.

As she searched the cupboards for dinnerware worthy of guests, she confirmed what she had already known; the house was ill equipped for special occasions. She removed plates, cups, and bowls from the shelves and stacked them on the dining room table, sorting out the chipped pieces, mixing and matching the intact dishes to make an adequate service for six. By alternating colors and patterns and adding pink napkins, fashioned from leftover fabric, she made the blend look purposeful.

From the bottom drawer of the banquette, she retrieved a yellowing lace tablecloth. Because it was too expensive to replace, Katerina decided to tea-stain the lace to give it a richer color. She filled a pail with boiling water and loose tea and let the tablecloth soak for an afternoon. After the cloth dried to a mellow brown, she wove pink satin ribbon around the perimeter, through openings in the lace, tying off a bow every twelve inches. She draped it over the table, stepped back to inspect the cloth, and smiled with pleasure at the effect.

On the Saturday afternoon of the dinner, before he went to the Pankos' for the night, she sent Aleksandr to pick wild bergamot. The rose-hued flowers made a fragrant centerpiece, and Yana had taught her that, afterward, she could dry the leaves to make a spicy tea.

"We expecting Prime Minister Meighen?" Viktor asked as he passed through the dining room.

"Just our friends." Katerina ignored his sarcasm.

By the time the guests arrived, she was as edgy as a cornered mouse. It wasn't due to the demanding preparations or inadequate dinnerware. She was nervous about what her husband might do or say and afraid that others would recognize how small she became in his presence. It was too late to retreat now, so she straightened her back and took one last look in the entryway mirror before answering the door.

Yana and Fedir arrived first.

"Evening, Fedir...Yana," Viktor said. "Glad you could make it."

"All day, he's been as excited as a boy on his first date," Yana said. "We can't remember when we've gone anywhere without the children."

"They're always welcome," Katerina said.

"Not on your life. I'm pretending my bride and I are courting again." Fedir squeezed Yana's arm and patted her backside.

"Fedir Panko, behave yourself. This is a formal occasion. Besides, I only let a man with manners court me." Yana clucked her tongue and gave a dismissive wave, but her eyes sparkled and she grinned like a schoolgirl.

The Klopoushaks arrived in their fancy truck. When they entered the parlor, Viktor strode toward them, extending his hand to Roman. "Glad you could join us," he said. "You didn't happen to see King George out there, did you?"

Roman looked puzzled.

"My wife's been acting like we're entertaining royalty."

Everyone chuckled.

Katerina smiled but her back stiffened and heat rose to her cheeks.

"That's the best kind of hostess," Roman said. "Any man who wants to get ahead in this world needs a high-class wife."

Alla beamed.

Caution streamed through Katerina's veins.

Everyone took their assigned seats at the table. At the women's places lay a single flower tied with a ribbon, at the men's, a cigar tied with a bow made of straw.

"How clever," Alla said.

Katerina had considered the seating arrangement carefully. Viktor sat at the head of the table, with Roman on his left and Yana on his right. Katerina placed herself at the end closest to the kitchen, with Fedir on her left and Alla across from him. She figured it was a kindness not to torture Yana by seating her next to Alla, and Katerina wanted to keep Alla—who had a knack of steering any conversation toward herself—within earshot so she could gently guide her to other topics. She also judged it best to keep her distance from Roman, hoping he got the message. Jovial Fedir could sit next to anyone and be at ease, and Viktor and Roman, the self-appointed titans, seated next to each other, could spar unimpeded.

First, Katerina served potato soup garnished with dill. She watched as everyone talked and ate, looking for signs of approval or disapproval. Not a drop remained in any bowl. She relaxed slightly. While she was in the kitchen preparing to bring out the main course—baked chicken in sour cream sauce, *nachinka*, beets and horseradish, and *varenyky*—Yana walked in.

"I came to help," Yana said.

"But you're a guest tonight."

"Remember the day you arrived, and Viktor came for dinner?" Yana said.

Katerina recalled it vividly. Everything and everyone had been frighteningly foreign. She'd been too nervous to sit and too nervous to eat. It seemed as though it were both yesterday and a lifetime ago.

"You said, 'Put me to work.' And I protested that you were a guest. You said, 'I promise not to step on your toes. I need to keep busy.' Remember?"

"You let me help," Katerina said. "But you also told me that when it came time to serve the meal, I became a guest again."

"Yes, but now we're friends."

Battling Yana with logic was a losing proposition, so Katerina handed her the bowl of chicken. "Thank you, friend," she said.

"Besides," Yana whispered, "you know how much I love to serve Her Royal Highness."

Katerina giggled, despite her nerves.

By the time she served the almond custard torte, Roman had not brought up the money-making opportunity, and Katerina began to wonder if he'd ever broach the subject. Maybe Alla hadn't been clear. There was no way to give a hint or signal without giving herself away, so she waited, playing hostess as if she had nothing on her mind other than the comfort of her guests.

"Time to retire to the parlor," Viktor said after finishing dessert. "Can't let these cigars go to waste."

"Excellent meal, Katerina." Fedir patted his rounded stomach. "You've outdone yourself."

"Thank you. Now if you'll excuse me, I'll clear the dishes and join you shortly with some tea," Katerina said.

"I'll help." Yana was already balancing an armful of plates.

Alla hesitated for a moment, then followed the women into the kitchen.

"Let's just stack the dishes for now," Katerina said. "I'll clean up later." She was on edge. Time was growing short for Roman to speak on her behalf.

When Alla and Yana entered the parlor—followed by Katerina, who was carrying a tray with teakettle, cups, sugar, and cream—the air was clouded with cigar smoke and Viktor had served drinks. Katerina noticed he'd already drained his first glass. She poured tea for the women while he continued as though they weren't present.

"Boris is driving his car along a country road," Viktor said, "when he meets Igor, driving his wagon. 'Hey, Boris, do you realize Olga fell out of your car three miles back?' says Igor. 'Thank heavens, I thought I'd gone deaf!' says Boris."

The men laughed boisterously.

"Fill it for you?" Viktor asked, nodding toward Roman's half-filled glass.

"Certainly."

"Fedir?"

"Maybe when I finish this." Fedir waggled his cigar in the air.

Viktor topped Roman's glass and poured a full glass for himself.

"I've got another one for you," he said. "Boris and his new bride, Olga, are riding home from the chapel in a wagon, pulled by a team of horses, when the older horse stumbles. Boris says, 'That's once.' A little farther along, the horse stumbles again. Boris says, 'That's twice.' After a little while, the horse stumbles again. Boris reaches under the seat, pulls out a shotgun, and shoots the horse. Olga yells, 'That was an awful thing to do!' Boris says, 'That's once.'"

"You're in trouble now," Roman said to Viktor.

Katerina knew better.

"Ach, you men," Yana said.

"Maybe it's time to change the subject," Fedir suggested.

Conversation turned to Roman's new implement business.

"Three weeks in and it's already doing better than expected," Roman boasted. "We're getting into this thing at the right time. Modern tractors and combines are going to revolutionize the hours of labor required and the amount of yield per farm. No question about it."

"Hell, maybe we'll have to build a second elevator," Viktor said.

Katerina watched as he drained his second glass and poured a third. If Roman didn't bring up the opportunity soon, it would be too late.

"Roman, can't say that having you next door has hurt business at my store. I should thank you for locating there." Puffs of smoke escaped from the end of Fedir's cigar as he spoke. "Don't get me wrong, I'm not grateful enough to pay you royalties."

"No need." Roman grinned around the cigar clenched between his teeth. "You scratch my back and I'll scratch yours."

Fedir raised his glass.

"Speaking of business," Roman said. "I almost forgot. Alla has a proposition for Katerina."

"Oh?" Viktor cocked his head.

The air thinned. Katerina's throat closed.

"As you know, your wife has been making dresses for Alla and for her niece in Regina. Well, Alla's family has connections to all the best people. It seems Katerina's work has caught the attention of...Alla, what's her name?"

"Francine Greenwood."

"Yes. She owns...what's the name?"

"La Belle Femme. Miss Greenwood was at the wedding we attended in Regina," Alla said. "She couldn't stop gushing about my dress. She went on and on about the cut, the detailing, and the quality, and she insisted on knowing where I had purchased my exquisite dress. Anyhow—"

Katerina was certain Viktor wouldn't want to know the minutiae, especially if they were supplied by Alla. It was time for Alla to hand the reins to Roman. Katerina's heart beat so rapidly, all she could manage was a weak smile. "That's very gracious of you," Katerina said. She spoke to Alla but made eye contact with Roman, who seemed none too eager to look away.

Roman cleared his throat. "Anyhow," he said, "Miss Greenwood has a business proposition for your wife. She wants Katerina to design and sew custom-made dresses for her most discriminating customers."

"How wonderful!" Yana exclaimed. "Remember what I told you, Katerina? I knew this might lead somewhere."

"What's involved?" Viktor asked.

"They want her to sew for them on an exclusive contract," Roman said, looking at Alla as if he were reading the words on her forehead. "As I understand it, La..."

"Belle Femme," Alla prompted.

"La Belle Femme would place an order for a limited number of designs, and when a customer wanted to purchase that design, Katerina would sew it for her."

"Sounds like a full-time job," Viktor said.

Katerina's stomach turned in circles.

"Actually, the store is a small, exclusive boutique, so she wouldn't be sewing a huge number at a time," Alla explained. "What do you think, Katerina? Could you do it?"

"I...it sounds like a great opportunity." The pounding in Katerina's ears made her voice a muted rasp. She wanted to shout and plead and celebrate all at once, but she forced herself to sound as placid as possible.

"Katerina is a smart, talented woman, Viktor."

There was a proprietary undercurrent to Roman's praise that made Katerina uneasy. She studied Viktor for any sign he'd heard it. His expression revealed nothing.

"You and Fedir and I are all businessmen. Certainly, none of us would pass up this opportunity if it fell in our laps."

"I have to agree with Roman on this one, friend," Fedir said.

Viktor puffed on his cigar and took another large swallow from his glass. "Would she have to go to Regina?"

"Probably, to set up the deal," Roman admitted.

"Lived alone once," Viktor said. "Not inclined to do it again."

"Viktor, I wouldn't agree to it if the job took me away more than that first time," Katerina said. While she struggled to sound conciliatory, she wondered if the others heard her desperation. They didn't see Viktor for what he truly was. They looked at his mask and believed it was his face, so why wouldn't they see her mask and believe the same?

Viktor looked at her intently. "Someone would have to go with you, and I doubt if I could get away."

The fact that she had traveled thousands of miles alone to get to Canada seemed to escape Viktor, but Katerina kept quiet because she could hear his defenses weakening. *Please, dear God, let him say yes.*

"Alla could go with her," Roman said. "We go to Regina pretty regularly."

"Yes," Alla said. "It would be my pleasure to accompany Katerina and act as intermediary, use my influence where needed."

"There's good money to be made here. You could reinvest the earnings in any number of ways," Roman said.

As Katerina waited for her husband to respond, each tick of the clock lasted an eternity.

"Viktor, you've got a talented woman there," Roman cajoled him.

Katerina squirmed.

"My advice is to keep her happy."

"Suppose there's no harm in it," Viktor said, finally.

After the Pankos and the Klopoushaks left and the dishes were washed and put away, Katerina went to Viktor, who was sitting in the parlor, smoking his pipe and drinking a nightcap. She touched his shoulder gently. "I'm going to get ready for bed," she said. "Can I expect you soon?"

"Soon as this glass is empty," he said, lifting it as if toasting the evening.

Katerina washed, selected her prettiest nightgown, and applied a touch of rosewater on her wrists and along the hollows of her collarbone. Unpinning her hair, she let it fall to the middle of her back, brushing it slowly and laying a single lock seductively over her shoulder, just the way Viktor liked it. She turned the lamp flame down until it cast a suggestive shadow along the wall.

Stepan had taught her well. He would have been the one creating the mood, telling her with his soulful eyes and tender hands what he wanted. She imagined him embracing her, his gentle fingers combing through her hair. He whispered in her ear. He inhaled deeply. *I want to drink you in. Ah, so beautiful. Let me untie that for you.* Teasingly, his tongue brushed her lips. At the thought of him, she felt longing in every part of her. Yes, he'd taught her well.

Viktor hadn't the first idea how to love a woman. He was a man with little regard for the needs of a wife. His occasional tokens—licorice or a bar of soap—sat like feathers on the scale compared with the weight of his angry fists and vicious tongue.

He'd been married before, to a woman who surely had known fear and helplessness, the way Katerina knew them. Often, she tried to picture faceless Elena from the scraps she'd pieced together. Yana had described her pale complexion and wide eyes, which looked "surprised by everything." *Not surprised, Yana, terrified.* Katerina saw the image of a young woman, small and delicate, whose features were a foreshadowing of Aleksandr's, a fragile thing Viktor could break with a slap and a brutal word.

What happened to her?

I don't know what happened to her. I know everyone says she drowned… I don't believe a word. What do you believe?…I think she was asking me to leave with her.

Had she gone or stayed? Was she alive or dead? Elena's tracks were as elusive as clouds. They led down a dead-end alley, where Katerina frequently wandered, lost.

She wanted to run. Every inner voice, every nerve, and every impulse warned her to flee. But there was Aleksandr—innocent, damaged little bird. What choice did Katerina have but to stay? She had to do whatever it took to survive and to keep him safe. With all her strength, Katerina pushed her shame, revulsion, and fear deep into her core, until they hit bedrock. Tonight, she would teach her husband how to love her. She would make him believe he was master of a woman who desired him. She would reward him for granting permission to use her talent, so that he would not change his mind on a whim, and she would will Elena and her fate from her thoughts.

When Viktor walked into the room, Katerina met him at the door. "I've been waiting," she said. As she stepped closer, she smelled liquor on his breath. She told herself it was not sour but sweet. Nectar of the gods. The alcohol would make him more pliable. He would not see her for the actress she was.

He looked at her as though he didn't recognize her. When he opened his mouth to speak, she put her finger to his lips. "Shh." She commanded him to be still. Beginning at the collar, she unfastened his shirt, lingering at each button before walking her fingers to the next. He groped for her breasts. She took his hands in hers and guided them to his sides. "Not yet," she whispered. He obeyed.

She led him to the bed and motioned for him to sit. Bracing herself against his knees, she knelt with effort, hoping her leg would cooperate. She removed his shoes. Next, she undid his belt and unbuttoned his pants. He stood, letting his trousers fall to the floor and stepped out of them.

He grabbed her wrists and lifted her so she stood before him. He was breathing hard.

Before Katerina could speak, he pressed his mouth over hers and slipped his rough hands under her gown.

Anxiety fluttered in her chest as she felt control slipping away.

Viktor wrapped an arm around her. He drew her to him, then ran his free hand from the small of her back up the base of her neck. Viktor closed his fist around her hair and yanked her head back until her face was inches from his.

Panic squeezed her throat.

"Who taught you this harlot routine? Roman?" His words dripped with vitriol.

"What!"

"Is he the reason you're seducing me like some cheap tramp?"

Katerina's eyes welled with tears. "Viktor, please. You're hurting me," she whimpered.

"Is this what you want?" He pressed his mouth over hers so forcefully she cut the inside of her lip on her teeth. Then he pushed her on the bed, pinned her hands above her head, and opened her legs with his knees.

"Please don't do this." Her voice caught in her throat.

"Is this how he does it?" He bit her nipple and she cried out in pain. He forced himself inside her.

"There's no one else." The words floated through the air as vapor. "I swear."

"Think I'm a fool? The way he looks at you, his little cripple fantasy." He spit in her face.

"Don't ever forget who you belong to."

She turned her head and stared at the wall through a prism of tears.

Chapter Twenty

Since the night Viktor had agreed to let her work for La Belle Femme and then forced himself on her, spitting in her face and bruising her in places that refused to heal, Katerina had been able to think of little else. Although she had feared he would withdraw his permission, he hadn't. He'd allowed her to go to Regina with Alla, but daily he reminded her that, like God, he saw and heard everything she did. Katerina feared he read her thoughts.

After that night, Viktor, as usual, acted as though nothing sordid had happened between them. Outwardly, nothing had. Katerina confided in no one. In her letters home, she wrote about innocuous things—the weather, neighbors, and small-town life—painting everything rose-colored.

When Viktor had come downstairs the next morning, she'd had breakfast waiting on the table. They'd gone to St. Kassia's together and Aleksandr had sat between them. Yet nightly, she prayed for deliverance and for God to forgive her for the hatred growing in her heart.

Her train trip to Regina had been a success. Although she'd had to put up with Alla's blather for 90 miles, she was grateful for her help plus relieved to be away from Viktor. Immediately, Katerina had liked Francine Greenwood, La Belle Femme's owner, who had a natural fashion sense and undisguised ambition. Katerina had never met a woman like her, confident and independent. Slightly older than Katerina and unmarried, Miss Greenwood apparently had no intention of tethering herself to a husband. Katerina had both envied and admired her. If circumstances were different, she had thought, they might have been friends.

This morning, she spread midnight-blue silk over the dining room table, pinned the fabric to the pattern, and began cutting. She'd drawn her fifth design for La Belle Femme, and today she planned to sew it.

Whenever Katerina used the gold-handled scissors, she thought of her childhood and her mother. She'd died when Katerina was so young that her memories of her were out of focus, embellished, or diminished by stories others had told, creating a soup of fact and fiction. Still, she was certain that the memory of her mother guiding her hand, teaching her to keep the blades at the perfect angle so each cut would be exact, was real. *Like this. See how straight. Now the pieces will match just right.* If only the pieces of her life fit together so easily.

Katerina remembered her mother's words, but, regrettably, the sound of her voice was lost forever. Other than the special scissors, only one tangible reminder of her mother remained—a small daguerreotype of her at fourteen, standing among three younger siblings. At the last minute, Katerina had taken the picture from Aneta's shelf and hidden it in her luggage, reasoning that claiming it had not begun to even the score in exchanged treasure.

Frequently, Katerina would search the girl's face in the photograph, trying to tease out the woman of her memory. She recognized the full mouth, so much like her own, but everything else about the girl in the portrait remained unfamiliar. What she recalled most vividly was not her mother's face but her hands—long, ivory-colored fingers into which her own child-size hands had disappeared; perfectly manicured nails that wouldn't catch on delicate fabric; and cool palms that caressed her forehead when Katerina was ill.

Now, as Katerina cut the pattern, the scissors slipped, causing her to slice an errant notch along the seam. She examined the scissors in the window's light and discovered that the screw holding the blades together had loosened. She considered waiting for Viktor so he could repair the scissors for her, but he'd be busy at the elevator all day and it was still early morning. Katerina didn't want to lose an entire day's work. Besides, even the smallest favors were added to the debit column of Viktor's imaginary ledger. She would borrow a screwdriver from his toolbox. Knowing he was fanatical about his possessions, she reminded herself to put everything back just as she'd found it or there would be a price to pay. There was always a price to pay.

She stepped down into the utility shed attached to the back of the house, where Viktor kept his tools stored in a large wooden toolbox, next to a workbench with a surface as neat as a church altar. His heaviest jacket, with a pair of perfectly aligned work boots below it, hung on the far wall. At times, Katerina had ventured into the shed to sweep and wash the floor, always careful to leave Viktor's possessions in place. Twice, she'd borrowed the ladder hanging on the wall, returning it promptly each time, before Viktor could suspect her.

Nervously, she looked around and again considered waiting for Viktor. Then Svetlana Sokur visited her thoughts. The day the family had departed for Edmonton, Katerina had gone to the train depot to say a final good-bye. Svetlana had seemed surprised to see her waiting on the platform and even more surprised when Katerina placed a strand of coral beads in her palm. "For good fortune," she'd said.

A single tear had escaped down Svetlana's cheek as she curled her fingers around the beads.

"I will never forget you," Katerina had said. "Never."

Svetlana had hugged her then and whispered in a voice so faint Katerina thought she might have imagined it, "Don't let him take your dignity. Once it's gone, you'll have nothing."

Although Katerina knew that she would never see the woman again, a permanent kinship between them had been forged, a bond that neither time nor distance could erode. She would write, she told herself, out of loyalty to the one person in Bilik who had truly understood her circumstance. But even as she vowed to do so, Katerina knew that their shared pain would never translate well on the written page.

Katerina gnawed the inside of her cheek as she silently repeated Svetlana's parting words: *Don't let him take your dignity.* Had she already been reduced to a woman incapable of acting, who feared the man she lived with more than she feared God? Would she let him take every last shred of her self-respect? Svetlana's battered arms pushed her onward, and her voice challenged Katerina to move forward.

She looked over each shoulder and listened. Nothing.

The toolbox was unlocked. Katerina realized Viktor had no need to lock it, because he believed she was too intimidated to cross him. His certitude proved as painful as her insecurity. She took a deep breath, then flipped the hasp and lifted the lid. It was heavier than she had expected. The tools were fastidiously arranged, the ripsaw and the crosscut saw nesting neatly next to each other and the various hammers grouped together. Before touching anything, Katerina took visual inventory. She saw one screwdriver but it was the wrong size. She reached into the toolbox, careful to avoid the adze blade, and then peeked inside a small tin box. It contained used nails. She noticed a wooden cigar box partially buried under a mallet.

When she lifted the cover, instead of tools, she found an envelope. Curious, Katerina removed the box and placed it on the workbench. She opened the envelope. It held the receipts from her sewing work, along with the money she'd been forced to turn over to Viktor. She counted the money: $124.50, the result of her talent and effort hidden unceremoniously, like an afterthought. She returned the money and receipts. As she was about to replace the box, she spotted a second cigar box hidden in the chest. Emboldened by the discovery of her hard-earned money, she lifted the cigar box out and opened it. This one contained a stack of envelopes, the top stamped with a Winnipeg postmark.

Her breath caught.

She fingered through the rest of the stack. Each bore the same return address: Two-zero- three First Avenue, Winnipeg.

Her heart beat faster. Put them back before it's too late. Katerina counted twenty-seven envelopes. *Put them back.* Her hands shook. *Coward!*

She opened the envelope with the most recent postmark and pulled out the single-page letter. The salutation read simply, Viktor. Katerina's eyes raced to the signature: Elena. She examined the postmark a second time—September 1, 1926—four weeks ago. The floor tilted. The room shrank. Katerina grabbed the workbench to steady herself. She rubbed her eyes, trying to focus as she read:

> *Viktor,*
>
> *Again, I beg you to send Aleksandr to me. I ask you for nothing else. I have work and am able to care for him. You are free to live your life as you please. In my heart, I know that is what you have always wanted.*
>
> *Elena*

Elena was alive!

Katerina threw the letter on the workbench, clamped her hand over her mouth, stumbled to the back door, and flung it open. Doubling over, she heaved until her stomach emptied. Hands planted on knees, she gasped for air and struggled for balance. Her limbs, her marriage, the very ground on which she stood turned hollow. Weight as heavy as an anvil lay on her chest. Her lungs filled to bursting. She closed her eyes and tried to think, but all that came were images. Black fear. Blue sorrow. Red hate. Katerina prayed she was dreaming. When she tasted Bilik's ubiquitous dust, she knew the truth. She grabbed the doorknob to steady herself and slowly uncurled.

Spent, Katerina limped to the workbench. As if the slightest movement would bring every lie precariously hanging between Viktor and her tumbling down like an avalanche, she stood death-still. The sour residue of vomit burned the back of her throat.

Katerina waited until she could no longer hear the thrumming of her heart in her ears and tentatively picked up the cigar box. In her hands, she held the past and the future. Staring at the letters, she resisted the impulse to destroy them, unread. She would force herself to read every betraying word. Katerina braced herself for what was to come.

She folded the hastily discarded letter lying on the workbench, put it back in its envelope, and returned it to the cigar box. From the remaining stack she pulled the envelope with the earliest postmark and sat on the toolbox. April 16, 1924. A lifetime ago. While Elena was fleeing Viktor, on the other side of the world Katerina was falling in love.

Her hands trembled as she opened the letter.

April 16, 1924

Viktor,

I know you will never forgive me for leaving. I haven't forgiven myself.

I tried to stay. I hope God will look into my heart and know I left to save Aleksandr, as well as myself. Leaving was the only way.

I beg you to send him to me. It is the last thing I will ever ask of you. I tell myself that Yana is looking after him and that you are providing a warm roof, if not a warm heart. From the first, you did not want him, and if your son had not already been growing inside me, I doubt you would have married me. It no longer matters. I plead with you not to punish Aleksandr for what I have done. My failings are mine alone. Please do not harm him. I know he is not the kind of son you would have chosen, but he is innocent of all wrongdoing.

No matter how harshly you judge me, you know I love my son and have been a good mother, even though I have not been a satisfactory wife. No child should grow up without his mother. I beg you to send him to me.

Blame me. Tell whatever tale you must, but do not look for me. I have taken great care that you should not find me, but I promise your message will be forwarded from this address. When I hear from you, I will send instructions for where to send Aleksandr.

Elena

From the first, Elena had been ephemeral, elusive. Hers had been a prosaic life—wife and mother—a story begun near the end, sliding toward a tragic conclusion. Now her letters, written in a looping script and bathed with maternal love, turned Elena to flesh and blood for Katerina in a way that living in the house she'd once occupied hadn't.

Carefully, Katerina placed the letter back in the envelope and read the next and the next, growing more agitated with each one.

She pulled the letter dated September 8, 1925. Elena had written it two days before Katerina's arrival in Bilik. The thought enraged her. God forgive her, if Viktor walked in at that moment, had she the strength, she would kill him.

September 8, 1925

Viktor,

If your silence is intended as punishment, you have accomplished what you hoped. I am sick with worry over Aleksandr's well-being. Does that give you satisfaction? I understand your desire for revenge, but revenge is not the way to show love for our son. Tell me how he is doing. Is he growing? Is he doing well in his studies? Is he safe?

Please, Viktor, I beg you to send him to me. Short of returning, I promise to meet your conditions whatever they may be. I do not believe you want to raise him on your own. It is a task no man would welcome.

I plead with you to answer.

Elena

Katerina stared at Elena's beseeching words: "I beg you to send him to me." She inhaled the heartache and felt it filling her. Who better than she understood a mother's desperation? Katerina imagined pleading with Aneta and Danya for Matviyko's return and knew they would never give him up. She also knew Viktor. He would never return Aleksandr to Elena. Never. Grief overwhelmed her.

She thought of Svetlana and Elena and how she'd once believed herself to be superior to both of them. In truth, all three were sisters, bound not by blood but by the sorrow of choosing unworthy men. She wondered, had they once loved their husbands the way she loved Stepan? Had they once believed in a golden future?

She had. Not with Viktor, with Stepan.

And once she'd realized that her marriage to Viktor was a tragic mistake, she'd deceived herself into believing that, at least, she'd known real love with Stepan. She'd thanked God for the love of a man unlike Josef or Viktor, men whose hands were unforgiving and whose hearts were calloused.

She'd clung to Stepan's promises as if they were written in stone instead of air. She'd convinced herself that his love was her salvation instead of her ruination. Like morning fog rising from the earth, Katerina watched her delusion slowly lift. It wasn't love Stepan had offered but the notion of it, wrapped in poetry and passion. Despite all that had happened, she'd awaited rescue by the gallant prince. Just as Viktor would never send Aleksandr to Elena, Stepan would never arrive. The admission wrenched her heart. What a fool! The sting of humiliation crept along every nerve. What a fool.

As Katerina returned to the letters, each more desperate than the one before, her fears grew.

She was wed to a man already married before God and the law. Although she knew nothing of Canadian justice, she felt certain she'd have no claim to support or to any of Viktor's worldly goods. At best, she'd be a castoff; at worst, she'd be held in suspicion. If she confronted him, there was no telling what Viktor was capable of. To what lengths would he go to keep his scandalous secret? Katerina knew how far she'd gone to protect her own. She shuddered. Other than the contents of the cigar box, Katerina had no proof of Viktor's duplicity, and if she challenged him, undoubtedly, he would destroy the letters. Then who would believe her?

Carefully, Katerina returned the letters to the box, making certain they were replaced in the exact order in which she'd found them. She must be above suspicion. She must take time and care, resist the urge to make haste.

She could wait until Viktor and Aleksandr left the house for the day, then board a train and flee. She didn't have much, but she could take the money Viktor had forced her to turn over to him. Plus she'd kept back money from sewing commissions and hidden it in the lining of her coat. She could use that secret money to buy a ticket. To where?

She saw Aleksandr's innocent face. He'd already been abandoned once. Katerina thought of Matviyko. Guilt dug its rapacious claws into her conscience.

I plead with you not to punish Aleksandr for what I have done. My failings are mine alone. Please do not harm him...he is innocent of all wrongdoing.

Katerina wondered, *Could I leave a second child?*

Chapter Twenty-One

"Aleksandr! Aleksandr! Boy, where the hell are you?" When Aleksandr heard his father's voice, he knew he should go to him, but his feet stuck to the porch floor. His heart beat so fast he thought it might explode. Why was his father so angry? He couldn't think what he'd done.

"Aleksandr! Goddamn it, boy!"

He considered running to the Pankos', pretending he hadn't heard him shouting. Maybe by the time he came home, whatever his father was angry about would have blown over. But it was getting dark. Besides, he knew better. When he got home, no matter what, he would be severely punished. Once his father's temper boiled over, nothing could stop it. As sure as there were stars in the sky, if he was seen running, his father would come after him. There was no telling what he'd do then. Whatever it was, Aleksandr knew he'd be lucky to live through it.

Don't cry. Whatever you do, don't cry. Regardless of what he'd done, if his father saw tears, it would be worse. The longer he stood there, frozen, the more paralyzed he became.

Move. Move. Move.

His father staggered around the corner of the house and into the front yard, carrying the short-handled coal shovel. Before Aleksandr could speak, his father hoisted him by the jacket collar, shoved him down the front porch steps, yanked him to his toes, and dragged him along the side to the back of the house. Aleksandr's feet skidded across the ground as he tried to keep pace.

"How many times do I have to tell you to latch the goddamned cellar doors?"

Aleksandr half hung in the air, staring at the ground. He couldn't see his father's face, but he could picture the large vein pounding in his forehead and his cruel eyes brimming with rage. He smelled the liquor on his father's breath.

When they got to the back of the house, Aleksandr saw that one of the clamshell doors had come off its hinges and tumbled into the yard. Bile rose to his throat. He swallowed, forcing it down. His father threw him to the ground. The back of Aleksandr's head hit the doorframe. Pinpricks of light popped behind his eyes. The ground spun beneath him. His father was speaking, not shouting, but talking through clenched teeth, as if venom were trapped in his mouth. Only certain words bobbed to the surface as his lips moved: stupid… never forget… pay...

He wanted to tell his father he was sorry for everything—sorry the bucket of coal was too heavy, sorry it took all his strength to haul it into the house, and sorry he'd forgotten to latch the doors. He wanted to explain that all he could think of when he lugged the bucket up the steep cellar stairs was getting out of the dark. When he was in that cellar, black as pitch, he couldn't think of anything but floating under murky water or being buried deep in the airless ground. But if he admitted that it made him really nervous every time he felt his way down the stairs, counting each step to keep from panicking, until he managed to light the lantern, and that, on his way up the stairs, he dreaded the moment when he had to extinguish that flame, his father would call him a sissy or worse. He wanted to tell his father he was sorry for being such a terrible son. He was truly sorry.

He watched helplessly as the short-handled shovel swung in an arc and landed hard on his arm—really, really hard. "Aahh!" It was his voice. At least, he thought it was his. Tears spilled from his eyes. He heard more screaming inside his head, but he didn't think it was coming from his mouth.

Then he saw his new mother limping from the house toward them.

She was yelling. He'd never heard her voice so loud. It was always soft and gentle. But not now.

"*Stop!*" she shrieked. "*Viktor! Stop!*"

Again, his father raised the shovel, this time turning toward her.

"I'll discipline my son any way I goddamn please!"

"I know," she said. "I know what you are."

Aleksandr sat up, his head as heavy as a bucket of coal. His new mother stood facing his father, her long, pointed sewing scissors gripped in her fist and held menacingly, like a sword. Her face was bright red, her expression wild.

His father stepped toward her. "You know *nothing*," he hissed.

"Two-zero-three First Avenue." She breathed really fast. "Two-zero-three First Avenue. I know enough."

To Aleksandr, the numbers made no sense, but his father stiffened as if every muscle in his body suddenly locked.

"Ungrateful whore!"

As his father lunged toward her, she swung the scissors wildly. The blades punctured his bicep. "Shit!" Stunned, he grabbed his arm and stepped backward.

Aleksandr clutched his father's pants leg, tugging with all his strength. His father swung the shovel behind him, missing Aleksandr's head by inches. His new mother slashed again and caught his shoulder.

"Fuck!" His father dropped the shovel, lurched, and fell to his knees.

"Aleksandr, run!" she yelled. "Run!"

Aleksandr wobbled to his feet.

"Run!"

He took one unsure step and then another.

"Run!"

She ordered his legs to fly.

In that moment, size and strength of foe meant nothing to Katerina. She had no plan, just hate and fury. Her actions were primal and her muscles as taut as a grizzly's defending her cub. To protect Aleksandr, she would fight to the death.

Katerina gripped the scissors so tightly that color drained from her knuckles. She remained focused on Viktor as she screamed for Aleksandr to escape. Whether the boy was seriously hurt she didn't know, but out of the corner of her eye she saw him scramble to his feet and run.

Still on his knees, blood leaking from beneath his tattered sleeve, Viktor spit between bared teeth: "You ignorant cripple. She's dead!"

"Liar!" Katerina's chest heaved rapidly. "I've read the letters." Her voice was shrill, crescendoing toward hysterical.

"Crazy cunt."

"Now everyone will know what you are."

"Think you can threaten me?" Viktor's lips curled.

"You're still married to her!"

"Keep your mouth shut or I'll—"

Katerina couldn't believe what she was hearing. Did he think life could ever return to the way it had been? Because he ordered it to? "It's *over!*"

Like a cornered animal, Viktor's gaze darted from side to side. He spotted the shovel and dived for it.

Katerina lunged toward him and plunged the scissors deep into his thigh.

"Ooww!" Viktor howled.

He stretched for the shovel. Katerina swung again. This time, Viktor seized her damaged leg and yanked. She landed hard on her back, the impact jarring the scissors loose. Pain coursed through her torso and limbs. When Viktor raised the shovel to strike, Katerina cocked her strong leg and drove her foot into his face with all her strength. Viktor's head snapped back like a swinging door, and he thudded on the ground, knocked out cold.

Katerina clambered to the porch steps. Grasping the railing for support, she struggled to her feet. Her ankle buckled. She clung to the newel post to keep from toppling. Whatever it took, she had to get those scissors. Gritting her teeth at every step, she hobbled over to the scissors and strained to pick them up.

Viktor lay motionless. She stood over him. Every fight-or-flight nerve was at the ready. Loathing swelled in her like a cresting wave. She wanted him dead. She imagined herself stabbing him through the heart. She imagined being free.

Katerina raised the scissors.

Kill him. End it.

Instead, she limped away, desperate to find Aleksandr.

Aleksandr's legs churned as he ran without thought or direction, ignoring his aching head and throbbing arm. Katerina's voice commanded him. *Aleksandr, run!* It wasn't until he reached the grain elevator that he thought about where he was or what to do.

He'd abandoned his new mother, left her alone to defend herself. Even with a pair of long, sharp scissors, she wasn't safe. His father was the toughest person Aleksandr knew, far stronger than Mr. Panko or Dr. Billings or even Jakob. Nobody could stop him. Nobody. Aleksandr tried to think. He had to save her. But how? Maybe, like Yuri Sokur, he could cut off his father's arm. But he didn't have an ax, and he didn't dare go back to the house to get one.

He tried the handle on the office door of the elevator. His father always locked it, but Aleksandr couldn't help hoping that, just once, he'd forgotten. It was locked. But even if he could get in, what difference would it make? He was too small and his father was too large.

There must be something he could do.

Viktor was nauseated, disoriented, and drunk. Shit, he must have blacked out. The chill running through his body told him he was on the hard, cold ground. The wet feeling on his leg and arm reminded him he was cut and bleeding. He touched his face and winced. As his thoughts cleared, he remembered. Katerina had kicked him. That cripple must have broken his nose.

He wanted to kill her.

He would when he found her.

Slowly, Viktor opened his eyes. The evening sky hung dusky silver overhead. Iridescent clouds drifted beneath the moon, creating the sensation of the ground moving beneath him. The earth smelled like night, fecund and damp. He sat up, his head pounding, his shirtsleeve soaked with blood, and his leg bleeding steadily. He had to take care of his wounds. He'd deal with Katerina later.

Viktor reached to unbuckle his belt and grunted. God, his arm hurt. Gritting his teeth, he unfastened his belt and pulled it from around his waist in one swift motion. Wrapping it twice around his upper thigh, he snugged it to stanch the blood flow and fastened it in place.

Next, he fumbled with his shirt buttons, cursing the slow progress. With the last one undone, he eased his arms from his shirt and held it in his teeth. The puncture on his bicep went several inches into the muscle. When he flexed his arm, the gash opened like a mouth. With his strong arm, he tugged at a sleeve until the threads ripped apart at the shoulder seam. He pulled the sleeve free and wrapped it tightly above the wound on his upper arm. Using his teeth and good arm, he drew a firm knot.

Gooseflesh covered Viktor's bare chest and back. He shivered but he had to ignore the cold. There were more important things to think about. He probed his shoulder wound. It was deep and bleeding. Wadding his shirt, he pressed it firmly against the cut. For now, there was nothing more to be done.

He hadn't seen Katerina leave. She could be hiding in the house but he doubted it. Probably, she'd cripple-limped toward Yana's. Christ, how he hated her ridiculous gait. He didn't want to take the chance she'd gone inside. At the moment, he couldn't afford another confrontation with the damned scissors. If he hadn't fallen, Katerina never would have gotten the best of him. By all that was holy, it would be the last time. He'd regain the upper hand. She was still afraid of him. He'd seen the terror in her eyes.

His biggest problem would be convincing everyone Katerina was mistaken about Elena. A misunderstanding, he'd say. He'd invent a story. He'd done it before. However, there was the matter of the letters. He should have destroyed them, but he'd never imagined Katerina would have the nerve to cross him. There'd be time to figure things out. First, he had to take care of his wounds before the loss of blood weakened him further. Couldn't afford to pass out again.

Everything he needed was at the elevator. With all the hazards lurking there, first aid equipment was in abundant supply. He could clean and bandage his cuts, sleep if he needed. The place was locked. Katerina couldn't get in there if she wanted to. The elevator was the last place she'd be.

"Aleksandr!" Katerina called out, her voice half whisper, half shout.

She listened.

"Aleksandr!"

Nervously, she checked ahead and behind, hoping to see Aleksandr's slight silhouette running toward her and praying she wouldn't see Viktor's hulking figure chasing after her. When she'd fled, Viktor had lain on the ground, immobile. Still, she was certain he'd come.

During the struggle, when Viktor had tripped her, she'd fallen hard. Now, not only did her damaged leg hurt, the ankle of her solid leg protested every time she put weight on it. Sprained? Or broken? She wasn't sure but it made the going extremely slow.

Desperation pushed her forward.

Thinking Aleksandr might run to the Pankos', Katerina opted to cut across the field toward the backside of Main Street. Although its openness left her exposed and footing would be uncertain, it was faster than following the road past the school and the livery. She imagined Viktor stalking her, hunting her. She had to find Aleksandr. Wounded or not, with weapon or not, if Viktor found her, he'd have the advantage in size and strength. He wouldn't be caught off guard again.

"Aleksandr! Aleksandr!" Her voice quavered.

Nothing.

Finally, she reached the rear of the bank. To take the pressure off her ankle, she braced her back against the brick wall and leaned heavily into it. Her ankle was swelling rapidly, puffing above her high-top shoe like rising bread dough.

She had to keep going.

In the distance, she saw movement. She squinted. A dark figure headed across the field toward her. Viktor!

She couldn't outrun him.

Think. Mother of God, help me.

She ducked into the doorway of the bank and flattened herself against a wall. Her heart beat with the cadence of a military march. She waited. Her bloodied fist coiled around the scissors handle.

Soon, she heard him coming, his footsteps landing heavy and irregular. Her body stiffened. She held her breath.

When he passed the doorway, so close to her that she smelled liquor and sweat, Katerina stifled a gasp. What if he'd heard her? After a minute, she exhaled—not a sigh of relief—a soft blowing like a mother soothing a child's scraped knee; yet in her imagination, her breathing sounded as loud as a gale-force wind. She prayed that Viktor wouldn't hear her, that he wouldn't return, and that he wouldn't find Aleksandr.

The night turned deathly still.

When she marshaled the courage, Katerina peeked out from the doorway. No one. Staying in the shadows, she edged her way along the outer wall of the bank for the entire length of the building. By the time she dared check around the corner and look west down Main, Viktor had disappeared.

Aleksandr struggled to figure out what to do. He had to help. No one else would challenge his father.

He shivered. It was getting colder. He thrust his hands in his pockets. His fingers wrapped around the matches he always kept tucked in his pockets, his protection from the dark in case the lantern in the coal cellar went out.

That was it! He could light a fire.

When his father saw flames, he'd have to come because the elevator was his responsibility. It was the most important thing in the whole world to him. Yes, he'd stop whatever he was doing to save the elevator.

Then she could run. She could hide. She would be safe.

Aleksandr picked up a fist-sized rock from the railroad bed, ran behind the elevator, and crouched in the tall grass. He'd never been back there at night. It was so scary and lonely; he might have been the only person on Earth. His drumming heartbeat and the swishing grass were the only sounds. With each passing second, it grew blacker, quieter, and eerier.

Then, as if the sky sensed his fear, the nearly full moon slipped from behind a cloud, bathing the field in gray light. The familiar smell of grain dust perfumed the air. Max's dog, Chaser, began barking in the distance. The sudden ordinariness of everything bolstered his courage.

He struck a match. It sparked and then fizzled. He threw it to the ground. He pulled another match from his pocket, turned his back to the wind, and struck it. The flame ignited. He held the match between his fingers as long as he dared, then dropped it into the crisp grass. Grabbing another match, he struck it and touched the flame to the tip of a paper-dry stalk until it caught. He watched the fire crawl quickly down the stem.

Aleksandr trembled as he removed the last match from his pocket. Falling to his knees, he struck the match and held the flame at the base of a clump of dried grass. The fire caught near the ground. Protected from the strongest gusts, it grew slowly and inched its way toward the building.

Viktor fumbled with the key as he tried to unlock the office door. His temples pounded and blood trickled from his nose. He cursed his shaking limbs. He was getting weaker. He had to stop the loss of blood. Finally, the handle turned. Stumbling into the room, he reached to switch on the overhead light but then thought better of it. Best not to draw too much attention. Moonlight, shining through the windows and glinting off the silver-painted walls, provided enough illumination.

He slumped into the desk chair. From the bottom drawer of the desk, he retrieved bottles of alcohol and Mercurochrome and a white tin box with a thick red cross on its lid. He pried it open and dumped the gauze and tape on the desk. In the middle drawer, he found scissors. Methodically, he made a pile of gauze squares, one on top of the other.

Viktor stopped. Had he heard something or someone? He listened and looked, heard nothing, and saw no one. Beyond the windows, the night was empty and still. Some mutt began barking. Maybe that was what he'd heard. Caution was making him skittish. He went back to his task.

Underneath the tourniquet on his thigh, he was beginning to lose feeling in his leg. Carefully, he cut off his pants leg, just below the belt. In place of stitches, he'd have to close the wound temporarily with strips of tape, but first he needed to disinfect the wound. He removed the cap from the bottle of alcohol and gritted his teeth, steeling himself for the sting.

Then he smelled smoke.

What the hell?

Aleksandr ran from the back to the front of the elevator. When he rounded the corner, he froze. A silhouette appeared in the office window. It was his father! Fear snaked along Aleksandr's spine. He ducked into the shadows.

What had happened to his new mother? Had his father already killed her? He hoped it wasn't too late.

He took a deep breath and dashed over the tracks and across Main Street. Except for the Ford parked in front of the bank—Sy's father was probably working late—the street was deserted. Hiding behind the car, Aleksandr hunched low and peeked over the hood. Smoke rose above the roof of the elevator and drifted like a low-lying cloud. He crossed his fingers, hoping that his plan worked.

Heading home, Aleksandr took the shortcut between the bank and the dry goods store. He was too worried about his new mother to fret about the dark. From this distance, he could see his house. Light shone in an upstairs window. A spark of hope flickered in his chest. As fast as his legs could carry him, he ran toward the house. He'd never felt more frightened nor more courageous. He was soaring like Ormer Locklear flying to the rescue. He hoped with all his heart that his new mother was still alive and that his father would be too busy fighting the fire to hurt them.

Winded by the time he reached the backyard, he bent to catch his breath. The shovel and the cellar door still lay in the yard. He checked the grounds, looking for his new mother. There was no sign of her. He hurried up the porch stairs and into the house.

That was when a gigantic explosion shattered the air.

With a roar as loud as speeding locomotives crashing head-on, the sky was rent in two. As she reached the Pankos' porch, the force of the blast knocked Katerina off her feet and slammed her against a newel post. The entire house seemed to shake off its foundation. Stunned, Katerina watched as a giant fireball shot high into the air in a burst of awful beauty. Night became day in a single flash. *Armageddon.* She bit down hard on her tongue, instantly tasting blood. Trying to break her fall, she landed on her left wrist, and it bent backward at an unnatural angle. Stabbing pain traveled up her arm. Splinters from the wooden stairs lodged in her palms.

My God, what was happening?

Confused and dazed, Katerina crawled to the front door.

An explosion. It had to be. My God, the grain elevator had exploded! Viktor. Had Viktor gone to the elevator?

Katerina had to get to Aleksandr. *Please Lord, let him be safe inside this house.*

A sound like a thousand thunderclaps crackled in the air. Windows rattled, dishes clattered, and the kitchen table shimmied toward the wall. Aleksandr heard unfamiliar banging noises in every part of the house. Could it be the end of the world? His heart hammered. What should he do? What if his father came back to the house? That scared him more than anything, so he decided the best plan was to find his new mother and run.

The smell of cooked cabbage hung in the kitchen air. Instead of hours, it seemed as though it had been days since he'd eaten. Aleksandr went from the kitchen to the dining room and to the parlor, calling out, "Where are you?"

Moonlight seeping through the windows bathed the rooms in gray, but the corners loomed, dark and threatening. In each room, he saw evidence of the blast—the stack of magazines tumbled from an end table, the hall tree toppled, the sewing machine wedged against the doorway. He ran upstairs, dreading what he might find. What if his new mother was lying on the floor? What if she was dead?

With the sureness of a blind man who'd memorized his surroundings, Aleksandr felt his way around his bedroom. The bed. The washstand. The wardrobe. Nothing.

Timidly, he peeked into his father and new mother's bedroom. The wall lantern still glowed. It was the light he'd seen from a distance.

"Where are you?" he whispered, as if he were in church.

He walked around the bed, careful to stare at the floor in case she was lying on it. She wasn't there either, but several dresser drawers lay open. Had his new mother gone away without telling him? Sometimes mothers disappeared without warning. But Aleksandr had witnessed her stand up to his father. She'd protected him. With his own eyes, he'd seen her face and fists full of fury and fight. She wouldn't just leave him. She cared about him, wanted him. He felt it with all his heart. No matter how long it took, he would find her.

Satisfied she wasn't in the house, Aleksandr flew down the stairs and out the back door, racing toward town.

Katerina hoisted herself up by the doorknob and pounded on the Pankos' front door. When no one answered, she opened it and shambled inside.

The parlor looked as though a giant wind had blown through and knocked everything from its moorings—Gram-O-Phone and radio on their sides, furniture upended, and stovepipe pulled from the wall. Not a single picture still hung on its hook. Windows were shattered and curtains billowed in the breeze.

Katerina heard shouts and movement in the house and limped toward the interior. She came upon Fedir and Lavro.

"Is Aleksandr here?" Katerina's voice was thick with anxiety.

"No."

"Was he here?"

Fedir shook his head.

"Everyone's got to get out. It's too dangerous," he shouted over the ringing, as though the explosion had rendered him deaf. Then Katerina realized the ringing was in her ears. "Yana's gathering the children. Lavro and I are on our way to the firehouse." Fedir spoke as if it were the most natural thing in the world to find Katerina wandering in his home late at night. "It will be all right. Yana will help you find him."

Yana descended the stairs, carrying Vera. Lilia held Marina's hand and Luka and Sasha, clinging to each other, followed close behind.

"Katerina?" Yana said. "What—"

"Have you seen Aleksandr?" Katerina asked. She realized she was crying.

"No." Yana looked confused.

"I don't know where he is."

"We have to get out of the house. The fire's too close," Yana said. "Don't worry. We'll find him."

Katerina grimaced as she shifted weight to her injured ankle.

"You're hurt," Yana said.

"I fell. It's just my wrist and ankle."

"Can you make it?"

Katerina nodded.

"Lean on me," Yana said, looping her arm around Katerina's waist.

"I have to find him," Katerina said, her voice breaking.

Above the buildings along Main Street, fiery tongues licked the night sky. Aleksandr had never seen anything like it. As he sprinted through the field toward the fire, he realized it was the grain elevator that had exploded. It wasn't the end of the world, but it might as well be. What had he done? He'd only meant to start a fire big enough to distract his father. Instead, Bilik rumbled with the roar of a monster flame. This was the worst day of his life, even worse than the day they had buried his mother.

Aleksandr wished he could snap his fingers and make today disappear. It would be yesterday, before he had forgotten to latch the cellar doors, before his father had hurt him, and before he had lit the fire. He wished tonight were like every other night, when all he could hear were grasshopper wings and train whistles. Mostly, he wished he could wake up from this nightmare. *One—two—three—four…*

From more than a block away, Aleksandr felt the heat. The sky glowed with light as bright as a hundred suns. Sparks danced in the air, then rained to the ground. Smoke fell like a veil over the town. St. Kassia's bell pealed steadily, sounding the alarm as far as the wind could carry it. With the strike of a match, sleepy Bilik had turned to chaos.

People gathered at the far end of Main Street, pushing as close to the scene as the searing heat allowed. Against the blazing orange backdrop, they stood as shadows and silhouettes. Aleksandr hid in the narrow alleyway between the dry goods store and the bank, his eyes burning, searching from face to face for his new mother and warily watching for his father. *Five—six—seven…*

At first, it seemed as though nobody knew what to do. Everyone stood in groups, hugging and counting heads. Then the shouting began as some of the town leaders took charge, but if his father was among them, he didn't see him.

As the volunteer fire brigade rushed the hose cart, pumper, and water tank from the firehouse into the street, Jakob shouted, "We've caught a break. The winds have shifted to the east. We can try to contain the fire at the base!"

Braving the oppressive heat, the men unfurled the hose, worked the pump, and began soaking the ground, so the fire wouldn't jump the rails or the road.

Mr. Panko, his face shiny and streaked with soot, hollered orders to a second crew as they rolled out the remaining equipment. "The elevator's lost. We have to save the other buildings!"

Max's father organized every other able-bodied person into bucket brigades. Pails passed from back to front until the last person threw water on the designated building. Battling against the fire's progress, one bucketful at a time, seemed like trying to hold back the tide with a wire fence, but as more farmers arrived by wagon, truck, and horseback, the collective effort began to pay off.

The longer Aleksandr hid, the more his anxiety grew. He still hadn't spotted his new mother or his father. *Eight—nine—ten...* Cautiously, he stepped from behind the corner of the dry goods store and squinted through the smoke to get a better look at the crowd. He saw Lavro, Sy, and Max passing buckets along the line in front of the bank, fighting the fire he'd caused. Guilt overcame fear. He ran to the line and wedged himself between Lavro and Sy.

"Your mother has been looking for you everywhere!" Lavro shouted.

She was alive! Aleksandr wanted to cry with relief. "Where is she?" he shouted back.

"She's with Mama!" Lavro yelled as he passed the bucket. "They were headed to the livery." He nodded toward the east end of town.

"Have you seen my father?"

"No."

Aleksandr broke from the line and ran.

As she made her way toward the livery with Yana and the children, Katerina shouted for Aleksandr until she was hoarse, coughing on smoke as she tried to amplify her voice. She asked every person they passed, "Have you seen Aleksandr?" Each no or shake of the head added to the stones piled in her stomach. "Please, if you see him, tell him I'm at the livery. Please."

Where had he gone? Where could he be hiding? Maybe he had gone to the school or the stable. She doubted he would have returned home. He knew what his father was capable of. Still, she wished she could check the house, but her legs wouldn't carry her that far. She'd have to wait for help and pray.

Oh Blessed Mother, who knows the anguish of watching your son suffer, who knows the heartbreak of losing that which is most precious to you, I implore you to keep Aleksandr safe from harm.

She had not forgotten Viktor. Among friends, she doubted he'd come after her. He preferred to show a neighborly face in public and use his fists in private. Still, wounded and furious, he was unpredictable. That both he and Aleksandr were missing was a terrible sign. It occurred to her then: What if Aleksandr had run to the elevator? A sob eddied in the pit of her stomach. As it swirled, threatening to pull her under, Katerina told herself she must be strong, not just for herself but for her son. She straightened her back, erecting a seawall against despair.

Aleksandr threaded his way down the middle of the street, pushing through bucket lines and bystanders. The smoke made his eyes water, and the acrid air burned his nostrils. After every few steps, he glanced over his shoulder, on the lookout for his father. Then, through the haze, he spotted his new mother standing next to Mrs. Panko. Relief burst in him like water breaching a dam.

As he drew closer, she saw him and waved frantically. Limping toward him, she threw her arms open. She was flushed and her eyes were red. Maybe the tears were from the smoke.

"Aleksandr!" Her voice sounded husky. "I was sick with worry." She hugged him fiercely.

He hugged her back.

She bent low and whispered in his ear, "I thought you'd go to the Pankos' house." Tenderly, she kissed the top of his head, careful not to touch the welt.

Aleksandr lowered his voice so only she could hear. "I thought he killed you." When he looked up at her, he saw dried blood on her lip.

"Where did you go?"she asked.

"To the elevator."

Her eyes widened.

Aleksandr looked at his feet.

Chapter Twenty-Two

"This isn't advisable," Dr. Billings warned. "It would be too gruesome a sight for most men, let alone a woman."

Still recovering from a broken wrist and a badly sprained ankle, Katerina sat, covering her mouth and nose with her opposite hand and nervously gnawing the inside of her cheek. The lack of certainty for the past two weeks had nearly driven her mad. Perhaps the doctor was right. But to believe, Katerina needed to witness Viktor's remains with her own eyes. Until then, she would have no peace.

"I appreciate your concern but I must see him."

Dr. Billings shook his head in resignation. He pulled the sheet from Viktor's body and stepped aside.

Katerina gasped. Her lids fluttered rapidly over watering eyes.

What lay on the table wasn't a body at all. No arms. No legs. No face. Only a charred torso. Any cuts or gashes, even the deepest, were undetectable. The scar above his eyebrow was gone, too, and with it, the secret of its origin.

The ashes of the elevator had smoldered, dangerously hot, long after the pump carts returned to the firehouse. No one could have gotten close enough to rummage through the ruins, so at first Viktor had been simply missing. During that time, for her and Aleksandr's benefit, their friends had maintained an optimistic front, keeping alive the hope that Viktor would reappear.

How could Katerina have admitted that their kind hope was her worst fear? She hadn't been able to rest—her every daylight hour tense, her every nighttime hour terror—imagining him lurking in the shadows, watching. In her entire life, Katerina had never wished someone dead. It would have felt wrong, unholy. Still, she'd prayed that Viktor would not miraculously rise from the ashes, come out of a secret hiding place where he had bided his time, recovering from his wounds and plotting his revenge. Only Katerina and Aleksandr knew that he'd left their house injured and bleeding. Only they knew that truth.

"You're certain this is my husband?"

"Positive."

Looking at the amorphous human form, Katerina wondered if Viktor had suffered as the flames consumed his body or whether the blast had killed him instantly, sparing him the pain of a gruesome death. Throughout the days of agonizing uncertainty, Katerina's heart had hardened. She couldn't help feeling Viktor's blackened remains fittingly reflected his stained soul. Perhaps his baptism by fire had bought his salvation. That was between Viktor and God.

Aleksandr was her only concern.

Katerina worried about him. Since the fire, he'd been closed and silent. The relief he'd shown when he'd found her that night had turned to anguish when he'd learned his father had likely burned to death. At first, he'd cried and repeated, "I'm sorry, I'm sorry, I'm sorry" in a monotone cadence that no amount of hugging and reassurance could penetrate. When he had cried himself out, he'd gone to his room, lain on his bed, and refused to talk. She'd tried to engage him in conversation but hadn't pushed. From experience, Katerina knew that heartache is a private matter that heals in its own time.

After seeing Viktor's body, Katerina decided that it would serve no purpose to publicly air their soiled linen. Let the good people of Bilik believe whatever brought them comfort. It no longer mattered. She and Aleksandr were free. And they were masters at keeping secrets.

"I've seen enough," she said.

Katerina held Aleksandr's hand as they waited beside Viktor's casket. She squeezed it gently and he squeezed back.

A solid gray ceiling hung overhead. The northwesterly wind brought unseasonably cool temperatures for late October, and it had rained steadily for the past three days. Although the air was thick with moisture, for the moment, the rain held off, but by the end of the graveside ceremony, rain would surely come.

Water seeped through the stitching in Katerina's shoes, making her feet feel clammy and cold. While others around her stood, she sat, unable to put full weight on her ankle. Beneath her stockings, a fleshy rainbow of purple, yellow, and green surrounded the severe sprain. Her splinted, broken wrist rested immobile at her side, the inconvenience and pain small prices to pay for all that was and could have been, partial atonement for both her and Viktor's sins.

At the gravesite, she and Aleksandr were surrounded by friends and neighbors, who'd come to mourn not only the death of a man but the loss of the elevator, the lifeblood of their community. Katerina found some comfort in communal sorrow, but she and Aleksandr shared secrets that set them apart, leaving them isolated in their clandestine grief.

The destruction from the explosion and fire had been so complete that there was no way to determine its cause. She'd heard the speculative whispers. An electrical fire. An overheated belt. Spontaneous combustion. She let herself almost believe that any one of those reasons could be true.

While the priest chanted the Trisagion and the mourners responded, Katerina's thoughts wandered and her lips remained closed. She glanced at Aleksandr, who stood as still as death, his eyes downcast, saying nothing.

"Blessed is our God always, now and forever, and to the ages of ages," Father Warga chanted.

The mourners responded: "Amen."

The Panko family stood somberly beside her. Even rambunctious Vera seemed to sense the solemnity of the moment and rested quietly against Fedir's shoulder. Yana chanted the responses. Katerina heard the quaver in her voice. She wanted to comfort her friend, but today she had little more to offer than the touch of her hand.

Since meeting Yana and Fedir, so much had transpired, and despite the gloom, Katerina knew that not all of it was tinged with regret. She thought of her wedding day, when Yana had loaned her one handmade *rushnyk* to bind her hands to Viktor's and another to stand on. She'd been overcome with gratitude by the unexpected compassionate gesture. *How will I ever repay you?* Yana's simple reply had stunned her. *No need. You are family.* At that moment, Katerina had no idea how deep the debt or strong the bond would become. Yana was mother, sister, teacher, and friend. Family.

"Holy God, Holy Mighty, Holy Immortal, have mercy on us," everyone repeated three times.

Alla and Roman stood on the side of the grave, opposite Katerina. From the first, theirs had been a complicated association. Alla's arrogance and self-aggrandizement were off-putting, yet Katerina owed much to her patronage. It had given her hope and now would provide a future. Roman was not above using his power and influence to unseemly advantage. He'd made veiled threats to excavate her past but hadn't, whether from a change of heart or because time had simply run out for implementing his plan, she couldn't say. Katerina looked across the casket at him. He was studying her the same way she'd caught him doing many times. She averted her eyes. Soon, she would be beyond his reach.

Dr. Billings stood next to the Klopoushaks. She remembered the day he'd amputated Josef Sokur's arm and how decisive he'd been. She also spotted Jakob, another kind and good soul, among the mourners. Ivan Zolyar caught her eye and nodded. The Bandarek brothers stood in the back, their identical faces solemn. Mr. Marko offered a gentle smile, as if reassuring her that everything would be all right. He was a fine teacher. She knew Aleksandr would miss him.

She thought of her family in L'viv and how little they knew of her life. The past weeks had been so full, she'd not even written to Aneta of Viktor's death. That would require time and thought. She doubted she would share the discovery of Elena's letters or the hateful confrontation with Viktor. Maybe in time she could bring herself to inscribe the truth on paper—but not now. Instead, she would describe the awful explosion that had taken her husband's life and devastated the town. She'd act the grieving widow, mourning the loss of her husband for all the reasons a wife usually grieves. That, Aneta could understand; the rest would leave her confounded.

Since the night of the fire, a steady parade of neighbors had paid respects and offered condolences. At the fringes, Katerina had heard them talking about more pragmatic matters, such as the replacement of the elevator and the hardship the situation presented for harvest. "We should thank our lucky stars, though." "The rain's a blessing." "It kept the fire under control." When she'd first arrived in Bilik, Katerina had found such talk tiresome, although she'd never said so. But in the aftermath of the elevator tragedy, she was grateful for the reminder that life continues, despite death and loss. Clouds rain. Crops grow. Farmers harvest. Birds still sing and wind still streams across the prairie.

Tears wet Katerina's cheeks. Grief sat heavily in her heart. It was not the singular grief of a wife for her husband but a larger sorrow. She mourned for the woman she once had been, the one who'd left her son an ocean away and fled to claim a different life. She mourned for Aleksandr, the boy desperate for his father's love, who now would never know it. And she mourned for a woman with four children who hadn't the wherewithal to leave her cruel, one-armed husband. Katerina grieved for an entire town, which, unknowingly, had paid dearly for her family's sins.

"Give rest to the soul of Your departed servant, Viktor, in a place of light, in a place of repose, in a place of refreshment, where there is no pain, sorrow, and suffering," Father Warga chanted.

Viktor's charred remains would rest, until the end of time, alongside the empty casket of a woman who had disappeared rather than endure another moment of life with him. The irony brought Katerina no joy. She cried not for the reasons the other mourners must have assumed, not for the loss of her husband, who, in everyone else's eyes, was a good and honorable man. She did not mourn for him. In her nightly prayers, she'd continually asked God to grant her husband the will to become a man worthy of the love of a wife and son, to wrest from him the demons that made him hurt most those nearest to him. Often, Katerina had prayed for deliverance, but until the very last she'd not wanted Viktor dead; she'd wanted him different. Today, she wept for what might have been.

"As a good and loving God, forgive every sin he has committed in thought, word, or deed, for there is no one who lives and does not sin," Father Warga continued. "You alone are without sin. Your righteousness is an everlasting righteousness, and Your word is truth."

With Viktor, there was much to forgive. Although God might absolve him, it would take prayer, soul-searching, and the Creator's grace for Katerina to find it within her heart to forgive him. It would take even more to forgive herself.

Father Warga sprinkled the casket with oil in the form of a cross. "You shall sprinkle me with hyssop and I shall be clean. You shall wash me and I shall be whiter than snow." Then he bent and picked up a handful of dirt, sprinkling it on the casket, again, in the form of a cross. "The Earth is the Lord's, and the fullness thereof: the world, and all that dwell therein."

As the wet dirt landed on the wooden box, it made a soft drumming sound. Among the mourners there was the sound of quiet weeping.

Katerina leaned down and kissed Aleksandr on the top of his head. "I will not leave you," she whispered. "We are together. We are safe."

Father Warga gestured toward the casket. "You are dust, and to dust you will return."

Slowly, the coffin descended into the grave.

Chapter Twenty-Three

Given all the terrible things that had happened in the house in the past year, Katerina was unprepared for the emotion that her departure evoked. Leave-taking, it seemed, was never easy.

Nearly three weeks had passed since Viktor's funeral. Friends and neighbors had tried to talk her into staying—none more ardently than Yana—but she'd known, even before Viktor's casket was in the ground, that it was best for Aleksandr's sake, as well as hers, to turn the page on this chapter of their lives. A frosty November day was not an ideal time to move, but she was determined to travel before the worst of winter set in.

The house stood empty except for the beds. Jakob would deliver those to the Zolyar farm after she and Aleksandr left. Katerina had sold the furniture, all of Viktor's tools, and even her sewing machine. She'd buy a new one once they reached their destination. None of it had ever felt as though it belonged to her anyway. Despite Viktor's obsession with erasing Elena's memory, Katerina felt as though she'd occupied that woman's life since she first stepped off the train.

She'd encouraged Aleksandr to save any possessions and mementos he wanted. Other than his clothes, he'd set aside little—a photograph of his schoolmates, a pouch of marbles, his model biplane, favorite stones collected along the railroad bed, and, of course, his skates. When she'd asked if he wanted to save anything of his father's, Aleksandr had looked at the ground and simply shaken his head. Katerina understood but she'd packed Viktor's pipe anyway, believing someday Aleksandr might want a tangible reminder of his father. Now, the wounds were too fresh.

There was time for one final survey of the house to make certain she was leaving nothing of value behind. It had been only a year since she'd moved into the place, yet it held strong memories.

She began her inspection upstairs in the bedroom she'd shared with Viktor. For the first week after the explosion, Katerina hadn't been able to bear sleeping in their bed and instead had slept on the floor. It was silly, she knew, but she felt him in the bed. He'd hurt her and shamed her there, and she felt his skin brush hers whenever she went near it. From years of wear, the mattress tilted toward the right, where Viktor had slept in the hollow created by his body, and she couldn't abide touching any part of it. His scent—a masculine mix of shaving soap, liquor, and sweat—clung to the bedding, and the odor of charred wood, blanketing Bilik, seeped through the windows. She'd laundered every inch of fabric in the room, including the curtains. She'd scrubbed the floors and walls. When she'd finally had enough of the hard floor, she'd slept on clean sheets, on her side of the bed, with a bar of Palmolive soap tucked in the pillowcase to mask any lingering hint of Viktor's presence.

Katerina peeked into Aleksandr's room. He sat on the edge of his bed, elbows on knees, head in hands. She worried about him. Since the night of the fire, he hadn't said more than a few words. He'd endured more than any eleven-year-old should.

"Jakob will be here to collect our belongings in ten minutes," she said.

He nodded.

This little, wounded bird needed sheltering. Leaving the only home he'd known was stacking trauma on top of trauma. Katerina hoped she'd made the right decision and prayed the fresh start would give Aleksandr the chance to be happy.

When she walked into the empty parlor, Katerina pictured Viktor sitting in his chair by the stove, a pipe in one hand, a glass of *horilka* in the other, and Aleksandr sitting in the corner, his head buried in a book. She'd spent many evenings in here with her stitchery on her lap, lost in private thought. It was the one room in the house where they'd played games and engaged in pleasant conversation. It had given her hope, if fleeting, that they could become a family.

The dining room table was gone now, too, sold with the rest of the furniture. Without it, the room looked larger but sterile. Katerina recalled the first pattern she'd cut on the table's sturdy oak surface, a flannel shirt for Viktor, a thank-you for the surprise gift of the Eaton's sewing machine. His purchase had given her a sense of optimism. How quickly her faith had given way to fear. How quickly her mother's gold-handled scissors had gone from treasure to weapon.

Every surface in the kitchen had been scoured clean. Instead of sweet aromas, the room now had a medicinal smell. Of all the rooms in the house, Katerina was the most ambivalent about the kitchen. It had provided the simplest pleasures and the rawest pain. She thought of the quiet mornings, after Viktor had left for work and Aleksandr had gone to school, when she had sat at the table, alone with her thoughts, savoring a steaming cup of tea. The kitchen table was also where she and Yana had shared stories and developed their friendship.

Out of habit, Katerina wandered to the sink and looked out at the side yard. It was at this window she'd learned to appreciate the prairie, with its constantly changing hues and transforming sky. It offered such simple beauty. Van Gogh could have painted *Wheatfield Under Clouded Skies* from the vantage point of this window. She wondered what the painter would have made of the random patches of silver sagebrush stubbornly camped among the tall, bleached grasses or the kestrel perched on the wire fence. How would he have captured the autumn golds, caramels, and yellow-greens?

Unforgotten was her darkest moment in the kitchen, when she'd lain in despair as the life growing inside her had leaked onto the cold floor. It was an aching memory that she had chosen to bury.

Katerina didn't check the shed. She already knew nothing of value had been left there. The day after the explosion, she'd retrieved the cigar box with her sewing profits and Elena's letters and taken it to her bedroom, where she'd hidden it in her bottom dresser drawer. She'd taken out the letters and reread them slowly, over and over. She'd sat for hours, thinking, arguing with herself, until she'd decided what to do. Now, the letters, tied together with a white ribbon, were tucked in her satchel, along with her sewing money.

There was a knock at the door. Katerina limped from the kitchen toward the parlor and called upstairs. "Aleksandr, he's here."

"Hello, Jakob," she said, opening the door. "Please come in."

He stepped inside. "I'm real sorry you're leaving." Jakob removed his hat and averted his eyes.

Katerina touched his arm lightly.

Jakob shifted his feet and nodded. "I'll load your belongings, then."

Aleksandr came downstairs, carrying a cigar box containing his few prized possessions, fastened with a belt.

"I guess this is it." Katerina peeked in her satchel. The money and the letters were safely tucked there, along with a more recent letter addressed to her. She took one final look over her shoulder and closed the door, as though turning the page on an unsatisfying but memorable chapter in a book. She hoped the new elevator agent and his family would find more happiness in this home than she and Viktor and Aleksandr had.

Katerina, Aleksandr, and Jakob rode the few blocks to the train station in silence. When they arrived, Jakob unloaded their baggage.

"Thank you for everything," Katerina said. "You're a good man." She embraced him. "I'll miss you." She knew it was true.

Jakob blushed and then shook Aleksandr's hand. "Good luck, son." He climbed into his truck and drove away.

Katerina thought of the day she'd arrived and wandered this same station platform, nervously looking for Viktor Senyk. Every sight and sound had felt mysterious and foreign. She'd had to talk herself into staying, instead of getting back on the train. Remaining had been an act of will. How different life would be had she made another choice.

Today, the rhythmical sound of hammers on wood thrummed through the air like drumbeats. A short distance down the tracks, a crew of builders, perched along giant timbers, framed a new grain elevator. The burned shell of the old elevator had been razed and disposed of like the skeleton of a putrefied carcass no one wanted to remember.

Katerina and Aleksandr stepped to the ticket window inside the station.

"One adult fare and one child fare to Winnipeg," Katerina said.

She and Aleksandr sat on the bench and waited for the train to arrive. Soon they heard the whistle of the 9:37 a.m. eastbound nearing the station. They stood in anticipation. When the train stopped, a loud hiss escaped from the engine, drowning out the hammering. Before long, their belongings had been loaded from a cart into the combine car, which carried both passengers and freight.

"Look!" Aleksandr pointed. He ran toward Lavro and the entire Panko family.

"We couldn't let you leave without a proper send-off!" Yana shouted as she climbed the stairs to the platform. "It's not too late to change your mind."

Katerina's eyes filled with tears. She kissed and hugged each of the children, embraced Fedir, and held Yana tightly. "I can never repay you," she whispered. "Never."

"Nonsense," Yana said. "You're family."

Aleksandr hugged Yana and the younger children, but when he came to Lilia, who at thirteen, looked like a blossoming woman, he hesitated.

She wrapped her arms around him. "You're not getting away that easily, Aleksandr Senyk," she said.

He blushed crimson.

Fedir shook his hand and ruffled his hair, the same way he'd done a hundred times before.

Lavro gave Aleksandr a little shove. "Someday I'll fly to see you," he said.

"Not if I fly to see you first." Aleksandr shoved him back.

The train whistled a warning blast. "All aboard!" the conductor shouted.

"It's time," Katerina said, touching Aleksandr's shoulder.

They edged toward the conductor.

"I'll write," Katerina said, turning a final time. "And you have the address where we can be reached."

"Two-zero-three First Avenue, Winnipeg," Yana said.

Aleksandr and Katerina boarded the train and made their way down the aisle to the third bench from the back. He slid in first; she eased in next to him. They waved through the window at the Panko family, still on the platform, as the train pulled away from the station.

As the engine picked up steam, they sat quietly while Bilik grew smaller and smaller."Katerina?" Aleksandr said meekly.

Her name, spoken in his timid voice, sounded strange. She couldn't remember him ever calling her by her Christian name. "Yes?"

"I—I want—I mean…" He looked at his hands. "I have something important to tell you."

"I know how hard it is to leave your friends."

"It—it's not that." His hands curled into fists.

She waited.

"It's about the fire."

"It will be all right, Aleksandr." Katerina put her hand over his. "I have something important to tell you, too."

Acknowledgements

I am indebted to all who helped make *To Reap the Finest Wheat* possible. Thank you to Carol Amour, in whose little "nest" the idea for the story was born, and to Anne Lindeke for inspiring the book's title. My appreciation goes to all members of the Campanile Writers Group, especially David Foster and Andreé Graveley, who read and critiqued my work often and honestly. The Writing Sisters—Roi Solberg, Lisa Kusko, Julie Holmes, Barbara Belford, Blair Hull—fellow travelers who held my hand from a distance, you have my eternal gratitude. Thank you Chris DeSmet, teacher and mentor, for your guidance and faith. My editor, Kathy Kaiser, corrected, advised, and prodded, filing the many rough edges of my manuscript into publishable form. I am also beholden to Wayne Hanson for his instruction on the nuances of starting a 1920's truck. So, you didn't just turn a key?

Numerous nonfiction authors provided source material for this novel. I am grateful to The Western Development Museum, "the keeper of Saskatchewan's collective heritage." Weeks spent pouring over exhibits and collections in Moose Jaw, North Battleford, Yorkton, and Saskatoon, gave birth to the fictional town of Bilik. The 1920's Heritage Village exhibit, complete with a Saskatchewan Wheat Pool elevator, helped me construct Viktor's world. The Ukrainian Museum of Canada provided a wealth of information, as did The Ukrainian Heritage Museum in Canora, a surprising little gem. And thank you to the welcoming stranger, who tended the gardens at Weyburn and Area Heritage Village, for allowing me to explore the grounds even though it was closed.

Finally, to my husband, Bob Hanson, there are no adequate words. I couldn't have written this novel without him. Period. For weeks, he camped with me in our RV, in Saskatchewan, delving into the museum exhibits with an enthusiasm that rivaled my own. He walked me through all things mechanical, discussed plot twists and turns, held my hand through episodes of writer's angst, and never doubted that it was possible for an old dog to learn new tricks.

To Reap the Finest Wheat

Book Group Discussion Questions

1. Discuss the impact of the prairie setting on the story.

2. Symbolism is used throughout the novel—e.g. damaged limbs, harvest, scissors, fire, etc. Discuss the significance of these and any other symbols you noticed in the novel.

3. Why did the author choose to give Katerina a limp?

4. How does Katerina's religious devoutness work for and against her?

5. What binds Aleksandr and Katerina together?

6. Although they are friends, Katerina does not confide her abusive situation to Yana. Why?

7. Katerina is both a victim and a risk taker. How does this create tension in the story?

8. Early in the novel Katerina is judgmental of Elena for leaving Aleksandr. Discuss the irony of her attitude, as well as the effect it has on her decision making. How does her attitude change over time?

9. Examine the relationship Katerina has with the various female characters in the story: Alena (her sister), Yana (her friend), Svetlana (the other abused woman), Alla (her wealthy patron), and Elena (Viktor's first wife).

10. Who is your favorite character in the novel and why?

11. What function do Yana and Fedir Panko serve in this story?

12. Katerina clings to the romantic memory of her affair with Stepan. What effect does this have on her relationship with Viktor?

13. Katerina is not guileless. Does this make her a more or less sympathetic character?

14. Viktor appears to show one face to the outside world and another face at home. Are these faces actually different?

15. Discuss Viktor's relationship with the men in this story and how it differs from his relationship with the women.

16. Aleksandr fears his father and is timid in his presence. However, there are occasions where Aleksandr shows inner strength. How do these occasions foreshadow the outcome of the novel?

17. While standing at the gravesite during Viktor's burial, Katerina imagines her physical discomfort as a small atonement for Viktor's sins and her sins. What does Viktor have to atone for? What does Katerina have to atone for?

18. The novel is set in 1925. If it were set in present day, how would Katerina's behavior and options be different?

19. Katerina's life becomes a sum of her choices. What are those choices? After Viktor's death, she faces a life-altering choice. What does she decide to do? Do you agree with her decision? If not, what other decision could she make instead?

20. By the conclusion of the novel, do you believe Katerina has taken control of her life?